Mary Wood was born in Maidstone, Kent, and brought up in Claybrooke, Leicestershire. Born one of fifteen children to a middle-class mother and an East End barrow boy, Mary's family were poor but rich in love. This encouraged her to develop a natural empathy with the less fortunate and a fascination with social history. In 1989 Mary was inspired to pen her first novel and she is now a full-time novelist.

Mary welcomes interaction with readers and invites you to subscribe to her website where you can contact her, receive regular newsletters and follow links to meet her on Facebook and Twitter: www.authormarywood.com

BY MARY WOOD

The Breckton series

To Catch a Dream
An Unbreakable Bond
Tomorrow Brings Sorrow
Time Passes Time

The Generation War saga

All I Have to Give
In Their Mother's Footsteps

The Girls Who Went to War series

The Forgotten Daughter
The Abandoned Daughter
The Wronged Daughter
The Brave Daughters

The Jam Factory series

The Jam Factory Girls
Secrets of the Jam Factory Girls
The Jam Factory Girls Fight Back

The Orphanage Girls series

The Orphanage Girls
The Orphanage Girls Reunited
The Orphanage Girls Come Home

Stand-alone novels

Proud of You
Brighter Days Ahead
The Street Orphans

The Guernsey Girls

Mary Wood

PAN BOOKS

First published 2023 by Pan Books
an imprint of Pan Macmillan
The Smithson, 6 Briset Street, London EC1M 5NR
EU representative: Macmillan Publishers Ireland Ltd, 1st Floor,
The Liffey Trust Centre, 117–126 Sheriff Street Upper,
Dublin 1, D01 YC43
Associated companies throughout the world
www.panmacmillan.com

ISBN 978-1-5290-8974-5

1 3 5 7 9 8 6 4 2

A CIP catalogue record for this book is available from the British Library.

Typeset by Palimpsest Book Production Ltd, Falkirk, Stirlingshire
Printed and bound by CPI Group (UK) Ltd, Croydon, CR0 4YY

Visit **www.panmacmillan.com** to read more about all our books
and to buy them. You will also find features, author interviews and
news of any author events, and you can sign up for e-newsletters
so that you're always first to hear about our new releases.

In loving memory of Kathy Dobson,
a dear friend who I met through my books
and came close to my heart.
Miss you dear lady. RIP.

PART ONE

A Friendship is Born

Chapter One

Olivia

January 1936

'Well, my dear, that's another year gone. And what a year! The Silver Jubilee of King George was wonderful – though many thought he wouldn't make it, such a sickly man.'

Olivia looked up from her embroidery, an occupation she hated, but it pleased her Aunt Rosina to have her sit with her sewing and chatting for an hour in the afternoons.

The saving grace was that during the times her aunt didn't chat but concentrated on her own creation, Olivia could gaze out of the window of this rambling house on the cliffs of the Cornish coast and dream of what the coming year would bring for her..

She, her father and her beloved fiancé, Hendrick, had spent a wonderful Christmas here with her aunt and uncle, but now her father and Hendrick had left and Olivia felt daunted and yet excited about staying behind to take up the study of languages in London.

She would so miss them, Hendrick in particular, and would live for his visits once or twice a month.

'Mind, he's better the devil you know, as Prince Edward, well . . . Such scandal surrounding him and his flirtatious

3

ways. Always married women, which makes it worse, but this latest one . . . Oh, my dear, she's an American!'

'Well, our dear king isn't dead yet, Aunt, and hopefully he won't be for a long time. I'm sure our handsome prince is just sowing his wild oats and will settle down with a suitable bride.'

A humph that spoke of Aunt Rosina believing it when she saw it brought the conversation to an end.

Feeling bored beyond endurance, Olivia stretched out her long slender legs and sighed. She seemed to spend her life with older people – her father, a widower and the owner of a bank in St Peter Port, Guernsey, had been forty when he'd suddenly married, and she was born.

He'd never married again and always said that Sylvanna, her mother, had been the love of his life, and no one could match her or replace her.

They'd met in France, fallen in love, and had lived with Father's mother – Olivia's adored Granny Lynne, who had sadly passed away last year. Now, Granny Lynne's house was still their family home: a beautiful, three-storey white house overlooking the sea in St Peter Port – a busy shipping port, with an ever-changing scene of yachts, ships, fishermen, either on the horizon or coming into dock.

A pang of sadness clutched Olivia's heart at not returning to Guernsey for so long but she couldn't dispel the excitement she felt at what the future held for her.

Her hand went to her hair, and she made a pretence of patting it into place, though the roll that Annie, Aunt Rosina's maid, had put into it this morning was perfectly fine and kept her shoulder-length locks neat and tidy. She loved the style.

She'd told Annie that she wanted to make sure that she didn't stand out like some alien being when she began her studies in London – such a fashionable city. But having browsed through a popular magazine that Annie had, she now felt confident that this was one of the latest styles, and a lot of the other students would be sporting it.

'So, my dear, changing the subject, how do you feel about your new life ahead?'

'I'm excited, and yet afraid. I'm looking forward to my studies but find the thought of living alone in London a bit daunting. And I'm missing Hendrick and my beloved Guernsey already.'

'Well, Hendrick and your father should be back home by now, and that's where you should be . . . Oh, I do wish you weren't going to London. Besides, there are rumblings of unrest in the world, dear. Ireland, New York, both had riots, and I don't like that Hitler fellow. He's making Germany into a dictatorship. It could all spell trouble.'

'Ha, Aunt, you've been reading Uncle Cyril's newspapers again. You know he doesn't like you to. I can hear him now: "Such things are not for the ears of you womenfolk, my dear."'

'Poppycock! Men make a mess of everything. They should leave it to us. I'm jolly glad that you're being allowed a proper education. It's right, too, that you should speak French as that was your mother's tongue and it's still widely used in Guernsey so it's useful to you. But why you want to speak German and Russian, I do not know! Urgh, such ugly languages. And what use will *they* be to you?'

'I just love languages, Aunt, and as you know, Hendrick is a linguist. We want to one day open a language school of our own. In the meantime, I need to gain qualifications to teaching standards.'

'Work, you mean? Good gracious!'

Olivia laughed. 'Haven't you just been saying that women should play more of a role? Well, we have to start somewhere. We need to be as clever as the men to achieve that. And that comes through equal education. You are a clever lady, but you are only able to find out about the world by sneaking a peek at Uncle Cyril's paper!'

For some reason this made Aunt Rosina burst out laughing. Though she didn't know what was funny, Olivia laughed with her. She loved her aunt. Father's older sister, Aunt Rosina had married a Cornish landowner and never returned to Guernsey. She had a broad view of the world and its affairs and, yes, though boring at times, was very interesting at others, which made staying with her a joy.

Here, in Wallington Manor, Olivia felt at home and everything about the house and the village nearby was familiar. Even the view from the bedroom that was always kept especially for her was very similar to the one she had from her bedroom in Guernsey – a vast expanse of blue sea and sky with hills either side.

'I've been thinking, Olivia. I don't want you travelling alone to London, and Annie is due her annual leave. She always goes home for a week after Christmas. She's a very trustworthy young woman and knows her way around. I'll buy her a ticket on the same train to accompany you.'

'That would be lovely, thank you, Aunt. I feel better already.'

'And you will have Mrs Cockley to take care of you when you get there. She's a northern woman, came down to London as a maid in 1920 and never went back. She now works for your father and looks after us very well when we stay in his apartment. She's a jolly good cook too – lovely home cooking with a northern flavour, stews with dumplings and meat pies, but she can also turn her hand to more fancy food if need be. She's a salt of the earth sort. Uncle Cyril fancies he takes her off very well, as he says, "Eeh, it's hot today, lass!"'

This made Olivia giggle. She had never heard anyone speak like that and thought her aunt was making it up.

'Anyway, I'm glad she's there to take care of you and to mother you, but I think you'll soon get used to London life and make friends. And you're right, of course, you should go to that college. Far better than finishing school. You don't need to learn to carry a pile of books on your head as I had to endure. Better to broaden your mind than straighten your shoulders, dear.'

'Thank you, and I really appreciate you giving me Annie to travel with me. My excitement is beating my fear now.'

'That's good.'

They were sat in Aunt Rosina's sitting room and as she said this she leaned forward and rang the bell on the table next to her – a carved occasional table in walnut, which matched the walnut bureau in the corner.

Always cosy, the room housed a large pink sofa and two dark green chairs. A French door led out onto the garden – a sloping, lawned area bordered by flowers in the summer, but with a dusting of frost tinging the blades of grass right now.

The floor of the room was a highly polished oak, with a large pink rug patterned with dark green feathery leaves covering the centre. The white marble fireplace was the centre point and it now crackled and spat its protest at Aunt having put a huge log on it.

Annie appeared at the door carrying a tray of tea.

'Thank you, dear. Now, Annie, I have something to tell you.'

Annie looked surprised, but said nothing. She just bobbed and then walked into the room and laid the tray on the table next to the bell.

'I want you to prepare Miss Olivia's things for her departure to London, and your own too. You are to accompany Miss Olivia on the express train from Penzance to Paddington on the fifteenth of the month. The train leaves at nine a.m. I will make all the arrangements. When you arrive, you are to see Miss Olivia safely to her address in Westminster, and then you may go home and spend a week with your family. Your yearly salary will be ready for you to take with you.'

Annie bobbed again. 'Ta, madam. It'll be me pleasure to take care of Miss Olivia. I'll see she gets there safe and sound, I promise. And I'm grateful for me week off too.'

'Very well, Annie, you are dismissed now.'

Olivia caught an excited glance from Annie and knew she could have skipped out of the room if she dared. Olivia thought how she would have happily joined her. She'd dance all the way along the hall outside the room and do a little twirl at the end of it, such was her pleasure at this turn of events.

It all seemed hustle and bustle from then on as Annie's work piled up and she was in and out of rooms carrying bed linen and brushes and pans. All the guest rooms had to be spick and span before she left and three of them had been occupied over Christmas.

Besides this, there was the packing and umpteen jobs that Aunt Rosina seemed to find for her, as if the poor girl was going to be away for months.

But Olivia did manage to get a chat with her one evening.

It was a particularly cold night and Annie had lit all the fires to warm the bedrooms. Olivia was getting ready for an early night when Annie knocked on the door and came in lugging a bucket of coal.

'For during the night, miss. Now, use them tongs or you'll end up with hands as black as the coalman's.'

'Ha, Annie, you sound like my father. I can put coal on a fire, you know.'

Annie ran her hand over her brow. 'I'm sorry, miss. I let me tongue run away with me. Me mum always says, "You've enough rattle on yer, Annie, to rival the bells of the fire engine. Me ears are ringing with your chatter, girl."'

Olivia giggled. 'Well, I wouldn't say that, but you do sometimes make me feel like I'm years younger than you. How old are you?'

'Coming up for twenty-one, miss.'

'Well then, I'm older as I'm already twenty-one.'

'Really! Well, that's something I got wrong. I suppose it's with you still going to school. It threw me.'

'Not school, but a college for languages. It's very different.'

'Oh, I see, but it's still learning, ain't it, miss? Mind, it weren't that I thought you younger, as you have a fiancé, just inexperienced in the ways of the world and I wanted to protect yer.'

'That's very kind, Annie. And I do need your protection. I missed out not having a mother to guide me. Sadly, she died giving birth to me.'

'That is sad. I'm sorry to hear that. Have you a picture of her?'

'Yes, it's in my bedroom at home. The resemblance between us is uncanny. She had the same dark eyes and dark hair, and father said that hers had a natural tendency to fall into waves, just like mine does. It seems my personality is very much the same too.'

'Well, that's something to hang on to, miss.'

'Yes. But if only she'd lived, I feel that I wouldn't have been such a novice in the big wide world. That maybe she would have taken me to places and encouraged Daddy to travel too. But as it is, I have only known life on an island . . . Oh, Annie, I feel so much better that you're going to be with me on my journey to London.'

Olivia liked Annie, but often felt sorry for her, as this rambling house had so few staff that each had to turn their hand to many tasks and work long hours.

For Annie, that meant laying fires, making beds and over-seeing the cleaning of all the rooms, but also acting as a lady's maid to Aunt Rosina – seeing to the laundering of her clothes, and carrying out any mending needed, besides dressing her hair and anything else that Aunt asked of her.

'Do you enjoy working here, Annie?'

'It's needs must, miss. I need to provide for me mum, and me sister Janey. Life ain't no picnic growing up in the East End of London.'

This hit home with Olivia, as she realized that though near in age, she and Annie had lived such different lives. Her own, privileged with every comfort, but for Annie, nothing but toil.

'But here, I'm well fed and warm, and I can give every penny of me wage to keeping me mum and me sister going. You see, miss, me mum can't work – she's crippled with arthritis and needs a lot of help from me sister. This means that poor Janey can only work a few odd hours a week at the local grocery shop.'

'I am sorry. It seems an awful situation. Maybe when I'm

in London, I can help out. Is where you live near to where my father's apartment is in St James's Street?'

Annie let out a loud laugh. 'Nah, crikey, miss, that's near one of the palaces, ain't it? Ha, yer may as well ask me if me house is like Buckingham Palace as compare me to that end of London. Up west? Blimey, I'd think meself someone if I did live up there, luv . . . I mean, miss.'

Olivia couldn't help laughing with her. 'Oh dear, I'm showing my ignorance. It's a good job you are taking me, or God knows where I'd land!'

'We'll be fine, miss. I'll say goodnight now. And I hope you sleep tight.'

'Goodnight, Annie.'

When the door closed, Olivia had an urge to call Annie back and ask her to stay a while longer. Suddenly, loneliness and the thought of living in a strange place and not seeing her home for a year crowded in on her and she felt near to tears.

Shaking the feeling off, she sat a moment by the fire and allowed its warmth to seep into her.

Putting her head back, she forced herself to think of the exciting things about her coming adventure, and she began to feel better. What lay ahead was a step towards brightening her future. A future she couldn't wait for – to be Hendrick's wife and to help him achieve his dream.

She hoped that she would find the skills she needed to improve her grasp of languages, especially Russian which she found the most challenging. German she felt she could hold her own with, but to learn more skills in putting the words into their correct context would make her fluent.

* * *

It seemed no time at all before Olivia found herself in a first-class carriage with Annie, speeding along at what seemed like a tremendous pace towards London.

The scenery flashed by. Fields, houses, factories, churches, all blurred into one. But looking out of the window didn't take much of their time as Annie amused her with tales of the East End of London and wanted to know all about Guernsey.

Olivia found she liked Annie more and more. And though she was the most unlikely person, she wanted to be on different terms than maid and mistress.

Annie was what you would call lovely to look at – not pretty and not beautiful, but with a pleasant dimply smile and honest blue eyes that twinkled when she smiled. She wore her hair clipped back into a bun at the nape of her neck, and had a slim, neat figure.

It was her ready humour and the kindness that shone from her that endeared her so much to Olivia. It was easy to sit with her on this long journey. She had the comfortable feeling of being with a friend.

This thought had hardly entered her head when the space around them was filled with the screaming, screeching sound of the wheels on the track as the brakes of the train jammed on.

Olivia shot forward; her breath left her body. Pain shot through her – unbearable, crushing pain – then all went black as she welcomed the veil that descended over her and took her into oblivion.

Chapter Two

Annie

Pain seared Annie's arm. She tried to move but couldn't. Something was holding her down. Her lungs were clogged with smoke, making it hard to breathe. Her nostrils stung with the tang of burning cloth and leather. She couldn't see. Opening her sore, gritty eyes hurt. Screams pierced her ears, and worse, the sound of children crying and calling for their mothers, with distress and fear in their voices.

Men shouted instructions, but she heard nothing from Miss Olivia.

Her throat rasped as she tried to call out. 'M – miss . . . are you hurt? Miss!'

Nothing.

Annie's heart beat wildly in her chest. Her mind screamed at her that Miss Olivia was dead, but she wouldn't accept this. Such a beautiful girl couldn't die! She wasn't going to let her!

Making a massive effort, Annie put her hands out. The agony of the movement made her cry out.

Feeling around her, she touched something warm. After moving her hand over it she knew it was Miss Olivia's leg.

Relief filled her as it dawned on her that the warmth meant Miss Olivia was still alive!

'Miss, miss!'

When there was no response, Annie wriggled her body, trying to free herself. She groaned with pain as something scraped her shin, but undeterred, she found a solid hold.

Ignoring the discomfort that she was in, she grasped what felt like an iron bar and pulled on it for all she was worth.

Inch by inch she freed herself.

Sweat poured from her. Her breaths came in gasps, each one giving her a feeling of suffocating and tasting of sulphur. Panic gripped her. She couldn't let Miss Olivia die!

Now she was free she could see a beam of light and feel a draught of cold air. Looking up, she saw the window that had been to her side was now the roof – a gaping jagged hole as shards of glass remained in its twisted frame.

'Miss? Miss?' There was no response. Her groping hands touched the soft material of Olivia's coat. Following the shape of her body with her hands, gently patting as she went, Annie found that something lay across Olivia's legs, trapping her.

A voice shouted, 'Fire! It's on fire!'

Fear trembled through Annie. 'We're here! Help! Help!'

No one responded. She had to get Miss Olivia out! But the light was fading. Looking up gave her the sight of black, swirling smoke covering the gap, some of it seeping into the cabin. 'No! No-o-o!'

Taking as deep a breath as she could, Annie made one more massive effort to shift whatever was holding Miss Olivia. It moved in an upward direction, creaking as it bent. Not heeding it, she grabbed Olivia and heaved for all she was worth, inching her along the floor and away from the object.

Just as she got her clear, a crashing made her heart stop. The carriage rocked. Annie clung on to Olivia with one hand whilst her other found something solid to grasp.

The strength drained from her as she held on with all her might. But then the rocking became a movement that dislodged her and sent her flying over the top of Olivia. She flung her arms around her and held on tightly but felt herself rolling.

Olivia was on top of her now, but soon by her side and then in front of her. Still, Annie held on to her with her agonizingly painful arms, trying to shield her all she could till the carriage came to a halt. The window was now in front of her. The shards of glass had gone. Catching her breath, little by little Annie pushed and pulled Olivia towards it, praying, crying, calling out as she did. Tears wet her face. Snot ran from her nose and dribble ran down her chin as she found a hold for her feet and pushed for all she was worth against it.

Reaching the window, she lay a moment, sweating, panting and coughing the smoke from her lungs, rasping her sore throat as she did, and then, as she slumped down, felt herself drifting away.

Wanting to go into the blackness that threatened to engulf her and to embrace the peace it offered, Annie lay still for a moment and allowed the stillness to take her.

A cough and a moan brought her back to reality. She had to get them out of there!

As she crawled through the window, her body shivered as an ice-cold wind stung her exposed skin. Looking this way and that, she saw the flames. Felt the heat instantly warm her as flames devoured the next carriage.

Once more the screams and shouting penetrated her ears.

The sound seemed to give her strength. She was out! Alive! Now, she had to save Miss Olivia.

Where she found the strength to drag Olivia from the carriage, she didn't know. But they lay side by side. Her gasping for breath, taking in the smoke-tinged air, Olivia unmoving. Silent.

'Miss, miss! Wake up. Help me to help you, luv.'

There was no response.

Looking around, Annie saw a figure through the swirling smoke. 'Help! Help me!'

Strong arms came around her. 'All right, miss, I've got yer.'

Annie slumped back into him. Saw another man bend over Olivia, felt released from fear for her mistress and allowed the darkness to take her.

'Open your eyes, dear. My, you've been lucky. That's if you can call huge gashes on your legs and arms and nasty burns lucky. But you got out. And they tell me you got your friend out too. Well done, you . . . Now, let's sit you up. There's a nice cup of tea here for you.'

Annie looked up into a kindly face swathed by a white veil that had fallen forward as she bent over, tending gently to her and helping her all she could.

'I'm Nurse Robbins, dear. You're all right. Nothing that won't heal or feel better in days. Your wounds are stitched and dressed.'

'H – how's Miss Olivia?'

'Oh, "Miss", is it? So, you're the maid. We did wonder how you afforded first class . . . Oh, I mean nothing offensive, dear, but you aren't wearing the usual expensive clothes.'

'Yes, I'm the maid, but I think a lot of me charge. How is she?'

'Very badly injured and in surgery as we speak. It's touch and go if her legs can be saved.'

'No!'

'Now, don't fret. Mr Godson is Oxford Hospital's top surgeon and has been mending limbs for ever. He worked in a field hospital in France as a young man, carrying out operations before he was trained to do so. He's saved thousands of limbs and lives. He won't let anything happen if he can possibly avoid it, but the young lady is going to take a while to recover.'

Annie looked away as the tears pricked her eyes. She couldn't bear the thought of Olivia being crippled in such a way.

'Now, dear, I need to ask details of your mistress's family. They must be contacted.'

'I only have her aunt's address and phone number. I'm her maid really but was given the job of taking care of Miss Olivia as she were travelling to London. I don't even know her surname. She lives in Guernsey, you see. I know that she's twenty-one and due to start some college or other to learn languages, but not much else.'

'That will help. And do you know if she is normally fit and healthy?'

'Oh yes. Fit as a fiddle. I'd know if she were on any tablets or anything, but she ain't.'

'That's good. The fit and healthy recover much sooner. Now, let me have those contact details that you do have.'

As Annie spelled out the address, the nurse scribbled it down with the telephone number. 'And what about your own family? Did they know you were on that train?'

'No. They knew I was coming home as I wrote to them as soon as I knew, but not which train I'd be on as I didn't know then. You can ring the local grocer who me sister

17

works for; he'd get a message to me mum for me.' Annie recited Mr Sutherland's phone number.

'Well now, leave everything to me and you try to rest.'

As she closed her eyes, Annie felt she could relax a little as she trusted Nurse Robbins, and though she hadn't met him, she felt she could trust the surgeon to do all he could for Miss Olivia.

Smarting pains woke Annie. She didn't know how much later, but guessed it was around four or five as it was getting dark outside.

At first, she felt disorientated, but then the horror of what had happened came back to her and she remembered her burns and gashes. It was a few moments before she remembered Olivia. When she did, she shot upright.

'Ah, you're awake. I'll just check all your dressings and make sure you haven't any infection. My, you've got a shiner of a black eye coming. Can you remember banging your face?'

'No . . . Is Miss Olivia all right?'

'Yes, Mr Godson has managed to wire the fragments of her broken bones together and is very pleased with the result. She's still unconscious and has other injuries, so she's very poorly.'

'She won't die, will she?'

'No. She's a strong girl. And I am happy to say that I managed to contact her family from the details you gave me. Her aunt and uncle are expected to arrive tonight. And I understand that her father and fiancé are chartering a boat and will arrive from Guernsey tomorrow. We don't know anything about your family yet, dear.'

'I don't think they will come. They'd want to, but wouldn't have the money, Nurse.'

'That's sad. I'm sorry. But we're here for you. And I'll let the night staff know you're on your own, so they'll watch out for you as well.'

'Ta. I'm all right. I just want Miss Olivia to be.'

'She means a lot to you, doesn't she? I don't know much about maids and their bosses – we only had a daily at home – but I didn't think the two became close.'

'Miss Olivia is special. She ain't got no airs and graces. She treats me like I'm her friend, not a lackey. Her aunt's nice too. But very formal with everything. The staff can't get close to her, but we all like and respect her.'

'That's good. So, you're not unhappy in your work? Mind, I'm surprised you work so far away from home.'

'I worked for a friend of Mrs Wallington's first, up in the West End, till she had to cut staff down. Then she recommended me to Mrs Wallington. Cornwall is a long way and I miss being able to get home for me days off, but the money's better and besides, work's short as there ain't that many toffs who can afford to keep a full house of staff on now, so I had to take it.'

'Never fancied working in the factories then?'

'No, them places ain't for me. I like me job.'

'That's good. Now, I must get on. Dinner will be around shortly. Just keep resting, but don't suffer pain. Let us know as we can give you something for it.'

'Ta, Nurse.'

It seemed to Annie that it was the middle of the night when she felt her bed being moved.

'Where you taking me to, mate?'

The young porter grinned at her. 'You're going up in the world, love. You're being shifted to one of our private suites to keep your charge company. Her family have ordered it.'

19

'Is she all right?'

'I reckon so. She ain't woken up yet, but I ain't heard anything that suggests she ain't doing all right.'

Annie relaxed a little. She was desperate for a pee but couldn't tell this bloke that.

When they arrived, it was like a different world. Instead of rows of beds there was just Olivia's and hers was put next to it. A nurse came over to her.

'Can I be doing anything for you, me lovely?'

'You're Irish, aren't you? I worked with a girl from Ireland once.'

'It is that I am. Now, let's be making you comfortable, eh?'

'I need to pee.'

'Ah, it is that we were hoping you would. It is a long time you have been here today, and you aren't for having passed any water. It's been a worry, so it is, for we can't always be seeing the internal damage everyone has suffered. I'll help you out of bed as we need for you to be moving about a little now.'

Annie cried out against the pain that gripped her stomach and legs as her feet touched the floor.

'Sure, it is that you're badly bruised, me wee darling. But that will pass.'

The bathroom was on the other side of Olivia. The sight of her filled Annie with worry. Olivia was deathly pale and had one leg hung from an iron bar.

'Now, don't be getting alarmed. That's called traction, so it is, and it's to keep the leg in a position to be helping it to heal, and she is still feeling the effects of the heavy sedation she was under.'

Once in the bathroom, the nurse stayed with Annie and told her, 'Don't be worrying about me, you do what it is you have to do. I'll busy meself in the cupboard getting you a clean gown and a bowl of hot water for giving you a wash down. Sure, you will feel a lot better as you've only been having your wounds cleaned and the rest of you is for looking like the coalman, so it is.'

Annie went to laugh but it hurt so she just grinned.

Everything hurt. Going for a pee, the washing down of her, and the fitting her into a clean gown, but she did feel better once it was all done and soothing cream rubbed gently into her bruises.

'There, it is that you are fit for your bosses to be arriving.'

Annie's face reddened at the thought of this. She'd forgotten they were expected and hadn't thought that she would have to see them when they were here. But when a few minutes later Mr and Mrs Wallington came into the ward, they were kindness itself to her.

'Oh, Annie, dear. We cannot thank you enough for saving our precious Olivia. We've been told that but for your actions we could have lost her. We'll never forget your bravery, dear.'

Annie just nodded. She hadn't thought of herself as being brave.

Mr Wallington gazed down at her. 'You're a good girl, Annie. Thank you very much. I've already done something for you. I've spoken to the shopkeeper, Mr Sutherland, and arranged for him to collect some money from the bank to take to your family. I know you have lost your year's salary among your other possessions, but we will make that up to you.'

'Ta, sir. That's kind of you, sir. Ain't me bags been saved then?'

'No. I'm sorry, my dear, but they've gone, along with Olivia's.'

He turned then and went to Olivia's side where Mrs Wallington was sitting crying.

'Now, now, Rosina, try to be brave. The doctor has said that he is expecting Olivia to make a good recovery.'

'But she doesn't even know we are here!'

'I'm sure she does. Just chat to her and hold her hand.'

For all his brave words, Mr Wallington blew his nose loudly and Annie saw him dab his eyes. She so longed to comfort them both, but it was unheard of for her to speak unless spoken to and to go near to them and to put her arm around them would be a cardinal sin.

It was during the night that Annie heard her name being called. She woke with a start to hear Olivia thrashing her arms and her croaky voice calling, 'Annie . . . A – Annie.'

Feeling the pain of sudden movement as she flung the covers back and went to jump out of bed, Annie gasped.

'Annie . . . Annie, are y – you all right?'

'I am, miss. I'm coming.'

'We've got to get out, Annie!'

'It's all right, miss. We're in the hospital . . . Miss Olivia, it's Annie, we're all right, luv.' Annie didn't correct the endearment but put out her hand to stroke Olivia's hair back off her face. 'Oh, luv, you're sweating. Are you in pain?'

Olivia nodded. 'Are . . . are you?'

'A bit. But we're safe now.'

Olivia's hand found hers. 'Don't leave me, Annie.'

'I won't, mate, don't you worry. I'll stay by your side for as long as you want me to. But we need the nurse . . . Here, wait a mo. I think this cord will summon her.'

As soon as Annie pulled the cord the door opened and the lights went on, making her squint and Olivia turn her head away from the glare.

'What is it? Are you all right? Is Miss Riverstone all right?'

'She's in pain and a bit distressed, Nurse.'

'Ah, it is that she will be. But it's not ten minutes since I came in and you were both fast asleep . . . Here, me wee darling, let me be making you comfortable and getting you something for your pain.'

Annie moved away from the bed, but had the strange feeling of sadness at doing so. She just wanted to stay close to Olivia.

As soon as the nurse left, Annie returned to be by Olivia's side.

'I'm here, luv. And I ain't moving. I'll sit on this comfy chair and hold your hand. Try to sleep, eh?'

'Thank you, Annie. I feel safer when you're near to me. Don't leave me.'

The next time Annie woke up, she had a blanket around her and guessed that Nurse Riley, as she'd told them she was called, had been in and covered her up. It felt to her that every part of her body ached, but she didn't care. Just to see Olivia sleeping soundly was enough.

When Mr and Mrs Wallington arrived the next day, she was still sitting there. She and Olivia had held hands for most of the time, only resting her own occasionally as it began to ache.

'Oh, my dear Olivia, how are you, dear?'

Olivia managed a smile for her aunt.

'You look so much better. More colour.' She bent and kissed Olivia and then greeted Annie. 'I've been shopping. I've bought you some essentials, Olivia, dear, and a couple of nice nighties for you and Annie. You can't be in those gowns when Hendrick and your father arrive. I'll ask the nurse to help you both get more respectably dressed and presentable. You both look like scarecrows!'

Annie managed a giggle, but Mr Wallington looked crossly at his wife. 'Rosina! Really!'

Unperturbed, Mrs Wallington said, 'Well, they do! And Olivia would be mortified for Hendrick to see her like that.'

Mr Wallington gave up with a meaningful sigh and went to look out of the window.

'Now, Annie. Here's yours. I chose lilac for you. Off you go to the bathroom and get washed and into it. And here, I have a bag with a hairbrush and some soap, a toothbrush and tooth powder. I want to see you respectable when you come out.'

Annie fought back a giggle. When she'd managed to sort herself out, she felt a million times better and even wanted to do a twirl as she thought she was dressed more for a ball than for going to bed.

She'd seen such finery – lovely soft, long silk nightgowns – but never thought she would one day own one. She loved it and the feel of it against her skin. And it felt so good to brush her hair and use the clips in the bag to secure the bun she made by twisting her ponytail and coiling it into the nape of her neck. A little bit of what it must feel like to be rich settled on her and she liked the feeling. Sighing, she told herself, *Don't be daft, girl. You're an Eastender born and bred, and'll always be. And it ain't a bad thing to be either!*

Still, she thought, *a girl can dream*. And she had every right to, having been close to death and knowing the panic of what one's last moments can feel like.

When she went back into the ward, Mr Wallington had left. It appeared he hadn't wanted to embarrass her and so was sitting outside the room until she was safely back in bed.

'You look lovely, dear. You could go to a ball in that.'

Mrs Wallington giggled and without thinking Annie said, 'I thought that. Ta for thinking of me.'

Mrs Wallington just smiled. To Annie, it all felt strange as she was seeing a different side to her boss – a lovely, fun-loving side – and she felt privileged to be doing so.

'Though we'll have to put plenty of powder on that black eye. Does it hurt a lot, dear?'

Annie nodded. This kindness and personal side of her boss was hard to deal with. She didn't want to say the wrong thing and felt she'd been too outspoken already.

'Anyway, dear, Olivia and I have had a little chat, and she doesn't want you to leave her side. So, from now on you will be her maid companion. I will of course speak to her father about your salary, but we hope you will accept and go wherever Olivia goes as you seem to give her confidence and, as she puts it, you make her feel safe. I hope you will accept.'

Annie wanted to jump for joy. She looked over at Olivia and felt a love for her surge through her. It was almost as strong as what she felt for her sister Janey, and at that moment, she felt she'd been given another sister to love.

'I'd be glad to. And I'll always take care of her. Ta for having me, Miss Olivia.'

'No. It is I who should thank you, Annie. You saved my life. And I don't want you to call me miss now, just Olivia . . . Come here, I want to hold your hand.'

Annie felt honoured. And she understood the feeling of wanting to hold on to one another. They'd been to hell and back together and needed each other and she had a feeling they always would.

Chapter Three

Janey

Janey stared at her boss. She'd been shocked to open her door to him; he'd never before visited her at home.

'I've bad news, Janey.'

As she sat on the sofa and listened to what he told her, her world seemed to collapse around her.

'Annie ain't hurt bad, love . . . I mean, they say she's got some burns, and deep cuts to her arms and legs and bruising all over, but she ain't gonna die. Her mistress is in a bad way, though, and her uncle said that, but for Annie, she'd be dead.'

'Annie saved her mistress? And they're in hospital together in Oxford? Where's that and who phoned you to tell you?'

A sob took her attention as Mr Sutherland explained.

'Mum! Oh, Mum, our Annie . . . in a train crash!'

Janey hugged her mum as best she could.

Mr Sutherland tried to reassure them. 'She's all right, love. I promise you both. The gentleman who rang stressed that Annie will heal in a matter of weeks. Here, he's given me an address to the hospital. We can look up the telephone number if you like, though I ain't sure where Oxford is.

I think it's a good way from here . . . I could get you a train ticket if you like, Janey.'

Mum tightened her grip on Janey's arm. 'Don't leave me, Janey.'

'I won't, Mum.' She was kneeling beside her mum now and had her head on her lap. 'Annie'll find a way of keeping in touch with us.'

'Yes, the gentleman said he'd ring with updates when he has them. I told him anytime, anytime at all and I'll see that you get them.'

'Ta, Mr Sutherland.'

'Is there anything you need, Janey, girl? Anything? What've you got for your tea?'

'I've cooked some spuds, and I'm going to make a gravy to go with them. But . . .'

'Hey, don't cry now.'

'Well, Annie usually brings us some money . . . I don't know how I'm going to manage.'

'Blooming 'ell, how could I forget that! This Wallington fella, he's sent a draft to his bank for me to pick up for you. He didn't say how much, but here . . .' Mr Sutherland dug deep into his trouser pocket. 'This is enough to run along to the pie shop and get a couple of hot pies. Then if you can come earlier in the morning, I'll go around to the bank and collect that money for you. How would that be, eh?'

'Ta, Mr Sutherland. I'll pay you back out of Annie's wages, as I expect that's what he's putting in. I should think Annie managed to arrange it with him, bless her. She's always thinking of us.'

'Yes, she's a good girl, though I never thought she should have left you like she did. You have too much on your plate for a girl of your age.'

Janey didn't comment. She loved Annie so much and missed her every day. And, she had to admit, what she brought home on her leave days kept them going throughout most of the year. What she'd earned up at the big house in the West End hadn't done that.

When Mr Sutherland had gone, Janey grabbed her coat. An old one of Annie's, it was tatty now and didn't do anything to keep her warm, but it was all she'd got.

'It's cold out there, luv. We'll manage with the spuds and gravy.'

'No, Mum, I can taste that pie now, and I've got to have it.' She grinned as she said this and was rewarded with a weary, but lovely smile from her mum.

'See if you can run to some liquor as well, me darlin'. We had a halfpenny left in the pot, didn't we?'

'I will. We won't need that if the money comes in to-morrow . . . I tell you something, the first thing I'll do is go and pay the electric bill, so we don't have to manage with the oil lamps all the time.'

'Oh, I don't know. They give a nice light and give off a bit of heat too. I like them, though it would be good to have the landing lit a bit better . . . That's if I can get up there. It's getting harder, Janey, luv.'

'I know, Mum. We'll see what we can do. We might afford a bed for down here, eh? We can take out the sofa and I can sit on the cushions on the floor.' She gave a laugh she didn't feel and then fibbed as she said, 'I'd like that, I like to sit on the floor. It puts me a little nearer to the fire.'

With her mum smiling, Janey made for the door. When she got there, she looked back at the pathetic fire trying its best to get a spark out of the green log she'd placed on it as she'd been unable to afford a bag of dried-out logs.

As she stepped out of her door, she was met with, 'Where you off to, Janey?'

'What business is it of yours, Harry Tyler?'

Living next door to Harry was like having a pest on your doorstep. At thirteen years old, he was into everything.

'Well, I just wondered if you wanted a share of the coal I've got? It's best kitchen grade.'

'What? You've got best kitchen coal?'

'A bag fell off the lorry, didn't it? I were just there when it did, and bucket loaded it back to our coal house.'

'Really? You've got a whole bag of coal?'

She didn't know why she was surprised. Harry was a wide boy, even at this young age.

'I have, and don't your Annie come home around this time of year with a wad of money for you? Well, you can have a half-hundredweight for tuppence, if you want it. Normal price is nearer ten bob. I'd bring it around for you too.'

'What, now?'

'Yes, now.'

'Right, if that's in me coal house by the time I get back, you'll have your tuppence!'

'I didn't see Annie come home . . . Have you got tuppence then? Mind, I trust you, so I'll take it round anyway.'

'Ta, luv. I'll have the money in the morning for you, but only if it's in me coal house tonight.'

'Show me your knickers and I'll make it a penny.'

'You cheeky beggar, I'll tell your mum what you said!'

'Ha, I were only joking. I've seen them anyway when you hung them on the line!'

'Get off with you, you little bleeder. But make sure I've got that coal. I've got some kindling. I bring wooden boxes home from the shop now and again. It'll be nice to have a fire to warm me mum up.'

'I won't let you down, Janey. You wouldn't buy from me again if I did. But if you can get me mum some of that kindling, I'd be grateful.'

'Help yourself. There's three boxes in the coal house, but mind you only take one. I'll bring you another when I can. Some of the fruit and the tinned stuff come packed in them.'

'Ta, Janey. And I'm sorry I asked to look at your knickers, I won't ask that again.'

Janey laughed as she walked on. Harry was all right really.

Though it was one of the saddest evenings they'd had, with wondering how Annie really was and not knowing if they could get to see her until she was discharged and came home, it was also one of the cosiest they'd known for a while and the first time they both felt full for as long as Janey could remember.

The pie and the liquor were the best ever from Jones's Pie Shop.

Mum had a smile on her face as she gazed at the flames. 'One thing, Janey, when we have electric, we'll be able to listen to the wireless. We might have known about the train crash then.'

'I did know, Mum. It were in the headlines of the papers at the shop, but I didn't read any of the stories. I just didn't think our Annie would be on it . . . Oh, Mum, I can't bear to think of her in a strange hospital on her own.'

They both cried as they held hands. 'She'll be all right, Janey, luv. The family she works for are seeing to that, and no doubt she's in the same ward as the young lady she was in charge of so she will have company . . . But a heroine!

30

Annie! Though I'm not surprised. I can't see her saving her own skin and leaving someone to die, nor you. You're both good girls, and caring girls . . . I just wish you hadn't to waste your life looking after me, though, luv.'

'It ain't wasted, Mum. I'd have it no different, and if Annie hadn't got to earn money, she wouldn't either. She's doing her bit in keeping us.'

Mum sighed. 'Anyway, it's nice to have a fire, ain't it?'

'It is. And I can sing for you. That'll give you something to listen to. We can have a sort of concert. Just me and you.'

'Oh, Janey, luv, it'll be lovely to hear you. I forget me pain when you sing, girl.'

As Janey cleared the plates she sang.

'Just whistle while you work
And cheerfully together we can tidy up the place
So hum a merry tune
It won't take long when there's a song to help you set the pace . . .'

Mum joined in the last line with her: *'So, just whistle while you work!'*

Janey wiped away the tears that had trickled down her cheeks as she'd started to sing and as they'd laughed together. She hugged her mum. It had been a shock, but Annie was going to be all right. She just longed for the day when she saw her and could hug her too.

The next day the living room was still warm but helping her mum down the stairs was wearing Janey out. Her arms ached and shook with the effort as her mum leaned heavily on her. As had happened before, Janey feared she would fall and Mum would land on top of her, but she clung on to the rail and used all her strength to support her.

31

At last, they made it – both sweating, both exhausted.

Janey made her mind up that she just had to get a bed downstairs. The ones they had were no good as they both had a double bed.

When she was little, she'd shared her mum's bed, but had moved into Annie's when she'd reached four years old. Mum had already been showing signs of arthritis and couldn't bear her little child leaning against her or kicking her even, as she wriggled about during the night.

'I'll give you your wash, Mum, then I'll get you some porridge before I go to work. I'll ask Mrs Tyler to look in on you as I'll be away a bit longer with having to go in earlier.'

'All right, luv . . . I tell you, I hate being such a burden to you.'

'You ain't, Mum, and don't think like that . . . Look, you'll feel better once I rub that oil into you that the doctor gave you. It always soothes the pains a little.'

'I think I might need those painkillers, luv. Have I many left?'

'Just the one, but I'll get to the chemist and get yer some more, eh?'

'They take a lot of our money up, though.'

'That don't matter. We get by, don't we?'

As she said this, Janey knew it would be the bed for downstairs or the painkillers, but then she knew Mum would rather have the pain relief.

'We'll start giving you one before you have to climb the stairs and before you come down them, it might help.'

'That might be an idea as they do make it easier for me to move meself, luv.'

* * *

The next day when Janey managed to get the painkillers from the money that Annie's boss had sent over, they spoke no more about getting a bed, as they'd never manage to survive if they laid out the amount of money it would take to buy one. The medicine had taken a good chunk of the amazing amount that came through for them, as Janey had made her mind up to get enough to last a while. She'd rather starve than have her mum in pain.

She'd also stocked up with tinned meats and bought a bag of spuds. Mr Sutherland had told her to keep them cool and in the dark to preserve them. And another precious buy was yeast and strong flour. Making her own bread saved them quite a bit, and for a treat, a box of Typhoo tea leaves. She gave the football card inside to Harry as she knew he collected them. Lastly, she paid the electric bill and a few weeks' rent, some off the back of the book that she owed, and some to take them forward.

The only thing she hadn't managed to do was to contact the hospital. But she just had to hope that no news was good news until Mr Sutherland located Annie.

Everyone who had come into the shop asked after Annie. News had travelled fast. But the one person she'd expected to contact her, Jimmy Blaine, who'd always held a torch for Annie and had even asked for her address once, didn't show up. But then, he'd gone up in the world.

With this thought, she told herself that she must remember to tell Annie that. Annie knew he'd moved away and that his fortunes had changed, but not by how much.

Why she was thinking about him even, Janey didn't know. From what she'd heard he'd become a womanizer. So, maybe it was best not to mention him to Annie.

'Well, what are we having for tea tonight then, luv?'

'I thought we'd open a tin of corned beef and I'd make a hash. You like that, don't you, Mum?'

'Ooh, I do, luv . . . But I wish you had news on Annie, I've been worrying all morning.'

'No news is good news. I know it's a worry, but we can't do anything but wait. Annie will write or something, you'll see. She'll sort something. We just have to hang on to the fact that she ain't in danger. No doubt she ain't feeling good, but we're not going to lose her and that's the important thing.'

'You're right, luv. Like you say, there's nothing we can do . . . Oh, I forgot to tell you that Mrs Tyler had some tales to tell today . . .'

Janey smiled. Mum loved a bit of gossip, but then, it was all she had in the world as hers was a humdrum existence of pain and more pain and either being in bed or downstairs on the sofa. She relied on folk calling in for a natter in the winter as she couldn't go out. Her trips to the lav in the yard were her only fresh air – if you could call the smog that lay almost constantly above them fresh air. She did manage to sit outside in the summer, though, and Janey loved to see that as then Mum would come alive, calling out to and having a laugh with the neighbours.

As for her own life, Janey couldn't see it ever changing, nor would she want it to as that would mean something had happened to her mum. But she did have her dreams. Like any young girl of her own age, she dreamed of meeting a handsome man who would sweep her off her feet and be able to support her and her mum – take her way from this drab street and think of her as beautiful. She couldn't ever see that coming true, but she loved to lie in bed at night imagining it.

Chapter Four

Olivia

After saying her goodbyes to her aunt and uncle, who'd had to return to their estate in Cornwall, Olivia didn't know why she cried when Hendrick arrived, but for the first time she shed tears and couldn't stop as he held her gently and kissed her cheeks, and her swollen black eyes, and whispered over and over how much he loved her and how he thanked God that she had survived.

It was as if they were the only two in the room as she drank in his presence – the tallness of him, his wide shoulders, his fair hair that tended to the unruly if he didn't tame it with Brylcreem; the feel of which she hated, so she was glad that he hadn't done that today.

They gazed for a long moment into each other's eyes – his blue and beautiful, set in his strong features.

How she wished with all her heart that they were alone.

But her father's meaningful cough showed he was embarrassed. Hendrick straightened and uttered an apology – one she knew he didn't feel. He would never apologize for his love of her.

'That's all right, my dear boy. I'm happy to know that the

feeling between you both matches what my darling Sylvanna and I had.' He grinned. 'But it is somewhat embarrassing for me and Annie to witness it.'

Annie giggled.

Olivia felt a little sorry for her. She'd only ever waited on them and tended to their needs and now she was in the situation where she was treated as an equal. She could see her discomfort. Only her head showed from above the covers, and she'd been looking the other way until her name had been mentioned.

After Olivia's father had kissed both of Olivia's cheeks, his worry for her showed in his face as he turned to Annie. 'It seems, my dear, that we owe our darling Olivia's life to you. Thank you for your bravery. The rescue workers told the staff here that but for your actions my Olivia wouldn't be here. We are so grateful and will always look after you.'

'Ta, sir, but anyone would have done what I did.'

'No, no. You could have saved yourself and not been so badly burned, but you didn't. And I understand you are to care for Olivia from now on? Once you recover, that is. Well, I want you to know that we are both very pleased to hear that and will make you very welcome in our home.'

Olivia wasn't sure about this last bit. 'Daddy, I want to carry on with my studies. I was thinking that I could still go to your apartment in London and continue with that.'

'Good gracious, that's impossible now, my dear.'

'Why? Surely I can continue with my studies even if I can't walk? I need to be able to . . . Hendrick, you understand, don't you? I will walk again and when I do, I want to continue with our plans.'

'And I will support you in that, darling. It was a huge sacrifice for us to have to be apart for weeks on end until I could visit you or you could visit me, but it was one we were prepared to make for our future. I think that with Annie caring for you, you could still work towards our dream of having a language school.'

'But surely Olivia needs to get well first! And this dream you speak of, I hope you realize that it will leave me without an international financial investment manager if you leave my employment, Hendrick?'

'Oh, Daddy. You will soon find another. Besides, it will be a long time before we achieve our dream of opening our language school. I just don't want to make that even further in the future by not taking up my studies. As it is I will need at least two months before I can actually attend classes.'

'How do you know that you will be well enough then? I think the whole idea preposterous. You are a young woman, for goodness' sake! And you, Hendrick, should never expect your future wife to prepare for work.'

'Oh, Daddy, don't be so old-fashioned!' Though she laughed so that this was a teasing way of quietening her father, Olivia didn't feel like laughing. She felt more like weeping her heart out as the weakness that had taken her made her wonder if she really could once more be the woman that Hendrick needed: a strong woman, willing to work by his side to help build the future he would love – not just a language school, but one that took boarders. One where young men and women could come to the island of Guernsey, be cared for, and learn the language skills that would help their future career.

'That was a big sigh, my dear. We are being so unfair to you. Here you are in pain and your father and I are showing our disagreement over your future. I'm sorry . . . I want you to know that you can give up the idea of your studies. I will take care of you, no matter what you decide.'

Olivia looked at the two men who loved her most in the world and wanted to please them both. But she couldn't do that. She had to think of the man she loved and would spend the rest of her life with.

'I do want to study, darling. And I want us to have the future we have talked so much about. And it is good to think that even if I never walk again, I won't be stopping us from achieving that. I can teach from a wheelchair just as well as on two legs.'

Saying this brought the reality to her of what her own life might be and once more the tears flowed. She couldn't understand why she felt weepy today when she'd been so strong.

Annie surprised her then as she spoke up – something she had never done without being spoken to first.

'Excuse me. I ain't one for speaking out of turn, but as the one who is to care for Miss Olivia, I'm not liking all of this, it's upsetting her.'

'My dear, it is admirable that you are ready to take up Olivia's cause and I am grateful for that. But with us living so far away, her immediate future must be decided. If she is to be residing in my London apartment block, I will need to make a few adjustments to the penthouse which I keep for our family's use. Luckily, the ground-floor entrance is on the flat and there is a lift installed.'

'Sorry, sir, I just didn't like to see Miss Olivia crying.'

'There is no need to apologize. I want you to feel that you can speak freely with me.'

'Daddy, please go ahead with any adjustments. I've no idea what, as I've never visited the apartment. But I think I should go there and initially put into place arrangements for a tutor from the language school to visit me. I have waited

38

so long to do these courses. This is a setback, but I don't want it to end my plans.'

'My, my, how did you become such a modern-thinking young woman? Just like your dear mother. She was all for women asserting themselves. They do so much more in France, you know.'

Olivia relaxed. She could so easily have just said, *Take me home, Daddy*, but she knew that if she wasn't strong when she felt at her weakest, she wouldn't be the woman that Hendrick needed. And she loved him with all her heart.

Two days later, it was announced over the wireless that King George V had died.

Father was most put out.

'Jolly inconvenient of him. Now the work needed to make the step that divides the sitting room from the dining room into a gentle slope for the wheelchair can't begin for at least a fortnight and we must return home!'

Though she giggled at her father's words, the feel of Hendrick's hand squeezing hers told her he didn't want to leave her. Her heart dropped as she felt she couldn't face saying goodbye to him.

'I will come over every weekend, my darling. It will mean we won't have many hours together, but it will be worth it to see you and to satisfy myself on the progress you're making. I'll charter a boat, so we won't be relying on the ferry.'

'That will be wonderful. It will keep me going knowing that will happen.'

'Well, now.' Father interrupted. 'I have other news too.'

Used to her father's ways, Olivia waited, but knew she wouldn't be surprised at anything he came up with as at times it seemed he could move mountains.

'I have been in touch with a private clinic, not far from the apartment in London, to ask about booking you in there. I've spoken to your doctor, and he agrees that the care they give will be adequate for you, my dear. And having you there, it will be easier for Hendrick to get to you. Annie can stay there with you, but as she gets better, she can keep her eye on what's happening with the apartment and get to know Mrs Cockley. You won't need to do anything, Annie, as Mrs Cockley will clean up after the workmen each day, but you can make sure all is in place for Olivia and check if there is anything else you will need installing to make her life easier.' Turning back to Olivia, he said, 'And I've also contacted the college, Olivia. They will be happy to provide a tutor for you. They say their numbers are disappointingly down for this new year's intake and so can easily provide two tutors – one will teach you German and French and the other Russian and Latin, though they would advise you to drop the Latin as it is a crowded curriculum you are taking on. I will leave you to discuss that with them, my dear.'

'Oh, Daddy, thank you. Being there will massively increase the time that Hendrick can be with me.'

The chat then was of the king's death and speculation over Prince Edward and what type of king he would be. None of them could imagine him in the role as he would be expected to settle down and there didn't seem any sign of that happening.

But when her father turned the conversation once more to arrangements and dropped the bombshell that he and Hendrick had to leave the next day, Olivia felt devastated. She and Hendrick hadn't had a moment alone as visits had been taken up by her father and his plans for her. She'd spoken to Annie about this and was grateful to her for speaking up once more.

'Excuse me butting in, but I think I'll go for a wander. Nurse Riley said I can and has given me one of the hospital gowns to put over me nightie. I can walk the corridors to exercise me limbs.'

'That's a good idea.'

At this from her father, Olivia almost giggled at Annie's face as she must have thought he'd decided to follow her.

But she was saved as he said, 'I too will make myself scarce. I saw a tea room not far from here, and I'd like to see a little more of Oxford after having refreshment. And then I want to finalize arrangements for the move to the clinic for you, my dear. I could do that on the telephone from a post office. I'm sure I'll come across one.'

With the room to themselves, Hendrick kissed her how she'd longed for him to, making her feel like a woman once more instead of a useless being that couldn't do anything for herself.

'I love you so much, Olivia. We will get through this year and then it will be our wedding day. It can't come soon enough for me. I want you as my wife, my darling, but . . . well, I – I feel I should talk to you about something that worries me about the future.'

'Oh?'

Still holding her hand, Hendrick sat down in the chair beside her bed.

'It's this Hitler fellow. He has made it compulsory now that all boys and girls join the Nazi Youth groups. He's indoctrinating them and the German mothers can't see it. They are proud to send their children along. But worse than that, my father has written about how many restrictions are being put on the Jewish people and how those who are

41

inflicted with a permanent disability are forced to be sterilized as Hitler wants only perfect children to be born German.'

This appalled Olivia. She'd never heard of anything so horrific, and why persecute the Jewish people?

Although she hadn't spoken, Hendrick knew what she was thinking.

'I know, it's awful, isn't it? And Father says there is a camp at Dachau that is for anyone who is thought to be opposed to Hitler's policies or of what some call dubious sexuality. Also, Jehovah's Witnesses. It's scandalous, but people are afraid . . . My father is too, as he expressed his distaste of the regime before it came to power and just after.'

Shocked at these revelations, Olivia began to feel afraid. She'd heard snippets, but never had Hendrick spoken in such depth about what he knew from his father was happening in his country and now he seemed worried for his father's safety.

Hendrick had been brought up by an aunt, who had married a Frenchman and lived on the island of Guernsey. Many times, he'd visited his father, who had remarried after his mother had died, but his father had never come to Guernsey. It seemed his new wife hadn't ever wanted children and didn't want to bring up another woman's child. Hendrick always excused his father of being so in love with his wife that he had to sacrifice being with his own son to be with her.

This acceptance that Hendrick had of his father's choice was something Olivia had never understood. To her, it was almost as if he was alone in the world as his widowed aunt had also died and he lived alone in the house where she had brought him up and that had been left to him in her will.

'Can your father not come to live in Guernsey?'

'No. It is not possible. He is being watched. And already

I fear that one day the conscription that is in place in my country will extend to my age group. It is for eighteen to twenty-fives now and I have missed it by just two years.'

'No! But surely you won't have to go? You're hardly German now, you have been brought up differently to German children.'

'I know. I hate Hitler and all he stands for. I cannot believe that the German people are just doing all he says, but he rules by fear. My father is terrified for his life.'

'Oh, Hendrick. Thank goodness you're not a part of all of that. And we don't know if what you fear will actually happen, my darling.'

'You're right. Surely no one would harm a man in his sixties just for disagreeing with his government? He hasn't voiced his opinions for a long time, but was very vocal about his views when Hitler first came to power. He swears he hasn't said anything since the rumblings of trouble for dissidents first began.'

'I'm sure you're worrying too much. Let's not talk about that horrid man, but how things will be for us.'

'You're right. And I do have news. I wanted to surprise you and have everything ready for when you returned, but I now think what I have done will help and encourage you to get better . . . I have made an offer and it has been accepted on that farmhouse we saw and fell in love with while we were out driving last year.'

'Oh, Hendrick, really? Oh, it will be perfect for our plans. When will you own it?'

'All is going through now. I have a copy of the plans in my briefcase. They show the layout of the house how it is now. I'm hoping you will soon feel well enough to look at them and we can begin to exchange ideas of how it will best work for us. There are about four acres of land with it, which initially can be for our clients to take walks in and enjoy, but eventually, if we do well, we can try for planning permission to expand the building. And even think about building a house for us on the field that juts out to sea, so that we're not living on the premises.'

'It sounds wonderful! Oh, Hendrick, it *has* enthused me. I will work hard this year, and with you coming every weekend, we can decide to just speak in one of the languages all the time you're here.'

'*Ya tebya lyublyu.*'

'Oh, Hendrick, I love the sound of you saying you love me in Russian. But I love you – in any language – my darling.'

'And for me that is my world.' Hendrick kissed her fingers as he said this and Olivia knew that no matter what, she would get better, and they would start out on their journey together next year.

'Well, love, your father will be back soon, and we will have to part, but I promise I will be back next weekend.'

'I will count the hours . . . But, Hendrick, will you do something for me?'

'Anything. What is it, Olivia, you look anxious?'

'I am worried about Annie. She hasn't seen any of her family, and yet she was supposed to be spending this week with them. I know she is worrying about them as they have been informed, but they have no money and can't get here to see her. And Annie's mother is crippled with arthritis so probably couldn't make the journey, but there is a younger sister – Janey. My aunt was sending some money to them because Annie lost her year's salary in the crash, but from what I know, they live on what Annie takes home each year and what her sister can earn in the corner shop.'

'Hmm, of course I will see to helping them to visit, but how? Do you know their address?'

'Yes. Annie wrote it down for my aunt, who put it in her notebook, but I have the piece of paper here that Annie used.'

Hendrick looked at the address. 'It means nothing to me, and yet I did get to know London quite well when I was at Cambridge University. We students used to take the train regularly at weekends to see the sights and to let our hair down. But I will come up with a way. Your father has many contacts in London . . . And this telephone number, is that relevant?'

'Yes, it's the shop where Janey, Annie's sister, works.'

'Ah, that makes it all much more possible now. It means I can contact the sister to arrange things her end.'

'Oh, that's wonderful. Thank you so much, Hendrick. I know it will perk Annie up to be able to see her Janey.'

'It may not be until you are in the London clinic, my darling, as here we are a long way from London, and it isn't easy to arrange something to cover the distance.'

'Daddy said that it won't be long before we're moved. I'm hoping he will know when by the time he comes back.'

'Yes, that would help . . . It's sad that there's so much poverty in this country, and yet so much contrast as there are many who are very rich. But we cannot put the world to rights, and I need us to stop talking and for me to just hold you, darling.'

By standing and leaning over her, Hendrick managed to hold her in both of his arms.

To feel his strong body against hers, though the position caused her pain, was all Olivia wanted.

His kiss tingled through her and held a promise of all that

was to come. For one moment, she was transported from this white-walled hospital room to a land of dreams. She would hang on to those and let them be her guiding light as she faced all she'd have to go through.

Chapter Five

Annie

Three weeks passed before Olivia was well enough to be moved to the private clinic in Ryder Street, London, just one street away from her father's apartment.

Annie had mixed feelings about the move. She'd felt comfortable in the Oxford infirmary. The nurses, and the patients she'd met on her walks, were mostly her kind of people, but in here the patients were all rich and the staff more impersonal. And yet it was progress for Olivia, and that helped, as did more than anything knowing that tomorrow she would at last see Janey and get news on her mum.

Olivia's leg that had been suspended had been lowered a few days ago from the harness that had held it and the surgeon had been pleased with the X-ray that showed it was healing well.

There had been times when Annie had struggled to keep Olivia's spirits up and to keep her thinking good things about the future, after she'd been told that even though she would eventually walk again, she would have a limp as her most badly injured leg would have little movement from the knee.

The room at the clinic had a high, ornate ceiling, white-washed walls and a dark blue, highly polished linoleum covering the floor. The huge windows, which looked down on Ryder Street and across at other elegant buildings, were hung with white Venetian blinds, which were a novelty to Annie. She loved the shade they gave from the low winter sun and how she could make stripes on the walls by moving the positions of the slats. Olivia laughed at the joy she found in this, but Annie didn't mind. To her, there was so much to discover, and she found it sad that Olivia took most things in her stride as they were all familiar to her.

They'd eaten breakfast – served on the bed tables that were on wheels and slid from the end of the bed to a position that allowed you to sit up to eat your meals. For Annie, the food hardly filled her as dainty portions were served up on pretty bone-china plates, but Olivia still hadn't much of an appetite so there were leftovers for her to fill up on.

'I can't wait for Mrs Cockley to arrive, Annie. I've forgotten what you look like in clothes.'

'I know, me too. I just hope she don't buy me anything too posh.'

'You'll look lovely in anything. I'm really looking forward to dressing in the day. It's lovely to sit out of bed. I so want to look nice for when Hendrick comes tomorrow.'

'You always look nice, luv. Even your black eyes suited you.'

'Ha! I felt like a panda! But now with how you've done my hair for me and with looking forward to getting dressed, I can hardly believe it has all happened.'

They fell quiet for a moment. The memories of the horror they'd survived trembled through Annie. In a way, she envied Olivia not remembering much about it. To Annie, it was a hell that visited her most nights and at moments like this.

'Annie, I can't believe what you did for me. A lot of people would have left me and saved themselves. I want you to know that I'll never forget it and will always care for you.'

They'd never spoken much about the train crash. They knew that two people had been killed, one being the driver, and a lot injured, but for Annie, it was difficult to revisit the terror, or to think about it all, let alone to talk about it.

She went over to Olivia's bedside. 'You have already. You've changed me life and that's thanks enough, luv. Oh, except all me new clothes you're buying me. They're a bonus.'

They giggled at this, and Olivia reached for Annie's hand. 'I've never met anyone like you, Annie. You're "real", somehow.'

'Well, I've never been described like that before. And I'm glad I met you, too. Though I can't get used to our new standing with each other and I still feel like bobbing when you ask me to pass you something.'

'With your bruised and gashed legs, you'd have a job!'

Once more they were giggling and, to Annie, it was nice to hear Olivia so cheerful. She knew some of that was due to her only having to wait one more day to see Hendrick, but even then, just a week ago, her pain was such that laughing hurt.

'It's good to see you on the mend, luv.'

'That's down to you too. You didn't have to stay with me. You could have gone home, and I know you were longing to. I prayed you wouldn't as having you by my side has made the pain bearable, and looking into my future a lot better than it would have been.'

'I won't leave you, luv. Don't you worry about that.'

'But what if you go to meet Janey tomorrow and meet a handsome young man? Have you ever had a boyfriend, Annie?'

'No. Unless you count snotty-nosed, ragged-arsed Jimmy Blaine. He fancied me when I were twelve. He wrote me a love letter once, then got the cane for passing it to me in the classroom. Poor fella, the teacher read it out before whacking him six times on his bottom for disrupting class.'

'Oh dear, did he go off you after that?'

'No. He still hung around. He even smartened himself up when Janey told him I wouldn't touch him with a barge pole as he stank.'

'Oh no! Oh, Annie, don't. It hurts when I laugh . . . How old was she then?'

'Eight, and she were a madam, I can tell you. Me and me mum spoiled her after me dad died. He was badly injured in the war and were never well. Janey can't remember him; she was only six months when he passed. But I see him every day in me mind. Me mum helped that as she told me when he died to think of his best face with a smile on and lock it in me head for ever. He were a lovely dad, kind and gentle. He didn't go to war at first. He worked on the docks, but when things looked bad, he was called up in the February of 1916. I was almost one and had me first birthday a week after he left. He came home a couple of times, but me first real memory of him was from late 1917 when he was discharged from the military hospital in the Midlands.'

'I'm sorry to hear that. I know how hard it is to lose a parent, even though I have no memory of my mother. But she's still in my heart, and I carry the picture of her in my head, from a photo that hangs in my bedroom at home . . . So, you must have had your twenty-first birthday in February? You never said!'

'We weren't in any fit state for birthdays, but yes, it were.'

'No, I can hardly remember most of it, it's just a pain-blur.

But that means there's only three months between us as I was twenty-one in November last year.'

A knock on the door – something that never happened in the Oxford hospital – interrupted their conversation. Olivia called out, 'Come in.'

A nurse entered. 'You have a visitor, loaded down with bags. A Mrs Cockley?'

'Oh, yes, we are expecting her.'

A rounded lady entered. She hardly took a breath, or even said hello before she spoke.

'Eeh, that weren't easy, buying for two lasses I've never met, and with only a few measurements from the secretary of this place to go on and her saying as one of you were the maid and the other the mistress. So, which is which then?'

Annie and Olivia looked at each other, and Annie thought it was strange to her that it wasn't obvious, but then neither of them had spoken yet and they were both in pyjamas.

'I'm, Annie, luv. I'm a maid to Miss Olivia, only we've become friends now.'

'Aye, well, being in the same boat is levelling, lass. Pleased to meet you, Annie, and you, Miss Olivia. And we all need a friend. I ain't got one, nor a relative in the world. You Londoners are hard to get to knaw. This city can be a lonely place.'

Annie had a surge of love for this middle-aged lady with her outspoken ways, her hairnet covering most of her greying hair, and her long coat of the fashion of twenty years ago.

Mrs Cockley's round, kindly face made you feel that she would take care of you no matter what.

'Well, you've two friends now, Mrs Cockley. Me and Olivia.'

'Eeh, you're a grand lass. I reckon we're going to get along fine and that flat that I rattle around in ain't going to be so quiet as it was.'

'And we're pleased to have you to make our lives easier, Mrs Cockley, and you needn't call me "miss", just Olivia will do. May we know your name as friends should be on first-name terms?'

'I'm Cissy. Short for Cecelia. By, I hope I've done right by you girls. I ain't much up on fashion, so I stuck to practical, but pretty, as you're only young 'uns and have been through so much. I were right sorry to hear what happened. Your da was very upset, bless him. A nice man. And your aunt. I love it when she and your uncle come to stay. And now tomorrow, I'm to meet your fiancé, Olivia, lass. Well, don't you worry, I'll take good care of him an' all.'

Annie loved the way Cissy expressed herself and just wanted to hug her.

As Olivia thanked her, Annie opened one of the bags.

'Now, that one's your under-bee-gums, lass.'

'Me what?'

'You knaw, knickers and things. Oh, and some thick stockings and lighter ones an' all.'

'Oh, righto. I like that name – under-bee-gums. I ain't ever heard it before but it sounds better than knickers and bras.'

Cissy giggled in such a way that a youngster would, as if she hadn't heard anyone call these garments their proper name and didn't think it quite right to do so.

'I have all the receipts, and charged it to your da's account, as were the instructions, Olivia, so we can take anything back if it don't suit or fit either of you lasses.'

When Annie pulled out a frock made of wool from the bag that Cissy had said held the clothes she'd chosen for her, she gasped. It was beautiful, and yet simply styled with sewn pleats in the bodice and false buttons down the middle to her waist and then a skirt that had only a slight flare. It could be worn during the day or evening, but only for special occasions.

'By, that'll suit you with your blue eyes, lass. Go and try it on, then we'll know if the other garments will fit. I've bought two plain frocks for daytime, a skirt and two different coloured twinsets for each of you, besides the undies and a warm coat. I reckon the coats you had on aren't much good now.'

Annie was too overcome to answer. She'd only ever owned her working frocks and her Sunday best before. And never anything of the quality these were. But Olivia thanked Cissy for them and showed surprise and pleasure as she took out a navy frock with a pleated skirt and white collar and cuffs. 'Oh, this is lovely. And it looks a good length for me too. Oh, and the lemon twinset and grey wool skirt . . . I love them all.' After this, she brought out a pale green twinset and two day frocks in linen. One a light blue and the other a light brown.

For Annie, there was a pink twinset, a navy wool skirt and a peach twinset. She couldn't think how Cissy had carried them all, besides the bag holding two thick wool coats, one for her in chocolate brown and one for Olivia in a moss green.

Clutching them to her, Annie trotted off to the bathroom. She'd already had the luxury of a hot bath that morning so didn't need to wash – though her bath wasn't without guilt as poor Olivia was still having to bear bed baths and bed pans, which she thought must be an awful experience for her. Humiliating too, having to do private things with others in the room, but she coped well and that made it easier for them both.

Before she slipped into the deliciously figure-hugging and pretty underwear, choosing the winceyette because she hardly dared to touch the silk ones, or even the lovely delicate white cotton set, Annie hugged them to her, wanting to savour the feel of them and the thought that they were hers. Part of her hoped that something would be too small and then she'd ask if the cost could be deducted from her pay, and she could give it to Janey.

But everything fitted her as if made for her, and she felt like a princess as she paraded each garment to oohs and aahs from Olivia and Cissy.

Lastly, she put one of the day frocks on, a plain, light grey with a white collar and white belt that buckled and showed off her slim waist.

'I nearly bought you both a pair of them women's trousers each, but I didn't knaw how you felt about them. Some say trousers are for men, not women, but by, if I were younger, I'd wear them like a shot. Why should the menfolk have all the comfort and warmth, eh?'

'I would have worn them. I've wanted a pair for ages, but Father isn't keen. I've never asked Hendrick, but he's very modern-thinking and I can't see him objecting. Once I'm well, I'll buy myself some.'

'Well, I can allus get them for you. Come spring, you'll want to go out of here for walks and trousers will keep you warm if the weather's still chilly.'

'Oh, thanks, that would be lovely, Cissy.'

'I'd love a pair too, but I ain't tall enough to carry them off, I'd look like a kid in long 'uns, so that makes me mind up for me.'

'We'll see, Annie. When you see them all wearing them about town, lass, you might change your mind . . . Anyroad, is there a chance for a poor shopped-out lady to get a pot of tea around here?'

'Oh, that's rude of us, sorry, Cissy. Annie, will you pull the cord and get someone here, love? I could do with a cup of tea myself.'

As she did this, making sure she pulled the right cord as there was one for emergencies, one for nurse assistance and one for room service, Annie said, 'A good idea, then after a cuppa, we can see about trying your clothes on, Olivia, luv. I can help you. I'm used to manoeuvring you and them plaster-cast legs of yours.'

'I don't think you'll get the under-bee-gums on me, though!'

They all laughed. It was always funny if Olivia tried to use slang, but this sounded hilarious with her posh tone.

'Well, we'll get a pair that would fit Grandma Buggins, they should do the trick, lass. And we can pin them around the waist.'

Their laughter increased at this as Annie recounted the episode of *The Buggins Family* on the wireless.

'Oh, *The Buggins Family*. I love that show, it has me in stitches. Remember the time Mrs Buggins managed to get them all to go on a picnic? They were on the top of a hill and Grandma says, "That 'ill's started me breakfast floatin', and I ain't goin' another step till it's perched." Then Mrs Buggins replies, "Well, that's yer own fault fer eatin' so 'earty." And Father clamps down on them both: "Now, now, now! I don't come out fer the day to 'ear you two spite at one another – I can 'ear that at 'ome!"'

Olivia's laughter was the loudest of them all at this. 'Oh, Annie, you sound just like them. I love the *Buggins* show, they tell how life really is for most. I go between feeling really sorry for poor downtrodden Mrs Buggins, to wanting to shake her!'

To Annie, it was good to see Olivia relaxing and enjoying the company, and this had brought some colour to her cheeks – a lovely sight. It seemed that it didn't matter where you came from, Guernsey, the north-east of England, or if you were a cockney, all had one thing in common – the enjoyment of listening to *The Buggins Family*.

They were still laughing as they said goodbye to Cissy a few minutes later.

'By, that were good to have a lighter moment, me lasses. I'll be back tomorrow and I'll bring you some nice soaps and some talcum powder. Ta-ra for now.'

As the door closed on Cissy, Annie turned to see Olivia's face glowing. 'Oh, Annie, Cissy's lovely, and she's chosen so well. I'd love to try one of my frocks on.'

'She is, and so easy to get on with. Come on then, luv, let's get started.'

Though they did their best, they had to call the nurse to assist them in standing Olivia up to get the frock to fall into place once she had it as far as her waist.

Everything fitted and Olivia looked lovely and almost back to new, and even though her pale face had grimaced in pain at some of the movements she'd had to make, Annie felt that at last they had turned a corner.

The next morning Annie woke with a feeling of excitement gripping the muscles of her stomach. At last the day had come for her to see her adored sister. Oh, how she missed her, and her mum. A tear came to her eye at not being able to have a visit from Mum, but at least she would find out today how she was.

And it helped to leave Olivia knowing she too was to have a visitor as Hendrick was coming today and one of the nurses had promised to come in good time to help her to dress as she so wanted to surprise Hendrick and not be in her night-wear for the first time.

Annie did her hair for her before she left but struggled as it seemed lifeless and didn't want to even fall into its natural wave. But eventually she managed to twist it into the rag strips and then leave them in place while she got herself ready.

She decided to wear the skirt and the pink twinset and once more felt like a princess as she twirled in front of the mirror. But she couldn't fully enjoy the excitement of wearing nice clothes as she thought of poor Janey in her cast-offs.

Deciding Janey must have filled out by now, as she had done herself by the time that she was seventeen, she put the pink twinset into the bag that Cissy had brought her clothes in. It would look lovely on Janey, and she would be thrilled.

Feeling really pleased with her decision, she told Olivia, 'I just can't have stuff like this whilst Janey has nothing. Are you all right with that, luv?'

'I am. Oh, Annie, I promise that when I'm better I'll make things better for your mum and sister, but in the meantime, would one of my twinsets fit your mother?'

'You don't have to do that, Olivia, but ta, luv, for offering.'

'I know I don't, but I want to. Which one would suit her best? I don't mind which one.'

Annie felt overwhelmed. To be able to take such a gift to her mum and sister was more than she had ever dreamed of. 'I think the green would suit her. She has hazel eyes and fair hair like me.'

'Good choice . . . Oh, Annie, how I would love to be going out too.'

'You will, luv. You just have to be patient a bit longer. Anyway, you've got Hendrick coming today, so that'll be good, won't it?'

Olivia brightened up at this.

'Now, let me get them rags out of your hair, you look so funny with them in. And let's hope they've done the trick, eh?'

They had. Olivia's dark brown hair fell into soft curls and looked lovely.

Once outside, Annie realized how weak she really was. The effort of dressing, seeing to Olivia and getting as far as the pavement left her feeling shaky. She leaned against the wall to catch her breath.

A familiar sounding cockney voice made her jump.

'Stone the crows, it ain't who I think it is, is it? Annie? Annie! Hey, it's me! Jimmy!'

Annie turned in the direction of the voice and her mouth dropped open. There in front of her was Jimmy Blaine! Though he didn't have a snotty nose any more, but was tall and handsome, in a cocky, rakish kind of way, with his flat cap worn at a jaunty angle showing a few curls of his dark hair. His smile showed lovely, even white teeth, and yet he hadn't changed, not really, as she'd known him immediately.

'Jimmy! What you doing up west then? I heard you and your mum had moved out of our area, but I didn't think you'd changed sides.'

'No, I still live in Bethnal Green, just a better area. And I had me own barrow, mate, only I ain't got it now, I've got a small van. I've done well for meself and have a regular round besides a stall in Covent Garden. That's me van over there, that green one with me name on the side.'

Annie's eyes almost popped out of her head as they followed the direction Jimmy pointed in. Standing next to the kerb on the other side of the street was a shiny green van and written on the side in large white letters was *Jimmy Blaine, Fresh Vegetables and Fruit Deliveries*!

'I deliver to this posh clinic here. You should see inside, mate. Talk about your fancy hotels, they ain't a patch on this.'

'I know. I just came out of there.'

'What? Are yer a nurse or something? Though you've a fancy coat on that makes me think you've done all right for yourself, Annie . . . Here, are you rushing off to somewhere? Only I could take a break once I've dropped off what veg the chef of this place wants.'

'I'm meeting Janey, she's being brought here by cab. I can't leave this spot; though I have come out early.'

'I can't take this in, mate. Finding you after all these years and here on me doorstep, so to speak. I heard you were down in Cornwall!'

'It's a long story, Jimmy . . . I – I . . .'

'Annie! Annie, mate, are you all right?'

Annie's legs felt as though they would give way. Jimmy grabbed her and held her to him. 'I've got you, luv. Hold on to me.'

There was a comfort for Annie as she laid her head on Jimmy's strong chest and his arms held her. She smelled the freshness of his shirt that came from it having billowed on a line to dry. And a sense of feeling safe came to her from being with one of her own kind. She willed the tears that had welled up not to spill over, but they did, and there, in an unfamiliar street, she wept her heart out on Jimmy's shoulder as an overwhelming sense of wanting to go home came over her. She wanted her mum.

59

'Annie, girl, what is it? I'm here for you, mate. I've never forgotten you. Let me help you, I'll do anything. Anything you want, luv.'

Annie managed to control herself. 'Ta, Jimmy . . . I – I've 'ad it rough . . . I – I were in that train crash outside Oxford.'

'No! Oh, Annie, were you hurt bad?'

'No, bruising, some burns and gashes. Me charge, a girl of me same age, were hurt worse. She's in that clinic . . . But I ain't told anyone that I can't get the horror of it out of me mind. I feel like me world is all changed, and yet I'm surrounded by kindness . . . and love. But it just ain't home and I miss me mum and Janey so much.'

'I'll take you home, mate. I've only got a couple of drops to make. Me mum runs the stall, so I've got time. Mind, she'll clip me lug 'oles if I'm late back as big as I am, so we'll have to go to the market first to let her know what me plan is.'

Annie loved hearing the cockney slang that Jimmy used. It seemed years since anyone had called their ears lug 'oles, and she couldn't believe she was going home. She came out of Jimmy's arms and looked up at him. He wiped a tear from her cheek, then held her face in his hands. 'I meant it when I said I'd never forgotten you, Annie. I know I pestered you when I were a ragged-arsed kid, but I'd like to see more of you now that I've found you again. Do you think there's a chance for me, eh?'

Annie couldn't believe what she was hearing, or that any of this was happening. How did she get from being in Cornwall, to being in a hospital, to being in Jimmy Blaine's arms and never wanting to leave them?

'I'd like that, Jimmy . . . Only, I have me job and me responsibilities.'

'You mean, you're going back down to Cornwall? Why? You needn't, you know. There're jobs around here.'

Annie's mind went back to how she'd started as a maid in one of the big houses on the edge of Bethnal Green – a place of contrasts with the rich living close by and yet as if they were a million miles away. And how it had seemed like an adventure when she had been offered a position in such a faraway place as Cornwall, and she'd jumped at it because of the better pay. But there had been a loneliness in her that she hadn't recognized until now.

'I have a job here. Well, just around the corner.' She told him about Olivia.

'That's smashing news, mate. It means I can see you again . . . I can even sell you the best fresh veg in London!'

Annie didn't know why, but she burst out laughing. Jimmy laughed with her then put his arms around her again and pulled her to him. She didn't resist. Didn't want to, but shyly put her arms around him and held him. It felt good. Like an old mate had her back for her. But no, more than that – like she'd come home.

Chapter Six

Janey

'Annie!' Janey called out to her sister, hardly believing her eyes.

There was Annie, who'd she'd longed to see, locked in the arms of a bloke she could've sworn was Jimmy Blaine!

Annie blushed as she came out of Jimmy's arms and looked towards Janey. Janey had the impression that she'd been far away in her thoughts and now that reality had hit her, she looked ashamed. She didn't want that. After what Annie had been through, she was entitled to seek comfort from one of her own.

'Annie! Oh, Annie, luv.'

Once Janey was in her big sister's arms, all thoughts of Annie's actions left her as she gave way to sobs of relief.

Holding her at arm's length, Annie looked into her eyes. 'Oh, Janey, it's good to see you. I'm all right, luv, don't cry. I'm all better now . . . Oh, Janey, I can't believe we're together at last! How's Mum?'

'She's not well, Annie. I didn't want to leave her, only Mrs Tyler said she'd see to her. Mum can hardly move now, she just sits on the sofa . . . I feel we're going to lose her, Annie. It were a big blow to her to hear what happened to you.'

'No! Don't think like that. I'm here now, girl. Together we can pull Mum through.'

'I thought I was going to lose you too, Annie.'

'I did meself for a bit, luv, but I got out and that's the main thing. Do you remember . . .' Annie turned back to Jimmy, but he'd gone. Annie's face dropped.

'Jimmy Blaine? Yes, I weren't sure it was him till I came closer. I saw him about a year ago. He asked after you then. He wanted your address, but I didn't give it to him – he's a bit of a womanizer. Thinks he's God's gift after going up in the world. I was shocked to see you in his arms, Annie! How did that come about?'

Annie smiled. 'I suppose it must have looked strange, but a womanizer? Oh, I didn't expect you to say that. Though he is handsome, so I suppose it goes with the territory.'

'Don't go falling for him, Annie, luv, you'll end up with a broken heart.'

But even as she said this, Janey wondered if it was too late for that as Annie looked hurt at finding out about Jimmy's reputation.

'Huh, 'ark at you. You sound like me mum.'

Janey didn't take umbrage at this as Annie's love for her showed in her look and her smile; she was only teasing her. It was so good to just be with her big sis and have her do that.

'Seriously, though, I can't believe how grown-up you are, and how your figure has filled out. Suddenly, you're a young woman. Mind, I ain't seen you since January of nineteen thirty-five – almost fifteen months ago!'

'I know, I've missed yer, Annie, and Mum has. It rocked our world when we heard the news.'

'Well, I'm here now, luv.'

'Yes. But how did you meet up with Jimmy?'

'He was just there! I came out of the clinic, and he was there! I know it looked bad, him cuddling me, but oh, Janey, I've been through horror, and it all washed over me as I left the clinic. It was like I was on me own in a strange world. To see Jimmy and to be offered comfort by him . . . well, I took it . . . and the strangest thing happened. I wanted to be in his arms, Janey. I did.'

'Ha, you wouldn't have said that when I were a kid! Do you remember me telling him what you thought of him?'

They giggled together. 'I do! Me and Olivia had a laugh about it . . . You'll love Olivia, she's the best friend I've ever had.'

'She sounds nice. Were it her that gave you your posh clothes?'

'It was.' She told Janey about Cissy too.

'I love them both already . . . Where are we going, Annie, luv?' Janey looked around her. Feeling trapped in a strange world, she said, 'I don't know anywhere around here, and I ain't comfortable. You're all right in your lovely posh coat but look at me. I can feel everyone giving me a wide berth as if I smell or something.'

'Ah, come here, luv. They don't know a lovely girl when they see one.'

They hugged then, and to Janey it no longer mattered what anyone thought of her, now that she was in her sister's arms.

When they came out of the hug, Janey asked again, 'So, what are we going to do, Annie? I'm getting cold standing here.'

'Jimmy'll be out in a minute. He said he'd take us home if we like . . . Would that be all right? Only, I really want to see Mum and, well, just be back in normality, as it don't matter how long I'm away, there's nowhere like our street, our folk and our home.'

Janey smiled. 'Oh, yes, please, Annie. We can check on Mum then and I've managed to get a coal house full of coal, partly through young Harry next door. I'll tell you about that sometime, but mostly I topped up the coal house and filled the pantry too with that money your boss had sent over to us. It seemed more than your normal wage and I've got loads of it left.'

'They're all kind-hearted. You wouldn't think it of posh folk and I ain't seen a lot of kind acts over me time with them, though all the staff are treated well in Wallington Manor and are happy.'

'That's good. I couldn't bear it if you were treated badly.'

They hugged again.

'I wish you'd never gone there, though, Annie.'

'I wouldn't have if things were as bad as they are now, luv. But Mum was coping well, and you were all right. And it's been good for keeping you well fed and the rent paid, ain't it?'

'It has, though I do get behind with the rent. But all that don't matter, I'd have rather starved and had you with us than not.'

A look of guilt flushed over Annie's face. Janey hadn't meant for that to happen and felt mortified. 'You're right, Annie, we needed the money, we would never have managed without it.'

Though she said this and wanted so much to undo what she'd done, Janey's thought was that it was possible for Annie to have earned as much in the factories, but she couldn't see Annie working in one of them places.

Janey could have, though, but she was never given the chance.

Jimmy coming out from the alley at the side of the clinic took these thoughts from her and she was glad. She didn't know what it was with her lately. This feeling of being Cinderella wasn't good for her, but oh, how she longed to have some fun like other girls of her age.

As she turned towards Jimmy, she caught her breath. To her, he looked beautiful as the sunlight caught him.

'Well, you two, are you all right now? Nice to see you, Janey.'

'And you, Jimmy.' As Janey looked up at him, for some reason her heart flipped over and the thought she had was confirmed. He really was good-looking. But then, she'd heard Jimmy had that effect on all the womenfolk and loved it.

'But I've warned our Annie of your ways, Jimmy, so you'd better be careful. I'll have me eye on you and'll soon tell you if you step out of line.'

'Ha, me ways? That don't sound good. And I know you'll be one for giving me a telling, Janey, I can remember from way back. How did you get to be so grown-up anyway?'

Janey laughed, and told him, 'While you weren't looking, mate.'

Jimmy laughed with her, then looked serious as he said, 'Don't take any notice of what you hear. I can't help it if the women throw their hats at me. Half of them I wouldn't touch with a bargepole. Besides, I've been waiting for me Annie and now she's here, she'll be the only one I want to win over.'

Janey didn't know why she felt a pang of jealousy. She was being silly. If Jimmy wanted any of them, it would be Annie, of course it would. Janey was only a slip of a girl.

She only wished she felt like one, instead of all grown-up and with the feeling of missing out on ever being young.

As Annie smiled back at Jimmy, Janey could see a special light in her eyes. She made herself laugh as Annie told him, 'Well, you men are all entitled to sow your wild oats, as I've heard said. But I ain't saying I'm available.'

'Well, I'll wait as long as it takes. So, are you two all right now? Only when I left you, you were crying.'

'We are. We like a few tears; it helps us to cope.'

'Well, Janey, luv, we were brought up on love and tears . . . Right, I've just got to put together the order and take it in. There's a tea room just around the corner. Go along there and get a hot drink, you must be frozen. I'll come to you when I'm ready and take you to see me mum before I take you home to see yours.'

'Ta, Jimmy.'

He hesitated as he went to cross over to his van. 'Oh, I didn't think, have you got some money?'

Annie answered him. 'I have. I've been looked after well, ta . . . Come on, Janey, let's hurry.'

In the tea room – a posh place with white cloths on the tables, and set with delicate bone-china plates and cups and saucers, with a cake knife at each place – Janey felt swamped by it all.

'You're as good as the next one, Janey, and don't you forget it.'

She managed a shy smile but her chest tightened with nerves and she hardly dared breathe. Annie distracted her as she asked, 'So, you don't think much to Jimmy then, girl?'

'He's all right. He's got a bit of a reputation. It's more by word of mouth than anything as I ain't seen a lot of him to know if it's true or not. If it is, it's probably like you say, sowing his wild oats, luv. I like him and how he's open with it all. He didn't try to cover it up, so that's something in his favour.'

'Well, it's no matter. It's nice to see Jimmy again, but that's all. It just meant the world to have a fellow cockney give me a cuddle.'

It wasn't long before they were on their way. The van had a bench seat and Annie positioned herself in the middle squashed up to Jimmy, making Janey wonder about her last statement as she didn't miss how every now and again, if the van had to slow, Jimmy put his hand over Annie's and looked into her eyes. Each time Janey felt a stab to her heart, but then asked herself how it was possible for her to feel this way about Jimmy Blaine!

She hadn't yet turned seventeen, so shouldn't even be having these feelings for someone so much older than herself! Besides, Jimmy was obviously besotted with Annie and always had been. She just hoped that Annie would heed her warning and take things slowly. She couldn't bear for her to be hurt.

Looking out of the window, Janey wondered how it had happened that the scruffy devil, four or five years older than her, who she'd stood in front of with her hands on her hips all those years ago and told a few home truths to, had turned into this man who seemed as though he was under her skin. And how was it that his life had changed from living in a hovel to being a man of business? She stopped herself thinking that he was not only that, but the most handsome man she'd ever laid eyes on.

After the last drop that Jimmy had to make to a hotel, it took only a few minutes to get to Covent Garden – a place that felt like a little bit of cockney land in the West End, as

68

voices called out, 'Lavely cabbages, luv! Look at the 'eart on them, enough to get yours ticking faster, and only a farthing each!' And, 'Get your spuds 'ere, the cheapest in the land and nothing but the best, mate! Fill your bag for a ha'penny.'

All around them there was cheerful laughing, but best of all, as Annie put it, was how familiar it all felt.

As they came up to Jimmy's mum, she looked quizzical for a moment. 'Who you got here then, Jimmy? . . . Janey! Hello, girl . . . And don't tell me this is Annie! Well, where's me Jimmy got you two from then?'

When all was explained, Rosie, as they'd always known her to be called, came around from inside the square of tables that made up her stall and put her arms out to Annie. 'I thought you looked peaky, luv. Well, you're all right now you're home, eh? Your mum'll be pleased to see you, poor soul that she is, or so I've heard. I don't get time to go to the street like I used to, we're always here or at our warehouse.'

The more she heard, the more Janey pondered how it was that the Blaines' fortunes had changed. Their own terraced house seemed like a palace compared to the one the Blaines had lived in. There'd been no dad that she remembered, and no other kids, but they'd lived in poverty and filth. It was all a big mystery to her and to most of the street.

It was on the way home that she found out as Jimmy said, 'I expect you're both wondering how the change in me and Mum's fortune came about? Though you've probably heard tales, Janey.'

Janey didn't answer, but Annie said, 'I am wondering. I'm pleased for you, though. I can't tell you how pleased, but it's a lot to take in.'

'Well, to start at the beginning, me mum's not wed.

She were raped by me granddad when she were eighteen and found she was expecting me.'

This so shocked Janey, she couldn't comment, and Annie just sat quietly as Jimmy carried on:

'She ran away from home and somehow, she found the hovel we lived in and scraped by . . . Well, you know how. And let's say, it weren't a nice way to earn a copper or two, but she did it to feed me and pay the rent. But she couldn't cope really and let the cleaning and washing side of things slide. You see, she'd come from a market garden family on the edges of Kent, so everything was alien to her. Anyway, one day this toff came knocking and it appeared me granddad had died, and she was next of kin. She didn't sell the land that was left to her but got a manager for it. As it turned out, a good one, and someone she'd known a long time. Alf, his name is. I'm still hoping they'll get together one of these days.'

His half-smile further fluttered Janey's heart.

'Anyway, everything began to improve and expand. We live near the park in Bethnal Green now. Mind, we don't forget our roots and Mum and me, we distribute any surplus produce around to the poor . . . They ain't where they were as them slums have all gone, but the folk who lived there are in tenements, which they hate, and with the slump, there's a lot of them that don't know where their next meal is coming from.'

'There's a few in our street, Jimmy, but you never came there.'

'No, Janey, it would feel like we were shoving our good fortune down their necks. Sorry, luv. Have you had it bad?'

'We have, but I see your point. They're a proud lot around us.'

'Well, I'm glad for you, Jimmy. It sounds like you weren't meant to be an East Ender in the first place, and you've regained your rights.'

'We have, Annie, but I wouldn't't've missed being brought up on our street and near to you.' Again, he squeezed her hand. Janey cast her eyes away from the look that passed between them. It seemed to her that Jimmy and Annie were made for each other all along and now they had found each other, she had to be content for her lovely sister's sake. What she felt was probably only an infatuation. She knew they happened to girls of her age. She'd have to stop being so silly!

Jimmy Blaine had only just come back into their lives, he was obviously besotted with Annie, and she with him, and he wouldn't ever in her wildest dreams have any thoughts of her – even if it was true that he was a womanizer, which she preferred to think he was!

Instead of drooling over him, she'd keep an eye on him and make sure he didn't ever hurt Annie. If he did, he'd have her to answer to!

Chapter Seven

Annie

For all the happiness Annie felt at the turn of events since leaving the clinic, her spirits plummeted, and her heart felt as if it split in two to see her mum sitting on the sofa. Her face was creased with pain and her eyes showed the agony she was in. Her poor hands and feet were even more gnarled and twisted than Annie remembered.

'Mum? Oh, Mum. I've missed you, luv. But I'm here now.'

'Annie, luv! Me Annie. I've missed you so much.' A tear plopped from her mum's eye onto her cheek.

Annie held her mum as best she could, trying to encase her in her love.

'Oh, Mum, your painkillers are still on the table. Didn't Mrs Tyler come in to give them to you?'

'No, Janey, luv. Her Harry got in a spot of bother with the coppers, and she had to go down to the station. I gave her a penny to get her there, but in her rush, forgot to ask her to put them near to me.'

'I'll get you some water, and you can take them. You'll soon feel better.'

Jimmy surprised them then. 'I'll do that, Janey. I remember

where the kitchen is. I tell you, it's like coming home being here.'

Annie blushed at Janey's reply to Jimmy.

'Ha, I don't think so, mate, we don't live how you did.'

For the life of her Annie couldn't think what was wrong with her sister. She'd never known her be rude to anyone.

But then it got worse as Jimmy retorted, 'No, and for all you go through, it don't come near to what me mum and me went through, either.'

As Jimmy went into the kitchen, Annie couldn't help herself but to tell Janey off. She'd never had to do it in her life before and felt disloyal starting now. 'That wasn't called for, Janey, you should apologize. Jimmy ain't done nothing to you. What's making you be so hostile towards him?'

'I'm sorry. I . . . Well, I worry that he's leading you on. You've only just met up and yet you're holding hands and giggling away with him.'

'You're jealous . . . Oh, Janey, luv, I'm all grown-up and can look after meself, I promise, and having friends – something I've never had – ain't going to take me away from you. Come here, you daft thing.'

They went into a hug. Janey's body was rigid at first, but she soon relaxed and hugged Annie back.

When Jimmy came back in with a mug of water, Janey apologized. 'I'm sorry, Jimmy. I shouldn't have said that. I were worried about me mum.'

'And your sister. I understand, luv. You've heard stuff about me, and you don't want Annie hurt. Well, I don't know how to prove to you that I ain't like the name I have, but I can promise, I ain't going to hurt her, luv.'

'I know. Sorry. And your mum did the best she could, I know that now. I just don't know what made me say it.'

As Jimmy put the mug down, he went to go towards Janey, but a funny look passed over her face that said, *Don't touch me*, and she turned away and busied herself giving Mum her tablets.

Mum took the attention away from the moment as she asked, 'So, I take it you're Jimmy Blaine?'

'Sorry, Mum. Do you remember ragged-arsed Jimmy Blaine?'

'I do. He were sweet on you as a kid, but was always snotty-nosed, so you didn't like him.' Mum grinned at Jimmy as she said this.

'That's me, Mrs Freeman. But I'm all grown-up now and making me way in the world.'

'I heard about that. Your mum came into some money or something and you left the area. Never seen sight of you since, though heard plenty of tales of your antics. So where did you go then?'

'Ha, me reputation has been built up from nothing, and travelled far, I see.'

As Jimmy told Mum his story, she was amazed but looked pleased for him. 'Well, your poor mum, we never knew . . . All sorts of stories used to circulate about her, and most weren't good, but I always found her to be a strong young woman who was kindly. I'm glad for you, and more than glad for her. You tell her I send me best wishes. But fancy you just coming across Annie like that! Ha, she used to dodge you all the time! Bet she didn't this time, eh?'

'She didn't . . . Well, let's just say, we're both glad to have found each other.'

He winked at Annie and Annie blushed as her mum looked at her with a knowing expression and smiled, a smile that went to her eyes and warmed Annie's heart.

'Anyway, Jimmy, don't go thinking that's it, and I've fallen head over heels for you. You need to prove yourself to me, you know.'

'Oh dear. You as well, Annie? I thought you'd have a bit more faith in me. We go back a long way, girl.'

'Ha, we do, and I ain't believing it all. But we've a long way to go too, so let's all stop talking as if I'm a signed and sealed deal, shall we?'

Jimmy put his head back and laughed out loud. This broke the tension as they all joined in with him, even Janey, who seemed a lot happier at the stance Annie had taken.

'It's good to have you back, Annie, luv.'

'And I'm glad to be back . . . Look, Mum, I wanted to say I'm sorry, I should have been here for you, but I promise you that from now on I will be. I'm only going to be working up west, so I'll be able to take care of you more and visit you all the time.'

'No, Annie, don't apologize, girl. You were looking after us by earning the money to keep us. And it did, didn't it, Janey? We've always managed to live for the year on what Janey can earn and you brought back to us each time you came home. When was the last time now?'

'A year ago, last January. But I was on me way to you this January, only . . . Well, you know what happened.'

'Oh, me Annie, I thought we were going to lose you and I couldn't get to you. Are you all right now, luv?'

'Almost. Still a bit shaken up. But that'll pass. It's poor Olivia that's come off worse. We're friends now, Mum. She ain't one of them as I have to cower down to any longer. Though I am going to look after her and be a sort of maid to her . . . well, more a companion, really. But she needs me after what's happened to her. She won't be able to walk for a long time, if ever. But even if she does, she'll have a limp.'

'Poor girl. But what's good is that you'll be close to us.'

'I will. And I'll be here as often as I can . . . I've brought you and Janey a present in me bag. Well, I didn't buy them. Cissy did from an allowance made by Olivia's dad to be spent on her needs.' Annie explained who Cissy was, as she pulled the twinsets from her bag. 'She got me and Olivia two each, so I've brought one of mine for Janey and Olivia sent one of hers for you.'

Both Janey and her mum drew in a breath of delight at the sight of them.

'The green one's for you, Mum, and the pink for you, Janey, luv.'

The excitement and joy they showed filled Annie with pleasure. She loved nothing more than to make these two precious people in her life happy.

Both wanted to wear them right then.

'You'll have to take Jimmy into the kitchen, luv, or he'll see a sight for sore eyes. Janey can help me on with mine and then put her own on.'

Jimmy laughed out loud.

Once they were in the kitchen, he took Annie's hand and looked into her eyes. 'Annie, luv, can I kiss you? I – I know it's a bit forward and will cement the tales that your sister and mum have heard, but if I don't, I'll not sleep a wink till I see you again.'

'Well, I've heard some chat-up lines, mate, but that's one of the best. But I think I'll say yes, as I'm never one to listen to gossip.'

She went into his arms, not able to believe what was happening, but a little afraid too, as she'd never been kissed by a man in her life and wasn't sure she knew what to do.

She needn't have worried. Just the feel of his lips on hers, gently at first, was enough to relax her.

It wasn't a passionate kiss, but a loving one. When they parted, Jimmy's eyes held a love for her as he said, 'Oh, Annie, I've never kissed a girl before . . . well, I mean, I have, but in a different way as it ain't ever meant anything to me. But if you'll have me, I promise, I'll never kiss another one, only you . . . I just can't believe you've come back into me life. I've dreamed of this moment . . . I tried to forget you, and yes, I played the field a bit as I thought I'd never see you again, but I couldn't get you out of me mind. From the moment I laid eyes on you, I've loved you . . . that snotty-nosed kid loved you with all the love he was capable of giving.'

'Oh, Jimmy. I can't believe this either. It's like I stepped onto that train and me life changed. It went into a pit of fear and horror, then pain, mixed with sadness at not being with me family and seeing Olivia hurt so badly, to finding you out of the blue and you being so different to the picture I had in me head. And yet, it's as if you're going to be the saviour of me . . . Does that sound daft?'

'No. It sounds wonderful.'

Jimmy kissed the tip of her nose, but as his lips descended towards hers again and she readied herself for the torrent of feeling this would bring, the door opened.

'Oh . . . sorry, but we're ready.'

They shot apart, but any embarrassment Annie might have felt vanished with the look of what she thought was disapproval on Janey's face and was replaced by feeling cross. But then that melted at her surprise of the beautiful picture her sister presented in her twinset.

Deciding to ignore the look, she lightened the moment

by crying, 'Janey! Me grown-up, beautiful sis. How did that happen? . . . Look at you, a young woman . . . Come here, luv.'

Hugging Janey gave Annie the feeling that all was as it should be for her, and she was back where she belonged in her beloved East End.

Suddenly, having to win over Janey didn't matter. All that did was the little back kitchen with its one window half covered by a net curtain, cast-iron stove, cupboards that needed painting, table and chairs under the window, and peeling walls with damp patches causing mildew to blacken the corners, as it seemed like the best place in the world to her – it was home.

'Mum's ready. She's like the cat that got the cream and looks lovely . . . Oh, Annie, we never thought to ever own anything like these twinsets. They're so soft.'

'Well, there'll be more like them for you both, luv. I'll see to that. You look lovely, girl.'

As she looked in wonderment at her little sis, suddenly grown-up, Annie had the sad thought that Janey had never really been a child. She'd always had an old head on her shoulders as they'd had so much to face from the moment she was born.

But nothing prepared Annie for seeing her mum dressed in her twinset. Tears filled her eyes at the lovely picture she made. The dark green brought out the colour of her hazel eyes, which now glowed with pleasure and with the warmth the twinset gave her, though the fire roaring up the chimney did that too, as both helped to wash away Annie's guilt at not being here and helping to care for her mum. She now knew she'd done that in a different way. She'd worked to pay for coal for the fire and food for the table. She'd done her best.

'I love it, mate. Say ta to your Olivia. Tell her she made me very happy.'

Going down beside her mum, Annie gave her a gentle hug. As she did, feeling the soft wool that had put a smile on her mum's face was everything to Annie. As was knowing she was only going to be a few miles away from them both in the future.

She turned on her haunches and looked up at Jimmy. As she did the thought came to her that the folk who really mattered to her were back in her life.

Chapter Eight

Olivia

A month had passed, and Olivia waited anxiously for Hendrick, as she had done every weekend. Annie had already left the clinic to go to her mum's and Olivia reflected on how lovely it was to see the happiness clothing Annie since Jimmy had come back into her life.

He visited Annie most days – well, them both really. He was a tonic, making them laugh, though it took a lot for her to stop thinking of him how Annie first described him to her or to imagine Janey telling him he stank. She wanted to reach out to the boy that he was and to help him.

When she'd said this to Annie, Annie told her there were still many living around her mum that were in the same boat and the best thing was to donate to the various charities that helped them and give her cast-off clothing to the jumbles held in the area. She'd made her mind up then that this was a way she could and would help.

These thoughts merged with the sound of Hendrick opening the door and calling out, 'Hello, darling.' But it wasn't him that came through the door first, but a wheelchair!

'What? Hendrick! What's this?'

'Your very own carriage, madam.' Hendrick parked the chair and came over to her, his arms open. He looked tired and drawn. It worried her that he was working all week and travelling at weekends and so getting no rest.

'Oh, Hendrick! My own?'

'Yes. Your father ordered it but didn't tell you as there was a long wait for it to be made and he didn't want you longing for it every day. So, my darling, it's a lovely spring day and I'm going to wrap you up warmly and take you out for a walk.'

Olivia couldn't speak. She'd longed for the day she could leave this room and just go outside as Annie had been doing for ages now. She looked up at Hendrick, saw him bending towards her and accepted his kiss, thrilling at the touch of him.

'Oh, Olivia, it seems to have been a long week since I was here last.' He went onto his haunches. Now she was face to face with him, the tired lines around his eyes and the bags underneath were even more noticeable to her.

'Darling, you must stop coming to see me every week. I wouldn't have seen you so often if the crash hadn't have happened. You need your rest. Now I have a chair and not just these four walls, the days won't drag so much as Annie will take me out and we can go shopping, have our lunch out or go to a market. Oh, my life will change! I love going to a market! And to parks.'

'Well, I'm going to take you for a walk today, darling.'

'Ooh, I'd like to see Buckingham Palace, and St James's Palace, they're all nearby. Oh, and Marble Arch – is it really made out of marble?'

'I'll get your coat, and yes, it is, from marble that comes from Italy. I'm a fountain of knowledge about it all as I knew you would want to know the minute you could visit it.' As he went to the wardrobe, he picked up on what she'd said earlier. 'And I don't want to come less often, darling. Not yet.'

As he helped her with her coat, he said, 'You see, I have something to tell you, darling.'

'Oh? That sounds ominous.'

'It is. I'm afraid the news isn't good from my country. Things are getting worse. Hitler has moved a huge army into the Rhineland against the law of the Versailles Treaty drawn up after the Great War.'

'Oh no! Are they really preparing for war? What's happening? Are there a lot of objections?'

'At the moment, no one is doing anything about it. France is in political upheaval with no clear leadership and Britain takes the view that the Rhineland belongs to Germany and so they should be able to use it as they see fit, that every other country bordering another has a military zone. But I don't trust Hitler and it could be a huge mistake to let him get away with this violation.'

Olivia was quiet for a moment. She didn't see the significance of it all as Hendrick did and was loath to ask him as she'd rather not know. But he continued: 'My father is urging me to join Hitler's forces very soon. He is afraid. It seems the regime is making examples of those known to speak out against it. As I have told you my father did, and not just lightly. He was a member of the Weimar Republic Party and spoke vehemently against the rising Nazis. He thinks if his son volunteers for the services, and says that his father urged him to, having had a change of heart and now seeing what Hitler is doing is the best thing possible for Germany, he will be forgiven his past and not be executed.'

'So, he would sacrifice his own son?'

'That's very harsh, darling . . . You see, well, he has been arrested twice. The second time, he was put into prison and is still there.'

'Oh no! I'm sorry. I – I shouldn't have said what I did.'

'No, it's understandable, but things do look bad for him.'

'Oh, Hendrick. Please don't go, I'm frightened.'

'There may not be a war, darling. Hitler may be all talk, or things may happen through negotiation. And I could of course come home on leave.'

'But there is bad feeling towards Hitler's forces. There were even rumblings in Guernsey before I left, and the nurses here have said odd things about how he frightens them.'

'At the moment, I am only thinking that I will offer to go back to Germany if they think I will be of use to them when I tell them the skills that I have. I'll also put it to them that as a banker in an international bank responsible for German accounts, I am taking care of Germany's interests. Your father suggests that this might buy me and my father more time.'

'Oh, please, please let it. I couldn't bear for you to go. If war comes and we are against Germany, it will pit us against each other.'

'It will never do that, my darling. My allegiance will never be to the Nazis. And if I am part of it, I will secretly do all I can from the inside to sabotage its aims.'

A shiver went through Olivia as if she was seeing the future.

'Let's just enjoy life as we always have, Olivia. A lot of things we are worrying about may never happen . . . I know there is already a lot going on that we hate – the discrimination against the Jews for one – but it may be that the German people will see sense and stop all of this before it spills out into the world.'

'How will you approach the Nazi regime, Hendrick?'

'I am here until Wednesday this time. This is at your father's suggestion. It will give me time to contact the ambassador of Germany, here in Britain, Leopold von Hoesch. He used to be a friend of my father's, though never held the same political ideals. I will ask him to speak for me. After that, I will have to let everything take its course, my darling.' He'd sat her back in her chair and was once more on his haunches in front of her, his head bent over her knees. He kissed her hands. 'I don't want to do this, darling. But your father helped me with the decision. He said, "What if one day you are given no choice and recalled to Germany and forced to join the forces? What if then they make a connection to your father and judge you as a traitor, as they are judging him at the moment? And what if they look with disdain at you having stayed away and not offered your services to your motherland when they are going through such a transition?"' Hendrick lifted his head. 'That way of looking at it made my mind up. This is my self-preservation, not just my father's.'

Olivia's heart became like a heavy weight in her chest. It felt to her as if she was losing her Hendrick.

As if he'd read her mind, he told her, 'It may not be as bad as we think. Yes, there is a lot of speculation as to what Hitler's intentions are and whether he will go through with his many threats, but none of it may happen and after serving for a while, I can apply to be discharged. But in any case, I haven't heard of any restrictions on travel, so I am sure that I will be able to come to see you as normal.'

This made Olivia feel a little better. She put her face forward to kiss his lips and smiled. 'Yes, it could all come to nothing. We're facing doom and gloom when maybe we needn't. Let's just enjoy our day, eh? Come on, my man, get my carriage ready!'

Hendrick stood, bowed and said, 'Yes, m'lady, where to today?'

This made them both burst out laughing and with the laughter came the feeling that, yes, all of this may turn out to be nothing and they were wasting their day thinking the worst.

Outside, despite it only being March, the sun was warm, though the breeze nipped her cheeks a little as there was still a chilly feel to it.

'So, where to first, darling?'

'Find a shop that sells blankets! I don't want to be out and about with this hospital one slung across my knees.'

'Oh, I have an idea. What if we walk by the apartment? You can see where you're going to be living and I could run up to ask advice from Cissy.'

Hendrick had a strange look on his face – a mischievous look. She had no idea why.

'Well, that sounds like a good suggestion. But why you look as though you have a secret, I'm not sure.'

'You'll see! Anyway, Cissy will love you calling round.'

'I'd love to see Cissy. I hope she comes down to me. She comes to see us a lot and I've grown very fond of her.'

'Me too, she's a lovely person, so easy to get along with.'

'We'll have to take her back to Guernsey with us . . . and Annie. Though I don't think she'd come as she's so in love with Jimmy . . . Oh dear, that makes me feel sad. Not that she's in love, but that one day we will have to say our goodbyes.'

'Well, she can visit us and we her, whenever we all can. That's the thing about friendships, they can stretch over the miles.'

Although Olivia knew this from those friends she had from

schooldays, she somehow didn't want that to happen with Annie. She couldn't bear not to be close to her.

When they came to the street where the apartment was, Olivia gasped and for a moment just stared. It was so different to anything she'd ever known – the hustle and bustle, the shops, and the magnificent, majestic white buildings that looked almost stately, as they lined both sides of the street. She was caught up in it all and loved it.

Cissy came hurrying down to her and clasped her hands with delight on her face. 'Eeh, Olivia, lass, to see you out and about at last!' She leaned over her and hugged her. She smelled of baking and freshly washed clothes all rolled into one, and Olivia felt a tear prick her eye. How she would love to go up to the apartment – just to see it and where she was eventually to live.

But then, as this thought died, Cissy gave her the surprise of her life.

'Well, we're all ready for you, lass.'

'All, Cissy? Where?'

'In the apartment. Come on, up you come, and I have a surprise for you.'

'As if this wasn't enough of one . . . Oh, Cissy, I can't wait to see it.'

When she entered the building, Olivia thought how beautiful the hall was with its tiled floor in red and navy, and grand staircase sweeping up from the centre, but she was glad to see the lifts on the left next to a reception desk.

'Morning, ma'am. Pleased to meet you. I'm Fred. I take care of everything and everyone in the apartment block. If you need anything, you just ring down to me and I'll do me best for you.' He winked at Cissy. 'Ain't that right, Cissy?'

Cissy blushed and giggled. In the lift she told them how

Fred had changed her life. He'd only worked there a short while, but always had a friendly 'hello' and loved to have a chat. 'Eeh I tell you, I sometimes used to talk to the walls before he came to work here, and I had you and Annie to visit in the clinic.'

This sounded sad to Olivia, but she couldn't give it her attention as her curiosity was such that she was excited to see who was waiting for her. When she got to the top landing and the door opened, she saw her father, her Aunt Rosina and Uncle Cyril, and she burst out laughing, which soon turned to tears – of joy mostly, but of missing them and realizing what had truly happened to her.

They all crowded around her. And for the first time, just being amongst them and away from the confines of the clinic, Olivia could see light at the end of the tunnel. She filled with self-belief. She truly was going to recover.

'We all wanted to be here to see this massive step of you coming home – well, to the home that will be yours, and very soon . . . I wish that it was back to Guernsey with me and Hendrick, but I understand this is a chance for you to shape your future together.'

'Soon, Daddy?' Olivia looked from her father to Hendrick. Saw Hendrick smiling and nodding and then felt an excitement buzz through her as he said, 'Yes, my darling. We, and the clinic, wanted this trial run to see if you can cope outside the hospital environment. So far, you are doing very well.'

'Oh, Hendrick, when?'

Aunt Rosina came and squatted beside her, taking her hand in hers. 'We all believe that is your decision, dear. You can choose to come before your casts are off and return to the clinic weekly to check your progress, and then when your casts come off, which is only a matter of two to three weeks, return there once or twice a week for help with your movements. They have an excellent gymnasium and instructor who will help you through exercise and massage to get you to a place where you have the best mobility possible.'

For a moment, Olivia felt annoyed that they had all discussed this and arranged it without involving her, though her doctor had said this would be the road she would take to getting her life back. But then, she knew they were doing their best to protect her and to help her through this, so she smiled, let the news sink fully in and told them, 'I want to come home. Annie is ready too. So ready. That room is driving us both up the wall. For me, well, it has been necessary, but for Annie, it has been a labour of love just to take care of me. Here, she can still do that with Cissy caring for us both, but we can go out and do so many things now I have my chair.'

'That's wonderful news, darling. We were afraid you may have lost your confidence.'

'No, Hendrick. I long to leave that shut-away place. When can all of this happen?'

It was her father who answered. 'Whenever you like. We have everything ready here for you. Your wheelchair has been designed so that it can get through the doors. Carpets have been taken up and replaced by staining the wooden floorboards, so you can wheel yourself around, and the college are ready with the two tutors I told you about.'

'It all sounds wonderful . . . Ooh, how can I thank you all?'

'By getting better and achieving your dreams, my dear.' Her father bent over her and kissed her cheek. 'We will do anything, anything it takes to make your life easier . . . We thought we had lost you.' His voice caught in his throat. Olivia lifted her hand and touched his cheek. She couldn't speak.

Her throat had tightened as the enormity of it seemed to be so close to her today that she suddenly felt like crying, but she swallowed hard.

'We owe Annie so much, my dear.'

'I know, Daddy. And I am hoping to meet Annie's family soon. I want to find out what we can do for them, as that's all Annie will want from us. You see, her mother is very ill, and I know they are poor. Annie had to sacrifice being with them to make her sister's and mum's life better.'

'An amazing young woman, and to think she has been under my roof for a number of years and I didn't even know her – not properly, but I know we miss her now. Nothing has run as smoothly since she left us to accompany you to London. But thank God she did.'

Aunt Rosina's hand brushed Olivia's hair as she said this. 'But anyway, my darling, this is meant to be a special day and we are all booked into Fortnum & Mason for tea! And we can walk there from here, so first a tour around the apartment with me, then freshen up and we can go!'

'And that's where me surprise comes in, Olivia, lass. I'll just go and fetch it.'

Olivia looked around at them as Cissy disappeared through a door. When she came back, she had a parcel wrapped in tissue paper.

'Eeh, I were hoping to get it done and I did. Late last night, I sewed the last square into place and quilted it, then put the backing on.'

Olivia giggled. 'Well, that gives the game away! The best clue ever to something I so need.'

When she opened it, the most beautiful, quilted blanket cascaded over her knees. Just the right size for her wheelchair and something she would be so proud to wrap around her.

'It's wonderful and has a cosy, warm feeling, Thank you, Cissy. I will treasure it.'

They all crowded around once more to examine Cissy's handiwork and cooed over its beauty. An oblong shape, the squares were all colours and patterns and yet, somehow, they blended into each other.

'Marvellous, Cissy. I will be giving you an order. I often sit in my sitting room with a blanket over me, but to have one of your quilts would be wonderful.'

'I'll make you one anytime, Mrs Wallington. And if you want any particular colour, I'll do that an' all.'

'Well done, Cissy. Now, are you going to show Olivia around, Rosina? We mustn't be late for Fortnum & Mason.'

'Ha, Cyril, thinking of your belly again.'

'I am. I can't wait to taste those ham sandwiches and cream cakes!'

They all laughed.

The apartment was lovely. Everything about it was huge. Each bedroom had space enough for three beds and each had a row of oak wardrobes covering one wall.

The main bedroom had its own bathroom, besides there being a guest bathroom. The colours in each room were restful light greens and greys and broken only by a rose pattern on the curtains, and a matching eiderdown. Most of the furniture was oak, and the sofas were a lovely rose pink that complemented the pale green. 'It's lovely, Aunt Rosina. I've never been here before. I always thought of it as a business stopover for Daddy. But all these feminine colours, they make it a home.'

'That's my influence. As you can see a lot of it is in the same colours as my sitting room, only a little more pronounced. Your father laughed when he saw it, but I loved choosing all the furniture and furnishings. So, you like it?'

Olivia nodded.

'That's good. Things are going to change for you, my darling. Life will become for living again.'

'Well, not too fast, I hope, as I still get very tired, but, oh, I am so happy to be coming home at last . . . There is just one thing, though. Can I have Annie in the same room as me? For my sake as well as hers. We need each other still. If I wake in the night and hear her gently snoring, I feel comforted and safe. And she has said the same. And if either of us really need anything, or we need the company of the other one, we are there for each other.'

'I don't see that is a problem.' Aunt Rosina went to the door and called out for Cissy.

'Cissy, dear, how can we move another bed into the main bedroom for Annie? Olivia wants them to be together.'

'Aye, I did wonder about that, but couldn't ask you, lass, as your da didn't want anything said until they were sure everything could be done. But don't you worry. Fred'll do that in no time. I'll see to it while you're all out.'

'That's wonderful. Well, we have to leave soon, so let me take you into the bathroom, Olivia, dear. Do you need much help?'

'A little.' Olivia felt suddenly shy and wished that Annie was there.

'Aw, you leave it all to me, Mrs Wallington. There's no room for us both to help. I'll soon have the lass sorted.'

And she did. Without any fuss, Cissy helped Olivia to stand, helped her with her clothes and then left as she sat down on the lav. There was no embarrassment, and Olivia found herself relaxing and seeing her immediate future as so much better than she had endured.

Chapter Nine

Annie

July 1936

At last, the day had come when Annie could take Olivia to her home.

It had been three months since they'd moved into the apartment, and Olivia, with all the casts off her legs, could now take a short walk with crutches.

'I'm excited at the thought of getting into a cab even. Doesn't seem possible that something you've done all your life can seem such a treat, does it?'

'Well, it has been a long time. But the cab is only the first step. Soon you'll be using the Underground!'

Annie shivered at her own words. She'd never been on a train since the accident and didn't think she ever wanted to again. Always Jimmy had taken her to see her mum and Janey.

'That thought scares me to death! Could you do it again?'

'No. As soon as I said it, I felt afraid. What's it like in Guernsey? Have you got trains even?'

'No. Just buses and cabs. But mostly I drive myself around.'

'You drive!'

'Yes. I love it. I don't know if I could now, though, with

these legs. Come on, we'd better start to get down to the ground floor, we don't want our cab to go and leave us here. I'm so looking forward to meeting your mum.'

But as they alighted from the cab, asking him to come back in an hour, nothing prepared Annie for Olivia's reaction as she looked around her.

'Oh, Annie, I never knew you lived in such a deprived area . . . Your poor mum and Janey. I'll speak to my father, love, and we'll get them out of here as soon as we can.'

Annie's face dropped. She sprang to the defence of her people as to her, this insulted them.

'It ain't that bad. The houses need repairing, but there ain't a step that ain't been scrubbed today. Or a front that ain't been brushed of debris. It just lies in the gutter 'cause the streets don't get cleaned like them up west, but the people who live here do their best.'

'Oh, I'm sorry. Oh, Annie, I didn't mean—'

'Come on, let's get inside.'

The afternoon was spoiled for Annie. She never thought that she would feel cross with Olivia, but right now she could tell her to sling her hook, as the dockers said when they wanted you to buzz off.

Once in her mum's living room, Olivia didn't look at all comfortable, but she greeted Mum with a kiss on her cheek. 'I've so looked forward to meeting you, Mrs Freeman. How are you?'

'I'm fine, girl. It's good to meet you at last. I've wanted to, and to thank you for being such a good friend to me Annie and Janey. Sit down, luv. You look all in.'

'I am. This is my first journey for a long time.'

Olivia sank down onto the sofa and leaned her head back.

Annie rushed to her side. 'Are you all right, luv?' Concern filled her as she saw Olivia's face drain of colour.

'Oh, Annie, luv. She looks like she's goin' to faint.'

Janey came in through the front door at that moment. 'Sorry, I'm late, Mum. The shop . . . Annie! You got here then? Oh . . . Olivia, are you feeling unwell?'

'Get a tumbler of water, Janey, luv. I think it's all been too much for her.'

Once she'd drunk the water, Olivia revived a little. Annie felt her reach along the sofa for her hand.

'It's all right, luv, I know you didn't mean it, not how it sounded. I were daft to take it how I did.'

'Have you two been falling out, Annie?'

'No, not falling out, Mrs Freeman, but I made a remark about getting you out of this poor area. I'm so sorry. I judged it by its appearance, and I upset Annie. I can't bear to do that, and your home is lovely. But if there is anything you need, anything at all, my father wants to help by way of thanking Annie for my life.'

'Oh, I see, girl. Well, that ain't nothing to get upset over, Annie. I think your pride was hurt, but it's a natural reaction of anyone of Olivia's standing.'

'I know, Mum. I'm sorry, Olivia, it just caught me on a raw edge. But you're right. It isn't what it should be for me mum and Janey. I've just forgotten what it's like living here, with a leaky roof when it's wet, and the cold when you move away from the fire. The draughts and the creaking windows. Me mum's arthritis would be better if they lived somewhere warmer.'

'I'd move tomorrow. Especially if it was all on the flat with no stairs to climb. Me and Janey have been trying to think of ways of fitting me bed down here, but it's pokey as it is.'

'I don't want to live up west, though, Mum.'

'I know, Janey. You're with your own kind here, but there were good tenement blocks put up. If we could get a ground-floor one, that'd do us, wouldn't it?'

'Could you help with that, Olivia?'

'I could, Annie. And would be glad to. My father is a property developer as well as owning a bank. He's so grateful to you, Annie, he'd even build something especially for your mum, if it came to that. He'll telephone tonight, I'll talk to him. But all of that will take a while. How can I make things a bit better for you now?'

'I don't think you can, love. The landlord won't do a thing. He's just waiting for the day that this street gets compulsory purchased and then he'll take his money and run.'

'Is he against you doing repairs yourself?'

'I couldn't mend a window, luv!'

Annie burst out laughing and felt better for it. The tension left her as she said, 'Oh, Mum, we don't expect you to get up a ladder!'

They all giggled at the thought and Annie thought how well her mum seemed to be and how she had lifted in her spirits. Life had changed for her now, with Jimmy bringing her fruit and vegetables. She had cabbage and carrots, and all manner of veg, and fresh apples and pears and the odd orange. It was all doing her good.

'I tell you what I would like, but it's asking a lot.'

'Anything. Honestly, just anything. And if it's possible, we'll get it for you. I promise.'

'Well, I like the sound of that chair you've got, Olivia. I can't remember the last time I left this street. The only fresh air I get – if you can call it that – is to sit on me stool outside me front door, but then it takes a bit of getting me there.'

'Oh, that's something we can do a lot sooner than your other needs. Father will order you one, but though I say a lot sooner, it will take about six weeks.'

'So, by late summer, I'll be going down to the park and to the market? I'll take that, girl, ta.'

Annie saw Olivia smile so wide at this, she seemed for a moment like the girl she'd first seen in Cornwall. It made her feel guilty at getting cross with her. After all, she'd only seen what she'd failed to see herself.

She looked around the poky room. The mildew suddenly seemed to have spread; the paint was peeling, like someone had ripped bits of paper and stuck them all over the wall; she even saw a brick exposed that she'd never seen before, up by the chimney where a whole slab of plaster must have fallen from. Getting up, she went into the kitchen, telling them she'd make tea.

Janey followed her. 'I'll help you, mate.'

She couldn't even smile her acceptance of this as opening the kitchen door, what always looked like a homely kitchen to her suddenly looked like a hovel. She turned to Janey. 'Janey, luv, I'm sorry.' Her tears flowed as she took Janey into her arms. 'I shouldn't have left you to care for Mum on your own and in this dump. I – I never saw it as that until today. Even when I visited from living in a posh house, it was always just home.'

'We knew that, Annie. We saw your joy, luv, and did our best not to spoil that by complaining, but it ain't been good for Mum's health here. Not for a long time. Her pain worsens with the damp and cold. Sometimes she sleeps on the sofa, which ain't really long enough for her, 'cause I just can't get her up the stairs.'

'Oh, Janey. You should have said.'

'What could you do, eh? Nothing, only worry yourself silly and that wouldn't have helped anyone. No, me and Mum made our minds up to give you a happy time as much as we could and just do our best to cope. But there were times, Annie, when we didn't eat hardly for the week before you came back as we'd run out of the money you'd given us on your previous visit and mine had to pay the rent or we'd have been on the streets.'

'Oh, Janey. I feel so ashamed.'

'No! Annie, don't. You worked hard for what you got, and you gave it all to us. We were glad you were being well fed and kept warm.'

'I should have gone into a factory.'

'There's been times when I've thought that, or that you should have looked after Mum and me gone into the factory, but at the end of the day, we didn't want that for you. We wanted you free from being around here, and look what all your hard work has led to, eh, mate? A chance for us all! So, please, Annie, don't blame yourself for all of this, luv. It's the rotten landlord that's to blame, not you. He keeps putting his rent up but does nothing. But if there's a chance for us to get out, don't block it. Be proud as you'll have done that for us – your bravery. Your saving of lovely Olivia's life. That's what will have got us a decent living.'

This was too much for Annie. She sobbed onto Janey's shoulders; her little sis, who she loved so much and who had such a wise head on her young shoulders.

'Come on, Annie, luv. Now's the time to be glad as life's going to change for us all.'

Annie dried her tears and looked into Janey's eyes. 'You remind me of Gran, luv. You've got her wisdom. I promise, I will make sure that things get better for you and Mum and then, if you want, we'll look at getting someone in and you getting a better job . . . I ain't one for taking, nor do I look on what I did for Olivia as needing paying for, I would have done that for anyone, but asking for things for you and Mum is different. I can see that now, and I know that Olivia's father will give me anything I ask for, so it's up to you.'

'I do love looking after Mum. But I'll think about it as I often dream of doing what other girls do and of having mates. But I don't want me life to change too much, just to get better for Mum.'

They hugged again. 'It will, me darlin'. It will.'

'I know it will. Now, shall we make that cuppa, luv, Mum's dying for one.'

'You should train to be a nurse, luv. That would suit yer.'

As Janey got their best cups out – four teacups and saucers, with a cornflower on each – Annie remembered the day they were going to be thrown out by the housekeeper of Wallington Manor as the rest of the set was chipped or broken, and she'd asked if she could have them.

Life in Cornwall seemed so far away now. And she was glad. Glad she was home, back here in London, so she could really take care of her mum and Janey. Not just with money, but to be here to love them and to help with Mum occasionally.

'I'd love that, but being a nurse ain't for girls of my standing. The cost of training is for the rich only.'

'You looked into it then, luv?'

'I did. I never mentioned it because I may as well say I wanted to go to the moon. Anyway, that tea'll be stewed if we don't pour it now . . . Are you all right now, Annie, luv?'

'I am. Let's take the tea in.'

But though this seemed to be the end of the conversation, it wasn't for Annie, as she hadn't missed the look in Janey's eyes when she'd talked about becoming a nurse. There would be a few years yet, as she understood it, before Janey could apply for training, but one day, Annie thought, she would make that dream come true for her.

Six weeks later, not only did they deliver the wheelchair to Annie's mum but the keys to a ground-floor flat. It was still in Bethnal Green – the only place Annie had found that her Mum and Janey would move house to, and she didn't blame them.

This flat was at the back of a shop and had been found by Jimmy. The shop owners were his customers but didn't live in the accommodation and it had stood empty for a long time. It was in good repair, though, but had taken a lot of work to get ready.

Annie had never thought to wield a paintbrush, or still less to see Olivia do so, but they had a lot of fun decorating the living room and had a good system going with her painting the top half of the walls from a ladder, Olivia the middle bit from her wheelchair and Janey the bottom half.

There'd always been more paint on them than on the walls by the time they'd stood back to admire their work each time one wall was completed, but now, with it all done, it was lovely – a pale lemon, which brought the sunshine inside.

Cissy had made the curtains, which were cream with a yellow rose pattern, and Olivia bought a new sofa and chair in cream. Cissy made antimacassars and chair back covers for these, to match the curtains. The floor they covered in a light oak-coloured oil cloth with a cream rug in front of the fire. To complete the picture, Janey found some dark green velvet cushions that added just the right amount of contrast.

They were all so pleased with the finished look that they celebrated with a glass of sherry, Mum's favourite tipple.

While they had been labouring away in the one room, Jimmy had whitewashed the walls of the two bedrooms and the kitchen, which was only tiny as it had been cut in half by the shop owner to provide him with a stockroom.

The only drawback was that the lav was in the backyard – not that Janey and Mum were used to anything else, but they had to share it with the shop owner, Mr Jackson, when he was at work.

But he was a kindly man and made them laugh as he told them he'd go really well before he left home and use the cafe toilets where he had his midday snack and so would rarely want to share theirs.

For Mum, Cissy had suggested a commode by her bed, and they'd found one in a second-hand shop that had taken an hour to clean up and paint but once Cissy had made cushions for it, it looked just like a nice chair in the bedroom and not at all what it really was. And Cissy promised to make a bed throw and curtains to match the cushions as soon as she could.

Annie and Olivia loved it when Cissy sat sewing in the evenings while they chatted or listened to the wireless.

'Well, Mum, are you ready, luv? This old place is all emptied out, and your palace awaits you.'

'I am, Annie. And I'm looking forward to the walk to me new flat as much as I am to be seeing it.'

When Annie pushed her mum through the door, the neighbours were all out on their steps. 'Good luck, Vera, luv.'

''Ope you'll be happy in your new home, me darlin'.'

And many similar things were called out.

Mum beamed at them all. 'Well, me mates, I'm only around the corner, and don't you go forgetting me. Call in when you come to the shops or the market.'

'We will, Vera, luv. You look after yourself. And keep that kettle boiling for us.'

They all waved, as Mum did to them. But when she was around the corner, she sighed. 'If it weren't for them, there were times I'd have been in the madhouse before now.'

Annie once more felt a pang of shame. And no matter what Janey and her mum said to placate her on this, she knew she would always feel this way. She'd had her eyes opened.

When they got to the corner, Janey looked back along the street they'd just left. 'Well, that's that then, Annie. But as I look at it now, I don't see the hardships. I see kids playing footie in the streets, and me and Peggy Bartram skipping and playing hopscotch. Poor Peggy, it was a terrible day the day she got run over. I ain't never had a friend since then. Not a close one like you've got in Olivia.'

Not picking up on the last bit, Annie allowed the pictures to come to her too. And she knew that there were many happy times, despite the poverty they'd endured. She saw her dad coming down the street, his cap at a jaunty angle, smiling and lifting her up in the air. And her mum chasing her down the street, then catching her and swinging her between her legs.

'It's good to remember the best bits, Janey. But it's good to know when it's time to say goodbye and put what were the worst bits away and go on to a better future.'

'You're right, Annie, luv. And it ain't as if we're going miles away. Ha, I can see the shop from here now.'

They turned into the side street just before the shop as this led to an alley that took them to the gate that led into what was to be their backyard. This still needed work to clean it up, but this was planned for Sunday when Jimmy could come. He was going to whitewash the walls and the inside of the lav, and she and Janey planned to scrub the slabs. Then, with some potted plants against the newly painted wall, it would make a lovely peaceful suntrap for their mum to sit outside and enjoy the sunshine in peace. Though on some of the busier shopping days, Mum had her own plans of being pushed around to the front to sit and watch the hustle and bustle, chat to folk and generally feel part of life again.

Cissy greeted them. 'Eeh, here she is, the queen of the palace. By, lass, you're going to love it, and be that cosy an' all. It's all ready and I have the kettle on. It'll start to whistle any moment now.'

Mum gasped when she was pushed inside. She'd chosen all the colours and been consulted on the fabrics used by Cissy.

She and Cissy hugged. They'd become good friends whilst the renovations of the flat had taken place. 'Welcome to your new home, lass.'

'Ta, luv. And ta, all of you. You've done me proud.'

'Well, this chair belongs to me, Vera, lass.' Cissy had sat herself down on one of the dining chairs under the window. 'And I'll park me backside on it every Thursday afternoon, as I came by Underground today to try it out and it's a doddle to get here. By, we'll have some giggles together. I can push you out easily and we can go for some fish and chips.'

'Ha, pie and mash with liquor more like, luv. You ain't converting me into a northerner, you know.'

To hear them laughing together was a tonic and warmed Annie's heart.

As Janey said, 'I'll make the tea,' Annie sat down next to Olivia.

Olivia grinned and winked at her as she whispered, 'I think that's a friendship that's going to benefit them both. Look at Cissy, she looks so happy.'

'They both do. We just need a mate for our Janey now. I only just realized that she ain't got one.'

'She's got us. Though she does need someone of her own age. Where do we find one for her, though?'

Annie laughed. 'We don't. What will help, though, is if she can have an outside interest. I found out that she'd love to be a nurse, so I was thinking about enquiring of the local Red Cross to see if she could join as a volunteer . . . Well, it wasn't my idea really, but Jimmy's. He knows everyone and he has a customer who is the co-ordinator. I'm going to see her as soon as I can.'

'What does Janey think?'

'I ain't going to tell her till I know she stands a chance; I don't want to get her hopes up. But I've put a bit by for her if it does happen as from what Jimmy tells me they'll need to buy their uniforms and pay their dues.'

'Well, you know that I'll help out if needed.'

'I know, luv. Ta. I just hope it works out as she's bound to meet a mate there, and even if not, I know she'll love it.'

When Sunday dawned, Jimmy picked Annie up in his truck. Hendrick was over and the two men chatted. Annie, thinking Hendrick might be offended, held her breath when Jimmy said, 'So, things ain't looking good in your country, Hendrick, are they? I hope it don't escalate again. Me best mate lost his dad in the last lot and he were a good bloke.'

But when Hendrick answered, he seemed to have taken it in his stride. 'I'm sorry to hear that. My own father was injured but survived. I've not lived in Germany since I was a child, but yes, the news from there and the things Hitler is saying are a bit disconcerting.'

'You're going to join them, aren't you?'

'Not in my heart, Jimmy. I'll never be your enemy, always remember that.'

Jimmy put his hand on Hendrick's shoulder. 'That's good to know. And I suppose like us all, you'll have to do your duty if you want to or not. Us mortals have no say in it, mate.'

'Yes. And I'm glad you understand that. If things escalate, we must remember that it will be the same for many men.'

'Well, we'll see. But one thing I do know is that though I'll never be your enemy, Hendrick, I can't say the same of your country if that Hitler fellow is stupid enough to repeat the last lot.'

'Well, if he does – and never say this to a living soul, Jimmy – but if I'm involved, I'll do my utmost to help Britain win. And that's my promise to you.'

The two men shook hands and then gave a manly hug to each other.

Annie's face glowed as she looked on. She didn't give her mind to affairs such as they were talking about, preferring to think that sense would prevail and all would be all right, but to know that if it wasn't, it wouldn't drive a rift between them all filled her with relief.

Annie set out with a sense of all being right in her world as she said her goodbyes to an excited Olivia, who today would finalize hers and Hendrick's plans for their wedding in September of next year.

Although happy for Olivia, a small part of her felt sad being away from her precious friend, but knew they were both soon to enter a new era of their lives.

PART TWO

New Beginnings and Broken Hearts

Chapter Ten

Olivia

July 1937

Olivia had continued with her language lessons at home, and now it was July they were complete, leaving her the proud owner of a certificate of merit for each. Everything would be wonderful in her life, she thought, if only world affairs hadn't been in such turmoil – she'd gone from not having much interest, to watching it all play out through listening to the news and reading the newspapers.

War raged between China and Japan, the Spanish were embroiled in civil war, and the Italians, who gained victory in their war in Ethiopia, were rumoured to be trying to make an ally of Hitler.

The one thing that gave her hope was that Britain had a new prime minister, Mr Chamberlain, who everyone believed would negotiate for a peaceful approach if ever all of this touched them and this gave them a sense of security.

Olivia even felt that her beloved Hendrick might now never be called to give his services to his country. His father had been released from prison and felt less threatened since Hendrick had put himself forward as willing to answer any call to duty.

All of this was forgotten, though, in the excitement of preparing for her wedding and she tried on this hot day in July to do Cissy's bidding: 'Eeh, lass, stand still. I've to get the last of the pins into this hem.'

But the pain in her hip prevented her from doing so, even with her best effort, as standing still for a long time caused her to jig from her good leg to her bad one.

'By, you're not helping. Look, take it off and I'll follow what I've already done for the rest. I should get an even hem that way . . . Aw, lass, you look beautiful, though, and you're worth all the effort.'

With the help of Annie, Olivia got down off the chair she'd been stood on while Cissy had been working on the hem of her wedding dress – a simple style in white satin, with a lace-covered bodice, a straight skirt and a long train attached from the back of her waist. She loved it and felt like a queen.

'Right, your turn, lass.'

Annie giggled as she stepped up onto the chair. She'd spoken of how special she felt too, in the long pale-blue satin frock that brought out her lovely blue eyes. Like Olivia's, the frock was a simple style with a fitted bodice and a straight skirt, but what made it so pretty was the tier of frills at six inches apart around the skirt.

'Good. Eeh, that was easier. Well, I'll have to get on. You two make yourselves scarce. Go on, get out me road and from under me feet!'

They both laughed at the flustered Cissy. She was doing a marvellous job in making the gowns, something she'd insisted on doing. She loved bossing them about too, whilst pretending that it was all too much for her. But if Olivia once suggested she got a seamstress in to do the work, or a daily to help her out, Cissy was up in arms. As it was, Annie struggled to get her to let her help more, though she had taken on quite a bit of the cooking since things had got easier and her full strength had returned so that she could manage to do more.

Coming out of the bedroom ready to go out, they hugged Cissy.

'Eeh, you girls, what will I do without you?'

Tears filled Cissy's eyes. Olivia swallowed the lump that tightened her throat. 'You'll still have Annie here, love. There's no room for her with her mum.'

'I knaw, but for how long, eh? She and Jimmy will soon be following in your footsteps, you mark me words.'

Annie blushed. 'Well, Jimmy has asked me. We thought to get engaged after you were wed, Olivia.'

'Oh, Annie, you didn't say! That's wonderful news.'

As they came out of the hug they'd gone into, they noticed how sad Cissy looked. But then Annie brightened her by telling her, 'I've something to discuss with Olivia first, love, and if she and her father are in agreement, it will mean you won't be rattling around in here on your own, but even if her father objects, then there will still be some arrangements we can make. So don't you worry about us deserting you, luv. We'd never do that.'

'We won't. I have plans of my own in mind if Hendrick does have to go to Germany, so no matter what happens, you'll never be alone again. We promise, Cissy.'

'Eeh, come here, me lovely lasses.'

They went into a huddle. 'I love you both, you knaw that. You're like the daughters I never had. I couldn't be without either of you for long.'

'You won't have to be, my dear. I won't be able to come back many times to see you, but I will telephone you as often as I can, I promise, and write letters to you and send you photographs. We'll have so much to share.'

'You will with all your plans, lass. I can't wait to hear you have your school up and running, but I'll need to see the progress of the renovations as they happen, you knaw.'

'I'll take loads of photographs to share and for us to treasure ourselves too. Ooh, it's all so exciting, like my life is going to start all over again after having been interrupted . . . But we won't talk about that, neither of us like to. We're just looking to the future now, aren't we, Annie?'

'We are, luv, and right now, I'm looking forward to having that cup of tea and bun you promised me in the tea room!'

They left, giggling as they went. Olivia was so pleased to leave her wheelchair standing in the hall by the lift that she blew it a kiss. This made them really laugh out loud. A laughter they hadn't controlled by the time the lift came to a halt. Annie had to use all her strength to open the inner gate to let them out, but they did put their hands over their mouths as the noise they were making earned them a look of disdain from a neighbour on the ground floor, who they called 'Miss Uppity'.

When out of earshot, Annie observed, 'We might be misjudging her, she's probably lonely. We should try being friendly to her.'

'Maybe, but it costs nothing to smile. I find her un-approachable. She tutted whenever she met us when I was in the wheelchair.'

Annie agreed, but they didn't chat further about it as linking in with Annie, Olivia had made it to the tea shop and felt so proud of her achievement.

'I will walk up the aisle, Annie. I will.'

'You will, luv. I'll be on one side of you and your dad on

the other. We'll be your crutches. You can hold your head up high and smile at your guests and your lovely Hendrick.'

Tears welled up in Olivia's eyes as Annie said this. 'It's all thanks to your devotion to me, Annie. And . . . well, when Cissy said she loved us, I thought that a lovely moment and it made me realize how much I love you, Annie. You have made all we went through so much easier than it could have been, as at times I felt so down.'

'I know, luv, and you made it easier for me too. You were always there with a cheery word, or lately when I've woken and found you sitting on me bed when I'd had a nightmare. That must have cost you a lot of pain, even though our beds are close to one another.'

'Well, it was worth it. And here we are, and our lives are going to change again.'

'They are. But we won't let it be anything but a happy change, luv . . . And Olivia, I love you too. With all me heart. You're like another sister, to me and to Janey, and another daughter for me mum.'

'Thank you, Annie, that's a lovely compliment. And I love how Cissy and your mum have become so close. It's done them both good.'

They fell silent as the waitress served their tea, then chatted for a moment about how Janey was loving her time at the Red Cross, but hadn't yet made any mates, saying they were above her station and whilst they were kind, they didn't seem to want to get close to her.

'But she don't care, she said she's happy just learning things and doing something different.'

'That's good . . . So, Annie, love, what are these plans you spoke of? . . . Though first, I can't tell you how thrilled I am about you and Jimmy . . . I mean, I never had a clue!'

'Ha, no, there were none, were there?'

They burst out laughing. When they calmed, Annie said, 'Well, Jimmy has his eye on a property in Bethnal Green that has three flats. Two of them are on the ground floor and the third one on the second floor which is huge as it takes up the space of both ground-floor flats. It used to be one house and overlooks the park. His idea is that me mum and Janey have one ground-floor flat and the other we rent out to Cissy. Then Jimmy can drop Cissy off at your father's apartment every day if he wishes her to be there that often, but in any case, any number of days he wants her there. So, she can still do her job of caretaker of the apartment, but not live a lonely existence within its walls when no one is visiting.'

'Oh, Annie! It's an amazing plan. I just know Daddy will go for it once I tell him how lonely she used to be. When will you know if Jimmy has got the place?'

'This weekend, and that's why I'm bringing it up now. He's put a bid in, and all bids are to be considered this Friday. Though he does know the agent and has been given a sort of nod that it's his.'

'That's wonderful! I can't wait to see it. Are the downstairs flats very big?'

'Bigger than where Mum is now, and best of all, as it was a house, there's a lovely, good-sized garden with a lawn and flower beds. Jimmy has plans to put a French door into each flat as they only have a kitchen door now and that's not convenient to get Mum's wheelchair through . . . Oh, I can just imagine Mum and Cissy sitting out there having a good gossip.'

They both smiled at this, and Olivia had a warm feeling that settled her worries over Cissy, as she had been on her mind a lot as to how she would cope if she was once more left on her own. In this flat Jimmy was proposing, Cissy would have Vera and Janey right next door and Annie above, and yet have her own privacy.

'And there's a fire escape from the top flat to the garden, so Jimmy said he'd paint that for me, and I can put a pot plant on each step and use it as a way down to the garden for us! Though we do have stairs that go up to the flat from the communal hall. And, as this is large, Jimmy said . . . well . . .'

'You're blushing, come on, what did Jimmy say?'

Annie gave a little giggle. 'He said there's plenty of room there for a pram and it won't be in either Cissy's or Mum's way of access but in a recess.'

They fell quiet. Then Olivia asked, 'Do you want children, Annie?'

'Oh, I do. Do you?'

'It would be a dream. Hendrick talks of having a rook of boys – very German in that, as he says they will all have blond hair.'

'Well, I don't care what colour hair they have as long as they are healthy, and boys and girls, all will be welcome.'

'That's how I feel. And I told him so too. He just laughed and said that as he understood it, it was the German man's way to want blond children. It upset me to tell the truth. But thankfully, he laughed and said he'd be more than happy if they all had dark hair like me and that he was only teasing. But it stuck with me, I don't know why.'

'Because we're all paranoid about the Germans, that's why. I'm sure Hendrick was only having you on, luv, just forget it.'

'If there is a war, will you come to Guernsey to live with me, Annie? And your mum and Janey and Cissy? You'll all be safe there. The Germans won't bother with it. It's only an island, it doesn't have anything Hitler would want, and isn't strategically placed to further any warmonger's campaign.'

'Let's not talk of war, eh? We're meant to be talking about your wedding. That's the main topic of this break together, nothing else allowed from now on, or I'll leave you sitting here, mate.'

Though Olivia smiled at this, she said, 'First, I have a plan, as I said. Part of it was to get you all to Guernsey if there was a war involving Britain, but if not and Hendrick is stuck in Germany, having to help blasted Hitler, then I would come back here to be near to you, Annie, as I would need your support more than anything then.'

Annie took her hand. 'We'll deal with it all when it happens, eh? Now, let's change the subject. We have a wedding coming up, so let's just concentrate on that, eh?'

Olivia released a sigh, but it was one of excitement as this was what she really wanted to talk about.

Her wedding had been brought forward to the first week of August because of Hendrick's increasing nervousness about being called up. Now, there seemed so little time. And she was glad to feel her excitement return to her as they began to talk about it. It was a much more comfortable place to be.

It seemed no time at all before, two weeks later, they were waiting in a queue of eager passengers to board a boat to Guernsey, with just four days to go before the wedding on the 7th of August.

The talk amongst the boat's passengers was mainly about world affairs and the invasion of China by Japan. To Olivia, it seemed there was a nervousness amongst the older ones who'd been through the Great War and there was an underlying current of hatred for Germany and its people. For the first time she wondered if Hendrick had suffered from this. But surely not as he was well known, liked and respected by the islanders.

And yet, as his fiancée, she could detect a change in attitude towards herself – a wariness of her. As if they were questioning whether she was still one of them.

Having an urge to test this out, she smiled at the Rundle family who she knew well but who hadn't yet acknowledged her. She'd thought that strange as they must have known what had happened to her. Hendrick had told her that her plight had been all over the local papers.

Mark Rundle nodded. So unlike him.

'Nice to see you again, Mark. Have you been on holiday in England?'

'London, yes . . . We were sorry to hear what happened to you, Olivia. But glad to see you are well on the mend. It's your wedding this Saturday, isn't it?'

Feeling better and thinking she'd been silly to think such thoughts, Olivia nodded and grinned. 'Yes. Nerve-racking but exciting all at the same time.'

He nodded again. 'Well, we hope you'll be very happy. Will you and your husband stay on the island?'

There was something in his tone that Olivia detected as him not wanting them to. A shyness came over her.

'Yes, we plan to open a language school.'

'Oh? You're not going to live in Germany then? We all thought Hendrick would have been called to duty the way that Hitler is going.'

'I think that's Olivia's business and not yours, mister.'

'It's all right, Annie, love.'

'Well, I beg your pardon, but I think it is the business of us all. We need to know just whose side Hendrick is on.'

'He's on no side. We weren't even aware that there was a side to take. How can you have this hostility towards Hendrick on speculation that his birth country is brewing trouble?! Besides, your brother Ian is his friend, and going to be his best man.'

'I'm not sure that Ian is going through with being best man. He hasn't liked how Hendrick has offered his services to the Germans, and, you will find, neither have many of your fellow islanders.'

Shock zinged through Olivia. Suddenly, she didn't feel welcome amongst what was mainly her own people sitting around her. It was as if they were already at war with Germany, but then, many had memories of lost sons, brothers and fathers just twenty or so years earlier and were afraid.

She wanted to say that Hendrick would always be on their side, but something told her not to say this. That sometime in the future it could mean harm for him. She prayed that it wouldn't. That what all these people feared wouldn't happen. Chamberlain would see that it didn't, wouldn't he?

In her distress, she felt Annie's hand find hers. The joy of her coming wedding had dampened. Somehow, she felt like an alien returning to her own country. How could that be right?

Annie leaned towards her and whispered, 'Tell them why Hendrick has offered his services, luv. Surely they'll understand then?'

She whispered back, 'I'm not sure. I mean, why didn't Hendrick tell Ian that? He must have a reason for not doing so. I think I'll leave it where it is . . . but I can't understand why Hendrick didn't prepare me for this?'

'I don't see what all the fuss is about. Most are going on what happened last time, but that ain't to say it will happen again. It's all daft to me.'

Mark Rundle coughed, bringing Olivia's attention back to him.

'Excuse us. There are some seats up on deck. We're taking the children up there.' He hesitated before saying, 'Good luck for Saturday.'

'Thank you.' She smiled in a friendly way, but he looked away. Mavis, his wife, had hardly looked at her, let alone spoken. She hadn't known her as well as Mark, but still hadn't expected this open hostility.

Her throat tightened.

'Don't let them bother you, Olivia. I'm sure they ain't the way everyone's going to be.'

'I'm not so sure. I know a lot of the people on here, but hardly any have greeted me, and most have avoided looking at me.'

'Well, it's their loss . . . Anyway, I ain't looked around much, I've been too busy trying not to be sick. I can't wait to get there.'

'Oh, Annie, we've got hours yet. But I did book us a cabin so shall we go to that? Our luggage should all be in there.'

'Blimey, luv, we should have gone straight away. I thought we'd have to sit here all bloomin' night!'

'Sorry, I – I just thought it would be nice to catch up with old acquaintances. I'd seen a lot of them while we were waiting to board. I'd thought them all too busy to speak with sorting tickets and luggage, and hoped we'd all have a chat up here, but no one seems to want to talk to me. I just can't understand it.'

Annie squeezed her hand. 'Perhaps they're just tired, I know I am, or feeling sick like me. You'll see, they'll be lining the streets on Saturday, like you said they always do for an island wedding.'

Olivia somehow had the feeling that they wouldn't be, and yet Cook would have baked hundreds of little tarts and Father would have arranged for lemonade to be set out on tables dotted along the route. Now, she was sure it would all go to waste.

The next morning, when they docked, Olivia clenched her fists as tension zinged through her. What kind of reception would she get?

Taking a deep breath, she steadied herself. This was her home, her beloved Guernsey. How could she be seen as unwelcome here?

A knock on the cabin door heralded the porter calling out, 'Can I take your bags, miss?'

'Yes, come in . . . Joe! Hello! Are you working on the port now then?'

'I am, Miss Olivia. And it's good to see you home, safe and sound. We've all worried over you, you know.'

Relief flooded Olivia. This was a welcome that warmed her heart. 'Thank you, I've missed you all.'

'You were nearly a gonna, they reckon. And is this the lady that saved you?'

'It is. This is Annie, Joe . . . Joe is one of the island's characters. He can turn his hand to anything.'

'Pleased to meet you, miss. We owe you a debt. Miss Olivia is one of our treasures. We've all been worried about her.'

Always forthright, as Olivia had found the cockneys to be, Annie said, 'Well, I hope you treat her better than she's been treated on this boat by folk who are supposed to be her own kind.'

Joe looked quizzically at Olivia.

'Oh, it was just Mark Rundle. He was a bit off with me on account of Hendrick being German. Don't worry about it.'

Joe pushed his cap to the back of his head. 'Well, there's been a few rumblings about Hendrick volunteering for the German army, and a few ain't that pleased . . . Look, come up top and you'll see for yourself.'

Olivia didn't know what he meant by this. Were there islanders on the dock ready to jeer at her? Surely Joe would protect her from that?

'Let me help you, Miss Olivia. Do you need your stick?'

'No, if I can take yours and Annie's arms, I'll be fine . . . I know you said up top, but I am on the level of the deck that we disembark from, aren't I?'

'You are. I'll help you out first then I'll make sure your cases get to you. Your father and Hendrick are waiting for you.'

When they stepped out of the cabin there was a roar of applause and people calling out, 'Welcome home.'

Olivia looked up into a sea of cheering people. The tears ran down her cheeks. All her fears were unfounded. Mark Rundle was amongst the few, not the majority. Happiness flooded her as she looked into the beloved faces of her father and Hendrick. 'I'm home, Annie, I'm home.'

Chapter Eleven

Annie

Annie couldn't believe Olivia's home. It was more sumptuous than her aunt's. Three storeys high, it had the usual kitchen and pantry and housekeeper's room on the ground floor, with a cellar leading off from the little hallway, which you could also enter through a door off the kitchen garden. There wasn't much more garden, just a small lawn fenced off from the vegetable patch at the back of the house, as the front opened onto the cobbled promenade.

The living rooms for the family were on the second floor and were normally only used by Olivia and her father, but they currently had two aunts visiting for the wedding. One of the rooms was Olivia's own sitting room, and Annie liked this the best, with its decor and furnishings in blues and very pale greens, and its shiny mahogany furniture. It seemed to bring the beautiful view over the sea inside. Annie loved to gaze at the many little boats bobbing around in the harbour.

The formal dining room also overlooked the sea and was across the hall, with the family living room at the back. The bedrooms were all on the third floor, with staff bedrooms being in the attic, though only two members of staff lived in – the housekeeper and the general maid.

The thing that struck Annie so much was that there was no class system. The staff were part of the family or treated like good friends – Annie loved it and felt at home. No one treated her as 'jumped up' because she shared Olivia's bedroom. Something which she couldn't imagine happening in Wallington Manor.

'Right, Miss Olivia.' Penelope, one of the maids, known as Penny, came into the living room, her arms full of freshly laundered clothes. 'I'm sorting this lot out . . . You said you wanted them bagging up and for them to be shipped to the mainland to be sold at jumbles, but we've no idea where to send them all.'

Olivia looked at Annie. 'I thought, if I have them all packed into a crate and sent home with you, Annie, you could sort through them and do what you think best. Are there jumble sales all year round?'

'No, mostly on occasions. Like at Christmas and such like. But there is an autumn fair run by our local church in Bethnal Green and I can donate them all to that. They'll really help families living in the area.'

'So, have they all to go, miss?'

'Yes, all of those, please, Penny. I've brought loads back with me, so I'm sorted as far as my wardrobe is concerned.'

When Penny left the room, Olivia said, 'Would you be offended if I suggested that you and Janey look through them first to see if anything suits you, Annie?'

'No, mate, I wouldn't. I'm just so grateful you remembered the poor. Anyway, I'm used to cast-offs and grateful for them. Though Jimmy said that once we're married, I'll never need anything like that again, as he can keep me – as he puts it – in the manner I should be kept.'

Annie strutted across the room with her nose in the air and they both burst out laughing.

'Oh, Annie, you will tell me if I go too far in trying to help you and your mum and Janey, won't you?'

'Don't worry, luv, we needed it, I just didn't see it that way, but I do now, and like I say, my mum is happier, and we're going to make her even happier with the move to be in the same building we are in. And you haven't overstepped the mark, you've just been a lovely kind friend. How that happened to someone like me, and to find meself invited as a guest to such a lovely home as this, I can't get into me head, but I'm glad and I'm honoured to be part of your life.'

'You've no need to be. You're one of the biggest parts of it, along with Daddy and Hendrick. I just can't believe that we'll be parting soon.'

This put a dampener on them both.

'What it will be like seeing you off on the boat on your own, I can't imagine, nor do I want it to happen, but you have your own life to lead, Annie, and a lovely future to look forward to. And I will be happy for you.'

'And you'll visit, won't you? Especially for me wedding, I want you as the maid of honour!'

'That would be lovely, and yes, we will, as Mr and Mrs Kraus!'

'Well, at least it's an easy name to remember.'

'Yes, Hendrick tells me it means curly, but he doesn't know what happened to the curls over the generations as his family all have straight hair!'

'Sad that his father can't come, luv.'

'It is. But his position is such that, though things have eased for him and he is no longer in prison, he is still watched, and doesn't think he would be granted travel documents . . . I wish that he would be, as then we could hide him, or smuggle him away somewhere and then Hendrick needn't go even if called on to do so.'

'Well, don't think of bad things. You're meant to be getting ready to take me on a tour of the island, remember?'

Annie was in awe of everything she saw from the back of Hendrick's open-top car as they drove through St Peter Port – a small, beautiful town with its whitewashed buildings, cobbled streets and many flowers. Everywhere there were flowers, and their scent filled the air.

Soon they were out in the countryside and driving along narrow tree-lined roads. The cool breeze rustling the leaves provided a welcome respite from the heat as it played with Annie's hair. Though when they sped down the hills she had to close her eyes against the pressure of it.

Her mind went to Jimmy and how much she was missing him. She so wanted him here with her, and made her mind up that they, too, would have a honeymoon. The thought came to her then that she would love that to be in Guernsey. She'd seen so many guest houses, with folk sitting outside enjoying a drink, or a cake and tea, she just wanted to do that with Jimmy.

'Here we are! Our farmhouse.'

The house was on a corner, whitewashed, with a sloping grey roof and black door and window frames. It looked beautiful – until they went inside, where work was going on, as that gave it a dusty feel, with windows you couldn't see out of.

This didn't detract, though, from the feel of the house. Each room had its own character, especially downstairs, which was once living quarters but had taken on the mantle of schoolrooms with the flat upstairs being almost finished.

From the windows of the flat, they gazed out over lovely views of green fields with cottages dotted here and there, and then the other way, they overlooked the sea.

'It's perfect, luv, just perfect.' Though she said this, Annie did worry about the arrangement and wondered how Olivia would cope on the stairs, but when they went up, she did really well, if a mite slow.

'It will exercise my legs well, as do those at home, though I do find them a strain more than these as the workmen have taken off the steepness of them here.'

'And we're hoping not to have to live upstairs for long, Annie, but to build on that land over there, look.'

Annie went to stand by the window with Hendrick and looked to where he was pointing.

'Oh, that's a lovely spot, so peaceful and like, well, some of the countryside I used to see on me way to Cornwall. It'll be smashing, mate.'

'So, Olivia tells me that Jimmy has bought a property. How are his renovations going?'

'They're going well, ta. Jimmy could get straight on with them as there were no change of use, so it just means getting all the flats liveable. Once he's done that, me and Janey'll take over and see to how we want it decorating . . . Oh, and Mum and Cissy, too. They'll have their say. So, I'm thinking it won't be long now before they're finished and in time for our wedding.'

'That's to be soon, isn't it?'

'Well, we haven't fixed a date yet, but yes, as soon as possible. Though I'm grateful for Olivia's father letting me stay with Cissy in the apartment until I can move into me own place.'

'It's a pity Jimmy couldn't come with you this time. You must be missing him. I like him. Salt of the earth kind of man.'

'He's always so busy, and he wants to get on with the renovations, but he always says that he likes you too, Hendrick, and that you'll never be enemies and that pleases him.'

'Well, best not to say that to anyone else, just know it yourself, Annie. Anyway, we're all hoping that any rumblings will settle down and it won't come that we must choose sides.'

Annie shuddered then; it was as if someone had walked over her grave and all she knew was going to change.

'You've gone quiet, Annie?'

'Oh, I was just thinking. I – I was wondering, Hendrick, you say that war won't happen, but do you really think that, mate?'

Hendrick sighed. 'Sometimes I do, my dear, but at others I don't. Things seem to swing one way and then another. At the moment, there is talk of the Austrian Nazi Party becoming more powerful and influential, so I do think Austria will eventually be annexed, but it's all supposition. None of us know. We read snippets in the paper, and of course, my father keeps me well informed now that he has more freedom. It's a real worry, but I think we have to live our life and enjoy it and try not to put so much store by what might be as it might never be. Let's make a pact of our own not to speak of war again. The first one who does will have to walk the plank off the end of the jetty!'

'Blimey, mate, that's a bit harsh, ain't it?!'

'Well, if it does the trick . . .'

Olivia, who'd been very quiet while Annie and Hendrick

had been talking, burst out laughing. 'Ha, Annie, don't look so scared, Hendrick's only joking. It was something we always used to say as youngsters here on the island. We were always playing pirates.'

Annie relaxed and laughed with her. 'He had me going there, but, oh, luv, I think your house is perfect. I'm really happy for you.'

Olivia took her hand. 'And yours will be too, and I'm happy for you, love.'

'Well, I'm glad everybody is happy. Now, I think we'd better make tracks for home. I don't want to tire you, Olivia, darling.'

With the gentle way Hendrick helped Olivia, and seeing her love for him shining in Olivia's eyes, Annie let go of all the feelings his remark had evoked, telling herself she was just being silly – it truly had been a joke that referred back to his and Olivia's childhood.

When she lay in bed that night, Annie thought of home – mostly of Jimmy. She loved that he'd made friends with Janey. She could tell he really liked her and had to admit to herself that at times she felt a pang of jealousy.

Restless and hot, Annie turned over, seeking a cold bit of the bed. As she did so, she told herself to stop having thoughts about Janey and Jimmy. It was good that they were getting on so well. She was seeing things that weren't there again, just as she had with Hendrick's remark earlier, when she'd thought he had a cruel streak.

With this, she tried to sleep, but for some reason she couldn't fathom, she felt very unsettled.

Chapter Twelve

Janey

Janey jumped when the shop doorbell rang. Hardly anyone had come in during the last hour and she had busied herself taking old stock off the shelves and putting new at the back, and then replacing everything, after dusting it – jam and tins of corned beef never needed this as they were good sellers that she was always restocking.

'Jimmy! What brings you here, luv?'

Though she tried, Janey couldn't help blushing as she looked at him. She wished this infatuation hadn't developed and tried her hardest to tell herself it was only what she'd feel for an older brother, but still she found herself dreaming that it was her and not Annie that Jimmy loved.

Jimmy gave her one of his lovely smiles and her heart flipped over. 'Is your boss in, Janey? I've a mind to try to pick up a bit of local business. I can offer him the stuff that won't be accepted up west for a fraction of the cost.'

'Huh! Rubbish for the poor, eh?'

'No, it ain't like that, Janey. Why are you always so harsh on me? I'm a businessman and saw an opportunity, that's all.'

'I'm sorry, Jimmy. I've been a bit crochety since Annie left. It's like the old days, and I can't get it into me head that this time she'll only be gone for three weeks, not a whole year.'

'I feel that too, luv, so I know what you're going through.'

'Mr Sutherland ain't in, I'm afraid, but I can give him a message.'

'Ta, luv . . . I've been thinking, if you're at a bit of a loose end later, I could do with a hand at the house. Nothing heavy, but I need to clear some stuff that's in me way. I've fitted up a bit of a shoot to a barrow in the garden, so it's just shovelling . . . You look nice and strong. I think you could help with that easily.'

Janey had a funny feeling zing through her as Jimmy said she looked nice and strong. Had his eyes travelled to her legs and then to her face? A heat spread through her as she looked away, knowing her face had reddened. Should she be feeling like this at her age?

'You want some cheap labour then, eh?'

'Ha, you've a sharp tongue and a mind like a fast train! But then like all kids from where we grew up, you've had to cope with a lot that's made you that way. We lived off our wits, didn't we?'

Janey's senses heightened. She was thrilled at being asked to go along and work with him, but if he brought them on a friendly level, she wasn't sure she could keep herself in check. It was easier to handle it all by snapping at him. 'I don't know as I'll have the time to help you, Jimmy. What with me mum and me job, I've enough on me plate.'

'Well, I'll leave it with you. You can just turn up any afternoon and I'll be there. I was there just before coming here when I had the idea of trying me luck. I work like that: I act on anything that comes into me head.'

His look didn't really go with what he said. Janey had the feeling that there was a double meaning. Was he really referring to the work he wanted her to do when he said he'd thought he'd try his luck?

'I'll be there till about seven tonight. What time do you leave here?'

'Four. But like I say, I have to see to Mum.' Something made her leave the way open. 'Though if Cissy's with her, that's different.'

'Well, I'll see you if I do, then . . . Here, them cakes look good. Bring them with you, eh? Or if you don't come, they'll be a treat for your mum.'

He brushed past her as he went towards the counter. Her nerves tingled.

'I'll leave the money for them.' The sound of his coins dropping onto the glass top zinged through her.

'See you later, luv.'

His wink made the feeling intensify.

Stop it! I must stop this. Jimmy will think me a fool. I'm picking up on the stupidest of things! None of them are real, it's just this daft longing inside me. Why, oh, why is it there?

She would never hurt Annie. And in any case, she had to hold on to it all being in her imagination! And yes, she would go to the house, and she wouldn't think like this but be the sister she was going to be to Jimmy. She could prove that much to herself and stop this nonsense once and for all!

With this determination, Janey made herself think of Annie and how happy and in love with Jimmy she was and told herself that she must never let anything spoil that.

* * *

Later, however, on her way to the house, having left her mum and Cissy happily playing cards, her stomach clenched with anticipation at just being with Jimmy. Clutching the box holding two cakes, having left one each for her mum and Cissy, she told herself over and over that she could handle it. She had to. She mustn't ever show Jimmy how she felt and if he ever guessed, she would be mortified.

'You came, luv! And very welcome too. I like them dungarees. How long have you had them?'

'I wear them for work sometimes if we have stockroom clearing to do. Me and Annie saw them on the market.'

'They suit you, luv. Right. Come upstairs and I'll show you. It's not heavy stuff, just plaster dust from chipping the old plaster off.'

Upstairs in the room Jimmy was working on, Janey's resolve melted when he stood close to her. She could smell the fresh sweat on his body, wanted to reach out and touch him.

'You seem nervous, Janey. Are you all right, luv? . . . You're not worried about being alone with me, are you? Honestly, that reputation I got wasn't warranted. There were a few women, as I said, that tried it on with me, but always I had Annie in me mind. I think the gossip started as a boastful thing when girls didn't want anyone to think they'd been rejected . . . Honestly, don't stay if you don't want to.'

But she wanted to. 'No, I'm all right, just feel a bit silly as I've never done men's work before, and I might not manage it.'

'Ha! You girls are stronger than you think or make out to be. And we men don't help, keeping you tied to the kitchen sink. Look, I'll show you.'

Jimmy picked up a shovel and set to work. 'There, you see, nothing to it. You have a go.'

When she took the shovel from his grasp, their hands brushed each other's. For her, it was like an electric shock, but Jimmy just stepped back out of her way.

Janey found the work lighter than she thought and began to enjoy it and as the pile got smaller her feelings began to settle down. Jimmy's presence didn't seem to affect her and once more she was able to talk to herself about her infatuation being something that would pass and that she must always treat Jimmy like a big brother.

It was on the third day of calling around to help that all her resolve went out of the window.

Jimmy had bought a second-hand sofa and placed it in the only room ready for decorating – what was to be his and Annie's sitting room. He'd told her that he'd decided to complete the upstairs flat first so that it would be ready for him and Annie to move into after they were wed.

The sofa was for him to rest on as he said his back was killing him with the work he wasn't used to doing.

'I think it's cup of tea time, luv. I see you brought some biscuits along with you. I'll have a couple of them with me tea. And we can sit on me new-old sofa! Do you think Annie will want to keep it when she sees it? I like it and think it really comfy.'

'No, she won't, you daft thing. She's dreaming of all new stuff that ain't ever been sat on by anyone else, though she said she'll look for sideboards, dressers and wardrobes in the second-hand shop, but not her bed. She's adamant that she don't want a bed that's been slept in.'

'Well, I'll just have to save a bit of me budget then as it sounds like me soon-to-be wife has a spending spree in mind.'

The kettle whistled. Janey lifted it off the paraffin stove

and poured the boiling water onto the tea leaves in the pot. She loved the smell of brewing tea as she'd rarely had the luxury of such a drink until recently. Now her whole life had improved, more especially with having Annie so close by, bringing them treats all the time and able to give them plenty of money to live on.

As she stirred the milk into the now poured tea, and handed a mug to Jimmy, she told him, 'Well, Annie's been saving as well, and she won't have to spend a right lot on a wedding dress as Olivia is letting her have hers. Cissy will alter it to fit. And I'm to wear Annie's bridesmaid frock when I'm your bridesmaid.'

'And a beautiful one you'll make, Janey.'

Her stomach muscles clenched. Her throat tightened.

'Come and sit down and enjoy your tea, luv.' He patted the seat next to him. 'You've done a good job with that rubble. It's about gone.'

When she sat down, she could feel his thigh next to hers. The clenching tightened. Annie came into her mind. Shame washed over her, making her ask herself for the umpteenth time, *Why do I feel like this?*

Jimmy leaned forward with his elbows on his knees and sipped his tea. He'd gone quiet. She felt sure he was feeling it too; it was like an electric current passing between them.

'Janey, I think we'll call it a day after we've had our tea . . . and, well, I – I think it best you don't come to help me again. I'll see you when Annie's back, eh?'

'Why? Have I done something wrong?'

'No . . . no, luv, I . . . well, it's for the best.'

Janey didn't want this. She wanted to be with him, just her and him working together, chatting.

'But I've loved it. It's something different for me.'

132

He turned and looked at her. Something in his eyes melted her heart. She saw him swallow hard, watched his Adam's apple jerk . . . 'Oh, Janey.'

Her body swayed towards his, without her making it do so.

Jimmy was so close when suddenly he said, 'This is wrong.' His voice had a husky tone; nothing he said held conviction. 'You have to leave, Janey . . . Please, get up and go, and let's forget this feeling between us ever happened.'

She knew he was right, but it was as if something had taken her over, was making her something she wasn't. She had no will power, and could feel nothing but a love for Jimmy that consumed her.

When his lips touched hers, it was as if their worlds collided and had found the place where they belonged. She clung to him and him to her.

Still keeping close when their lips parted, she saw tears glistening in Jimmy's eyes. One rolled down his face. Her own misted over.

'What do we do, Janey, luv?'

She shook her head. This released her tears to wet her cheeks.

'How do we get out of this mess? I – I realized a long time ago that it was you that I love, Janey. Me coming to the shop, well, I shouldn't have done it, but I felt compelled. I don't really want an account with your boss.'

'Oh, Jimmy, why did you let it go this far? Why did you keep courting Annie when it is us that should be together?'

'I thought what I felt on seeing Annie was love, but, oh, Janey, how do we go forward?'

'I don't know, Jimmy. I love you and have done from the moment I set eyes on you outside that clinic. I thought at first that it was just an attraction, a silly younger sister thing for her older sister's boyfriend, but it isn't . . . I even thought you were making a pass at me after the things I heard . . .'

'Janey, they weren't true, luv, they weren't. Like I said, a woman customer got a thing for me. I refused her, but she put it about that I'd been with her. She was married as well. But her talk set the rumours growing . . . Being a young man with feelings, I did go with one of them that threw themselves at me, and that was that: I was known as a womanizer from then on. But I ain't. This is breaking me heart. I can't bear to hurt Annie in this way.'

'No, we can't. I'll move away, Jimmy. I'll tell Annie that it's my time to see a bit of the outside world now that she's able to take care of Mum. Maybe her old boss will take me on down in Cornwall and that'll mean we're apart for a year and you can get on with being a good and loving husband to Annie . . .' Her throat tightened into a sob. Jimmy pulled her close. She clung on to him as if this would be the last time ever.

But then he was kissing her. Her eyes, her cheeks, her neck, and then his hand came onto her breast, and she was lost. She couldn't resist, and knew he couldn't stop.

She didn't resist when the braces holding the bib of her dungarees were slid off her shoulders. Or when her jumper was gently taken over her head, but thrilled at the kisses Jimmy planted on her naked skin.

Then it happened and, after a moment's discomfort, her world burst into a frenzy of joy and pleasure like she'd never dreamed she could experience. Jimmy's lovemaking took her through exquisite sensations that she knew he was feeling too when he joined her in crying out their undying love for one another.

When it was over, they lay together on the sofa, clinging to each other as if their lives depended on them never letting go.

'Run away with me, Janey. Let's just go. I can't give you up, not now.'

'But Annie? Oh, Jimmy, me love, we can't do that to Annie.'

'Would it be better that I married her when it's you that I love?'

'You must, Jimmy. Annie doesn't deserve this. She loves you. She talks of nothing else but your wedding day, your new home, the babies . . . Oh, my God! Jimmy! Will I have a baby?'

Jimmy gasped. 'I – I didn't think. I don't know. The other woman I went with, she made me pull away from her . . . Oh, Janey, I should have, but I was lost, me darling. I was in a cocoon of love and feelings. I didn't take care.'

'Don't talk about that woman, Jimmy. It hurts me . . . Have you and Annie . . . ?'

'No. I haven't touched Annie, only kissed, and cuddled . . . I, well, I've always had this feeling for you, but thought it was a silly thing born of your indifference to me – you know, wanting something that you can't have. Somehow, though, it held me back from ever making those kinds of advances towards Annie. That and, well, the feeling wasn't right. It wasn't there. I knew I loved her, but did I? Have I been thinking myself in love with the girl I was infatuated with as a youngster and not allowing myself to think of anything, or anybody else? And I could always tell myself not to make love to Annie until we were wed. With you, Janey, I could never have waited, I just couldn't. We were meant to be.'

'Oh, Jimmy, I love you . . . but it's hopeless . . .'

Jimmy held her tighter; he kissed her hair and then her forehead, found her lips, prised her mouth open and played with her tongue with his. The sensations began to build in her once more.

This time, she explored him as he did her. Both discovered places that made them cry out with the joy of being touched.

Somehow, without stopping the pleasure happening, they managed to pull the cushions off the sofa and lie down on them. Jimmy guided her to sit on him. The sensation of this transported her to another world. Even the soreness she'd felt at first didn't stop her. She gave her all to him until she collapsed in a heap of sheer ecstasy, calling out her love, screaming for a release.

When it came, she hollered his name and her love for him.

Afterwards, they lay sobbing in each other's arms. Unable to bear a future apart, and yet unable to bear what it would mean to be together – the hurt it would cause Annie.

When they untangled themselves from each other, they lay quietly sobbing, their predicament feeling like a horrendous choice to them.

Kissing her on the cheek, Jimmy said, 'Let's get dressed and talk, eh?'

Janey never wanted to dress again. She wanted to lie for ever next to Jimmy's naked, strong body, and to keep on making love to him, and yet, she felt spent of energy.

As they sat together on the sofa holding hands, Janey said, 'I'll have to go away, Jimmy. There's no other way.'

'Maybe Annie will understand.'

'How can she? How could we ask her to? The man she loves and is looking forward to marrying telling her he loves someone else would be bad enough, but telling her that that someone is her little sister would devastate her. We can't do that to her, nor to me mum, or your mum, come to that . . . Look, I've got the address of Annie's old boss. I used to write to Annie when she lived there. I'll write tonight and I'll talk to me mum about me leaving. She'll want me to see a bit of the world. She's always saying it ain't fair on me being stuck at home looking after her and never going out. Well, when she moves in here, she'll have Annie and Cissy and you on hand.'

Jimmy's head dropped. 'I can't bear it, Janey. I love you. You're right here in me heart . . . But I can't bear to hurt Annie either. I've loved her since I were a nipper, though then it was more that I couldn't match up to her, and now I know it ain't the kind of love that takes you through your life on a wave of happiness, but a love that'll always be good to have. Can you understand that?'

'I can . . . I hope I find a love like I have with you again in the future, Jimmy. But for now, we have no choice.'

He kissed her so many times before they got into his van, even stopping halfway home and pulling up to kiss her. 'I love you, Janey. Always remember that. But be happy. Promise me you'll be happy.'

'And you, Jimmy. I want that for you too.'

'I'll find a happiness with Annie. But always it will be you, Janey, always.'

'And you for me, Jimmy. When I visit . . . Well, we must never be alone . . . I couldn't be alone with you without making love to you.'

'Somehow, we'll do it. We'll do it for Annie.'

As Janey got out of the van, her heart was breaking, but Jimmy was right: somehow they would do this for Annie.

Chapter Thirteen

Olivia

Four days after arriving back in Guernsey, Olivia woke to beautiful sunshine streaming through the bedroom window.

'Happy the bride that the sun shines on, luv.'

With this from Annie, Olivia stretched, her body filling with nerves as she did.

To combat this, she jumped out of bed.

'Well, I'd better get on with being that bride then. I'll get my bath first, love. Will you organize a cup of tea and some toast for us? Oh, unless you want to go down to the dining room and have a big breakfast?'

'No, I just want to do what you want, it's your day. I'll ring down to the kitchen – ha, I've always wanted to say that! Never thought I would.'

Olivia laughed with her. But she didn't miss how all of this must be for Annie. She had a feeling that something was troubling her. She was restless at night and seemed far away in her thoughts at times. She told herself she was being silly. That Annie was feeling out of her depth and, more than anything, missing home.

* * *

A couple of hours later when they both were ready, Annie held her hands. 'You look a picture, luv. Hendrick will fall in love with you all over again.'

Olivia smiled. A smile that hid her nervous anticipation and the turmoil of emotions she felt as she thought about her mother and how it would have been if she'd been here today to help her into her gown.

As Olivia entered the church, just a few paces away from her home – a walk cheered on by what seemed like hundreds of people calling out good wishes and throwing petals to give her path a lovely scent – all her concerns left her.

She glanced up at the beautiful window in the church that was dedicated to her mother's memory. At that moment the sunbeams came through. They glistened with the colours that made the glass mural of Our Lady so vivid. To Olivia, it gave the feeling that her mum smiled down on her. She smiled back.

Hendrick looked beautiful in his dark morning suit, white shirt and blue cravat. As did Annie, her hair suiting her so much, caught up on the top of her head and falling into ringlets, for which she'd endured having rags twirled in it all night long.

The day went by happily, with the wedding breakfast held at home and everyone waving them off as they left to spend a few days on the neighbouring island of Jersey where they'd booked a hotel. Neither had wanted to go far, but both had wanted privacy from folk they knew and a few days to adjust to at last being married.

It was just as they were to board the ferry that she looked around her and caught sight of Annie, standing on the edge of the crowd, tears rolling down her face. Turning, she ran as best she could to her. 'Oh, Annie, don't be sad. Soon it will be your own wedding day, love, and we will be there.

You'll be so busy from now till then you'll hardly have time to miss me.'

'I know. But, oh, Olivia, I will miss you, luv.'

'What's wrong, Annie? I feel there's something.'

'It's me being silly, but well, I keep having doubts.'

'Ha, is that all?! That's every bride's prerogative, darling. I had so many, but like you, didn't feel I could talk to anyone about them. Oh, if only you'd said before, love. We've no time to talk now, but I promise you, they are natural, every girl has them, or so I read in my magazine that you say is all about daft stuff!'

'Do they? Did you doubt that Hendrick really loved you?'

'Well, no, not that one, but loads of other things. But of course Jimmy loves you and has done since he was that snotty-nosed kid you told me about.'

They both laughed and Olivia felt better, though she did wonder why Annie was having these thoughts.

'Look, I've got to go now, but everything will be all right, I promise you. Would Jimmy have bought a house for you and all your family and even Cissy because you love her so much, if he didn't love you?'

'No, you're right. I don't know what's got into me. I just don't want me or him to make a mistake.'

'You do love him, don't you?'

'I do, with all me heart.'

'Well then. And he loves you in the same way.'

A loud ship's horn blew, and her father called, 'Olivia, dear, hurry. We'll look after Annie.'

'Oh, I have to go! Wish me luck, my lovely, lovely friend, I will miss you so much.'

There was just time for a quick hug before Olivia reluctantly had to leave.

Why, oh, why hadn't Annie spoken of her doubts before? Olivia wondered as the boat got ready to sail. Now she would have a niggly worry hanging over her.

What can have happened to make her doubt Jimmy? *Please God he isn't the womanizer Janey said he was.* But surely, if Annie had known something like that was true, she wouldn't entertain marrying him?

All of this went out of Olivia's head as she held Hendrick's hand, and they stood on the deck to a cheer that went up as the boat slowly pulled away from the harbour.

She was married! Married to her beloved Hendrick!

Both feeling tired when they arrived at their lovely hotel on the promenade, they relaxed over dinner, talked of everything and nothing, drank a couple of glasses of delicious French wine, and finally found themselves going up in the lift to sleep together for the very first time.

Feeling so relaxed, Olivia didn't worry about what was to come, but instead enjoyed the delicious anticipation, though a shyness did come over her as she prepared for bed.

Hendrick made it easier for her by tending to her gently, helping her with any items of clothing that she needed help with and telling her, 'I have longed for this moment, my darling.'

He kissed every part of her as it became exposed, taking away any embarrassment as he caressed her scars, calling them beautiful medals to her bravery.

And then they were on the bed, holding each other, caressing each other, finding how to give and to take pleasure. To Olivia, it was a glorious journey of discovery. She felt a frenzy take over her as she moved towards something she knew she wanted – needed. And then it happened. A feeling that grew, and which she almost wanted to stop, and yet begged to take hold of her. She cried out when it did – a sound that was akin to agony, but this was a blissful cry of almost unbearable pleasure, the giving of her whole self to her beloved husband.

His own hollers joined hers as he pressed himself even further into her. His body rigid, his hoarse voice crying out his joy.

They clung to one another, a bundle of sweat, giggles, tears and happiness, as they allowed their bodies to come down from the place that had captured them and changed them for ever.

It was the next day when they were walking along a winding clifftop path with the sun beaming down on them that Olivia told Hendrick of her concerns about Annie.

Hendrick was quiet for a moment, then shocked her.

'You remember that day over Christmas when they all came to the apartment?'

'Yes. Why?'

'Well, I . . . look, I'm wrong, I'm sure, but well, I saw Jimmy looking at Janey. She didn't see him, or even look over towards him as I made a point of watching her, but well, Jimmy's expression was of a man yearning for something. I told myself I was seeing things because in an instant, he turned his attention back to Annie and put his arm around her.'

'No! You don't think . . . ? But Janey's only young . . .'

'Janey strikes me as never having been young. She is a beautiful young woman, who I am sure doesn't feel like a girl . . . I'm not saying that this has anything to do with anything, but it has stuck with me, and alarm bells rang for me when I saw it.'

'Oh, Hendrick, that would be disastrous. Annie is so happy. So in love! It can't be . . . Please don't let it be.'

'Well, I'm sure it's not now. I'm sure I was seeing things. Let's forget it, darling. I am sorry I told you. Only I don't want anything to spoil our day today. We only have a couple or so together.'

'Huh! I thought we had the rest of our lives! That's what you vowed – forsaking all others!'

Hendrick laughed out loud.

'You goose, I meant on holiday! Our honeymoon. It will be all work after this, and I want to enjoy every moment we have now. You won't do that if you're worried about Annie. Anyway, I think she just has wedding nerves, we all have them.'

'Did you? Did you have doubts?'

'Well, I read that it was natural to have them, but mine were only centred around if things change, not anything else . . . Well, I did worry that I wouldn't . . . we wouldn't . . . well, do things right . . . you know.'

'We did things perfectly. I still cannot believe how it feels and how we ever waited for our wedding night. If I'd have known, I'd have had you in that hospital bed . . .'

'Olivia!'

She laughed at him. 'Don't be shocked! It was you that made me feel like I did and made me wish I'd felt it a long time ago!'

'Ha, I've married a different person!'

'And so have I . . . Kiss me, Hendrick.'

She was in his arms. He was kissing her and saying her name over and over.

Happiness and desire burned every sinew of her.

Hendrick's need for her showed as he pressed himself against her.

Drawing breath, they looked around them. They were on a lonely path with a bank next to them covered in beautiful heather of purples, pinks, greens and yellows. They could smell the lovely scent of it as they lay down together amongst it and once more joined in an ecstasy of giving and taking love to the sound of the sea lapping on the shore far below them.

When it was over, they adjusted their clothes and sat looking out over the horizon.

'I wish the world could stay like this for ever, my darling.'

'Hush, it will. Our world will, Hendrick, we must make it so.'

'But—'

'Don't tell me if you know something different, just let me do as you say and enjoy this wonderful peace and all we have found together, my darling. If there is something we must face in the future, we will, together, but don't let your worries crowd out our peace now.'

'I'm sorry, darling. It's all never far from my mind.'

As she watched him gaze out to sea, his face creased with anxiety, she so wanted to take away his thoughts of war in the future, but she knew she couldn't. Maybe it was better to let him talk.

'In that case, share it with me. We must be able to talk to one another about anything that worries us. I'm sorry I tried to block you from doing that. I'm ready to listen.'

'Thank you, Olivia. It worries me that I have had to be careful what I say, and to pretend none of it is happening. I want us to make plans, to know what we will do if our worst fears happen – and they may. I heard from the German consulate. He has asked me to learn Italian and Japanese and to be ready if called.'

'No! No, Hendrick! Just a short while ago you said there had been nothing from any of them. Why? Why now?'

'The Italians already have a pact with Germany, but Hitler must be leaning towards making one with Japan. Of course, they will already have interpreters, but the more countries that enter an alliance, the more they need . . . I am preparing myself for being called up – or rather, they are preparing me, which means we have time on our side. It also means that they are keeping an eye on me. But above all, to me, it is a relief. It tells me that they are considering me for a role in the translation of documents. And that means that if there is war, I won't be called to be a fighting man – something I am not.'

Olivia couldn't see this as the positive that Hendrick was making it. 'How will you learn Japanese? Italian will be easy and can be picked up from textbooks, but Japanese?'

'I don't know yet. I may have to go to London and attend the language college that your tutors were from.'

'Oh, Hendrick! I never dreamed you would say that! But what of our plans – our home, our school?'

'We could get plans drawn up, and commission builders to do the work, and you could oversee it. I would come home every weekend, just like we have been doing.'

'I wouldn't come with you then?'

'No, my darling. It would only be for six months at the most . . . It's just that I have a niggly worry that . . . Oh, I don't know . . .'

Olivia waited.

'Look, I think there may be an ulterior motive for the ambassador to suggest all of this. I think he wants me to increase my knowledge of Britain and the ways of the country. He said something about how pleased they were that I appeared to have connections here and . . . Well, as I said, I think I am being watched . . . not by someone following me, but by methods of intelligence. They knew all about my schooling in Rugby, my time at Cambridge University. My finance career and qualifications. The latter astounded me, as did how all of it seemed to be what they are looking for. But there was a sinister note, as he did say my loyalty to Germany would be tested before I was accepted.'

'So, how does that affect me not coming with you?'

'Well, it might look like I wouldn't be willing to leave you now that we are married . . . I'm afraid, darling. They will want to indoctrinate me. I don't want you involved in any way. They aren't nice people and if it looks like someone is a hindrance to them, well, their methods are ruthless.'

Olivia's spine crawled. A shiver trembled through her. This was no longer something that might happen, but something very real and terrifying.

'I hate your cowardly father!'

Hendrick's hand took hold of hers. They sat there in silence. Olivia could feel his fear and knew a deepening of her own. There were greater forces than them at work here. Her bright, happy future seemed to be crumbling around her and she was powerless to stop it.

'I'm sorry, darling, I should have told you all of this earlier.'

'Yes, you should have.'

'All I can say is that I wanted you to have the dream of us settling down in the farmhouse together and beginning our new life. I couldn't shatter that. To all intents and purposes, the prospect of me having to go back to Germany had receded and life had got back to some normality. I just didn't want to have this new turn of events hanging over your head throughout our wedding day. I'm so sorry, it was the wrong decision.'

'It was, and we should make a pact now that we keep nothing from each other, nothing! Good or bad, it affects us both. It all has to be faced and cannot be so if it isn't planned for together – oh, I know things will crop up, but this hasn't. You've known about it, formulated plans to accommodate it, and then sprung it on me when I least expected it.'

'Darling, I'm so sorry. Are we having our first row?' He pleaded in a childlike way. 'Please don't let us, not on honeymoon.'

Though inside she felt infuriated with him, she couldn't help but smile.

'Just promise me that from now on you will always consult with me, darling . . . I know I am partly to blame as I had shut myself off from the thought of you going back to Germany and having anything to do with Hitler's regime, and you knew that. But neither of us must do this again. Apart from anything else, it has meant you carrying the burden on your own . . . Does my father know of it?'

'Not my plans to go to London, no. I just don't know how to tell him. He will have to find a replacement for me. That's not going to be easy, but he has known for a long time now that the prospect of me having to go away was on the horizon. He's been keeping abreast of my portfolio so can take over himself as his own responsibilities are just in the capacity of overseeing all accounts now.'

'He should be thinking of retiring really, not taking more work on.'

'I know. But he has always been expecting me to leave, as once the school was off the ground, I was to devote my time to that.'

Olivia bowed her head with the weight of her sadness at

the school not happening now, and probably not for a long time. It was as if their dreams were crumbling at the whim of that horrid little moustached maniac who'd taken power over Germany.

'I need you to be strong, my Olivia.'

Olivia took a deep breath. 'I will be. We're in this together.'

'Are we? I mean, how far would you go in the extreme circumstance that Britain is involved in a war with Germany?'

'What sort of question is that? Of course I will support you as my husband, but I would never betray my country.'

'I will. I will betray Germany.'

'What? How?'

'Think about it, Olivia. If I work on highly confidential documents, I will have access to information that could help those fighting Germany.'

'Be a spy, you mean . . . But, Hendrick, you would be in extreme danger.'

'I would be willing to do that. There is nothing about the Nazis that I can admire or follow. I don't want them to succeed. The world they would create isn't a world I would want for my children. I'd do anything, anything to stop them.'

They fell silent. Olivia broke this with one word. 'How?'

'I don't know. I will need contacts – someone to pass the information to. But if I am being watched, then I cannot make them myself. I will only have you and your father. Somehow, I would have to pass information to you, and you would have to get it to where it will be of help. Would you do that, Olivia?'

Olivia didn't have the slightest doubt that she would. 'I don't know how we would do it, but yes, if it is possible, then we will.'

'I have thought about it a lot. We need someone we can trust who can approach the Foreign Office with the suggestion. I cannot, and neither can you. If they know what I am doing, they know what you are up to and possibly our friends too.'

For Olivia, this was all so far away from what these three days were about that she had the strange sensation of being drawn into something that was unreal. Which she knew it was, as it might never be real, and yet she felt in her bones that Hendrick was right. That he could be a channel of information that would be so useful to Britain if they went to war.

It was strange, but though classed as British, she'd never felt that as she'd always just thought of herself as an islander of Guernsey, and yet what happened on the mainland always affected them – they were part of Britain. The king was their king too, even if the government was not theirs, nor the laws of Britain. There was just this affinity that couldn't be broken.

'I have no idea how we can do that, Hendrick, but now that I do know of what you plan, a way may present itself . . . But now, please, darling, all of this is scaring me and spoiling what we are here for – to celebrate being man and wife at last.'

'It is. But I am glad I have shared it all. It has played on my mind for so long. Together, we might find solutions.'

'One is that I will study with you. I find it fascinating that you are taking Japanese.'

'Wonderful. I can bring my coursework home and pass on to you what I have learned, then we can practise together. It always helps to have a study mate . . . You are my mate in every way, Olivia. Never forget that I love you with all my heart, no matter what happens or how things look in the future.'

This frightened her even more, but she smiled and said, 'I won't, I promise.'

It was an easy promise for her to make and she meant it with all her heart, for no matter how much they were tested, they would always be linked in the faith of their love.

Chapter Fourteen

Annie

As Annie stepped off the gangplank a voice called her name. She turned to see Jimmy running towards her.

'Jimmy? . . . Jimmy! What the . . . ?'

His arms grabbed her, lifted her up in the air and swung her around. 'I couldn't see you travelling on a train, luv, I knew you'd be terrified and sick all the way home. So I took a day off.'

'Oh, I am pleased to see you, luv, I've missed you so much. I love you, Jimmy.'

Jimmy held her close, but didn't say he'd missed her, or loved her. His hold on her was as if she was a lifeline.

'Are you all right, Jimmy?'

He hesitated, looked into her eyes. In his she saw something she couldn't detect. 'Jimmy? What's happened? Is Mum all right, and Janey?'

He flinched, then took a deep breath. 'Yes, luv. All are fine. I'm just so pleased to see you. I worried you'd be lost to me again. But you're not. I love you, Annie.'

Her fast-beating heart settled with this. Why was she so oversensitive? Why couldn't she just accept that they had found one another, and that Jimmy could love her?

151

When they arrived at his van parked on the dockside, Jimmy surprised her by saying, 'Let's get wed soon, Annie. I can post the banns tomorrow. We could do it in three weeks. I've concentrated on our flat and will see about getting help from builders to finish it off. It's almost ready for you just to buy the furniture. Janey told me you wanted to do that side of things, and I've put a bit of money by for you to put with what you have . . . Though it looks like you've brought a load of stuff back with you – that porter's heading our way and calling out your name!'

'Oh, that'll be Olivia's cast-offs. I'll explain all. They are booked onto the train for the goods van, so I can tell him to take them there, unless you can get them in?'

'I can. Me van's empty, luv.' He called out to the porter, 'Here, mate. Over here for Miss Freeman.'

'Righty-oh.'

After the van was packed and Jimmy had tipped the porter, Annie got into the passenger seat. Her excitement at all Jimmy had said lifted her out of any thoughts that gave her doubts. Jimmy loved her, and he wanted to marry her so much that he'd pulled out all the stops to get their home ready while she was away. She couldn't wait to go shopping now.

When Jimmy got in, Annie slid along the seat to be close to him. He took her hand in his but didn't look at her.

'So, you and Janey have—'

'What? I – I mean . . . Sorry, luv. I wasn't concentrating. I – I was thinking about how to get out of this place. I ain't been here before . . . What about Janey?'

'Nothing. I was just going to say it sounds like you've been plotting behind me back with—'

'We haven't, Annie. She helped me out at the flat, that's all.

152

She told me then about you wanting new stuff and I agree. We should have it.'

'Jimmy, what's wrong?'

Jimmy's face had coloured to a bright red.

'You seem on edge, luv. Has something happened?'

'No, Annie. Look, do you have to question me? I haven't questioned you. I've a mind that you believe the talk about me. Well, that ain't a good starting place, Annie. You've to trust me or we have nothing.'

Annie fell silent. Whatever she said had touched a nerve. She'd only been joking about him and Janey plotting – had tried to make him laugh. Why he'd taken it like he had she was at a loss to know.

They'd gone a few miles before the hand he'd snatched away from her found hers once more.

'I'm sorry, Annie. I'm oversensitive about me reputation and you believing it . . . I'm tired, too. I've worked long hours, up at three to get me produce off the train from Kent and stock the stall and start me rounds, then instead of a few hours' kip in the afternoon, I've been working till dark on the flat. Janey's been a big help, like I say, and we're getting on better now. She's shovelled and painted and cleaned. We had one mission, to get the flat ready for you and me. The rest can be done afterwards.'

'It's all right. But I want you to know, I do trust you. I'd trust you with me life, Jimmy. I didn't mean to touch a raw nerve, I was just joking about Janey and you plotting behind me back, but I'm pleased to hear that you've got on well. She had her ideas about you in the beginning because of all the stories about you womanizing, but she's over all of that. The constant banter she has with you is the way she would be with a big brother if she'd had one. You're a good match for each other!'

He squeezed her hand in his. 'I think you should prepare yourself, luv. Janey's been talking about seeing the world – well, Britain – now you're going to be on hand for your mum. She's talking as if it's her time now. I agreed with her; she's given all her young years to caring for your mum.'

This shocked Annie. 'Oh? But I will need her. I've been looking forward to having her close, and being there for me if . . . well, if those babies come along that we joked about.'

Another shock hit her then as Jimmy took a stance against this.

'That's just it. Janey is seen as the stay-at-home, the one to be depended on. It ain't fair, Annie, the girl needs a life. Just let her go with your blessing, luv, and stop thinking she'll always be there for you and your mum.'

'I didn't think that . . . Well, of course I did. But I won't stop her. What is she planning?'

'I'll let her tell you, luv.'

Another change came over Jimmy, and his face creased in a frown. He sighed and looked away, glancing out of the side window. Annie just knew there was something on his mind, but she couldn't think what. Was he going to miss Janey? She knew he enjoyed the banter they had. Had they become close while working together? *I must stop this, I must! What am I thinking? Jimmy has loved me since he was a boy! Janey's like a kid sister and nothing more! I must stop this jealousy. Jimmy has given me no reason to be jealous . . . none!*

They didn't speak much for the rest of the journey. To Annie, it was as if there was a barrier between them and it broke her heart. She made her mind up that she must show Jimmy her love for him in everything she said and did. She couldn't bear for him to be unhappy.

* * *

At Mum's home, there was a flurry of hugs and kisses, including from Cissy who was waiting for her too.

'Eeh, lass, we've missed you. I've rattled around in that empty apartment again, only it were worse after living with you both and then you were gone. I'm so glad you're home, me lovely lass.'

The welcome from them all, so different to what she'd had from Jimmy, warmed her heart. 'How have you been, Mum?'

'I've been grand, as Cissy would say. I'm sure being in a nice dry place and having company and being able to be pushed out on walks and to the shops is doing me the world of good. I've hardly taken me pills, have I, Janey, luv?'

Janey nodded.

'And you've been helping Jimmy, I hear, Janey, luv. Ta for that. I'm so excited to see your handiwork.'

'Only a couple of afternoons or so . . . He wanted to get it done for you, didn't you, Jimmy?' A look passed between them. But Annie noticed that when Janey saw that she'd seen the look, she coloured and turned it into banter.

'The lazy sod wouldn't have got it done if I weren't there. He just wanted one pot of tea after another brewing, but I hid the matches to the stove. I tell you, Annie, you'll have to keep the whip on him.'

'You cheeky madam, I did all the work! You were the one wanting to put the kettle on!'

'Well, all that dust, what do you expect, eh? Anyway, it's all done, Annie. You'll love it. I can't wait to go shopping with you to furnish it. Only don't let that daft sod have a say in any of it, he's got no taste. He wanted me to paint the woodwork in brown! But I chose a nice cream with a pastel shade of lemon for the walls as that would make a nice backdrop to whatever colours you choose.'

Annie felt at a loss, as if she was the outsider, but she just smiled and nodded.

'Take no notice of them, Annie, they're like this all the time. I need to hear all about Olivia's wedding, and I know Cissy does.'

'Well, before you get gossiping, ladies, I've got to go. Shall I come back in a bit and take you and Cissy up west, Annie?'

Suddenly, Annie didn't want him to. She'd had enough, she wanted peace. She wanted to think and to sort out her feelings. Her thoughts went to the beautiful wedding gown in her case, and she wondered if she'd ever want to wear it now. 'No, ta, luv. I'll get a cab. I'm not sure when I'll be leaving. I'm tired too, so I'll see you tomorrow, eh? Pop round when you're on your rounds and we'll arrange something.'

Jimmy looked surprised but she didn't care. She felt hurt and confused and wanted time.

'What shall I do with this bundle of stuff then? And do you want all your cases bringing in, or shall I drop them off at the apartment and leave them with Fred? I've to go up there to get Mum.'

'Yes, that'll be good, ta. I don't need anything till I get back there. I'll see you sometime tomorrow.'

Jimmy hesitated. 'Will you come outside to me van a mo, Annie, luv? I won't keep you.'

Annie sighed. She felt the eyes of them all on her. Her mum looking worried, Janey a little afraid, and Cissy unsure, but Annie didn't react to any of this, she just followed Jimmy out into the back alley.

When they reached his van, he turned and looked at her.

'Annie, are we all right – you and me? We're not falling out, are we? You seem different.'

'It's you that's different, Jimmy. You're snapping and snarling at me, and there's an atmosphere. I can't put me finger on it, but it's like something's happened and it's changed you.'

'Oh, Annie, I'm sorry, luv. It is just tiredness, I promise you . . . But, well, if you feel differently about me, you will tell me, won't you?'

'I don't feel differently about you, Jimmy, I love you. It's not me that's causing it. But do you still love me?'

Jimmy stared down at her. His mouth opened and then closed again. But then it didn't matter what he was going to say as his lips came down on hers and the touch zinged through her.

His kiss was gentle at first, and then deepened. Annie clung on to him, feeling his passion and matching hers to his until a sound, like a cry, made them pull apart. They turned, but there was no one to be seen. When Annie faced Jimmy again, tears ran down his cheeks.

'Jimmy . . . Jimmy, luv, what is it? Talk to me.'

For an answer, he kissed her again. Once more with a passion she'd never known. His body pressed into hers. She felt his need. Thrilled at the sensations tingling through her body and clung on to him, ready to give herself to him right there in the alleyway.

Abruptly, he pulled away, leaving her suspended, gasping for breath and for control of her emotions.

'I must go, Annie. If I don't, we'll be doing things we shouldn't till we're wed. But Annie. I love you. I love you . . . with all me heart.'

She giggled. More for a release of her feelings than anything. 'We'll be wed soon, luv. Post them banns. Who cares if our flat's finished or not. I'd live in a shed with you, me darlin'.'

'Oh, Annie'.

The painful sound of this bewildered Annie, but she told herself it was just his frustration.

'I know how you feel, luv. We needn't wait till the wedding night, you know.'

Jimmy looked shocked. 'I – I couldn't do that, luv. I can wait . . . I . . . it wouldn't be right.'

Annie's cheeks flushed.

'But I know what you mean. I do feel it . . . I'll sort things, luv.'

His kiss didn't hold a promise, but was a light peck on her cheek. She'd upset him. She hadn't meant to.

But then he laughed. 'You're a bit forward, Miss-soon-to-be-Mrs Baines!'

Annie laughed with him, but the same niggly feeling that all wasn't right visited her as he got into his van.

When she waved him off and turned to go back inside, she wouldn't allow herself to think anything but smiley thoughts, and with this she was grinning when she opened the back door.

'Is everything all right, luv?'

'It is, Mum, we had a bit of crossed wires, but it's all straightened out . . . Like you said earlier, it's grand, just grand . . . Where's Janey?'

A look passed between Cissy and Mum. It was Cissy who answered. 'She's gone to her room, love. Lass has got a headache. She's had it all day. I reckon her monthlies are coming on the way she's been acting this last couple of days.'

'Oh? I wanted to talk to her.'

'What about, luv?'

'Has she said anything about leaving, Mum?'

'Oh, Jimmy told yer? Yes, she has been on about it. Well, more than talk, she's written to your ex-boss.'

'Mrs Wallington?'

'Aye, lass. I'd leave her to it if I were you. She's feeling restless, and me and your mum can understand it. She's young and hasn't had much life.'

Annie sat down. 'Well, it's no life lackeying in a manor house for folk who can't get enough staff to work down there, I'll tell you. I mean, they're lovely people but they have no idea of the life they gave to us downstairs. The days can be fifteen hours long, and time off is always being cancelled. The wages aren't bad to what maids get around London and the counties, but they have to be to keep any staff working down there at all . . . We can't let her go there, Mum. There must be something else.'

'She's adamant. And I mean, where else would you feel safe letting her go to? Like you say, they're decent folk and they thought a lot of you, so they'd look after Janey. And I'd feel she was safe.'

'Well, there is that to it. Oh, I don't know. I always thought I'd help her into nursing – she loves her time at the Red Cross.'

'She's given it up, luv. She said she didn't fit in and doesn't think it's for her. She found the book work a struggle too.'

'She never mentioned anything like that before.'

'No, well, she said she didn't want you to feel let down. But, well, it's no good her doing it in that case. I'd let her go and try things out.'

Annie had to admit that part of her would welcome Janey going. She never thought she'd ever think this way, but Jimmy and Janey had been acting strangely since her return.

Her beautiful sister would attract any man. She had a way that teased and yet got them going so that they bantered a lot with her.

Annie sighed as she thought of herself as ordinary against Janey, but then thought, *Well, I'll just have to be more than ordinary to keep Jimmy*. And with this she knew that she was ready to fight for him and do whatever it took to keep him. Even go to bed with him before they were wed!

As this came into her head she had to turn away and walk towards the kitchen as the feelings that she'd had when Jimmy had kissed her had hardly quietened, and now revisited her, making her blush again.

'Well, we'll see. Let's have a cuppa, eh? I'm parched.'

'I'll do that, lass. I have everything ready laid out and I brought one of me cakes over in a tin. I came by bus; it were better than the Underground. That makes me feel claustrophobic.'

'Blimey, Cissy, that were a big word, luv.'

'Eeh, I don't knaw where it came from, Vera, lass, but I knaw it means not liking closed-in spaces. And that's me to a tee.'

As Cissy overtook Annie and opened the kitchen door, Mum's giggles at what Cissy had said changed the mood for Annie and she felt she could go back to sit with her as her emotions calmed and she felt ready to chat about the wedding – anything but thinking about Jimmy and how he'd made her feel, or wondering how to cope with Janey's new idea.

The thought of her going had shocked her but now she thought about it, she felt sure that something was troubling Janey and maybe making her want to run. Her conscience pricked her – she should help her. She always had done whenever Janey was troubled.

'I'll go in and see Janey, Mum, she may need me. I've hardly said hello. She's probably feeling guilty about her decision.

I know I did when I made it. We have to show her that we support her.'

'Yes, luv. Do that. I'm glad you've taken it this way. It's for the best. Poor kid's at odds with herself. We all went through it.'

Annie wasn't sure what her mum referred to and didn't want to ask. She didn't want to know what Janey was going through as somehow, she thought it would rock her world. Why she thought that she didn't know, it was just a feeling.

Knocking on Janey's door, she called out, 'Can I come in, Janey, luv?'

'I've got a headache, sorry, Annie. I'll see you next time, eh?'

Annie frowned. Janey's voice sounded thick with tears. She opened the door. Janey was lying across the bed, sobbing.

'Janey. Oh, Janey, me darlin'. What is it? Oh, Janey, come here and let me hug you, luv.'

Janey sat up and put her arms out to Annie. 'I'm sorry . . . I'm sorry, Annie.'

Annie sat on the bed and held Janey to her. 'What's happened, luv? You can tell me. I know that something has.'

'Nothing . . . only, well, I feel trapped, and it makes me feel bad . . . Did – did Jimmy tell you me plans?'

'He did, luv, but why are you so upset?'

''Cause . . . 'cause you'll hate me for leaving you and Mum, when she needs us both.'

'I won't, luv. I understand. I do, honestly. And I support you. I'd support you in anything you wanted to do . . . But Cornwall? Oh, Janey, that ain't right for you. It's no better than slavery. Let's think about it, eh? We can come up with ideas, and look into them. I can ask Olivia to help. She's always saying she and her dad would do anything for me.

Anything I want, I only need to ask. I ain't wanted anything for meself. And they didn't even have to help when Mum moved here as Jimmy found this place for her.'

'What kind of thing? A job?'

'I don't know, we need to think. What about that idea of you taking up nursing? Mum said you'd given up? Only, it ain't all for toffs, luv. I've met a few who were from a working-class background, it's just that their parents worked hard to educate them and save the money to pay for them to take up nursing. You've always been the brainy one so . . . Well, I'm thinking that maybe you could get an education. We could find out what you'd need to have for nursing – qualifications and that, and then ask Olivia to help you get them.'

'But it has to be away from here, Annie, it has to!'

'Oh, Janey, I never knew you felt like this, luv. I thought you were happy looking after Mum. I'm sorry, I'm sorry to the heart of me for putting it all on you, luv.'

'I were happy. I'd do anything for Mum, and I'll miss her so much when I move. I just feel that me life ain't going anywhere. That you've seen other places, even lived up west and been abroad to Guernsey, but me, I've been stuck here and seen nothing but the East End!'

'What brought all this on, luv? Was it me going to Guernsey, eh?'

Janey looked down at her hands. For a moment she didn't answer. When she did it was to nod her head . . . 'But don't apologize, you deserved it, Annie. You deserve it all – having a nice friend, nice clothes, posh place to live, and . . . and getting wed. You've sacrificed a lot for me and Mum, and then all you went through and how you saved Olivia . . . And you're the best sister anyone could wish for, so I'm happy for you, I am.'

'You just want something to happen for you. Well, I want that for you too, and we can make it happen. Why don't you wash your face and come and have a cuppa and then we'll go for a walk, eh? We'll go to the park and sit on a bench and talk.'

'I'd like that, ta, luv. I won't be a mo.'

As Annie went out of the room, she sighed with relief as she thought that everything was going to be all right. That all her doubts were unfounded. She would help Janey to find what she was seeking as her happiness meant so much to her, then she would get on with her life with Jimmy. She couldn't wait.

Chapter Fifteen

Janey

As Annie held her hand and they walked along to the park, shame washed over Janey, as did heartbreak at the thought of soon having to witness her lovely sister getting married to Jimmy. *I won't be able to bear it, I won't.*

They didn't speak much until they got through the park gates – a different world, as here they gazed on the green of the grass and the trees, not the bricks and mortar of endless buildings. Here you could take a deep breath to fill your lungs with fresh air, and listen to birds tweeting. Yes, the traffic hummed in the background, but still this was a world away from the fumes they belched out.

Here, too, Janey felt that she could forget who she really was and what she'd done to her sister and think about making a new future for herself. With this, some of her heartbreak lifted, and she knew she could be strong enough to face everything she had to.

'Let's sit on that bench, Annie. The one under the tree over there, luv.'

When they sat, Annie took hold of her hand again, further reassuring Janey that all could be put right.

'Have you thought on what you'd like to do, luv? I know going to Cornwall is an easy solution, but though I had kind employers, they could never get enough staff, so believe me, you won't get any life, only humdrum. Looking back, I don't know how I stuck at it. And you've been used to a lot more freedom than I had before I left to go there. Oh, I know, you haven't had as much as other girls of your age, but you never had anyone bearing down your neck, criticizing you as the housekeeper did constantly, even though you'd done a good job. Nor have you ever been expected to do two jobs at once and to be in two places, leaving you feeling that you can't please anyone, and longing for some fresh air and to be on the deserted beach far below the clifftop on which the manor sits, so that you could just scream and scream and no one would hear you.'

'Oh, Annie, luv, I didn't know it was like that. I imagined you paddling in the sea, having lots of friends, having good food and a nice warm bed to sleep in.'

'Only two of those things: the food and the bed. The rest was akin to torture at times, but I didn't see a way out. In some ways the train crash, though it gives me nightmares, was the best thing that happened to me. It released me from a living hell!'

'I've sent the letter now, Annie.'

'Don't worry about that. Like I say, Mr and Mrs Wallington are the nicest people. If they think you've a chance to better yourself, rather than just be a maid, they'll be happy for you.'

Janey couldn't understand this. How could nice people treat others so badly? But then, she'd never worked in such a household so didn't know the way of things.

'I'd love to train to be a nurse, Annie. I know I told Mum that I didn't like it, but I did. It was just a struggle with some of the written work. But I am a quick learner. Where do you go to get an education, though? And would I have to stay at home?'

'I don't know. But it might not be so bad if you're out at college for a lot of hours, as when you're away from home, you'll be with girls of your own age, and you'll make friends and arrange things with them, that sort of thing. You might even meet a handsome doctor one day and fall in love!'

Janey flinched. She had fallen in love, and it hurt. It hurt so much. She wanted to lie with Jimmy and make love to him. To have him hold her, to marry her, to have his children.

Her hand went instinctively to her stomach and her heart missed a beat as the constant fear she was under bore down on her.

But with it came the deeper fear of how she was to live her life seeing him every day, imagining him at night making love to Annie – maybe even hearing it if she lived at home in a flat beneath them. No! She couldn't. She just couldn't!

'Janey? You're crying! Oh, Janey, I feel something bad is troubling you, luv. Tell me what it is. Please, me darlin'. Nothing's as bad when shared.'

With Annie's arm around her, Janey almost blurted out the pain she was in, but that would give the pain to Annie, and she didn't deserve that.

'It – it's like, I don't know who I am any more, Annie. I need different things to what I did. I never saw meself wanting to escape me home, and leave Mum, but now I do. But I don't know if I do. Mum says she'll be all right with it, but she's so unselfish. She let you go without a word of protest, but I know it broke her heart to part with you. She'd cry herself to sleep at night for weeks after you left. I don't want to put her through that.'

'Oh, Janey, I didn't know. But Mum's right not to hold us back. She's right to encourage us in all we want to do, so don't feel guilty. If we had a mum that tied us to her apron strings, we wouldn't love her so much . . . But, Janey, there's something else. You're me little sister. And I know when there's something not right. Please, please, tell me. If you don't, it will eat away at you and ruin the rest of your life. Please, Janey.'

It was too much for Janey. Before she could stop herself, she blurted out, 'I love Jimmy . . . Oh, Annie, I love him with all me heart and he loves me . . . I'm sorry . . . Annie, I'm sorry!'

Annie stood. Her stare held disbelief and pain.

Janey slid off the bench, onto her knees, and held on to Annie's legs. 'I'm sorry . . . sorry . . . I love you, Annie. Forgive me, forgive me.'

'Excuse me, is everything all right?'

Janey looked up and saw a young man standing just a few feet away.

'Can I help you both?'

Annie's voice shook as she said, 'No, ta, mate. No one can. But we'll be all right, ta.'

The man bowed slightly and left, but he'd caused enough of a distraction to them both to calm them. Janey felt Annie's hands come under her arms and lift her. When she stood, she was being held by Annie. Her hair became wet with Annie's tears. Never had she heard Annie sob like she did now. She'd broken her own sister and, in doing so, broken herself.

After a while, Annie took a deep breath. 'Let's sit down.'

Janey obeyed. Fear of her actions trembled through her. She wanted to blame someone. 'You shouldn't have pushed me for the truth, Annie, you shouldn't. We'd made a pact.

Jimmy was going to make you happy, as he does love you. I was going to go away and leave you to get on with your lives. Now, I've ruined it all . . . But, oh, me agony was too much to bear, and I couldn't hide it from you.'

'Shush, Janey. Leave me alone, please.'

This cut through Janey. She'd rather that Annie screamed and shouted, ranted and raved, than sit there calmly thinking things through.

After a while, Annie turned to her. Never had she seen her beloved sister look so wretched. 'You say that Jimmy loves you, not me?'

Janey nodded, then shook her head. 'He does love you, Annie. Has done since being a lad, but . . . we – we fell *in* love. We didn't want to. We didn't try to. It just happened. And I promise you, we weren't going to hurt you. It was the last thing we were going to do. You should have let it go, Annie, you pushed and pushed me.'

'Don't put the blame onto me, Janey. I was just concerned for you. I never expected . . . But then, that's a lie. I've thought for a while . . . I didn't know what, but I knew there was something not right. And I knew it was to do with you, Janey . . . you and Jimmy.'

'But we never . . . I mean, I didn't know . . . Jimmy didn't know . . . I . . . Well, I did have an infatuation with him – I thought it was just that, but he had no idea. I was always awful to him, as it wasn't a nice feeling for me. I wanted to hate him. But then . . . I'm sorry, Annie, sorry to the heart of me, but, well, when we were working together . . .'

She didn't say that Jimmy had sought her out, that he was feeling the same. She had so little in the way of lessening the hurt she was causing, but at least, she thought, she could take all the blame off Jimmy's shoulders.

'I need to be on me own a while, Janey.'

'No! No, don't leave me . . . What will you do?'

'I'll just walk. Go to the Thames and just walk.'

'But that's miles away. Please, Annie, please stay and talk to me.'

'If I stay, I feel I'll tear you to pieces. At this moment, it's what'll release all me pain. But I don't want to do that. It would be easier if you were a stranger, but me own little sister! Why, Janey? Why? Were you that jealous of everything I had that you had to take the one thing that I loved the most? At this moment, I hate you. I hate you with everything that I am. Go home. Go home and tell Mum and Cissy what you've done, and I hope you can live with yourself!'

Annie stormed off.

Janey stared after her. It was as if her world had come to an end.

Hearing her name being called brought Janey out of the stupor she'd been in, and awoke her to how cold she felt, and how folk had stared at her, and how some had stopped and asked if she was all right.

'Aw, Janey, Janey, luv . . . Where's Annie? Eeh, what's happened, lass?'

Two chubby arms enclosed her.

'Janey, Janey, speak to me, me darling lass. What's happened? Your ma and me have been out of our minds with worry over the pair of you. You've been gone hours. In the end, I persuaded your ma to let me come and find you.'

'Oh, Cissy, Cissy, help me.'

'Aw, me little, lass, I'm here . . . Is it Jimmy?'

Janey shot out of Cissy's arms and looked at her with astonishment. 'How did you know?'

'We older ones knaw a lot more than we say. Me and your ma, we hoped you'd get over it, lass. That it were an infatuation, sommat as can happen to young girls and is natural. Jimmy's a handsome man, and a lovely man, and even I have a soft spot for him, as does your ma, so it follows that you were attracted to him an' all . . . Have you said owt to Annie? Is that why you're sitting here in the depth of misery and Annie's missing?'

'Oh, Cissy . . . She made me. She wouldn't let it go . . . But it's not infatuation, I love Jimmy and he loves me and that's why I was going away. We agreed that we couldn't hurt Annie . . . Oh, why did I give in and tell her?'

'Aye, well, if that's the state of affairs, it's a good job you did. Annie's pain would have been far worse if she'd have married Jimmy and then found out. But are you sure, lass? You don't think that Jimmy was just saying he loved you to . . . well, sort of let you down gently?'

'Yes, I'm sure. I've never been more sure about anything in me life. He is me life, Cissy. Now Annie knows and, oh, Cissy, I never meant to hurt her. She means the world to me.'

'I knaw, lass. It's a terrible situation. Love can be like that. We don't choose who we fall in love with. But it's a tragedy when two loving sisters fall in love with the same man. Though didn't Jimmy love Annie from being a lad?'

'He did and he never forgot her. When they met up, it seemed as though it was all he'd dreamed of, but then he realized that though he loved Annie, it was me he was *in* love with, but it was all too late. Plans had been made; Annie was happy. We couldn't . . . didn't want to hurt her.'

'By, it's a mess, I'll tell you. But then, greater messes have been sorted out. I say we use that telephone box at the end of the road to telephone Jimmy and put him in the picture.

He should never have let it get this far, so he's the one who needs to sort it out. We'll get him to go and find Annie and give them some time to talk it all through. I'm sure it'll all come out in the wash, lass. Most things do one way or another.'

Janey allowed Cissy to help her up.

'Come on, lass, let's go home and get a hot drink down you, eh?'

They stopped at the phone box on the way. Janey didn't know how she was going to do this, and yet the one thing she wanted in all the world was to hear Jimmy's voice. 'I ain't got me purse, Cissy.'

'Eeh, I never thought of that . . . Wait a minute, you can reverse the charge, can't you? I've heard tell you can, anyroad.'

'Yes, I forgot that.'

As the operator asked Jimmy if he'd accept the charge from a Miss Janey Freeman, Janey's heart raced when she heard his voice say 'yes', followed by the operator saying, 'Go ahead, caller,' and him saying, 'Janey! Janey, me love, is everything all right?'

'No . . . Oh, Jimmy, she knows. Annie knows.'

There was a silence.

'Jimmy? Jimmy, I'm sorry. I – I . . . Oh, Jimmy!'

'It's all right, luv. I were just shocked, but well, now it's done, I don't know how I feel. I feel happy, relieved, and yet sad, and as if something terrible's happened . . . How is she, Janey? . . . Oh, God, I – I . . . Oh, Janey.'

'She's gone off somewhere. She said the Thames . . .'

'What? No! Janey, she wouldn't . . . Please tell me she wouldn't do anything to harm herself!'

'I don't know. I've been in a bit of a stupor, but now I'm scared. I – I thought she'd gone home by now. I – I was in the park; Cissy came for me.'

'I can't make any sense of all of this. I just know I have to try to find Annie and make sure she's safe. I'll have to ring off, Janey . . . But, Janey . . . remember, I do love you. And maybe this will be for the best when it's sorted. We none of us wanted to hurt Annie, and never would. But if it's happened, all we can do is try to make it right. We both love her. We'll do the best by her, luv.'

'I love you too, Jimmy. But find Annie, luv, please find her.'

'I will. I won't rest until I do.'

The phone went dead. Janey stood a moment holding the handset, but then a voice said, 'The call is disconnected, please replace the handset,' and that jolted her into doing so.

'Well, I heard your side, lass. What did Jimmy say?'

'He's going to look for Annie. But he ain't cross with me, he's relieved. Just so upset that Annie's been hurt . . . But, Cissy, I know it sounds bad, but me and Jimmy, I don't think we could have lived without each other, no matter how much we tried.'

'Naw, not if you love one another. Better that it's out in the open. But by, Annie's going to suffer, poor lass . . . Let's get home, your ma's at her wits' end.'

When they opened the door, Mum made a kind of moaning sound. Janey screamed out. Mum was slumped over the side of her chair.

'Mum, Mum . . . Oh, Mum!'

'Eeh, Vera! Vera, love.'

'It's all right, I slipped. I was stretching to reach me book. Help me up, for God's sake, help me. I'm in such pain.'

All hurt of her own went out of Janey's head as she helped Mum to sit up straight again. 'There you go, luv.'

'Eeh, me lass, I shouldn't have left you, but as you can see, I found Janey. Let me rub your side for you.'

Cissy doing this gave a moment of respite to Janey, as facing her mum with it all was almost too much to think of.

'Ta, luv . . . Now, Janey, what's going on, girl? I've been out of me mind.'

'It's as we thought, Vera, love. It's all about Jimmy.'

'Oh, Janey, why didn't you talk to me, luv? I might have been able to help you. It's natural for you to have feelings, luv. Jimmy's a smasher and a nice bloke – kind too, and no doubt he ain't known how to deal with your obvious feelings for him. We'll sort it, luv. Where's Annie?'

'Eeh, Vera, love, it ain't that simple. Jimmy's in love with Janey, not Annie.'

'What? Oh, my God! Does Annie know? . . . Where is Annie? Ain't she with you? . . . Oh, Annie, me Annie.'

Cissy put her arms around Mum. Janey could do no more than slump down on the sofa. Her heart was breaking. She'd never meant to cause all of this; how would anyone ever forgive her?

Cissy explained to Mum about Jimmy going after Annie. 'They'll sort this out, lass. Poor things have naw choice now. But I have to say that Janey and Jimmy didn't choose to fall in love. Naw one does. It's just sad that it's caused this pain, but they both tried to avoid it. Jimmy weren't going to let Annie down.'

'So, that's what all your talk of moving away was about then, Janey, luv?'

'It was, Mum, and I would have. I promise.'

'Annie forced it out of her . . . Eeh, now we're in this mess.'

'Annie's never been able to rest if she thought there was

something wrong with Janey, and she always knew. Even before I did. I can imagine her wheedling it out of you, luv. Now she's left with more than she wanted, or needed to know.'

'Aye, well, it would have been worse down the line. At least this way Jimmy hasn't married the wrong one, as to me own mind, that would have been a disaster in the long run, lass.'

'You're right. But what a mess.'

'Eeh, Jimmy'll sort it, he'll have to.'

'He will. Like you say, Cissy, he'll have to. Come here, Janey, luv.'

Going into her mum's arms soothed Janey a little. Just not having her accusing her meant the world.

'I'm sorry, Mum.'

'I know. But like Cissy says, none of us can choose who we fall in love with. It ain't your fault. You tried not to hurt Annie, and that's all you could have done. Though you're no good as an actress, luv, don't ever try to go on the stage. Your heart was on your sleeve for Annie to see.'

'I know. It was when I saw them kiss.'

'Well, you shouldn't have put yourself in that position. I did have me suspicions when you went out to the lav just after they'd gone out, but then you can't put an old head on young shoulders. And that's what you have, Janey. And I want to be sure before this goes any further that this really ain't an infatuation on your side. If it gets sorted, I want you to court Jimmy for at least a year before there's any talk of marriage. Will you do that much for me – for Annie too? I mean, you can't expect her to turn around and attend your wedding, instead of getting married herself, poor girl. Me heart breaks for her.'

Janey knew hers did too but waiting to marry wasn't something she wanted to do. She had a funny feeling, too, that it wasn't what would happen, as there was something different about herself, something only she knew. A feeling she couldn't put her finger on and which might be proved wrong next week if her monthlies did start. But somehow, she didn't think they would.

Chapter Sixteen

Annie

Annie's tears had dried. But still she felt numb with the shock of having confirmed what she'd suspected.

How she'd arrived at the side of the Thames, she didn't know. Her mind had been blank as she'd trudged along oblivious to her surroundings.

Exhausted, she'd sat on a bench and stared at Tower Bridge without really seeing it. Had watched boats bobbing up and down, some in transit; one a large freight carrier that had to have the bridge raised for it to pass under, something that always fascinated her, and yet today hardly impacted on her.

Her mind had gone from thinking that Janey was fantasizing to knowing it was true that she'd lost Jimmy.

Did she ever really have him? Had it all been something that happened, and they'd been carried along with?

Were all her dreams to come to nothing?

Her heart ached as it took the weight of her grief and her loss cut deep into her.

The life she thought she would have had gone from her. What would she do? Where would she go? How could she ever forgive Janey and be a sister to her again?

It felt to Annie that her world had ended. Janey was lost to her, Jimmy didn't want her, and Olivia had gone home to Guernsey and no longer needed her. Even Mum didn't really need her as she had Cissy and Janey, and . . . No! She couldn't think of them together or link their names in this way!

Not knowing how long she'd sat there, and not having any solutions, she looked at the swirling water – imagined herself sinking into it, finding a release from pain, and then her body floating in a blissful peaceful state, leaving behind all the pain.

She wasn't aware of standing up, or of walking to the water's edge, only of wanting to plunge into its depth and take the solace it offered her.

'Hey!'

The voice broke the spell.

She turned to see a policeman coming towards her.

'Now then, miss. Nothing's that bad that we can't fix it. Come on now, come back from the water's edge.'

Realization hit Annie. What had she been thinking? How could jumping into the filthy Thames ever be a solution?

And yet, she couldn't move, and felt that if she did, it would topple her. Looking down, she realized that her feet were over the edge, she was balancing in an almost no-man's land. 'Help me!'

The policeman's arms came around her. 'I've got you, luv. You're safe now.'

He was huge. Towering over her. Annie clung on to him.

'It's all right. Shall we sit down and have a talk, eh?'

She didn't want to leave his arms but allowed him to guide her to the bench. When they sat, she felt compelled to ask, 'Will you hold me?'

When he did, Annie leaned on him. His jacket felt rough on her cheek, but the comfort she felt made up for this.

He smelled of fresh air and she could sense his goodness. A wholesome goodness – someone who cared.

'You're all right now. But you gave poor Aggie Brown a shock – she's the flower seller and she saw you from her stand. She ran for me – huh, didn't know she could move that fast. Now, tell me all about it, luv, as like I said, nothing's ever as bad as you think.'

'It is, though . . . I – I were to get married, but . . . me fiancé, he loves me sister!'

'Blimey! Well, that is bad – well, it is on the face of it. How did it happen? . . . No, that's a daft question as nobody knows how love happens, it just does. So, I take it you've just found out?'

'Yes. She didn't want to tell me, only she's me baby sis – she's four years younger than me, and I've always looked out for her. I know when anything's troubling her . . . I didn't expect . . . well, I did in a way . . . I knew there was something.'

'See what's happening, luv? You're answering yourself with saying that you did know really but couldn't put it right in your head . . . Anyway, that doesn't help matters. What you've got to do is find a way of coping with it and even to come to a place where you and your sister are all right with one another. Anyway, we're working backwards, so let's start at the beginning by you telling me your name and where you live, luv.'

'Annie. Annie Freeman. I live up west . . . I'm – was – a lady's companion to me friend. Me family live in Bethnal Green.'

'Well, shall I take you back to them, or put you on a train

to where it is you live? Mind, that's a bit posh, ain't it? So, you still live there even though you don't work there?'

'I do, but no, not the Tube, I can't. Besides, the house-keeper needs to get home, she's with me family,' Annie explained, not able to stop once she'd started. She told him of Olivia and Cissy and the train crash and how she met Jimmy, finishing on a sob, saying, 'Now, I feel as if all me dreams and me new life have gone.'

'Oh, Annie. A train crash! And then all of what has followed . . . I remember now reading about it. You saved your friend's life, didn't you?'

'I only did what anyone would.'

'Well, not anyone. I'd have done it, but a lot wouldn't. I think you're made of special stuff, Annie. And that will get you through this. I think you're best to start by thinking how your sister is feeling as that might help . . . You say she didn't want to tell you, that she had plans to move away? Well, I think she must be suffering now that you know she's betrayed you, and because she thinks she's lost you, whereas from all you've explained, she wanted none of that and wouldn't have spoiled your happiness.'

'Oh . . . I didn't think, and yet, I did . . . I mean, I know Janey, and all what you say is right. I just don't know what to do! Me heart's broken and I don't know if I can just . . . But I have to, don't I? I have to follow me first plan and go away, leave them to find happiness, but how, when it happens, am I going to face their wedding that should have been mine?'

'You faced trying to get your friend out of that burning carriage, luv, and I reckon you can do this, too . . . Let's get you back to your family, eh? There's no time like the present to make a start. Not that I'm saying it will be easy, not for any of you, but once it's done it'll get easier.'

179

'Ta. I can see that. What's your name?'

'Ricky. PC Ricky Stanley.'

He said the last with pride.

'Ta for saving me, PC Stanley, I'll never forget you . . . It sounds silly, but I don't want to leave you. It's as if I won't be able to cope without you.'

'I'm the local around this patch, you'll always find me here if I'm on shift. And if not, any copper'll know me, so just give them a note and tell me where to meet you and I'll come and help you, Annie, as I'll never forget you either.'

Annie looked up at him. Saw him for the first time and thought that sitting down he didn't seem so large, though his shoulders were broad. His face wasn't handsome – his broken nose spoiled that for him, as did a scar down his cheek – but his blue eyes held kindness and his dark curly hair softened his looks. He smiled at her. 'I'm no oil painting, am I, girl?'

They laughed together and it felt right – like she'd known him all her life.

'Are you allowed to be friends with the waifs and strays you help, PC Stanley?'

'I am. As long as they ain't criminals. And call me Ricky. Friends can't go around being formal.'

'I'm going to need a friend, Ricky.'

'Will I do?'

She smiled and from her heart said, 'Yes.' Then thought that a bit forward, so, feeling more like herself, qualified it with, 'Well, you're in the running anyway. Unless you're married. Wives don't like their men to have girls as their friends.'

'No, I'm not married. No one would have me with this ugly mush. So, friends it is. And as friends go out together, I'm off duty tomorrow afternoon so would you like to go somewhere with me? That's if you feel up to it after your ordeal, luv, or even want to . . . I mean, we can be just friends who chat to one another when we see each other if you like.'

Annie liked how he had no side to him, and that he didn't mean anything other than what he was saying – but she knew it had cost him dearly to say it as he seemed to expect rejection.

'I would. Ta for asking me, Ricky. I would love that . . . I – I'm going to be a bit lost. I – I haven't even got me job with Olivia going back home and married now, though her dad were generous with the leaving wage he gave me. But that won't last me. You see, I didn't know I would even need a job.'

With this, her throat tightened once more.

'Don't get upset again, luv. You've done well. You're bound to be fragile but fight it. Be strong. Call on the strength you've proved that you have.'

'I'll try.'

'Well then, I do think now is the time to get you home.'

Annie stood. She felt so much better. Life seemed to have opened a little for her and she was no longer looking at a dismal end.

When they reached the top of the steps, the flower lady came over to them clutching a white rose. ''Ere you are, luv. You had me worried there, girl. This is to bring you healing. And next time, come and talk to me, don't let despair take you. Us cockneys are always ready to help anyone.'

'Ta, luv. I know. Born and bred in Bethnal Green.'

'Well, with your posh clothes I didn't guess, girl. Now then, luv, you know where I am. Aggie Brown's the name. Good luck to you.'

'Ta, Aggie. See you around.'

As she left, Aggie said, 'You'll be all right with Ricky. He's one of the best.'

'Ha, you're only saying that 'cause I get you a mug of tea when I'm on duty. And you never give me a flower!'

'You big soft sod!'

With this Aggie went back to her stall, leaving them both giggling. For Annie, it felt as though her own folk had healed her a little and she felt glad to be back amongst them. Whether she would stay, she didn't know.

'I don't have a vehicle, luv, but I can walk with you, and push me bike, if that's all right?'

'That would be fine as long as you won't get into trouble. Bethnal Green ain't on your patch, is it?'

'No, but I have a duty to see you're safe. I'll have to pop into the phone box and report in with me whereabouts and why, though.'

As they walked together, they talked. Annie found that Ricky loved the theatre and music hall, and this had come from his grandmother, who used to be a music hall singer and dancer. He talked on and on about this before saying, 'I'll take you one day, Annie, it's magical. I like to sing meself, but only when on me own.'

He told her how he only had his mum now. 'She's called Lilly. Even I call her that, as I thought for a long time that she was me much older sister! She had me out of wedlock. She was going to marry, but then he went to war. She said it happened when he came home on leave, but after he went back, he never returned.'

'Ah, your poor mum. Good that your granny took you on, though.'

'I loved me granny, and as I say, I thought she was me mum till I grew up and they told me. It was hard to take at first, but when I did accept it, Lilly was still, and always will be, just Lilly.'

They chatted on and as they did, the feeling Annie had that she'd known him for ever deepened and the pain of her loss lessened.

After a while, they walked on in companionable silence in which Annie felt comfortable.

It was Ricky who broke it. 'I like walking, which is a good thing given me job. A lot has to be done on foot.'

'I do too. Shall we go for a walk tomorrow? Where I live is near to St James's Palace – we could walk amongst the trees and up the Mall to see Buckingham Palace, and I'll treat you to a cup of tea and a bun in a cafe . . . Oh, I mean, if you still want to see me, that is.'

''Course I do, luv. We're friends now. And that sounds right up me street – well, as far away from me street as you can get actually, but I'd love to do that. A good suggestion. I get off work at two so can be up west by three.'

Not feeling at all embarrassed, Annie said, 'That would be fine, and we could meet outside Piccadilly station. I'll wait outside.'

'Good idea. I'm looking forward to it.'

He'd only just said this when a van pulled up. Annie cringed to see it was Jimmy.

'Annie! Annie, luv. Thank God I've found you.' Jimmy was out of his van and running across the road to her.

'I take it this is the fiancé. Will you be all right, or do you want me to stay?'

She desperately wanted Ricky to stay, but knew she had to face Jimmy and that was better done alone.

'I'll see you tomorrow, Ricky. Ta for everything. You saved me life.'

'I don't think you would've done it. You're made of stronger stuff.' He placed himself between her and Jimmy. 'Now then, sir. Take your time. I know all about what has happened. Annie has been through a lot. I hope you'll respect her feelings and tread carefully.'

'I will. I – I didn't mean to hurt her . . . It . . . well, it just happened. I'm sorry, Annie. Sorry to the heart of me, luv. Will you come home with me?'

Annie just nodded. The pain that had sliced her wouldn't let her speak.

'Come on, luv. It'll be all right, I promise. I – I just don't know how this mess happened. I didn't want it to.'

They said their goodbyes to Ricky and walked across to the van. Annie didn't slip across to the middle as she was used to doing but sat as far away from Jimmy as she could.

'What do we do, Annie? I – I still love you . . . It's just that . . . Oh, I don't know.'

'You're *in* love with Janey.'

He didn't answer.

'Tell me, Jimmy. I need to hear you say it.'

Jimmy put his hands on his steering wheel and dropped his head onto them. When he lifted it, he said the words she'd dreaded hearing. 'I am, Annie. I'm deeply in love with Janey.'

Her gasp made him turn towards her. 'Oh, Annie, I . . . we didn't choose for this to happen, we didn't, and I promise you, I was going to marry you and would have made you happy . . . But for all that, I have to be honest now. You deserve that of me . . . But I'm glad in one way that none of us have to live a lie. It may have destroyed us all in the end.'

Annie knew he was right, but that didn't help her to accept it. She wanted to claw at him, hurt him how he had hurt her, but then he said, 'I'm hurting too, Annie. I'm hurting because I feel that I've lost you for ever, and because I've caused a rift between you and Janey, and because me dream that I've had since being a lad is in tatters . . . But I think that's the problem. I loved you then so much, and I never got over that. So when we met, I thought what I had for you was true love that could take us through years and years, building a life together. I was happy, but for one thing. I couldn't get Janey out of me head. From the moment she challenged me for being a womanizer – something that looks true now – she was there, in me heart . . . I shouldn't have pursued our relationship. I should have brought it to an end then.'

'Has nothing we had meant anything to you?'

'Of course it has. I told you: I love you, Annie. If I could have stopped me feelings for Janey, I would have done, but I couldn't. They ate away at me very soul. They drove me to seek her out when you'd gone away. I should never have done that, but how do I make amends for it now? I can't, Annie.'

'Well, that's true.'

'Annie, please.'

'Don't "please" me, you sodding coward! You've wrecked me, me sister and ruined our relationship, not to mention what all this has done to me mum!'

Jimmy's head went down onto his steering wheel again, his body heaving with sobs.

It took a moment for some compassion for him to enter her, but it did. 'Let's go to me mum's. She and Cissy must be out of their minds with worry. You've broken a lot of people, Jimmy . . . No! Don't say you couldn't help it. The minute you knew how you felt, you should have told me and finished with me . . . I ain't saying it would have been easy, but it would have been easier than this way. You strung me along, and now I'm shattered. Like I say, you're a coward, Jimmy. A bleedin' coward!'

With this her temper broke and she slid along to him and hit him on the back of his head. Once she'd started, she couldn't stop. He staved off the blows, but then grabbed her arms.

Her tears mixed with her snot and her body shook. 'I HATE you!'

Still, he held her arms, his face wet with tears. When she went slack, he slipped his arm around her. She collapsed into him.

'Annie, Annie. Please forgive me . . . I don't deserve it, but I don't want you to lose Janey.'

She took the large handkerchief he offered her and wiped her face. Feeling calmer, but exhausted, she told him between rebound sobs, 'Take me home to the apartment up west, please, Jimmy. I just can't face anyone. And arrange for Cissy to be brought home in a cab. But make sure she's got the money, and tell Mum and Janey I just need a little time.'

'Are you sure that's what you want, Annie?'

'It is. I'll be all right, but I won't if I go to Mum's now. What I just did to you, I'd do to Janey, and she don't deserve that. She's innocent in all of this – well, mostly she is. She should have resisted you and told you to go to hell!'

'All I can say is that we love each other, Annie. We didn't choose to, but it happened and neither of us could have resisted each other. The only way we could have done is if Janey had gone away as planned . . . Well, you know what happened to that plan. Maybe you should think about that, and let Janey be a grown-up, as she is, you know. If she says she's all right, and you know she ain't, well, let her deal with what's troubling her in her own way. She ain't the kid you had to watch out for any more.'

'Don't you dare put the blame on me, Jimmy! That lies firmly with you! . . . Just take me home, please.'

By the time they reached the apartment, Annie had dropped off to sleep. Jimmy helped her to get out of the van, his touch meaning nothing to her now. She didn't even turn to say goodbye.

Once in the apartment block, Fred greeted her. 'There's a few parcels and a case here for you, luv, shall I bring them up? Hey, are you all right?'

'Yes, ta, Fred. Yes, bring them up.'

With the parcels and the case holding her dreams, in the form of the wedding dress she was to wear, stored away in a cupboard in the hall, Annie went through the silent apartment to the bathroom and ran a bath.

Lying in the hot water, she lay back and let her tears flow once more. It felt to her that every part of her body wept as she realized that life was never going to be the same and her earlier plan to leave was the best.

She'd ring Olivia in a few days, give her time to settle back in Guernsey, then she would beg her to help her, telling her she would work for nothing, only board and food, doing anything. Anything at all, just as long as she could be with her and not here suffering this awful agony.

Chapter Seventeen

Olivia

Moving in with her father on their return, Olivia and Hendrick's first task was to prepare Hendrick's house for sale. And as they drove towards the house to make a start, Olivia was glad they had something to concentrate on as it would leave little time to think about the enormity of what lay ahead. This, she thought, was a good thing as the dampener that dealing with the future had put on the beginning of their marriage threatened to send her into the doldrums.

She just couldn't imagine her life ahead. Yes, she'd have the renovating of their farmhouse to oversee, but that wouldn't really occupy her mind. She knew she would live from one weekend to the next, with the in-between days dragging.

If only Hendrick thought it safe that she should go with him to London, but for some reason he didn't, and she had to respect that, even though she was sure he was overreacting to the 'clues' he believed he'd detected of him being watched.

It all sounded so ridiculous to her now that they were home and she'd mulled it over. And as she had, her anger at Hendrick's father had grown. How could he put his own son in this position? He'd ruined their future and put this terrible cloud over them of having to part, and possibly for a long time, because she would never consider going to live in Germany if it happened that Hendrick did. Not with how it was today. And she knew Hendrick wouldn't ask her to or want her to.

More and more the strain was telling on him too. He'd tossed and turned in the night, and stared vacantly, seemingly in his own world for most of the time. There were times when he held her after they'd made love and cried, tears of anguish and sorrow.

Olivia didn't know how she was going to cope with him gone all week. It had been hard enough before, but then she hadn't had their lovemaking to miss! Yes, she'd always longed for it, and they'd come close to doing it, even. But she hadn't known how truly wonderful it was and how much her body would need it, as it did now that she'd been awakened.

Hendrick cut into these thoughts as he drew the car up outside the cottage. His sigh was deep. 'Oh dear, I don't know where to start, darling.'

'Let's get in and tackle one room at a time. We can judge what we keep and put into storage to furnish the farm with, or because it is a precious memory to you. And then decide about the rest.'

'That sounds like a good idea. I think the kitchen will be easy as we will need all the utensils, crockery, cutlery . . . Well, just everything as we are going to essentially be a guest house as well as a school.'

Olivia agreed but as they went inside and set about the task, they found it such hard work, making up the boxes, wrapping each item and packing, taping, and labelling.

Hendrick made it worse by not wanting to let things go.

Olivia managed to persuade him over most things, but when it came to a radio set that looked like a case, she had no chance.

'But it still works and is part of my own history – what little I have with my father.'

As they worked on, Hendrick told her how his father had bought the set for him and had one himself and how they used to contact each other using it.

By the time the tales were over, and the set was labelled along with a mound of stuff they'd sorted, Olivia felt exhausted. Still, she hadn't the strength she used to have and still her leg pained her if she stood too long. Reaching for a kitchen chair, she sat down.

'We're not going to be able to do this on our own, are we, darling? Are you all right?'

'No, I just feel drained with everything, and I don't know what possessed us to think we could tackle this.' Olivia sighed. 'I now think we just need to label everything we want and get the removal men to pack it all and then take it into storage.'

'Yes, I do too. Especially as I must work tomorrow, and from then until I leave for London. I want to make sure the accounts are in order . . . But I do worry about you, darling, your poor leg.'

'My ugly leg you mean!' Olivia looked down at her misshapen, scarred limb and wanted to cry.

Somehow she had to take it as part of her. It reminded her of all the pain she'd been through and brought back to her the awful sound of the screeching brakes – the only thing she remembered of the terrible crash.

Annie came to her mind then and she wondered how things were going for her. Imagined her happiness as she and Jimmy planned for their wedding and worked together to get their home ready. But her heart felt heavy with these thoughts. *Oh, how I miss you, Annie.*

Hendrick's arm came around her. He didn't speak. She placed her hand over his. She knew without asking that he was torn between the memories evoked by tackling the undoing of his dear aunt's life in this house, and his worries about the future. She tapped his hand. 'Your aunt would be so pleased to be helping us with our plans, darling. And so proud of you . . . And, darling, a lot of what you fear may not happen. Yes, with them asking you to learn to speak Japanese, it is looking likely that they will call on your services, but they haven't done any more than that. They aren't going to pay for your course, or pay you a salary while you take it, so they've made no commitment to you.'

'You're right, of course, darling, but I want to show them that I am committed and not just saying so to save my father.'

Olivia could see this. And how it also increased his anguish to have her constantly putting obstacles in his way. Turning her face up to him, she saw a glimpse of this anguish.

'We'll get through it all, darling.'

'Are you sure? I'm putting a lot on your shoulders.'

'No, not you. The situation you are in. But you have to deal with it, and I will support you, I promise. I'll stop raising objections or making you feel guilty. I know it's not what you choose to do.'

His hand stroked her hair.

'Anyway, it's a nice day. Let's leave this, I can cope with the labelling while you are at work. Let's go home and pack a picnic and go for a drive, eh?'

Hendrick smiled. 'That's a much better idea. I don't think

I am up to this anyway. I know Aunty would be pleased for me, but it's still a sad task.'

'It is. I can manage it, darling. It'll keep me out of mischief. And I know the things you will want to keep as heirlooms, so you don't have to worry.'

He leaned over her. 'Thanks, my darling.' He kissed her hair, and then as she looked up at him, her lips.

The kiss lightened her mood and gave her a promise. Standing with his help, she went into his arms. He held her gently to him. 'I love you, Hendrick, I love you with all my heart.'

'And that's all I need, ever.'

After a moment, he said, 'That picnic is calling me. Shall we go?'

When they reached the house the first news that met them was that Annie had called. That she'd asked that Olivia call her back as soon as she possibly could.

'Oh dear, this doesn't sound good, Hendrick, I can feel there's something wrong.'

'Well, all you can do is to telephone and find out, darling.'

Olivia dialled the operator and gave her the number of the apartment, hoping that Annie would be there.

Cissy answered. 'Eeh, Olivia, lass, there's trouble.'

'What? Is Annie all right?'

'Naw . . . Look, I'll put her on, but just to say, congratulations, lass. I ain't heard much about your day yet, but sommat bad happened here and it's took all the time up.'

'Thank you, Cissy. I'll speak to you soon. I'll write a letter telling you everything and send a photograph.'

'By, that'd be grand. Ta-ra, love.'

When Annie came on the phone, she burst into tears.

'Annie! Oh, Annie, my dear, what's wrong?'

As she listened, all that Hendrick had said came back to her. He hadn't been wrong about the look he'd seen Jimmy give to Janey. What a mess! 'Oh, Annie, Annie, love, my heart goes out to you. Have you spoken to Janey?'

'No . . . Well, it ain't her fault. I mean, me knowing . . .'

'Oh dear. Well, love, my honest opinion is that it is better this way. Horrible, painful and destructive, but better. If not now, it would have happened, and by then, you might have had children even. Because the strength of love is such that they would have had to have been together in the end, no matter how much they tried not to be.'

'Oh, Olivia, I know. I do. But what about how I feel?'

'I can hear that you're wretched, my dear Annie . . . I want to hold you . . . I – I . . . oh, Annie, I'm so sorry.' Tears ran down Olivia's face. She tried to keep them out of her voice, but her lovely Annie didn't deserve what had happened.

'Don't cry, Olivia. I never meant to make you cry, I just needed to talk to you and to ask you something.'

'Anything, my darling, anything.'

'Can I come and live with you over there? I wouldn't be in the way. I'd work as a maid to you, and not interfere with yours and Hendrick's life, only I must leave London. I can't bear to be around them, I can't.'

'Yes . . . yes, yes! Oh, Annie, that would be like a dream to me . . . I have news of my own . . .Oh, Annie, you don't know how much I need you.'

They chatted on and by the time the conversation ended, Olivia could feel that Annie had cheered, that she was looking forward to her walk with her policeman friend, though hearing how they'd met had run a shiver through Olivia.

'Please promise me you won't think of harming yourself again, Annie.'

'I won't. I don't know how I'm going to face Janey, but I know I must. I just cannot forgive her . . . I can't, and yet I keep telling meself that she ain't done anything wrong. She fell in love. Like I did and you did . . . But why did it have to be with Jimmy? And why did he return her feelings? That leaves me out on a limb.'

Annie was crying again. Olivia was at a loss as to what to say. She could only cry with her.

Hendrick's arm came around her and he took the handset from her hand.

'Annie? Annie, it's Hendrick. I'm so sorry for what has happened. I have stood next to Olivia and heard most of it . . . Annie, try to think that this was meant to be. That neither Jimmy nor Janey would have wanted it – in particular Janey. She loves you more than the world and her heart must be breaking. Try hard to put things right with her before you come, dear. If you don't, you may live to regret not doing so for the rest of your life. And do it quickly as the longer you leave these things, the harder they become. Please, Annie, you and Janey have such a deep love for one another and that is why this is hurting you so much more than if it had been a stranger to you.'

'I – I'll try. I will . . . I'm so confused, Hendrick. One minute I hate her, the next I understand.'

'Yes, that will happen, and probably for a long time, but time will heal this terrible pain you must feel, and when that happens, it would be a tragedy if your rift with Janey is so deep neither of you can overcome it.'

'I – I know.'

'We will help you all we can. Olivia will make all your travel arrangements, and you will be welcomed here by us all. And tell Cissy that if the plans for her new home materialize, she's to go ahead. We're all happy with the arrangements you made, dear. And we know how much she is looking forward to being close to your mum.'

'I – I will. I just don't know yet what will happen.'

'Well, dear, that is up to you . . . Look, this may sound harsh, but you either release Janey and Jimmy to be happy together, or you hold on to your hate and bitterness and not only ruin your own life but any chance they may have . . . I'm so sorry to put it as bluntly as that, but think about it, dear. And we are waiting to welcome you and take care of you.'

'Ta . . . ta, Hendrick . . . I – I know you're right.'

'Oh, my dear, I wish we were there with you. Try not to cry. Have you anyone you can turn to who isn't involved?'

'I have. Olivia will tell you . . . I have to go now. But ta ever so much, Hendrick. Tell Olivia I love her and will speak to her later.'

'I will, dear. Take care and know that you have friends here. Friends who love you.'

Hendrick put the phone down. All Olivia could do was to hug him and tell him, 'You're a very special man, my darling, very special.'

Hendrick swallowed. She could see he was upset by the experience. Then he said, 'I was right. I saw the love Jimmy had for Janey. What a mess. What a tragedy. Poor Annie. Poor, poor Annie.'

Tears brimmed in his eyes and at that moment, Olivia knew she was right in what she'd said, Hendrick was very special. He was gifted with an insight that was far-reaching. But that troubled him too, as he seemed to know what was coming and she knew what he perceived for the future wasn't good, but that he was doing his best to turn it into something positive. She would do her part. She'd try to learn the code he was working on so that he could pass on information. Even though it seemed so complicated.

She put her hand on his arm. 'Like you said, we'll take care of her. We'll make her happy. And one day, I'm sure she'll meet someone who will fall in love with her. I pray that is so. Now, let's go for that picnic. And let's not talk of anything other than good things. I'd like to go to our field, the one where one day we hope to build our home.'

At the farmhouse, they enjoyed going over what they were going to do and imagining how it would look before they went through the garden gate that led to their field.

'So, where do you want the kitchen and the living room to be, darling?'

Olivia turned around to face the sea. 'Right here, with a huge window or French doors so I can always see that beautiful view.'

They stood a moment and gazed out to sea. To the left of them a rocky peninsular jutted out and to the right the coastal road snaked up and around a bend, disappearing into the hills.

'It's beautiful.'

'And it's ours, darling . . . Hold on, let's collect stones and mark out our house. I'll be able to imagine it then.'

Olivia giggled. 'You can collect the stones, I'll sit here and plan.' She lowered herself onto the soft grass and watched as Hendrick made many trips backwards and forwards to the farmhouse garden, the roadside and even the beach.

It was taking ages, so she decided to pitch in and help.

At last they had a kitchen to the right of a living room, and a front door leading to a hall, all marked out on the grass.

'Is it big enough?' Hendrick asked. 'Remember, we need to have enough space above it for at least three bedrooms and a bathroom.'

'No, but we haven't got a dining room and an office yet. I'm exhausted, though!'

'Ha, you weakling! What will you do when we come to build it?'

'We're building it ourselves?'

'Ha, no. Sorry, just teasing. You go back to planning where to place these rooms and I'll carry on and fetch more stones. I want to get one big one for each area. There's some paint and brushes in that old shed behind the house. I'm going to paint on the stones what will be built above it. I want to imagine it all and leave a little of my imagination right here for you to visit.'

As Olivia watched Hendrick working, her heart weighed heavy in her chest. Hendrick was preparing both himself and her for a time she didn't want to think of. Did he think he might never come back if he was forced to go to Germany? Did he mean he was trying to leave a bit of himself here in case that happened?

When he was done, he came over to her. 'Can you manage to come and look? I'll help you.' Taking her hand and helping her up, he said, 'We'll start in our living room.'

A stone had been placed in the centre and on it Hendrick had written, 'Above here, Olivia and Hendrick's bedroom – love nest.'

He dropped her hand and put his arm around her. They stood there gazing down on it. In her mind, Olivia saw the bedroom. 'I want it to be in restful colours – the walls white,

197

the carpet in a soft, pale green. Then the eiderdown in peaches and greens, and the curtains to match. I might set Cissy on making it for me. I'll find some samples and send them home with you and you can give her an allowance to buy what she will need. She makes such beautiful patchwork quilts.'

'Hmm, that sounds wonderful. And we'll have a huge bed so make sure you tell her to make a gigantic one.'

'I will, I'll explain it all in the letter I promised to write.'

'Now, before I show you more, I want our first cuddle in our imaginary bedroom.'

'You're a romantic, Hendrick, my darling, and I love you.'

They stood there entwined in each other's arms. What Hendrick's thoughts were, she didn't know, but her own were prayers to God to let it happen. Let them know a time when they built this house and did cuddle in their own beautiful bedroom.

To lighten the mood, she said, 'Well, we've picked a good-sized room in the farmhouse to be ours in the beginning, so we can still have it in the way I'd like it, can't we?'

'Yes, we can, as I think it will be two or three years before we make enough money to build this house, darling. I just like to dream . . . So, over here . . .'

They stepped over the stones to a much smaller room.

'This is to be the office.'

On the stone in the centre of this one, he'd written, 'bathroom'.

And through here, again, they stepped over stones to their right. 'This will be the dining room.'

On this stone he'd written, 'Olivia and Hendrick's eldest child.'

Olivia hugged his waist.

'I thought by the time we move here our children will be

old enough for their own rooms, so they will both be above the kitchen and dining room, and both rooms the same size, so no falling out.'

'Oh, we're having two children then?'

'Yes. Karl Hendrick and Sylvanna Olivia . . . That's if you like those names.'

'Oh, Hendrick, I love them. For our little girl to have my mother's and my name would be a dream. Is Karl after anybody?'

'Yes, my grandfather. It is spelled with a "K". He was a wonderful man, I loved him very much. My father is always saying that I have his nature.'

'Then I would have liked him too.' Wanting to bring this to an end as her emotions were high, and yet not wanting to as it was a beautiful moment, Olivia moved away from Hendrick. 'I'll set the picnic up in the dining room . . . Oh, I just thought, maybe the kitchen should be on the back and the dining room on the front so we can eat and still enjoy the view.'

'No. I'm going to have you tied to kitchen sink, so you'll need the view there.'

'Ha! Of all the cheek!'

Hendrick laughed. 'I'll tell you what, I'll design you a stunning garden and then we can have French doors going out from the dining room and eat outside when we want to.'

'All right, that's a good compromise, I'll take it.'

As they sat eating their sandwiches and the lovely light Victoria sponge slices that Cook had wrapped for them, they talked of Annie and her plight.

'Let's get her over soon, darling. I need her here. And I need to take care of her.'

'I know you do . . . Wait a minute, why don't we fetch her? I could fix up everything that needs doing for me to take lessons, or find a freelance tutor while we are there.'

'I wonder if you will find a tutor. It isn't a normal language of study, and I thought you were afraid of taking me with you.'

'Just for a short visit to fix things up will be fine, I'm sure. Anyway, I'm going to take the chance for Annie's sake. As for the Japanese, I do know of several financiers who deal with Mitsui and Co., a Japanese firm with headquarters in London. I'm hoping if all else fails, I can find a tutor amongst the middle managers, who may want to earn extra money. I shall ask the ambassador to help too. But I need to be there to do that, so I can tell him that I am bringing my wife over to collect a maid who is her companion too.'

'Won't that bring Annie to their attention?'

'I don't think so. They have no need to want to know about serving staff. Besides, I am being overcautious with what I told you before. It could be just me that they are checking up on, to see if I have any politically minded friends or acquaintances, that kind of thing. I think being brought up and living on Guernsey has probably helped me as there is no real political involvement here.'

This settled Olivia's mind. 'In that case, yes, I would love to fetch Annie over ourselves, and she'll need our support.'

'I'll organize it, get the tickets and see to all travel arrangements. You just see to the packing, and we'll be all set!' He moved closer. 'But now, I have a job to do. You've some jam in the corner of your mouth that I want, so I'm going to pretend to kiss you and then nick it.'

Olivia didn't argue but melted into his arms. His kiss took all the dread and the worry over Annie away from her as finally, she gave herself to the moment, in this almost deserted part of the island, that would one day, she hoped with all her heart, be where they lived together for the rest of their lives.

Chapter Eighteen

Annie

Annie had managed to splash her face with enough cold water to make her puffy eyes look a bit better and had fixed a smile on her face as she'd met Ricky.

Now they were sitting on a bench in Hyde Park after what seemed like a marathon walk sightseeing the nearby palaces.

A light breeze rustled the trees and wafted a cooler air over them. Around them, children played and nannies pushed babies in prams. It was a place where you could forget you lived in a dusty, smoky city and imagine yourself out in the countryside.

It was Ricky who spoke first and Annie had the feeling he'd mulled over her situation since meeting her. 'I know you used to work in service, Annie, but I wondered if you've ever wanted to do anything else?'

'What was there that I could have done? Work in a factory, or a shop? I couldn't stand the thought of the first, and the second, well, there ain't that many unless you travel back and forth, and I needed every penny I earned to give to me mum and Janey. A job where at least I was fed without touching me pay meant I could do that.'

Ricky nodded. 'I can see that. It seems a waste to me, but needs must and they dictate our choices a lot of the time.'

'What about you, Ricky? How did you come to be a copper?'

'It was something I wanted from a kid. We had a copper whose beat took in our street. He was a good bloke. He kept us kids in order, but in a fatherly figure kind of way. He always had time for us: he'd play ball with the boys, and even skip with the girls. He was funny, kind and yet strict. He'd give you a wallop if you were naughty, but a hug if you needed one. And at Christmas, he'd bring a big bag of toffees with him and dish them out. We could always go to his house if we needed help. I just wanted to be like him. To wear his uniform and his boots. I told him so one day, and he sort of channelled me this way. He told me to join the army first to learn discipline. So I was a soldier for two years.'

Annie so admired Ricky as she listened to his story. He'd made good from his humble beginnings. She wanted to say so but didn't interrupt him.

'Me proudest moment was knocking on his door in me police uniform for the first time. He told me, "Right, Ricky, you're now the bloke who looks out for folk, protects them, guides them when they're going wrong, comforts them when they need it, and keeps them safe. Always remember that a thief is a bloke in need. Help him and he won't need to steal again." Sadly, he died not long after, but I've heeded his words and carried on his legacy.'

'That's a lovely story, mate. The copper around our way ain't like that. We were all scared of him as kids.'

'There's a lot like that who like the power the job gives them . . . So, if you had the choice to do anything you wanted, be anyone you wanted to be, what would you do, Annie?'

'I've never thought about it. Us girls were never encouraged to think of ourselves as anything other than doing a job until we got married. But now you've told me the story of the copper that influenced you, I'd like to be like him too. There's a lot of kids go wrong for want of the guiding hand of someone who cares, but you don't see many women doing your job.'

'No, there ain't as many as men and most do the office work. Some work with kids who've been brought in for committing a crime and take the case through to the juvenile courts. And they take care of any women offenders too, besides sometimes helping at parades. It's a good career. Only problem is, if a woman police officer marries, she has to leave the service.'

'Well, I ain't planning on marrying since yesterday.'

'No. Sorry, Annie. Do you want to talk about it? I've not mentioned it as I was waiting for you to.'

'I still can't get me head around it all. It's like me heart's broken in two pieces. Janey's broke it in one and Jimmy in another. I'm going away from them both. I'm going to me mates in Guernsey.'

'Blimey, that's a long way away! Will it be for a break, or . . . ?'

'For as long as it takes. I told you about her, she was in the train crash with me. We're good friends, almost like . . . well, sisters. Only I can never see Olivia letting me down . . . But then, I didn't see Janey doing it either. Not ever.'

'I don't think she did. And I think you know it really, Annie. It's the pain you're in. You want to blame someone, lash out and make others hurt like you're doing. Have you thought about going to see her yet, or your mum?'

'I can't.'

'I did.'

'What? When? You shouldn't have. You had no right!'

'I'm sorry, Annie, but I did it for them. I couldn't stop thinking about you last night, nor about them. I asked the copper on your beat if he knew you and for your address. I went this morning.'

Annie couldn't believe what she was hearing. How dare he do such a thing!

'Your mum needs you, Annie, and your sister's in bits. She's not come out of her room, not even to help your mum. A neighbour from the street where you used to live has been doing what she can. Jimmy fetched her apparently, as he can't do anything with Janey. She's sort of collapsed. But what the neighbour can do ain't enough. Your poor mum's in a state.'

'No!'

'Yes, I'm afraid she is. So much so that I fetched the doctor. He wanted to put your mum in hospital till some-thing was sorted out, but she wouldn't go. He checked on Janey too. He gave her something to make her sleep, but said she was on the brink of a complete breakdown and might end up in a mental institution. This made your mum distraught, so the doctor gave her something to calm her and make her sleep too. Between him and me we put her to bed. But if Janey don't see to her, I don't know what will happen!'

'God! Oh, God! What have I done? Oh, Ricky, I never meant . . . She hurt me. She hurt me so badly. I couldn't think . . . I . . . Me mum, me poor mum . . . I've got to go there, I must. Right now!'

'Yes, Annie, it's the best thing. Your mum said that Janey won't eat, that she screams and cries. She needs you, Annie.'

Annie's mouth dried; she couldn't swallow. The bottom had dropped out of her world. Suddenly it seemed that the park was spinning around her. That the children's voices were screeching. She wanted to stand up and scream, but if she did that, she knew she would never stop.

'Annie, I can take you to them. I can get a cab. I'd stay with you and support you because it won't be easy for you. But calm yourself first, luv. Take deep breaths.'

'Why didn't you tell me as soon as you got here? All that walking and talking! We've wasted almost two hours!'

'Because you were in no fit state. Your eyes were swollen with crying, Annie. You're shaky, going from one subject to the next. You never calmed till we got to this park, then I waited for the moment. I knew both your mum and Janey would sleep for a few hours. So, I had time. The bloke in the shop was going to keep an eye on them. The doctor said they'd wake up a lot calmer and be rational, so I made a judgement.'

'It wasn't yours to make, Ricky. I should have been told. I'm going right now, and you don't have to come with me.'

'Annie, please. I'm sorry if I did wrong, but I acted how I thought best. You're in charge of yourself now, you've become stronger. You can see straighter and know what you must do. I didn't think it right to pile all of this on top of the anguish you were in when we first met. Once you were able to speak about it I knew the time was right.'

Ricky looked appealingly at her. Her anger died. 'I'm sorry, you're right. If you'd have told me when we first met, I wouldn't have been able to cope. It was just such a shock. All I've thought about is how all of this has affected me . . . I must go to them, Ricky. Will you take me, please?'

Ricky smiled. 'I'll be with you every step of the way, luv. Come on, we'll get the Tube.'

'No! No, not the Tube. I've enough money for a cab.'

'Oh, sorry, luv. Yes, of course, we'll take a cab. I did intend that, but I'll pay half as you're going to get a sizeable doctor's bill.'

'Ta, Ricky. Did the doctor mention how much?'

'No. He said your mum paid into a penny insurance with him when she could, and that despite her condition, she didn't bother him much, so he said she'll only have to pay for the medicine for her and Janey.'

'I didn't know she did that. She ain't never said, and I've never known her to have the doctor to her, she's always bought her own medication.'

'Well, maybe now she can start to get her penny's worth. Come on, there's loads of cabs around, though whether any'd be willing to take us to the East End, I don't know.'

They found one that would and sat in silence. After a while, Ricky's hand found hers. She looked at him and he mouthed, 'Are you all right, luv?'

She nodded. He took his hand away, but she hadn't wanted him to. The contact had been a comfort.

At last, they arrived, and split what seemed like an enormous amount, but other than thinking she would offer Ricky's half back to him, Annie's only thought was to run down the alley to the back of the shop and Mum's flat.

As soon as she got through the gate, she called out, 'Mum, Mum, Janey! I'm here, me darlings. I'm here!'

A moan came from the direction of Janey's bedroom.

'I'll look in on your mum, luv. She's probably still asleep as she had her draft a bit after Janey. Then I'll put the kettle on. I'll find everything, don't worry . . . And, Annie, luv, this ain't no time for recriminations. You can't change the situation, but you can change the future.'

Annie knew he was right. She took a deep breath and opened the door. The sight that met her wrenched at her heart.

Janey was naked, her clothes torn in shreds around her, deep scratches gouged out of her skin, her hair matted with her own blood from a gash on her head and her eyes swollen and bruised.

'Janey, Janey, me darlin', it's all right. Everything's all right. I'm here. Nothing matters. Oh, Janey, Janey.'

Janey sobbed – a dry sound – then from her kneeling position, she fell forward.

Annie went to her, climbed on the bed, took her into her arms and lay with her, holding her, rocking her. 'Janey, everything's going to be all right, I promise you. You and Jimmy can be together. I'll be all right about everything. We can be as we were. I'll go and stay with Olivia for a while to give you a chance to get yourselves sorted.' Then she told a lie that cost her dearly. 'I don't love Jimmy any more I mean, I ain't in love with him.'

Janey clung on to her.

'How did you hurt yourself, Janey, luv?'

'I – I . . . Oh, Annie, I had so much pain inside me, I wanted to get it out. Me only way was to bang me head, but when that weren't enough, I scratched meself, and it helped, Annie. The more physical pain I had, the less me heart hurt.'

'Oh, luv! Oh, me darlin' . . . No!'

'Can you forgive me, Annie?'

'I have nothing to forgive, me darlin'. You did nothing wrong. I know that now. No one chooses who they fall in love with. It happens. And you weren't going to take Jimmy, even if he did love you. You would have suffered so much to save me. You're one in a million, Janey. I shouldn't have acted how I did.'

Janey looked up. 'No, Annie, don't blame yourself, you're the least to blame.'

'Well then, as I see it, no one's to shoulder any blame. We've to find a way to go into the future.'

'You won't stay away for ever, will you, Annie?'

'No. Not for ever. I feel how you did, luv: I need to escape, and it'll be better for you and Jimmy if I do, too. When we've all healed, I'll come back and sort a life out here for meself. By that time, I'll be over it all, and things'll seem normal for us.'

'Will they? Will everything get back to normal?'

'It will, of course it will. Hearts have to heal. New things must take the place of old, and then all will be natural once more. But me and you, Janey, we're back to how we've always been now. You're still me little sis, though now you're a little big sis! All grown. We're two young women together.'

They hugged the best they could, then Annie said, 'I'll go and sort a bath out for you and make sure that Ricky's all right.'

'Ricky? Who's Ricky?'

'He's me new mate – a policeman. He was here this morning, luv. I met him yesterday by the side of the Thames. He told me what was happening here. He's putting the kettle on right now. I'll bring you a cuppa and then get your bath ready while you drink it, eh?'

Janey nodded.

When she came out of the bedroom, Ricky was waiting for her in the living room, his face full of concern. 'How is she, luv?'

'Not good. I'll just go in to Mum, I won't be a mo.'

'Take her tea with you, eh? She's all right. She's relieved you've come back.'

Annie didn't answer but went through to her mum carrying a mug of tea.

'Mum, oh, Mum, I'm sorry.'

'Annie, me darlin', you've nothing to be sorry for, luv. Come here.'

Putting the mug down on the dresser, Annie went into her mum's open arms, taking care to be gentle.

'How's Janey, luv?'

'She's all right, Mum. I'm going to bath her. I'll bring the bath in here to give her privacy as this room's bigger, and also, I don't want to tell Ricky to leave.'

'He tells me he's your friend, luv. He's a nice young man. Nothing to look at, I know, but a lovely way with him. Look how he checked up on us this morning.'

'I know. I like him. He . . . well, let's say, he's been me saviour.'

'Oh, luv, are you sure you're all right?'

'Well, not fully, that'll take a long time, but I'm coping. That's down to Ricky. He said that I can't change things, but I can make a better future, and that's what I'm going to do.' She told her mum about her plans.

'I'm going to miss you, luv, but I'm with you in that. You need to be with Olivia, you all need time to adjust. So, you and Janey? I mean, you'll be like before?'

'We will. I love Janey with all me heart, I'm just to stop looking on her as me kid sister and treat her as an equal with the same feelings as I have. I – I . . . well, I'm not sure about Jimmy. I'd rather not face him for a while.'

'You take your time. He has to allow that.'

'I will . . . Right, Mum, poor Janey was expecting me to bring her a mug of tea . . . By the way, she don't look good. She's hurting herself.'

Mum looked shocked as Annie explained. 'Oh no! Oh, Annie, luv, we have to help her. I've never said, but your dad's sister were like that, your Aunty Rita. She'd cut herself to make herself hurt somewhere else and not feel the pain of her broken heart when her husband went off with a floozie.'

'We will, Mum. I won't go anywhere till I know she ain't hurting any more. See you in a while. Enjoy your tea, luv.'

She'd hardly shut the door of the bedroom when Ricky said, 'Shall I pour Janey one now?'

'Yes, please, luv, and me. I could really do with one. Then I need to get the tin bath in. Oh, and while you're in the kitchen, will you turn the heat up under the pot on the stove? It's always on keeping warm for washing the dishes and things.'

When Ricky came out with two steaming mugs of tea, Annie had already pulled the bath inside and taken it into her mum's room. Taking one of the mugs from him, she took it into Janey and was glad to see that Janey had her long nightdress on now and had propped herself up against the headboard.

'Feeling better, me darlin'?'

'Yes, Annie, ta. And I really need that cuppa. I've had nothing pass me lips since yesterday.'

'Ah, it was bad for us both, luv. Get this down you and I'll sort things ready to clean you up, eh?'

Janey managed a smile.

'And, Janey, never hurt yourself again, promise me. If you're hurting inside, turn to me. I'll always be there for you in the future, no matter what happens between us, and even when I am in Guernsey, if you call me, I'll come to you. That means anything, even if it ain't to do with me. I'll always be by your side holding you. I promise, luv.'

Janey managed a weak smile as Annie left the room.

'Well, how did it all go, luv?'

'Better than I thought, ta, Ricky. Me and Janey are going to be all right. But how I'll face Jimmy, I just don't know. I don't think I can.'

'Well then, that's the next hurdle. But if everything is truly to be all right, luv, you're going to have to eventually.'

'I know.'

'I'll always be with you, if you need me, Annie.'

'Ta, Ricky. It was a good thing when you came along. I'd never been so desolate in me life as then.'

'I know, you had me worried. So, what do you want me to do now? I was hoping we'd have tea out together. A nice pie and mash, or fish and chips, or I can go to a proper meal in a restaurant, but not up west.'

'I'd like that, ta. Pie and mash in a pub would be lovely and if they have a piano and singing, that would be even better.'

'I know just the place, The Blind Beggar.'

'Ain't that a bit rough? A few years ago a man stabbed another man in there.'

'Ha, that was a long time ago. It's a decent place now and they have a good old sing-song and pie and mash. And you'll have me to protect you, don't forget.'

Annie laughed at this.

'Right, you're on. But I'll get some for Mum and Janey first and bring them back for them.'

'I can do that. I'll help you to fill that bath, then I'll nip out for a bit. I'll bring the pie and mash back in about an hour. We'll all be ready to eat then.'

Tenderly bathing Janey seemed to bond them together again.

'I love you, Annie. You're the best sister anyone could want.'

Annie leaned forward and kissed Janey's hair. 'No, you are, luv, by a mile. And I want you to be happy, me darlin', not full of guilt or anything. Just be happy with Jimmy, eh?'

'I will. I love him so much.'

Annie felt her heart contract, but not nearly as badly as it had done yesterday. 'Ah, and I know he loves you. You were meant for each other, I can see that now . . . There, you're all cleaned up, me darlin'. But you need some dressings on. I'll get Mum's box of magic potions. Ha, we used to rely on that as kids. Besides the kiss that made everything better.'

'You needed the potions the most. You were a clumsy devil, Annie.'

They all laughed.

When they calmed, Annie asked her mum, 'What about you, Mum? Are you stopping in bed, or getting out for a bit, eh?'

'I'll stop here, luv. I'll get up tomorrow. Only, whatever the doctor gave me is still making me feel sleepy.'

'Well, I'll get you a nice warm flannel to wash your face with, and then I'll empty and clean your commode. I can do the latter with a bucket of this water.'

'It needs it, luv. It didn't get done this morning. Ta, Annie . . . It's good to have things back to normal between us all. You're a strong young woman, and I'm proud of you.'

Annie went over and kissed her mum's cheek. 'You taught

me that, Mum. You always said that there's nothing we can't get over. And you're right. I'll be fine. I just need a little time away and there's nowhere better than with Olivia . . . Anyway, I'm going for me tea with Ricky tonight, so I'd better get me skates on and start to bucket this water out . . . Are you all right now, Janey?'

'I am, Annie. Ta. And Annie . . . I love you.'

Annie hugged her. 'I know. And I love you, me little big sis.'

Once more they giggled, and to Annie, it suddenly felt that nothing was as bad as it had seemed. She'd get through this. They all would.

Chapter Nineteen

Janey & Annie

It was two days later that Janey felt she could see Jimmy. Ashamed of what she'd done to herself and him having witnessed it, she hadn't been able to face him and had stayed in her bedroom each time he'd called to the house.

Somehow she thought that her actions in hurting herself had marked her as not being old enough to cope in situations, but also felt afraid of how, in a strange way, it had helped by giving her a release. That fear had increased as she'd listened to Mum telling her of their Aunt Rita and she'd made up her mind that she would never do anything like that again.

Jimmy looked wonderful to her when he arrived. Though his expression showed his worry.

Mum didn't let him off the hook. 'Jimmy, I know you keep saying it, but I want you to be sure. I know you tried hard not to break me Annie's heart, but I worry that you thought yourself in love with her and now you say you're in love with Janey. What if you change your mind again?'

'Mum!'

'No, Janey, we cockneys are straight talkers, and Jimmy knows that.'

'I can understand how you feel, Vera, and I don't blame you. But though you keep asking me, I don't know how to make you feel reassured. I can only tell you that I'm sorry about what happened and that I love Janey with all me heart.'

Janey felt a smile coming from deep within her. Jimmy loved her. Surely nothing else mattered but that?

Jimmy turned to her. 'Let's take a couple of chairs outside, eh, luv. We need to talk. Is that all right with you, Vera? Then we'll take you for a walk in that chair of yours as it's a nice day. I'll buy you an icey and you can enjoy a bit of fresh air, eh?'

'Ha, blackmail will work every time with me, Jimmy. I'll look forward to it.'

Once they were outside, Jimmy held Janey to him. She felt his hand stroke her hair and heard his words whispering, 'Janey, me Janey. We never meant for this to happen, but I'm glad it did, luv. How was Annie with you?'

Janey told him what had happened. 'She doesn't want to see you yet, Jimmy. I hope she does before she goes away.'

'Just let it be her decision, luv. Don't press her. Oh, Janey, look at your lovely face. Why? What made you do this to yourself?'

'I can't explain, luv. And I don't want to talk about it.'

Jimmy clasped his hands together and leaned forward, resting his elbows on his knees. He gazed at the concrete floor of the backyard.

'I promise I'll never do it again, me darlin'.' His hand reached for hers. She rested her head on his shoulder. 'It all hurt me so badly. I couldn't bear to lose Annie.'

'And you never will, she's told you that. But other things in life might one day hurt you, Janey.'

'Well, if you're not able to help me, I've promised Annie I will turn to her. I've to face things, I know that. This was me first time feeling such pain . . . Just leave it, Jimmy. I just want to enjoy us being together without having to feel guilt. I know Annie is still hurting, but she's given us her blessing. We can't spoil that by going over and over it all and picking at bits of it, that's not helpful.'

'Oh, Janey, I said it before, and I'll say it again, you've a wise old head on your young shoulders.'

'Well then, listen to me. And you're meant to be kissing me, not lecturing me!'

'I feel like you may break. You look so fragile, and your poor eye.'

'I won't, Jimmy. It's all made me stronger if anything. I feel able to go through anything now, as nothing can be as bad as that.'

'All right, luv. Come here.'

His kiss thrilled her. Gentle at first, it became passionate and awoke the feelings of what she'd experienced with him. She clung to him, showing him her need, loving him, and wanting to experience the feeling of safety he gave her.

When their lips parted, he looked into her eyes. 'I love you, Janey. Will you marry me, and soon?'

'I will, Jimmy. But I can't too soon. I want Annie to have time away and to heal, as I can't have a wedding without her.'

'That may be months, luv.'

'I know and it'll be hard, but we've got to do it. One thing, we've got to prove to all that our love is true.'

'You're right. If we rush it, it might be said that I took advantage of your age . . . It's, well, with us having done what we did, I've worried meself sick that we . . . well . . .'

'Might be having a baby?' Suddenly Janey felt more grown-up than Jimmy and she thought of her mum's words that girls always matured more quickly than boys. 'Look, if I am, we'll change our plans, but let's not rush, let's wait and see, and enjoy our courting days.'

'You're not changing your mind, are you?'

'No. Never. I just think it wouldn't be right. Not to us, and not to Annie. I want to be sure that she's all right and she can be in your company . . . I suppose I'm hoping she meets someone who will make her happy, then we'll know for certain that she's over it all.'

'Yes, I can see that. That copper who was here the other morning seems a nice bloke. He took a lot more interest in Annie's affairs than is his job to do, even checking up on you and your mum.'

'Ricky? He's nice, I like him. I'd love it to be him, and not someone she meets in Guernsey. Then she'd live around here near to us . . . Oh, Jimmy, that would be lovely.'

'Ha, hark at us. Just because we're in love, we want everyone to be, especially Annie. We'll be marrying her off to anyone who takes an interest next.'

This made them laugh and lifted Janey's spirits as now the focus wasn't on her and the harm she'd done to herself.

As the afternoon wore on and they walked Mum to the park, the feeling grew that everything was going to be all right. That it had all been a bad dream and that nothing would ever happen like that again.

But when they got back home, an exhaustion came over Janey like none she'd ever felt. With dinner to get and Mum to put to bed, she didn't know how she was going to cope.

'Are you all right, luv? You've gone very pale.'

'No . . . Jimmy . . . me head . . .'

'Janey! Janey, me darlin'.'

'Get her to the sofa, Jimmy, and fetch the doctor. Hurry, luv. I've noticed her speaking with a bit of slur in the last half an hour. Hurry, Jimmy!'

Not conscious of Jimmy lifting her, Janey had the sensation of floating. The feeling was nice. It took away her headache and left her feeling peaceful. She didn't want to be anywhere else but in this blissful state where it seemed that nothing could hurt her.

How many days had passed before she heard Annie calling her, she didn't know, only it seemed Annie was at the end of a long tunnel. At the other end was a man. A nice man who Janey felt she should know. He was calling her too. Only his voice had a beautiful echo to it. The way he said her name, she knew he loved her very much. She wanted to go to him, but then the desperation in Annie's voice and her calling, 'Don't go, please don't go, Janey,' made her turn towards it.

Jimmy's voice came then. 'Janey, me darlin', don't leave me. I love you, Janey, please, please don't leave me.'

She turned to look at the man again, but he was smiling and nodding, and not calling her any more. He put up his hand and waved to her, then he faded, until she could no longer see him.

'Open your eyes, Janey. Come on, dear, open your eyes. You're all right. You're on the mend now.'

This was a male voice that she didn't know. A posh one. She tried to open her eyes. They were so heavy. She just wanted to sleep.

When she did manage to, she felt encased in white. White walls, a man with a white coat on, and a woman wearing a white veil. 'Where am I?'

'You're in hospital, dear. You had an accident and bumped your head a few days ago. You'll be all right now.'

'Jimmy? Annie?'

'We're here, luv. We'll come nearer once the doctor has made his checks.'

Fingers opened her eyelid and a bright light shining made her flinch. 'Try to keep still, Janey. I'm just doing some checks.'

After a moment, the doctor said, 'I think she may have had a bleed on her brain. It's hard to tell, but that would render her unconscious. She's a very sick young lady. I think we should sedate her and keep her sedated for at least another two days.'

Janey couldn't sort out in her head what sedated meant.

The doctor enlightened her. 'Janey, we're going to help you, dear. We will let you sleep for a while so that you can heal.'

'Will she heal, doctor?' Jimmy asked.

'We hope so. It's difficult for us to know but she isn't showing signs of this being serious. Her speech, for instance – we would have expected it to be incoherent if this was a serious bleed, not just slightly slurred, which can be caused by the sleep state we induced. Many small bleeds just heal like a cut on the surface, and this is showing all the signs of being that. We will rest the brain and give it more of a chance to heal.'

He whispered something to Annie and Jimmy then. And Jimmy said, 'We will, Doctor. We'll bring her mum in as well now we know it's better news.'

'Yes, that will help her. But tell her the same as I told you.'

'I've got your hand, Janey. And Annie has your other one. I won't let it go. Annie will have to care for your mum, but will come back when she can, luv. You're going to be fine, me darlin'.'

'Me and Jimmy are going to care for you, me Janey. Get better, luv. We won't leave you. Mum's coming in. See if you can manage one of your smiles, eh?'

Mum was there then as if in a flash of time.

'Oh, me Janey, me precious girl! The doctor says you're going to get well. Oh, Janey, I love you. Enjoy your little sleep and have lovely dreams, me darlin'.'

Janey did as Annie had said and smiled. Then it seemed they all swirled around her, and their voices drifted away from her, but somehow she knew that Jimmy was there. That Jimmy and Annie had been together and were all right with each other, and that her mum would be all right. Annie would bath her and put her to bed and get her meals.

With this thought, Janey drifted away and once more saw the man at the end of the tunnel, but he wasn't calling her name, he was calling to Mum. He faded, but his voice said, 'Tell Vera I love her.'

Janey wanted him to stay. She loved him. He was important to her. And yet, she somehow knew she had a choice. The lovely man, or Jimmy, Annie and Mum. She let the man go.

Annie tenderly washed her mum down, then rubbed her dry, knowing that every movement caused her pain, seeing her twisted body, feeling heartbroken for her mum and for her sister, and yet powerless to do anything other than be there for them, something she couldn't be for long.

Being with Jimmy, talking to him as if he was her brother, wrenched at her heart. Part of her wanted to claw at him, spit at him – just make him pay in some way – and yet she wanted to hold him, to have him hold her, to hear him say he loved her.

Hating him was easier.

This firmed her resolve that she was doing the right thing in making a life for herself. How long it would be for, she didn't know, but she had to carry it through for her own sanity and to give Janey a chance to be happy.

There was no other way.

'There you go, Mum. Are you comfortable now, luv?'

'I am, ta, me darlin'. And I slept well, so feel a lot better. I just need me pills with me cuppa, then I'll be set for the day.'

It wasn't long after they'd eaten breakfast that the door opened. 'Eeh, it's only me, lass. I caught an early Tube as I've news for you, but first, how are you all? I've been out of me mind worrying.'

'Oh, Cissy, come in.' Annie opened her arms to Cissy and hugged her. At this moment she seemed like a link to a different world. A world that was sane, where men didn't flit from one sister to the other, and sisters didn't inflict physical pain on themselves and come near to death, and where mums weren't mangled with arthritis.

'Are you all right, lass?' Annie felt Cissy pat her back. This gesture nearly broke Annie. She felt that she could weep her heart out, but she swallowed hard. 'I've been better, luv.'

'Aye, well, life is allus kicking you in the teeth, lass, but what don't kill you makes you stronger, and you're the strongest young woman I knaw. You and Olivia an' all . . . Now, let me take the weight off me pins as I've news about Olivia for you.'

'Oh? Well, I was just going to make Mum a cuppa, so I'll

do that, and get us one too, then we can chat, luv . . . I hope it's good news, I need some of that!'

This last Annie said as she went into the kitchen.

After turning the heat up under the simmering kettle and with having the tea things all ready, she added another mug to the tray, then took a breather and stood with her hands on the pot sink, leaning heavily on it. *Please let this news be of my transport! Though not too soon, I must see me Janey better first.* How long that would take, she didn't know, but it was what she wanted most out of all the things she needed to happen.

Bracing herself, she took the tea through. 'Here we are. I've put milk and sugar in for you both.'

'Ta, luv. I'm ready for this.'

Annie held the cup till her mum had a good grip on it and then turned to pass Cissy hers. Sitting down on one of the kitchen chairs that stood next to the small table under the window, she asked, 'So, you've heard from Olivia then, Cissy?'

'Aye, she phoned last night. First chance I've had to tell her what's been happening. She was devastated to hear of Janey's plight. She's coming over. She'll be here in a couple of days.'

'Oh, that's wonderful news.' This did spill Annie's tears. She dabbed at her eyes. 'Sorry, there's just so much to contend with. Carry on, I'm fine.'

'Well, lass, it's understandable for you to shed a few tears. Like you say, there's a lot to cope with at the mo. But, yes, Olivia and Hendrick are coming. They planned to anyway, to fetch you back with them, but that was going to be next week. Now they want to be with you all and to do what they can. And Olivia's plan is to stay until it's all right for you to go back with her. Hendrick has some business or other to see to here, then he will return to Guernsey – but not for long! It seems he wants to study more languages and so will live over here for a few months, visiting Olivia at the weekend.'

'Oh? Will he need you to stay with him, Cissy? Only . . . well, I was hoping that if Jimmy gets the flats ready, you and mum could move in there, and . . . well, maybe till they're w – wed, Jimmy will let Janey sleep in the flat that they – they'll share.'

'Eeh, love, this is all costing you dearly. And the best thing is for you to go and begin a new life, lass. We all knaw that. Me and your ma have talked about it. We want her happy, don't we, Vera?'

'We do. And it is me that'll hold her back. I'm sorry, luv.'

'Naw. There's naw need for that. I am going to do as Annie just said, love. I talked it over with Olivia, and they both agree that it will be fine for me to travel to work at the apartment, so if the flat's ready for me, I'll move in and be here in the evenings, and all weekends. And until Janey is strong enough, Olivia is engaging a nurse to help with your care, Vera. She'll come mornings to get you up, bath you and dress you, then at night come and put you to bed. I'll be in the next flat, and Janey just above you. And another thing, Olivia's going to make sure you can communicate with either of us at any time, though she didn't say how.'

'Well, there you go, Annie, luv, it sounds as though nothing need hold you up from going. I'm so pleased for you . . . Though you will come home regular to see us, won't you?'

'I will, once me heart mends, Mum, I promise. I can't believe Olivia is going to do so much for us. Or how lucky I was to ever meet her and become her friend.'

'You're more than that, lass. You're the sister she never

had. Aye, and sometimes the ma she never knew an' all. Not to mention the saviour of her life! You deserve everything she does for you . . . So, you'll go then, eh?'

'I will. Part of me doesn't want to, but if I'm to keep sane, I must.'

A knock interrupted them and Ricky poking his head around the door warmed the cold places of Annie's heart. 'What're you doing here? You're on duty!'

'Blimey, that's a nice welcome. No come on in, we've tea in the pot then?'

Annie laughed. 'You daft beggar! Come in, I'll get you a cuppa.'

After saying hello to Mum and Cissy, he followed Annie into the kitchen. 'I've been up to the hospital, luv. Janey had a restful night, and all her signs are good. They said to tell you they may consider bringing her around later, and not wait until tomorrow.'

'Oh, that's wonderful news, Ricky! Ta, mate.'

'Annie . . . I – I . . . well, I wouldn't speak, but for you going away, but will I always be just a mate to you, luv?'

Annie froze. She didn't need this and was shocked that Ricky could be so insensitive when he'd been just a wonderful friend that she could rely on.

'I'm sorry. Forget I said that. I wasn't going to, and I shouldn't have . . . I just couldn't help meself. It's seeing you so miserable, it cuts at me heart.'

'I wish you hadn't, Ricky. I can't think like that at the moment. I don't want to feel awkward around you. I wanted to have you here, someone to rely on, a good friend. Now that's spoiled for me too.'

'It doesn't have to be. Don't let it be, Annie. I – I, oh, Annie, I don't want to lose you, luv.'

His face looked full of anguish. She held his gaze, saw his scar twitch, and his eyes fill with tears. She felt immediate remorse.

'And I don't want to lose you, Ricky. Like I said, you're me saviour. But will what you've said be between us now?'

'No, it won't, luv. We'll carry on as always, and if ever there comes a time when your feelings heal and you can look on me differently, then that will be me life complete. But if it doesn't happen that way . . . well, we'll always be friends.'

His face had a look of fear. She knew he was dreading losing her and loved him for that as she did need him. Stepping towards him, she leaned forward and kissed his scar. He didn't make a move towards her, just smiled his lovely smile, 'Phew! I thought I'd blown it then. Blimey, Annie, you're a beautiful, kind soul and I'm honoured to have you as me friend.'

She kissed him again. 'And me you. It's your kindness that I love and need, nothing else, not yet. Maybe not ever. I don't know. But for now, just carry on being you, eh?'

His hands came on her shoulders, and he looked deep into her eyes. His voice croaked as he said, 'I will. I'm yours for ever, Annie, in whatever guise you need me to be.'

'Ta, Ricky. Now, I'll pour that tea. It'll be a bit stewed, mind, but that's your own fault!'

They laughed together as they went back into the living room.

Annie felt Mum's knowing eyes on her, so stopped anything being said by telling them, 'Ricky has brought more good news for us. Janey may be brought round this afternoon, and not have to wait till tomorrow.'

'Really! Oh, Ricky, ta. That's good news. Have you seen her then?'

'I have. Jimmy still sits with her, holding her hand . . .'

Annie was surprised that this didn't stab at her heart as deeply as she thought it would. She couldn't have said why, but what she felt wasn't much more than if he'd said a nurse was doing that. She smiled at everyone.

'Well, that's done you good, lass, and it's good to see. So, Ricky, lad, tell us all about it.'

As he did, Annie realized that it wasn't just the news, it was something else. As if Ricky's words had started a healing process. She couldn't understand it and wouldn't pursue it. She would go to Guernsey, heal properly, and see how the future panned out.

Chapter Twenty

Olivia

The sight of Annie tore at Olivia's heart. And then to have her burst into tears and almost fall into her arms as soon as they closed the door of the apartment was almost too much to bear.

They sat down together on the sofa. Offering comfort didn't help but ended with them sobbing together. For Annie to have lost the happiness she'd found tore at Olivia's heart. 'Oh, Annie, I'm so sorry. Dry your eyes and talk to me, love.'

As she said this, Olivia looked around her. Hendrick was nowhere to be seen. She heard the click of a door and guessed that he'd left the apartment to give them time together. She was grateful to him. Annie needed to be able to talk openly.

'I just feel broken, Olivia. Then I don't and I can see hope in the future, then I do again.'

'Does the hope come from having met Ricky?'

Annie nodded. 'A bit . . . He's so nice, Olivia. He makes me feel safe.'

'You said he's a policeman, didn't you? Well, he'll be trained in dealing with people, but does it go deeper than that for you?' Olivia knew it was a little insensitive to ask this, but she wanted something, anything, to hook on to that would give Annie hope. And herself too as she so wanted that for Annie.

'I don't know. Me pain feels so raw. There was a moment . . . but I can't even think like that about him.'

'No, of course not . . . Have you not come to terms with Jimmy and Janey's love for one another at all, love?'

'No, not really. I just want to come and be with you, away from here, where I can't see them, or hear about . . . Oh, Olivia, it's so awful.'

'I know. I hope it helps you to come home with me. Life in Guernsey is so different to here and, as you say, you'll be away from everything that reminds you.'

'But I can't go yet. Janey's still not well. She can't look after Mum.'

'But it isn't just your mum. Someone must look after you. You've worked all your young life to take care of them and now it's time to take care of you. Cissy told you I was looking into getting a nurse in until Janey can cope, didn't she? Well, let's see how far Jimmy has got with the flats and look at getting Cissy next to your mum as that will put your mind at rest and Cissy will like that too. She really loves your mum. They remind me of you and me.'

'Oh, they do. They light up when they see each other. And talk for hours. They play games – cards and snakes and ladders. And I managed to get Mum a gramophone, so they have a sing-song. Mum would love a piano, always has wanted one as her granny taught her to play, but there was never anywhere to put one.'

'That all sounds lovely for them and maybe there will be room for a piano when they get their new place . . . So, your mind would be at rest if they were together and if we engaged a nurse until Janey is well enough to cope?'

'It would, as Janey may need help for a while too. But I can't let you do all this when I'm capable of doing it. I should be the one to care for me mum and me sister.'

'Should be perhaps, but are you able to? I don't think so. And you know that we will do anything for you. Anything in the world.' They hugged again, only this time Annie didn't cry and that to Olivia was a relief and filled her with hope that Annie would heal given time.

As they came out of the hug, Olivia said, 'I can stay for a while, love. Well, as long as we need to set everything up and for you to feel able to pack your things and come back with me.'

'But Hendrick can't stay, Cissy was telling me. She did say, though, that he will be back to study? I couldn't understand all of that.'

Olivia tried to explain without saying too much. 'It's all to do with what might happen.' Suddenly it occurred to her how she could tell the truth but not reveal what might be best kept to herself. Hendrick hadn't said she couldn't speak of him being approached and advised to learn Japanese, but she thought it best for Annie not to know too many details. 'You know how he feels strongly that he doesn't want to be in a fighting unit if forced to go back to his own country? Well, he's decided that if he knows the languages of all those countries that are involved with his own, he'll be so useful as an interpreter and translator that it won't even be considered to train him as a pilot or some such. So, he is going to study Japanese and maybe a few more languages.'

'He's amazing. I have a job speaking English, I only know the cockney way.'

For the first time, Annie smiled.

Olivia caught on to this. 'Well, maybe you could teach him that as even I feel I need an interpreter with those who speak broad cockney!'

This made them both giggle and the mood lightened.

Changing the subject, Olivia said, 'I can't wait to meet your Ricky. Why don't you ask him to dinner tonight?'

'No! I mean, well, he ain't that kind of friend. Maybe one night we could go for pie and mash at the pub, after Hendrick's gone home. That'd suit him. He took me for a lovely one the other night.'

'I'd love that. You've mentioned pie and mash before, and I've wondered about it. It seems a real Londony thing to do.'

'Ha! That's a new one, Londony! But it fits well. So, that's how you'll meet him then. When we do the Londony thing.'

They both laughed now, and Olivia could see some of Annie's old spark returning. 'So, have you got to get back to your mum's, love?'

'I have. She'll want her tea, bless her. This is the longest I've left her, though the man who owns the shop is good. He'll pop in and take her a cup of tea when he makes his own.'

'Well, maybe you'd better get back now. We'll get you a cab. I would come, only my leg is giving me a bit of pain after the long journey, and I know Hendrick will want to get unpacked and organize some meetings he needs to set up. So, how about I come over to your mum's tomorrow and we'll all talk about things, and then go and see Janey?'

'Oh, luv. I didn't realize. You're doing so well, and hardly ever complain, that I sometimes forget about your poorly leg.'

'I do myself. It's only when it hurts that I remember how ugly it is.'

'It's not. No part of you can ever be ugly, Olivia. You're the most beautiful person I know.'

Annie opened her arms as she said this.

Leaning into the embrace, Olivia's heart warmed. She thanked God every night for bringing Annie to her.

Janey was propped up when Olivia and Annie arrived at the hospital the next day. Jimmy was with her. For a moment, Olivia felt embarrassed at seeing him, even though she knew he was going to be there, but then her concern for Janey took these thoughts away for she looked the picture of misery and cried when she caught sight of Annie. It was good to see them hug, cry together and to hear Annie use a kind voice when she said to Jimmy, 'Go and get yourself a cuppa and something to eat, Jimmy. We'll stay with Janey a while.'

Jimmy didn't hang his head, or look ashamed when he said, 'Ta, Annie. I will.' Then he turned to Janey, 'Will you be all right, me darlin'?'

'I will, Jimmy. Go and have a break. Me Annie's here now.'

When Jimmy left, he nodded at Olivia. She smiled in return. She couldn't help but feel sorry for him, even though at times her anger at him almost spilled over.

'Hello, Janey, love.'

Janey said a quiet hello and then looked down as if she was feeling shame.

'Janey, I've been thinking of you, dear.'

'Ta, Olivia . . . I'm sorry I worried you all. I don't know what came over me.'

'Look, there's no need to explain. We just need you to get better.'

'Will you go when I'm better, Annie?'

'Yes. You know that I must.'

'But you've been all right with Jimmy. I thought . . . Well, I thought everything was all right now.'

'Janey, these things take time, luv. I am all right. But well, me life's changed . . . I'm not saying it's anyone's fault, it ain't . . . Least of all yours and Jimmy's.'

'Oh, Annie, you don't blame us for it then?'

'You know I don't, I told you. All I want is for you to get better and to be happy.'

Janey put her hand out and Annie took it. Olivia had to swallow back the tears.

'How will we all manage, Annie?'

'While you explain the plans we have, Annie, I'll go and find Jimmy. I expect he's gone to that cafe I saw down the road. Only I need to inform him of the plans, Janey, and to see if they are all possible. You two enjoy some time together.'

As she walked the long corridors, Olivia felt her leg getting more and more painful, so was glad to at last see a bench. Easing herself down onto it took the pressure off. But she wasn't there long when Jimmy appeared. He couldn't have had time to have a cup of tea and a bite to eat so she deduced he'd only been able to relieve himself.

'Jimmy!'

'Olivia! I thought you were with Janey.'

'No. I need to talk to you . . . No need to look so defensive. I just want to talk about some plans we want to put into action. Can you sit with me a moment as I don't think I can walk much further?'

'Oh? Are you all right, luv?'

'I am. It's just this leg. Anyway, never mind about that. Can we just have a talk?'

Jimmy sat down. He cleared his throat. 'I – I didn't mean for this to happen. I feel awful about it all.'

'I know. We're not blaming you – you fell in love, it happens, we can all make mistakes with our first choice. We just feel that things could have been handled differently.'

'Ta for that and I know you're right . . . It is a terrible thing, I admit that, and I wish it hadn't happened. Me Janey . . .'

He leaned forward and placed his head in his hands with his elbows resting on his knees. His head shook from side to side. 'I was nearly the death of her.'

Olivia instinctively put her hand on his shoulder. 'It will all be all right, Jimmy, but it will take time. I want to give Annie that time by taking her back with me. That will give you and Janey a chance too, but I need your help.'

He sat up as she began to outline the plan.

'I can do that. I can employ a team of builders to finish off the bottom flats. I've done the top one now, it just needs furnishings and carpet . . . Oh, Olivia, you don't know what you've done for me. To think you're going to take care of poor Annie, and that your plan will mean everyone will be all right and cared for. You're a marvel.'

'Well, I wouldn't say that. I just love Annie very much and owe her a massive debt.'

'I know. You leave it with me. In fact, if you and Annie can stay with Janey, I'll go right now and arrange things and then come back later . . . I didn't feel like eating before either, but now I could eat a scabby cat, so I'll have something to eat while I'm away too.'

Olivia laughed. 'Well, I hope you put salt and pepper on that cat!'

Jimmy laughed then. He had a lovely deep laugh, and she was glad to hear it. 'I can't thank you enough, Olivia . . . I tell you what. I'm going to carry you back to just outside the ward before I go.'

'No! Jimmy, no!'

But her protests went unheeded. He lifted her up and walked with her.

'There you go. You've only about five yards to go now. Explain everything to Janey and tell her I'll be back to stay with her.'

A few days later, Olivia said goodbye to Hendrick as he was to go back home. For her, it seemed her life was always to be like this – seeing Hendrick coming and going. How she longed for their life to be normal, for them to be able to settle down together, have a family and achieve their ambition of getting the school successful and their forever home built.

When the door closed on him, she leaned on it and allowed the tears to flow.

'Eeh, Olivia, lass.'

Cissy had come in from the kitchen. 'I'll make you a pot of tea, lass. That allus cures all.'

Olivia didn't object. She felt exhausted with heartache for herself, for Annie and for Jimmy and Janey. But she knew she was doing her best for them all and the report that Janey could go home had cheered her. Though how they were going to manage in the three rooms and a kitchen they had, she didn't know. It was then that it occurred to her.

'Cissy, Cissy, love!'

Cissy came running through. 'I've had an idea. Until the flats are ready, I'm going to bring them all here! We can take care of Vera and Janey between the three of us. Jimmy can come and visit, if Annie is all right with that, but if she'd rather not be here, she and I can go out to eat, or to the theatre. What do you think?'

'You've took the wind out of me sails for a mo but, eeh, I reckon it's a grand idea. They all need taking care of, Annie as well. And it was all going to land on her shoulders, but now it won't . . . We'll have that cuppa then I'll set to and get the rooms ready. Annie's bed is still in with yours, and Vera and Janey can be in the guest bedroom that has the twin beds in. Eeh, you have some good ideas, lass. I feel excited. Especially at having Vera with me.'

Olivia smiled. Her own mood had lifted, and she felt that this way, both she and Annie could go to her home sooner knowing Cissy, Vera and Janey would be fine here until Jimmy could move them all into the flats. She couldn't wait to see Annie to tell her.

'Leave the beds, love. Let's get a taxi over to Annie's mum's and then if they'll all come back, Janey can be brought here as soon as she leaves the hospital. Me, you and Annie will soon sort out what needs doing. And like you say, I'll move out of the double room, back into my old room to be with Annie . . . Ooh, if only they will agree!'

Later that evening, Olivia smiled as she looked around her – her wish had been fulfilled.

Annie's face glowed with a happiness that radiated around the room, infecting them all as they sat around the dining room table in the apartment. The meal was the most delicious Olivia had ever tasted – pie, mash and liquor, brought with them from Jones's Pie Shop in Bethnal Green.

'Eeh, Olivia, lass, you've brought the East End to the

West End. I never thought I'd see the day, and it's making me feel so happy and relaxed.'

Cissy put her hand over Vera's. 'And with Jimmy saying he's secured builders to finish off our flats, lass, we'll soon be able to do this once a week – you come to me, or I come to you. I can't wait.'

Vera beamed. 'Nor me.' She turned towards Olivia. 'Ta, luv, you're an angel sent to care for us. All our lives have changed since you came into them.' She raised her glass of wine then – something she'd said she'd never tasted as sherry was her tipple. 'To Olivia and her Hendrick. With love and thanks and wishing you both a happy and long marriage. No one deserves it more than you two.'

They all raised their glasses, and Olivia felt herself blush.

'I can never thank you enough for what you've done for me, Olivia. You're the best mate anyone can have.'

'Well, that I can answer. What you did for me, Annie, and keep on doing, surpasses anything I do for you. We just need Janey here now to make it all complete . . . Oh, and to organize a nurse tomorrow to come here and then to continue for as long as you need her at home for you and Janey too, Vera. And then, though it will be sad to leave you all, I know Annie and I can, knowing that you're all cared for, and your lives are going to be so much better.'

Just one week later, Janey came home to the apartment to a lovely welcome – another pie and mash supper, and best of all, Olivia experiencing her first ever cockney sing-along as Vera played the piano that stood next to the window in the dining room.

Olivia didn't think she would ever forget all of them belting out:

'She'd got a hole in her frock,
Hole in her shoe,
Hole in her sock
Where her toe peeped through'

as they sang 'On Mother Kelly's Doorstep'.

And never had she felt so happy for Annie, who stood with Ricky, his arm around her shoulder and hers around his waist, swaying as they sang, seeming to be oblivious to Jimmy singing his heart out while he sat on the chaise longue with a frail but happy-looking Janey.

To Olivia, this was a pivotal moment for Annie, as though she was unaware of it, her healing had begun. And maybe the process would complete once they were in Guernsey. Who knew, maybe Annie would find that she could return the love that Ricky was offering her. She prayed that she would.

PART THREE

Parting is Hard to Take

Chapter Twenty-One

Olivia

1938

For Olivia, her first Christmas as Hendrick's wife had been wonderful, even though she'd missed Annie, who'd gone home to spend it with her family – her first trip home since she'd arrived here in early October. She now wasn't expected back for another week at the earliest, and then only if any boats were sailing. Often they were docked in the winter months due to bad weather.

But Annie not being here had been softened by the wonderful news that Olivia couldn't believe – Hendrick wouldn't be going back to England! He'd already mastered Japanese, and to her he was a whizz. Languages just weren't a barrier to him. It seemed that one day he didn't speak a tongue and the next he did!

Her thoughts went back to Annie. Since being here, she'd grown in confidence, had cried less, and had taken to island life like an islander. She had a job in a sweet shop and loved it. Of all things, she thought the best bit was weighing the sweets out into quarters of a pound and pouring them into little cone-shaped bags, twisting the tops and arranging them in trays for display.

Olivia hadn't wanted Annie to work and would have been happy to continue paying her as her companion, as would her father, but they could both see that it was what Annie wanted to do – that and cycle everywhere when she wasn't helping Olivia to oversee the renovations of the farmhouse.

It was good to see her blossoming once more, though she did worry over Janey, who'd had many bouts of being sick, and as Annie put it when she telephoned, seemed to be putting on weight and yet looked wan and frail.

Olivia had her own theory and couldn't see why it hadn't occurred to Annie, but then, Olivia thought, being in the same boat and suffering the same symptoms, she had clues to go on. The reason for feeling as she did gave her such joy, though she was sure it wasn't so for poor Janey.

With her hair brushed till it shone and falling into the bob that she loved, she leaned towards the mirror and ticked her finger each side of her mouth to remove lipstick that had found the crease there, and then sat back and gazed at her reflection. She couldn't see any difference in herself despite her wonderful news – well, a bit of a glow perhaps.

Twisting this way and that, Olivia was pleased with her appearance. Her pleated grey skirt and pink twinset didn't quite cover the slight bulge in her tummy, but she didn't mind. All would be revealed today – something she hadn't wanted to do until Hendrick was home for good, as she knew he'd worry about her and that would have made their parting even more difficult.

But today was Saturday, and Hendrick didn't have to go to work – he'd been giving her father a hand since Christmas to train a young man who Father had taken on some time ago, and who was proving to be a genius with figures. His only training required now was in the intricacies of foreign currencies and markets.

'Penny for them, darling.'

'Oh, Hendrick, you made me jump.'

'You look like someone with a secret and have done for days. When are you going to spill the beans then?'

'This afternoon. I want you to drive me out to the farm and I will tell you in our imaginary bedroom.'

'Ha! Well, it'd better be good, it's freezing out there.'

Olivia smiled. She'd wanted to discuss her thoughts over Janey with him but thought that might lead to her telling him about their own expected event, which she didn't want to do yet. She wanted that moment to be special and connected with the home they would one day bring up their children in.

Already work was progressing well on the farmhouse, and most of it had been completed towards the beginning of December, so they had high hopes of taking up residence in their flat there once the last job – the pointing of the chimney – was completed. Sadly, the weather had held everything up of late.

At last, they stood within the square of the stone that proudly stated 'Olivia's and Hendrick's bedroom' and held hands facing the sea. The wind whipped around them as Hendrick hugged her to him.

'A baby! Our very own baby! Oh, darling, when?'

'Well, the doctor thinks I am four months, and will deliver our child in June – probably the beginning of the month.'

'So, we made a baby within weeks of practising how to do so! Oh, Olivia, I love you. Thank you, this is the best news.'

He hugged her close, kissing her hair. She could feel him shivering with cold, though suspected some of that was due to shock and excitement. She'd been able to conceal her condition well from him and he hadn't a clue that it had happened.

'Shall we go before we freeze ourselves and our child, darling?'

With chattering teeth, Hendrick agreed. 'But while we're here, I'll just check the last of the plastering on the schoolrooms has been done and then we'll go and have a hot cup of tea in Florrie's.'

Once inside the house, Olivia looked around her; she couldn't believe how big the rooms now looked as she listened excitedly to Hendrick.

'I won't order the furniture for down here, darling, but what you chose for upstairs, from the shop's catalogue, is being shipped over next week! So, we should get in before I hear when I go . . . I mean . . .'

Olivia froze. Her excitement and happiness splintered.

Hendrick turned towards her. 'I – I haven't wanted to say, darling, but Ambassador Ribbentrop told me that a place is being found for me. Apparently, Dirksen, the German ambassador to Japan, shares Ribbentrop's views and is also pro-Japanese. Together, they will try to persuade Hitler to see things their way. And so, Ribbentrop thinks a lot more interpreters will be needed for any negotiations that may take place between Germany and Japan.'

'Oh no! I'd managed to put it out of my head as something that won't happen.'

'I know. And I allowed that because I didn't want it to be.'

With her heart thudding in her chest, but trying to be brave, Olivia asked, 'Should we continue with our plans here then?'

'Yes, I think so. Even if you don't want to live here, it can be a bolthole for you, darling, and for us when I'm home on leave. And maybe you and Annie will want to live here. She can take care of you while our baby grows inside you.'

As he held her close, Olivia once more felt in tune with his feelings and knew his sorrow and fear matched her own.

Not feeling like going anywhere, they went home to Olivia's father's house and had tea served in Olivia's sitting room, a room they had made their own each time Hendrick had returned after his week away.

A little bit of him had made it his too – his bookcase, brought from his aunt's old home, now stood against the wall near to the window with his bureau in the same walnut wood next to it, though he'd never used it much as time had been limited to weekends only. But as they finished their tea, he went over to it.

'I think I will work on that code we always talked about, darling, as you should rest. You mustn't do too much now you are with child.'

Olivia laughed. 'I've been "with child" as you put it for months, darling. I don't need to rest. I'll work with you. I've had some ideas, but it's all very complicated as we don't know what, if anything, is going to happen.'

'It already has. And at last, the world seems to be taking notice. Hitler is having more and more of an influence on Austrian politics. It is his ambition to expand the Reich by having them as part of it. And now Poland is in a precarious position as both Germany and Russia have expressed their desire to take back their previous possession of it.'

'Back? You mean, to how it was before the Great War?'

'Yes. The treaty of 1918 reunited Poland as an independent state, but it appears that with the advance of Germany, Russia is making rumblings about their claim. As you know, before the treaty, Russia occupied the whole of eastern Poland, and Prussia, as it was then, held western Poland which then founded the German Empire.'

'It can't happen, can it?'

'To me, it looks likely. Germany has rearmed and has a sizeable military force. That has been allowed to carry on despite the Versailles Treaty. We must not go around with our heads in the sand, we must prepare.'

Olivia didn't put up any argument to Hendrick's theories. He was passionate about the politics of his country and others, whereas she couldn't see it all happening the way that he did. To her, the Great War ended all such wars, and as time had gone on from when Hendrick first got nervous about it all, she'd felt more and more convinced that he was wrong. Everything seemed so normal in her part of the world; it couldn't all be destroyed again, could it?

They sat for the afternoon, working out different ways of saying things in code. They laughed, got angry, but then laughed again, and finally settled on key words that they would use when talking on the phone that would alert her that Hendrick was about to relay a secret message to her. She would know then that the next few sentences would need decoding.

The main key word was to be 'Rupert'.

Rupert was Olivia's treasured teddy bear.

Hendrick would ask something like, 'So, how's Rupert then?' And after she told him, she would know that as he'd mentioned Rupert, he was going to speak in code.

He'd give her the key to the code by mentioning numbers. These would indicate the word in each sentence he would utter that she would need. And with them, she could decipher the message.

He might say, 'Did you say four or five toes that Rupert has now?' And then laugh before saying, 'Has he cuddled you this week?' After allowing time for an answer, he would continue with something like, 'That time at the docks? You mean in St Peter Port? . . . Oh, you mean London?' Again, he would leave time as she told him the real news, before he might end by saying, 'Yes, a real explosion of colour. I love the eastern colours.' Again, a pause, and then he would end the message in the same way, each time indicating there was no more to convey to her, by saying, 'I love you, so much, my darling.' And then hopefully, the conversation could flow between them normally with a few references back to the beginning to blend it all in for any listeners.

From this, she would work out that 'this week' were the fourth and fifth words in his first sentence and then 'docks' was the fifth word in his second sentence. And so on. 'This week, docks, London, explosion, huge, eastern', meaning that there was a planned air raid on the docks in East London.

Somehow, and they didn't know how yet, but if such a thing ever occurred, Olivia had to get such messages to London.

To help herself cope with all of this, Olivia kept telling herself that it was just in case.

'Are you all right, darling?'

'It won't happen, will it, Hendrick?'

'I hope not, darling, but it is said that if there was another war, it would be fought on English soil too. It was tried in the last war. Only nothing was accurate, and it was houses, not strategic targets that got hit by mistake. A lot of advances have been made since then. Anyway, I enjoyed that exercise, and you were brilliant, darling. You cracked every code.'

'Once I got into it, I found it easy.'

'I did too. Mind, I found it difficult to make up a few of the sentences, so I might have to use longer sentences as we go along, and somehow let you know the number of each word. Though how, if it is something like the ninth and the tenth, I just don't know.'

'Well, you could try mentioning a memory we shared that you were thinking of and then say, "By the way, was that the ninth or the tenth of December?"'

'Brilliant! You're a genius, my darling. If ever we need this, it really is going to work. I think we should start to play games around it from now on, giving each other a code, and then see who can crack the other ones and in the shortest time, that sort of thing. It'll all become second nature then.'

'Oh dear, I can see me looking for codes in every conversation that numbers are mentioned!'

They giggled, but then Hendrick said, 'That's the beauty of the key words. We can have conversations without messages, but once I say one of the key words, and I think we need a few, then you will be on the alert and write down everything I say. But then you will have to eat it, darling.'

'Eat it! Oh no, I'll have a stomach like papier mâché.'

Again, they nervously laughed to cover up their fear and their knowledge that the day they had dreaded for a long time was almost on them and soon Hendrick would be gone – this time, they wouldn't know for how long.

A knock on the door broke this pretence of normality and the real world came into focus as Father came through. 'Sorry to interrupt, darling, but I didn't see you come in, only Annie rang earlier. She sounded upset.'

'Oh no. I hope nothing else has happened! Thanks, Daddy.'

'Well, I'll leave you to it and get back to my book. I'm at an exciting moment. Agatha Christie is a genius!'

It never ceased to amaze Olivia that such an intelligent man as her father found pleasure in reading books such as Agatha wrote. She was sure he worked out the plot long before the end – but then, maybe that's what he enjoyed.

Frustratingly, there was no joy in ringing Janey's flat as the operator told her that there were no connections to the mainland for at least two hours.

Poor Annie was reluctantly staying with Janey in the home that was to be hers and Jimmy's. She'd have preferred to stay over in the St James's Street apartment, but that would mean travelling backwards and forwards and over Christmas that wouldn't have been easy. Besides, she hadn't wanted to upset Janey.

When at last she got through, Annie sounded tired. 'The worst has happened, Olivia. Janey is pregnant . . . That bleeder must have done it while I was away at your wedding . . . I don't know how much more I can take of this, I just want to run and run and run and never stop.'

'Oh, Annie. I don't know what to say. I expect everyone is telling you to accept it, that it would have happened one day anyway and you would have had to face it, but I'm not going to say that, love. I could punch Jimmy. All right, he fell in love with Janey, but the least he could have done is respect her and, more so, you! He could have broken his commitment to you before he did anything about his love for Janey. That way it would still have been painful, but not half as painful as his deceit and finding this out. Come home, love. Come back here so I can care for you.'

'I can't. We must get them wed. Mum can't do it all. Jimmy's mum's being a brick and helping as much as she can. But the banns are up now, so somehow I must face it all.'

Olivia wanted to ask if Annie had Ricky's support. She'd hoped with all her heart that what Annie looked on as a safe friendship would develop into love for her. It seemed that somehow Annie was being left behind now, with both herself and Janey expecting babies, and Janey soon to be married too – if only that wasn't to the man Annie loved!

'I will try to come over to support you, Annie. We could both live in the apartment then and you needn't face everything every minute of the day.'

'Oh, Olivia, will you? With you by my side I would cope with it all.'

'I'll speak to Hendrick, only . . . well, he may have to go soon, so I don't think he can come.'

'Then you're not either! I ain't dragging you away at such a time. Oh, Olivia, I'm so sorry that's happening, I'd hoped it never would.'

'Me too. But it is imminent now . . . And, Annie, I'm pregnant!'

There was a silence.

'Annie, you will come back, won't you? I don't think I could get through it all without you.'

'I will, luv. And it's wonderful news about the baby, though I know you're torn at the moment . . . Oh, Olivia, it's all giving me strength. Knowing you need me – I mean, well, I know you always do, but it's more so if Hendrick is going and with a baby on the way.'

'It is, and I do need you. Oh, Annie, it feels as though it's all going wrong for us.'

'We'll get through, luv. We always do, don't we?'

Olivia smiled to herself despite her anguish. Annie was taking on the protective role of her and that would help her.

Now she could relax, knowing that Annie would face what she must and then would be back here by her side.

Three days later, a call came for Hendrick. He was to return to Germany and report to the Nazi headquarters in Munich at once. He would go by boat to France and then overland to Germany.

Olivia felt deflated – it had begun.

They cried together, clung to one another. Tried to cheer each other. But nothing stopped the time arriving when Olivia stood on the dockside and waved off her beloved Hendrick, not knowing when she would ever see him again.

Chapter Twenty-Two

Annie

Annie had fixed a smile on her face even though she felt broken.

Janey had been through so much; she didn't need her bridesmaid showing any signs of hurting.

What helped Annie was that Ricky had been asked to be best man. He'd become like a brother to Janey, supporting her and Mum, though she had to admit that Jimmy had done that too.

Mum and Janey had wanted for nothing. They ate well, they had a lovely warm home. Mum was happier than Annie had ever known her as she had Cissy living within the same building, just across the hall.

As well as being near in proximity, they were as close as sisters too, and this was lovely to see.

Janey, too, had made a lovely home in the top flat and with Cissy's help cared for Mum as she'd always done. Theirs was a house of happiness and Annie felt that all three deserved that.

But she couldn't help thinking that it was as if Janey had taken over her life.

Ricky, offering his arm as they followed Janey and Jimmy out of the register office, took these thoughts away. Her smile to him was genuine. He'd come to mean so much to her.

'You look beautiful, Annie, girl.'

'You look dapper yourself, mate. Never seen you dressed so posh.'

'I made the effort for you, luv.'

And he did look handsome. She no longer saw the flaws that marred his looks, just him, lovely, kind, gentle Ricky who today was her rock as he had been so many times.

'That frock looks lovely on you, Annie. You should wear pale blue more often, it really makes your eyes stand out.'

'This was the frock I wore for Olivia's wedding . . . I – I brought it over when I came back after her wedding . . . It was meant . . .'

'Don't think of that today, luv. I know your heart's breaking. I won't leave your side; you're doing so well.'

'Ta, Ricky, and ta for understanding.' Annie quickly wiped away the tears that had filled her eyes.

She didn't really understand them. She hated Jimmy for what he'd done to her, and yet even hate was too strong a word. She just couldn't forgive him was more how it was for her.

'Eeh, me little lass, you look lovely.'

'Ta, Cissy.'

'Let me give you a hug, love. You look like you need it.'

It was the last thing Annie needed, she thought, but couldn't deny Cissy as she held out her arms.

Controlling herself took all the effort she could muster as having the understanding and the love Cissy gave almost undid her.

'Annie, Annie!'

Annie came out of Cissy's hug and turned towards Janey. She'd never seen her looking more beautiful than she did today. Her long cream silk frock, made by Cissy and Mum, had a little flared overskirt flowing from under her bust to cover the slight bulge of her tummy. She looked like an angel with the ringlets caught up in a comb and falling around her shoulders completing the vision.

Getting Janey's hair into this style had taken Annie quite a while to do but had been a distraction, as though Janey had prattled on about her happiness, the intricate work involved had kept Annie's mind busy.

'Jimmy has a photographer here! We're all to be in a photograph!'

'Ah, that's lovely. You'll be able to remember this day for ever and show your children what it was like, luv.'

'Oh, I will, Annie. I've never had me photo taken before.'

Jimmy's mum joined them. 'What a wonderful day this is, Annie, girl . . . I know it should have been your day . . .'

Annie gasped.

Ricky saved the day. 'It is her day. Annie was just saying she couldn't feel happier for Janey and Jimmy and how glad she is that a huge mistake wasn't made.'

'Oh . . . I – I didn't mean . . . I'm sorry, Annie, it was thoughtless of me, luv. Can you forgive me?'

'I can, Rosie. I know you'd never say anything spiteful; it was just something that was in your head and came out of your mouth. I'm always doing that.'

'Ta, Annie, that's exactly what it is. But it was me love for you that prompted it, duckie, I just feel so much for you.'

'Please don't. I'm fine with it all and happy for me Janey.'

'You're a lovely girl, Annie.'

'Ta . . . Look, I have to go to me mum. I'll see you in a bit, eh?'

As she turned to walk away, Ricky's arm came around her. Annie had the sudden thought to show Rosie and them all and laughed up at Ricky. His eyes held hers. His face came nearer to her. She didn't look away as suddenly, she knew that she was no longer using him as a shield. She wanted his kiss.

It was just a light brushing of her lips but it sent feelings zinging through Annie that she'd never thought to feel again.

He went to speak, but she put her finger on his lips.

He sighed. 'Oh, Annie, Annie.'

'One day, Ricky. I'm just not ready yet but I promise I almost am.'

His smile, a wide, grin-like smile, made him look as if he'd just won a prize. 'One day'll do me, luv. I can live on that for years.'

She grinned back at him but didn't say any more. It would take her a long time to trust another man – the words they said, the kisses they gave you, how would she ever know they weren't like those spoken and given to her by Jimmy?

'Annie, come on! The photographer is waiting!'

Annie took a deep breath and walked over to the wedding party gathered for a photo. Standing beside her mum, she bent and kissed her. 'Are you having a good time, Mum?'

'I am, but how're you, luv?'

'Fine. Absolutely fine. I promise you.'

'I am too, Vera. Annie has promised to love me one day.'

Mum laughed, but Annie hit out at Ricky. 'You idiot! I love you now, but as a dear friend.'

'Ah, but a little birdie told me that might change.'

'Oh, Ricky, you're incorrigible!' But despite being cross with him, Annie found herself smiling and feeling something like a veil lift from around her heart. She turned and beamed at Janey. 'It's a lovely day, mate, and I know that Jimmy's going to make you very happy.'

'Oh, he is, Annie, I love him so much.'

No pain sliced Annie's heart, just a love for her sister. 'Well, you two get off when you can, it's quite a drive to Southend. And you have the best couple of days you've ever had, luv.'

'Ta, Annie, we will.'

They all posed for what seemed like umpteen photos, and then it was time to wave the happy couple off.

Amidst all the hugging and kissing, Jimmy came up to her. 'Ta for today, Annie. We couldn't have got through it if you'd been upset.'

'I've nothing to be upset about, Jimmy. That's all in the past, like your snotty nose and irritating ways when you were a boy.'

Jimmy grinned. Then became serious. 'I still love you, Annie. And look up to you. You're going to make me a smashing sister.'

Suddenly, all animosity left Annie. She leaned forward and kissed his cheek. 'And I love you, too, me big brother . . . Mind, that's in size, not age. I'm still senior to you, and don't forget it.'

He put his head back and laughed out loud. She laughed with him, then was shocked as he took her into a hug – a lovely, brotherly hug.

As she came out of it, she looked around. Mum and Cissy both had hankies to their eyes, and Janey and Rosie had visible tears running down their faces. She looked back at Jimmy. He too was crying.

Realization dawned on her that the pain caused had affected them all, not just her, and not least Jimmy and Janey.

She motioned Janey over and put her arm around them both, though the one she put around Jimmy only reached into the middle of his back. 'Go and be happy, me darlin's. This is how it was meant to be. I love you both . . . Now get going before big sis blows her top at the prospect of you not reaching Southend till after dark! Besides, it's bloomin' freezing and we all need to get inside!'

They both cuddled her. To Annie, it was the ultimate healing. She was all better and could look to her own future.

As the van drove away, with old boots rattling and banging on the floor and everyone cheering and waving, Ricky's hand found hers.

'I know that I promised never to speak about this, and I've already broken that promise once today . . . But I can't help meself. I love you, Annie, I love you with all me heart.'

Annie turned and looked up into Ricky's eyes. 'Never say never, Ricky.'

'Oh, Annie . . .'

'Just give me time, Ricky. I still need that, though what just happened took me a long way forward. I need to go back to Olivia, and be very, very sure . . . You see, I've had me heart broken by one man already and it takes a lot of learning to trust again.'

'I'll never do that to you, Annie . . . Don't make me pay for another man's sins.'

'If you love me, let me come to this in me own time, Ricky. Please, just allow me that.'

'I can wait, luv . . . Will you do one thing, though? Will

you come out with me tonight? I've tickets for the theatre. I got them especially in case you needed cheering up, luv.'

'I will and would love to, if you promise you'll not badger me.'

'Ha. I promise, just for tonight. But I can't say after that.'

His grin made her smile and put them on a lighter footing. She grinned back. 'Well, you'd better keep to it.'

'How long for?'

Annie sighed once more.

'I'm sorry, luv. I'll tell you what, anything along them lines has got to come from you. I'll never mention it again, nor make any suggestions or advances towards you. I'll wait. You deserve that. And while I wait, I'll pray that one day, you will know that you love me – I mean, that you're *in* love with me and want to marry me and have me kids.'

Annie could have burst out laughing, but held it in. Ricky was travelling far too fast . . . kids! But she didn't say this.

'Ta, Ricky. That's the greatest thing you can do for me. I found healing today. But the sores are still just a little raw.'

'I know . . . Right, let's get your mum and Cissy out of the cold. I'll call a cab, eh?'

'That'd be grand, lad, as Cissy would say! I'm frozen stiff too . . . But just a minute . . . Rosie, Rosie, luv!'

Rosie came over to them. 'I was just going to make me way home. Are you all right, luv?'

'I am, luv. We wondered if you'd like to come back to ours and have a bite to eat? We'd love you to.'

'Oh, Annie, you've always been a kind girl. Ta, luv. I was feeling a bit lost then.'

Ricky took her arm. 'Never feel lost amongst family, luv. You're all in-laws now. Ain't that right, Annie?'

'It is. Rosie, you're one of us now . . . But hurry up and get that cab, Ricky, mate, before we all die of cold.'

When they got home, the pot of stew Annie had left simmering on the stove smelled delicious. 'See to the fire, will you, Ricky, while I cut some doorsteps off that loaf Cissy baked.'

'Aye, aye, boss.'

Annie burst out laughing. 'Glad that you know your place, mate.'

To her, it was as if they were back on the friendship footing within which she felt safe.

In the kitchen Annie looked around her and seemed to see it for the first time and what a good job Jimmy had done.

The entrance door was wide enough for Mum to wheel her wheelchair through, something she was adept at doing now; she could manoeuvre it all over the place. And everything in here was low so that she could reach it. And even though it broke Annie's back to work bent over the sink and the surfaces, she thought it an amazing thing for Jimmy to have done.

Even the iron stove had had its legs cut down. Jimmy had sent it off to a blacksmith to do the work, and now it was just the right size for Mum, though she had to sit on a pile of cushions to make her high enough to work with anything hot.

Annie had been amazed, too, at how nimble Mum had become. Having things in her grasp made her determined to make that bit of effort to make the most of them, and so she would slide herself onto one of the kitchen chairs, then pile the cushions onto her chair, before getting herself in place. And all done safely.

This gave her so much more independence and she loved it. She could make tea, spread herself some bread and jam and even make porridge for her breakfast. But best of all was how she had an inside lav and could slide herself on and off it. This had been a revelation to Mum and made her so happy.

When Annie went back into the living room – a large room that Mum could easily get around and which was furnished with a new sofa and chair in brown leather with red cushions too – it all looked lovely. Besides this, Mum had brought along the bits she'd always loved: her dresser and her old footstool that had belonged to her own mum.

But best of all, against one wall stood a piano!

For as long as Annie could remember, Mum had wanted one but even more so since she'd played Olivia's.

The room was now turned into a dining room too, as Cissy had the leaves of the table up, a cloth on it and Rosie stood ready with the cutlery.

Putting the plate piled high with chunks of bread in the centre of the table, Annie told them all, 'I think the best way is for you all to come and grab a bowl and ladle the amount of stew you want into it.'

When they were all sitting, with the fire crackling its pleasure at a new log for its flames to lick, Ricky said, 'I got a couple of bottles of a nice sherry the other day and gave them to Janey to put down here for when we got back. Have you seen it, Vera, luv?'

'Seen it! Me and Cissy have had a tipple out of one of them, luv. And a very good sherry it is as well.'

'Aye, it's grand as owt, lad. I'll get it, it's in the dresser.'

As the laughter flowed as naturally as the golden liquid did into Mum's best sherry glasses, Ricky stood. 'It's me duty as the best man to toast the bride and groom. Ladies and . . . well, me! I give you Jimmy and Janey!'

They all giggled as they raised their glasses.

'And now it is me honour to toast our most beautiful bridesmaid – I give you Annie. Please raise your glasses.'

A huge cheer went up that sounded more like a room full of people instead of just five of them. Annie blushed. 'Ta, everyone. And no one else ask me to do this duty . . . You know what they say, three times a bridesmaid, never a bride! And I've done two already!'

'Ha, and I were thinking of asking you to be mine too.'

They all looked at Rosie.

'Well, I've let the cat out the bag, but, yes, I'm getting married. I know . . . it's about time! Me mum always said I did things in the wrong order . . . Only . . . well, anyway, his name's Alf. He manages me farm in Kent. I were in love with him as a girl, and still am. So, we're getting married now that Jimmy's settled, and the business is doing well. Jimmy can run that now. He can afford to employ workers to do what I do. So, I'm going to be what I was meant to be – a farmer!'

After a moment's silence, Annie clapped her hands. 'That's wonderful news, Rosie. I'm so happy for you, mate . . . Ricky, another toast!'

The glasses were filled up again, and a toast to Rosie given.

Then Mum, her cheeks glowing from a little too much sherry, suddenly said, 'Right, let's have a sing-song now we're tiddly, eh?'

Annie's heart warmed. She'd felt the amazement of discovering this talent her mum had when she'd heard her at Olivia's, despite knowing she played and having a vague memory of her doing so. But how, even with her gnarled fingers, she could master the keys and would play anything she was asked for after just hearing a few lines of a song seemed unbelievable and yet wonderful.

Before long they were all singing 'Down at the Old Bull and Bush' and then 'The Lambeth Walk', but when it came to 'Knees up Mother Brown', Annie would never forget Ricky taking hold of her and kicking his legs up high. His face bright red, his lips stuck in a permanent smile; as to Annie, in that moment, he looked beautiful.

Getting into the spirit of things, she kicked as high as he did while belting out,

'Knees up, knees up, don't get the breeze up, knees up, Mother Brown!'

When it ended, they fell onto the sofa laughing till Annie felt fit to burst. She'd landed on Ricky but found she didn't want to move. His arm came around her and it felt right. She lay against him for a moment, but then warning bells sounded and she jumped up.

'Wow . . . I'm out of breath now and look at this mess!'

'Oh, leave it, luv. It'll do later. But I could do with you helping me to bed, me darlin'. I need a lie down.'

This surprised Annie. She knew her mum could do it all herself now, but then, she thought, it had been a long and emotional day.

'I will, Mum . . . Ricky, I'll see you tonight, luv. I need to get this frock off and have a bit of a rest meself!'

'All right. I'll pick you up at about seven, eh?'

She smiled and nodded, hoping the smile told him that all was all right.

Cissy took the moment. 'You come and have a cuppa with me, Rosie, lass, then we'll get you a cab home. By, I was glad to hear your news.'

'That would be lovely, Cissy, ta . . . And I want you all to come to me wedding. I've plenty of room in me farm-house to put you all up. But I ain't asking you to be bridesmaid, Annie. Not after what you said, luv, but I will ask you, Vera, and you, Cissy, to do that honour for me, as we've become pals since you all moved in here.'

'Ooh, get me! A bloomin' bridesmaid at my age, Annie, luv.' Mum playfully shoved Annie's arm. 'Ha, I'd love it. You can make the frocks, can't you, Cissy?'

'I can, luv, and eeh, they'll be like no other, all frills and knickers!'

The laughter acted as a cover for the feelings Annie was experiencing, and those she knew that Ricky was too.

She was glad of this, and for the respite created, as it would now be easier to keep things normal when she saw him tonight.

What would happen then, she didn't know. She hoped nothing, as she couldn't deal with it all. Not yet, and maybe not for a good while. She really needed to be with Olivia, maybe more than Olivia needed to be with her.

Chapter Twenty-Three

Annie

As she kissed her mum once she was comfortably lying on her bed, Mum took hold of her hand to stop her from leaving.

'Annie, luv, Ricky loves you. Really loves you. You ain't no pipe dream to him. You're real and so is he. He won't let you down in the way that Jimmy did, girl.'

This surprised Annie. Mum had kept neutral about it all and had just been there for both her and Janey.

'Yes, Jimmy did wrong, we all know that. Very wrong by you and by Janey. But it's been handled and you're coming to realize this was how it was meant to be, so just don't lose Ricky as you hang on to the pain of the let-down you suffered. Give him something to hang on to, girl.'

'Don't worry, Mum. It'll all work out. I'm in a better frame of mind about everything and I even found some healing after the service.'

'I know, it was a good moment, luv. I was proud of you.'

'Get some rest now.'

* * *

The evening was magical. The music from The Little Theatre musical *Nine Sharp* stayed with them both as they walked along holding hands.

Ricky behaved and only chatted about the wedding, Rosie's surprise announcement and Mum's playing.

When they said goodnight, Annie allowed Ricky to hold her, needed him to, and she lifted her face to his. 'If I kiss you, Ricky, it won't seem bad of me, will it?'

'No, luv, it'll be something for me to treasure and revisit while you're away.'

The kiss frightened her with the feelings it unleashed and yet she couldn't draw away.

When they did part, Ricky whispered, 'That's all I wanted to know, me darlin'. I'm happy now and I can wait.'

Once more he hugged her before leaving her at the bottom of the fire escape – the stairs that would now lead to Janey's garden, not the one she had planned.

But with the feelings ignited by the kiss still swirling around her, Annie didn't feel any hurt at this but just sighed happily.

Two days later, making the excuse that she had a lot to sort out, not least to take what she and Janey and Mum hadn't wanted from Olivia's cast-offs to the local church for their next jumble, Annie went back to the apartment on the day that Jimmy and Janey were due back.

'Tell Janey that I'll give them a couple of days to settle in, will you, Mum? Then I'll visit them. I don't want to be delayed from going back to Guernsey once I hear from Olivia that there's a boat going, so I need to be ready.'

'All right, me luv. But everything's fine with you, ain't it? You've accepted it all now?'

'I have, Mum, I promise. But I've me own future to sort out, and at the moment, that's going to be with Olivia. She needs me the most right now. Janey will have Jimmy, you and Cissy to see her through till she has the baby, poor Olivia will have no one once Hendrick goes. Though I'll try to visit, and will definitely be back for the birth, or just after, of my little nephew or niece.'

'All right, luv. I'm going to miss you, though, as I'm only just getting used to you being home.'

'I know, I'm sorry, Mum.'

'Don't be. You have your life to live, and God knows mine's a million times better than it was, so you can go and not have so many worries about me, luv.'

'Ta, Mum. Cissy said she'd be in later to make sure you've eaten, so I'll go now.'

Memories assailed her of the mum she used to be – fun-loving, happy, carefree – and how now, though unable to do a lot, how patient, kind and understanding she was.

'I love you so much, Mum.'

Her mum's hand patted hers. 'And I love you, me darling, more than words can say. Be happy, luv. Don't be afraid for ever. Not all men are the same, and what happened to you is something that rarely happens . . . Ricky's a lovely bloke. Don't lose him because you can't let yourself love him.'

Annie put her arms around Mum's neck and leaned on her shoulder. 'I'm so confused and unnerved by it all. When Ricky kissed me, I knew I did love him, but then I thought I loved Jimmy. And, well, I keep thinking, how will I know that the same thing won't happen again? So I stop myself from loving him more than I would love a friend.'

'Well, luv, if it's meant to be, there'll come a time when

you won't be able to do that. Your heart will rule. But let it heal first, me love. Go to be with Olivia and let all of this settle down, eh? Then see how you feel. If it's that you want Ricky, then you will have to choose between him and caring for Olivia. Don't make the wrong choice, me darling.'

'I'll try not to. I'm hoping that all that Hendrick thinks might happen will blow over and he'll be home again. Or, if he has to serve, that it's safe for Olivia to go to be with him wherever he's stationed.'

'Well, Hendrick ain't the only one thinking that things are brewing up for another war . . . But, God, I hope not. The last took a lot from us, another might destroy us.'

'I still remember Dad, you know, Mum. I talk to him and know he watches over me.'

'Me too. He's with me for me every waking hour, and I think he was with Janey when she was so ill . . . You know, that man that she remembered seeing at the end of a tunnel, who she didn't know but knew she loved? I think that was your dad.'

'Yes, I've had the same thought. I'm so glad she didn't go to him, though . . . Mum, you will keep an eye out for any signs that she's hurting herself again, won't you? I still feel terrified by that. I'd never heard of it before, but with you saying that Aunt Rita did it, I'm scared that any upset could trigger Janey into doing it again.'

'I will. I can't see it happening again. She was open about doing it, which Rita weren't, not at first, and not for a long time, so I think that bodes well for Janey. We just have to hope for her, luv, and be here for her if we need to be.'

Annie sighed. 'Yes, you're right, Mum, that's all we can do . . . Anyway, I'd better go. I'll pop my head in and let Cissy know I'm leaving. And don't worry about Janey, it may never happen again. Just keep your eye on things so that you can call on me to come back in plenty of time.'

'All right, luv. Now get going or it'll be dark and then it'll be rush hour.'

The apartment felt cold and lonely. Annie turned the radiators on knowing that Fred would have the boiler in the cellar lit.

She'd left her cases just inside the door and picked up one or two bits of post as she'd come through the lobby, and now sat down and kicked off her shoes and shuffled through it, surprised to see there was a letter for her.

It was from Mrs Wallington.

Dear Annie,

I hope this finds you well.

I was sorry when your sister decided not to take up the post I offered her in response to her enquiry as I sorely need a maid.

I'm writing to ask you if you would like to come back? Olivia told me what had happened. I am very sorry, my dear.

It wasn't that she broke your confidence, it was rather a slip-up as I spoke to her on the telephone after her wedding and asked her if she would soon be going to yours. So, please don't be cross with her.

Then recently she said you were home for Christmas, and she was wondering if you would go back to Guernsey or not, but so wanted you to.

Have you made your mind up, my dear? If you are staying in England, and your family are all right once more, then do consider coming back here. Terms and conditions would be different. Like you were to Olivia, you would be my maid and companion as I feel we are more like friends now.

Looking forward to hearing from you.

My sincere good wishes,

Rosina Wallington

Annie put her head back and smiled to herself as she thought that, yes, she might have considered going back if Olivia hadn't needed her. But now? No, and she would ring Mrs Wallington later to give her apologies.

Her thoughts went to something else that had kept popping into her head, to do with work. She'd not forgotten how she felt when Ricky had told her the story of the lovely policeman who had inspired him to take up the same career.

Often, she'd thought of how he'd said that women police officers did the office work, which she wasn't sure of, but how mostly the young offenders were the responsibility of these women officers and how they followed their cases and assisted at the courts. The idea of it all really appealed to her.

She hadn't discussed it with anyone, not even Ricky, but she somehow knew that she had a calling to that kind of work, and this had grown when listening to Ricky relating tales about his day-to-day life as a policeman. The thought came to her that if she wasn't needed by Olivia, she would fight this urge to run away again and instead begin studying so that, one day, it might be possible.

She closed her eyes and imagined herself in the uniform. Suddenly, to be a police officer was what she wanted more than anything in the world.

Making her mind up that she would ask Olivia if there was a chance that she could work towards getting the school certificate she'd never gained, she got up out of the chair ready to tackle the jobs she needed to do. She so wanted to be ready once Olivia secured a passage for her.

When this was done, the quietness of the apartment began to close in on Annie. She wasn't used to being alone.

Picking up the receiver, she thought to try the police station to see if Ricky was there, or if not, if a message could be got to him. He'd given a number she could use that wasn't for important police business.

It wasn't long before his voice came down the line.

'Are you all right, luv? Nothing's wrong, is it?'

'No . . . well, apart from the fact that I've got Cissy's disease.'

'Oh . . . is Cissy ill? . . . You're not ill, are you, luv?'

'No. I mean that I'm rattling around in this empty apartment, like she did, and so wondered if you would rescue me? Do you fancy going out tonight?'

'Oh, mate. You had me scared there. Yes, of course I will . . . do . . . I mean, are you asking me out on a date? As I'm not like that, you know!'

'Ha! Yes, I am, and you needn't get ideas, I'm asking you as a mate.'

They both laughed.

'Look, I've got to go, Annie. I'm in the middle of writing up me notes. As soon as I've finished, I'm off duty. So, I'll go home and change out of me uniform and jump on the Tube. I should be there in an hour and a half.'

Annie smiled as she knew that could be done, but he'd have to move like lightning.

'That would be lovely, ta, mate. I'm going mad here and I ain't been here five minutes.'

'You've got used to having the family all around you. But I understand why you want to escape for the next couple of days at least.'

'Well, I did have stuff I've got to do . . .'

'I know. Anyway, I don't care where you are, I'll come running when you call, luv . . . How about we have our tea out and then go to the cinema? Me mate were saying that he and his girlfriend went to see *Head Over Heels* starring Jesse Matthews. It's playing at the Astoria which is about fifteen minutes' walk, or we can get a cab . . . It's a musical, and I'd like to see it if you fancy it.'

'Oh, I do. Ta, luv. See you when you get here.'

As soon as she heard the click of the receiver going down, Annie jumped up and ran to the bathroom to have a bath, not acknowledging the feeling racing around her that had been triggered by knowing that Ricky would soon be here. Instead, she put having collywobbles in her tummy down to excitement at going to the cinema, something she'd only done once before in her life and had loved!

Choosing to wear the costume that she'd picked for herself out of the bag of Olivia's cast-offs, Annie did a twirl in front of the mirror.

Ricky had said he'd liked her in blue, and this was a navy blue, which she'd teamed with a light blue blouse. She loved the effect, and how the broad, puffed shoulders accentuated her waist and slim hips.

Her hair had grown quite long lately, so she'd caught it up in a bun as she always did but left a few tendrils around her face to soften the look. Then she did something she'd never done. She delved into Olivia's make-up drawer and applied lipstick to her mouth. It felt and tasted funny at first, but she was pleased with how she'd been able to follow the bow of her own lips and at how stunning it made her look.

Feeling brave, she rubbed a minute amount into the palm of her hand as she'd seen Olivia do, and then carefully dabbed it onto her cheeks before smoothing it out and then wiping off the excess.

The young woman looking back at her just didn't look like her, but a much prettier version. She giggled at her reflection, then leaned forward and said, 'Hussy!'

This made her giggle even more. Yes, the women from her old street would have called her that with her face painted, but this was the more sophisticated West End and none of the ladies would be seen without their make-up. She only hoped Ricky liked it.

When he arrived, he once again looked dapper in his brown striped suit with wide shoulders that made him seem even bigger than he was. With this he wore a white shirt and a brown spotted tie.

'My, you look lovely, luv. I've never seen you looking prettier. Make-up suits you.'

He offered her his arm. 'Your escort for the evening, madam. Where to as we're too early for the film?'

'Oh, Ricky, behave yourself, you idiot . . . Anyway, I was hoping that you had somewhere in mind.'

'There's a pub called the Palace Tavern on Charing Cross Road. Never been, but you can bet they sell pie and mash, which we both love.'

'Up here in the west? You think so? . . . Right, you're on, but I ain't walking, not in these shoes.'

'Righty-oh, mate, a cab it is.'

The pub served them the most delicious pie and mash, which they both were surprised to find in the West End, and both conceded was the best they'd ever tasted with the liquor being just right . . . Well, it at least matched that from Jones's Pie Shop.

Afterwards, the film was magical, and in a strange kind of way helped Annie as the story of the heroine, Jeanne, played by the beautiful Jessie Matthews, was about a girl falling in love, but her partner runs off with another woman. It was then that she met her true love – a man that helped her with a new career. *Will that happen for me? Will Ricky help me to become a police officer? But then, if he did, I wouldn't be like Jeanne in the film, or do what she did, fall back in love with the man who had abandoned her! But will I ever marry Ricky? Oh, I'm so confused!*

As they came out of the cinema and walked along the road to where the cabs stood waiting for fares, Ricky, still caught up in the glamour of the film, suddenly took her hand, twirled her and began to sing:

'These nights
Can't sleep a wink
And I can't even think
And I miss about half of my meals
'Cause I fell
I fell, I fell head over heels in love.'

Looking around and feeling embarrassed, Annie told him, 'Stop it, you idiot!'

But though he let go of her hand, he danced around her and carried on,

'Every night I'm the mooniest one
The juniest one
The looniest one
Love made me the crooniest one
Spring has sprung
Oh, tra-la-la.'

Annie fell about laughing. It no longer mattered what the little crowd gathered thought, but to her surprise, they clapped and cheered. One said, 'Go on, mate, propose!'

Ricky bowed, and then went down on one knee. Annie wanted to shout, *No, go away all of you.*

But she was caught between them and Ricky saying, 'Please, Annie, will you do me the honour and promise one day to marry me?'

For a moment she didn't know what to do. The last thing she wanted was to embarrass Ricky by refusing, but then, he had said one day.

'One day I might, if you stop dancing in the street!'

A cheer went up. 'Well done, mate, you've only to behave yourself and you've bagged the best-looking girl I've seen in a long time.'

Everyone laughed, and Annie joined in with them, though secretly had a tinge of pleasure at being called pretty. She'd never considered herself that.

As the small crowd drifted away, Ricky got up and asked, 'Did you mean it, Annie?'

'Please, Ricky . . . I . . . well, yes, but not yet, not for a long time. I want to talk to you about me ideas for the future.'

'I meant it when I said that I can wait, luv. Shall we go into the same pub again? I could just down a pint to celebrate, what about you?'

'A pint! Beer, you mean? I ain't never drunk any beer, and I ain't starting now.'

'Ha, no, I didn't mean . . . but you do enjoy a little glass of sherry, so you can have one of those.'

'All right. Yes. That would be lovely, ta, Ricky.'

Once they were seated and Annie had taken a sip of sherry,

then coughed when it hit her throat, Ricky said, 'So, what's this about the future?'

'Don't laugh at me, but I want to become a police officer and wanted to ask how I do that – I mean, when Olivia's settled and all right for me to leave her.'

Ricky had his mouth open. 'A policewoman, you mean?'

'Yes . . . I – I just can't stop thinking about what they do and how much I would like to do that.'

'Well! That was the last thing I expected you to say, Annie. But well, you need to have passed your school certificate, and there's an entry exam. Oh, and you need to be able to type, I suppose . . . I mean, that's what they do a lot of. And be a certain height, of course. Five foot four is the minimum, but you are that easily.'

'It's the exam that worries me.' Annie explained how her schooldays were scant at the crucial time and how she was going to ask Olivia about helping her to become educated.

'So, you really mean it then? Only, well, you won't be able to marry me.'

'Oh, Ricky. I – I just feel that I want to do something with my life rather than serve. I mean, of course a police officer serves the community, but, well, mopping and lighting fires. I've broken away from that. Marrying will put me right back there, mate. I want to do something with meself before that happens.'

'You'd never be me lackey, luv. But I understand and will support you in this. I'll speak to some of the women doing it now, eh? Just to give you an idea of what you need.'

'Ta, Ricky.'

'Will you write, and maybe phone me while you're away, luv?'

Annie put her hand over his. 'I will, I promise . . . You know,

I remember me dad saying to me that love can allow many things if it's strong. But the hardest of all for it to bear is separation. I know I'm going to feel that, Ricky, but you know why I have to leave – I want to be sure. I don't know if I will be if I don't follow different paths after the hurt that I've been through.'

'You're right, luv, though it breaks me heart to say so.'

They sat in silence for a while, neither touching their drinks. Their hands were linked. Annie still felt full of anguish – a barrier to letting in the love she should, but though she knew this, she couldn't deny having to find her way before she let herself love Ricky to the exclusion of everything.

'Shall we go, luv?'

Ricky nodded.

Outside they walked to the cab in silence.

Once outside the apartment, they stood at the front door, Annie looking up at Ricky. He looked so forlorn. Hesitating for a moment, she suddenly found herself in his arms.

'Oh, me darlin', me Annie. It's all right. I love you enough to give you all the time you need.'

She lifted her head and looked up at him. 'Ta, luv.'

His lips brushed hers. 'Goodnight, Annie. Don't forget, call and I will come running.'

As he turned away, hot tears ran down Annie's cheeks. For a moment, she could have run after him, but she didn't. She had to believe that she was doing the right thing. That for once what she planned – something just for her – was how she should go forward.

Then, one day, she would be ready to let love in. Ready to fall head over heels. And she knew that would be with Ricky.

Chapter Twenty-Four

Olivia

The telephone ringing as she passed by it made Olivia jump. Picking up the receiver, a voice spoke in German. Then a crackling noise and her beloved Hendrick's voice came down the line – distorted, but his!

'Oh, my darling!'

'Olivia! I can't believe you've answered. That's a huge help as I am calling from a telephone kiosk.'

'Hendrick! Oh, darling . . . But the line isn't clear, my love, you'll have to speak up.'

'I'm near to my father's house. I have so much to tell you, darling, but so little time. You see, as a serving civil servant my letters will all be vetted so will never contain anything other than what concerns our life together. Nothing of what I do or what others are in my life or what is going on around me, so I need you to understand if they seem stilted. They will also praise the regime. But you will know I mean the opposite.'

'Oh, my darling! You sound afraid.'

'I am. But I will get used to it all and will adjust.'

Worry for him caused an ache in Olivia's heart. She still couldn't link his distress and urgency with the world as she knew it and wondered just what was going on in Germany to make him feel so unsafe that he had to take these measures.

Then she understood as he said, 'But, oh, Olivia, I have had to swear my allegiance to, and join the Nazi Party. And I have to do their ridiculous salute and stand to attention every time anyone new comes into the room. I hate it, darling, and all it stands for. Never, ever think that anything they do is me doing it, will you?'

She reassured him that she wouldn't.

'It's huge, darling. You may have read that Hitler had seized power of the German army and put Nazis in charge of every unit? Well, hearing of these things is not like witnessing them. Our youth march through the streets in uniform, they are all indoctrinated. Jews are segregated. I cannot understand it, and yet dare not break the rules and so pass by on the other side of the street to a known Jew.'

Olivia tried to comfort him in his misery, to tell him to think how much help he would be if ever Hitler's threats became a reality, and how he had saved his father's life by doing what he was doing.

But though he was brave and said he would carry on, there was no consoling him. When he broke down, her heart broke too.

'I have to go, darling. There is a queue, I'm afraid someone may hear me. But I do have a system in place for ringing you from now on. Father has a friend with the same views as he has, and who lives in the same block. His house can be accessed through their adjoining attics. His name is Mr Meyer. He has a telephone, so when I can call you, it will be from there that I'll ring with anything important. Otherwise, we will use our code, darling . . . Though, well,

Meyer's wife is a Jew and I fear for her. He says that no one knows about her, and I have checked, and she isn't marked as a Jew. Her family died a long time ago, but I am worried about her and mine and my father's connection to them. Mr Meyer understands that I will never converse with him in public, or even in his garden for fear of my sympathy with the Jews being found out. He and my father are supporting me every step of the way.'

'I am too, my darling. Remember that. I love you, Hendrick.'

The phone went dead. She knew he hadn't disconnected it himself as he would have answered her but guessed his credit had run out.

Reaching for her coat, she called to her father that she was going to walk to the dock to await Annie's boat arriving. She had to do something, or she would go mad.

The walk along the promenade chilled her to the bone as a bitter northerly wind whipped around her. She looked out to sea, saw how rough the waves were and hurried her steps.

As soon as she caught sight of Bertie, the port master, she called out, 'Has the boat from the mainland been cancelled, Bertie?'

'No, this only whipped up a couple of hours ago and wasn't forecast – they rarely get the forecast right these days. Have you someone on the boat?'

'Yes, my friend. You know, Annie, from London, she's coming back.'

'Poor girl had better be a good sailor, or she'll be suffering in this lot.'

Olivia felt full of despair. What with her heart breaking for Hendrick and Annie hating sailing even when the water was calm, her nerves jangled.

279

'So, Hendrick went to Germany then? They say he's serving that Hitler fellow.'

An alarm set up in Olivia. The way Bertie said this was with a disdain bordering on hate. She understood and wanted to yell that he had no choice and would do all he could to undermine the Hitler regime, but she couldn't. Folk had to believe that Hendrick wanted to go, that his alliance was with Germany.

Now more than ever she realized that this must be so, and she must warn Annie of this too. 'Well, he is German. We would all pledge our alliance to our country, Bertie.'

'Aye, I suppose so. But if me country were anything like Germany is, I wouldn't do it.'

Olivia looked away. Had they ever liked or accepted Hendrick, or were they always just polite to him? All at once, Olivia wasn't sure. And with the revelation came fear for herself. What if eventually they turned on her?

Bertie shouting, 'There she blows. Look, on the horizon,' took her attention. She looked in the direction he was pointing and saw the outline of the ship.

'She'll be another hour coming alongside, Olivia. I should come back if I was you. You'll catch your death.'

There wasn't a trace of animosity in his voice now, nor did his kindly smile show any sign of him feeling any towards her. She was being silly. The islanders were bound to disapprove of Hendrick going. She was just oversensitive after their conversation on the phone.

She waved as she left, and Bertie gave a cheerful wave back. A real character, Bertie looked the part, with his red face, twinkly eyes and long beard. He was an important man to the islanders and had the last say for those with boats as to whether they could sail out or not. Some said he was involved in smuggling between the islands, too. And Olivia knew you had to give him a backhanded payment at times to be able to leave the shore and most felt it wise to give him a share of their catch if they'd been out fishing. But for all that he was a loved and respected man, so Olivia feared that if he expressed views against Hendrick serving in Germany, then the mood of the whole island would be one of antagonism towards her beloved husband.

After going for a walk to nowhere in particular, Olivia felt better as she met others out and about and found that everything was as it always was. People greeted her, some stopped for a chat, others even asked after Hendrick.

To those that did, she told them about her news of expecting a child and revelled in their congratulations, hugs and promises of giving her help if she needed it. A few even said they would get busy with their knitting needles!

It all helped to lift Olivia, especially as she'd realized that Hendrick hadn't even mentioned their unborn baby or asked how she was. This, above anything, told her just how upset he really was, and she wondered if he would cope and be able to pull off his guise of being a true Nazi!

Fear clutched her. The regime in Germany sounded ruthless and unfeeling. *Oh, my darling, be careful and be strong.*

The walk back to the port side did little to clear Olivia's head. But by the time she arrived there she was calling herself all sorts of silly beggars for letting her imagination run riot along paths that would give her nightmares. She'd to be strong too . . . Could she be?

It seemed like moments before she was in Annie's hug and still thinking these thoughts, when she'd imagined that

Annie just being here would be able to wipe them all away and make everything better.

'Oh, it's good to have you here, Annie. Are you all right? Were you seasick?'

'No, though me legs feel like jelly. I reckon they're proper sea legs now, luv, as there were a few in distress, but I managed all right.'

'Oh, I'm glad . . .'

'Olivia! You're crying. Oh, luv, they don't look like tears of joy at seeing me either . . . We're together now, luv. You'll be all right. You can bet that Hendrick will be back before you know it.'

'He telephoned—'

A voice interrupted her.

'Can I take your bag for you, miss? Oh, hello, Miss Olivia . . . Is everything all right?'

Young Joe, Bertie's son, who had most likely come to act as a porter, came up to them.

'And I didn't realize it was you, Annie. Nice to see you back with us. Do you need a hand with anything?'

'If you can see Annie's bags are delivered to my house, Joe, thank you. Here . . .' Olivia searched for her purse and put a coin into Joe's open hand. *Like father, like son*, Olivia thought, but it made her emotions settle as this was something normal to everyday island life.

As Joe nodded and touched his cap, she told him, 'And my tears are those of joy, Joe. Haven't you ever shed them?'

'I have, Miss Olivia, when I got me first wage packet. I still have it unopened in me drawer.'

'Ha, Joe, you should read the Parable of the Three Servants.'

Joe looked bewildered, as did Annie.

'Well, if you're given something, or earn it, you should

always do your best to make that an even better and bigger prize by investing it. Let me see, you began work here at the age of thirteen . . . about four years ago? Well, suppose you earned sixpence. Now, if you had put that into my father's bank, by now you would have a shilling or more, and yet you still only have the sixpence! That way you will never reap the rewards of your labours – the man in the parable who buried his coin wasn't let into the kingdom of God but had to be in no-man's land and would be gnashing his teeth for ever.'

'Flipping 'eck, Olivia, that's all a bit deep and religious, ain't it?'

Olivia laughed, glad of the distraction. 'Well, it's all there in the Bible, love.'

'I ain't much for religion, Miss Olivia, and I didn't think you were, but I tell you what, you've made me think. When I get home tonight, I'm going to take me money out of me drawer and try to double it.'

Annie must have felt sorry for him, as she took out her purse and handed Joe a coin too, saying, 'There you are, that'll help you to begin with. That's for taking me bags, Joe. It's already doubled what Olivia gave you. Ta, mate. See you around, eh?'

Once they were out of hearing, they giggled over the incident and Olivia linked in with Annie. 'I don't want to go home yet, love. Shall we go to Florrie's? Could you stomach a hot cup of tea and a cake?'

'I bloomin' well could, luv. I didn't eat on the boat just in case that set me off. I tell you, I was scared at times, Olivia, luv. But it was worth it to be with you. How have you been? I'm so excited about your news, and with Janey's too! You're leaving me behind, the pair of you.'

'Oh, Annie, I've worried about that, dear. Are you all right about everything?'

'I am. I've a lot to tell you and to ask you, and well, I think me future will change, and I'll achieve things.'

They were sitting in Florrie's cafe, just a few minutes' walk from the quayside, with the delicious smells of baking and the chatter of others gathered to take afternoon tea making a cosy atmosphere, before Olivia felt able to ask, 'What things? Have you made plans, Annie?'

To say she was amazed by all that Annie told her was an understatement, but happy too. So very happy that Annie was thinking of making a niche for herself and had ambitions, and more than happy that one day Ricky would feature in those.

'How exciting, love. I can help you. We can get a tutor for you . . . Only, Annie, I have an idea too. I'm thinking that you and I could go and live in mine and Hendrick's farmhouse, once it is completed. You see, I'm hoping our furniture was in one of those crates on the boat, as the last I heard, it was at the docks on the mainland awaiting shipment. If it is, I should receive a notification from the warehouse here soon, and then we can furnish the flat upstairs and once we're sorted, I could help you with basic maths and English until you feel confident enough to have a tutor.'

'Ta, Olivia. I would love that, and living out at the farmhouse too. Ooh, I'm excited now and ain't bothered about me job. I'll give me notice in at the sweet shop.'

'And wouldn't it be lovely if Ricky could visit? He'd be comfortable out there with just us two and the daily I intend to employ.'

'Oh, he would . . . But I'd rather wait a while. I keep raising his hopes and then letting him down with a thud. I don't want to treat him like that any more. He knows where we stand now.'

'Well, we'll go to England, eh?'

'England? To live, you mean?'

'I have thought of it. I'm bored here.' Olivia didn't say that she was afraid too, as still it played on the back of her mind how Bertie had been about Hendrick. 'I love London.'

'Blimey, mate, I've only just got off the bloomin' boat. I don't want another journey like that, and you won't be bored now I'm here. You're missing Hendrick and that's making you feel restless and want to take flight. You need an aim, we both do. Mine will be to get meself educated, but what about you? Ain't there anything you've ever wanted to do? I mean, being a language teacher and having a school are really Hendrick's ambitions that you've gone along with.'

'I suppose they are. Though I have always wanted to teach, but young children, not older students that we would expect to come to live in at the farm from all over the world.'

'Well then, why not do that, luv? Why not teach children?'

'I can't now, not now I'm pregnant, the local school wouldn't entertain me.'

'But what about other types of classes and running them at the farm? You must have other talents. And I'd help you.'

'As it happens, I play the piano to teaching standards.'

'Really! See, you've never mentioned that or ever played the one at your home.'

Olivia felt stunned. It was as if Annie had made her realize that she'd taken on all that Hendrick wanted to do as being what she wanted to do too. Along the way she'd lost her own identity. All her ambitions were Hendrick's. How did that happen? How could she have known Annie all this time and not even mentioned that she had high grades in piano playing?

'You look as though a light bulb's been switched on inside your head, luv.'

'It has. Let's go home, Annie, I've an urge to play the piano.'

As they finished their tea, Annie chatted about Janey's wedding.

'It was good to hear Mum play again, and Ricky was as daft as a brush. He got hold of me and made me do "Knees up Mother Brown"!'

It was lovely to see Annie so animated, funny and, well, living life with the outlook she always used to have before she was hurt so badly.

'Your Ricky is a dark horse! I thought him a serious young man, I didn't see him as an all-singing, all-dancing person.'

They laughed then as Annie told of the night they went to the cinema. 'I tell you, Olivia, he really showed me up. I could have killed him!'

'He got a promise from you, though, didn't he?'

Annie blushed, the kind of blush that admitted that Olivia was right. 'Oh, Annie, love, I'm so happy . . . I know you aren't planning anything just yet, but technically, you are engaged! Congratulations!'

Annie's blush deepened, but she didn't deny anything, just smiled happily. For Olivia, it was so lovely to see Annie find healing and happiness, even if she was denying herself the path it took. But then, as she sipped the last of her tea, a thought occurred to her. 'Oh, Annie, you haven't put your own life on hold for me, have you?'

'No, silly. I haven't put it on hold even. I told you, I want to be a policewoman and I'm going to do it, Olivia. It just might take time, but Ricky is prepared to give me that.'

'I haven't taken that in yet! A policewoman! Oh, Annie, you'll make a perfect one.'

'Ta, luv.'

As they walked home, they linked arms and chatted about this and that and Olivia began to feel that she could cope as long as she had Annie by her side. She made her mind up. If Annie did have to go back to the mainland, then she would go to.

When they reached home, they only took time enough for Annie to freshen up and unpack before going to the drawing room where the piano was, and Olivia sat down to play.

She chose a gentle piece: Beethoven's 'Moonlight Sonata'.

After a moment, Annie said, 'Oh, that's lovely. It makes me think of a child skipping along in the rain, and then when that deeper sound suddenly comes in, it's as if he's jumped into a puddle!'

'Well, I've never heard it described like that before, Annie. You've an ear for music, love. Did you ever want to be like your mum and play?'

'I've never thought about it. You see, she had to sell Granny's piano when I was little to help get us through. She and Granny sold a lot of stuff just to keep us going. Though I've never heard her play anything like you've just played, and I don't think she even had lessons. She told me once that she just tinkered on me granny's piano and found she could just play tunes.'

'She does what they call "playing by ear", I should imagine. I can do that too. We should have a knees-up of our own. That would really cheer me up.'

'Do you know any London songs?'

'I've heard a few on the radio and those that your mum played are still in my head. I love them, they always lift you and make you want to laugh, or like you and Ricky: dance and act the fool.'

'Well, try one now then, eh?'

Olivia thought a moment. 'Well, the one that comes to mind is "Any Old Iron". It reminds me of hearing the rag and bone man going along the streets of London.'

After a moment of humming and tinkling with the piano notes, Olivia had the tune and how to play it. It only took a couple of trial runs before they both belted out the lyrics and Annie began to strut up and down in time to the tune. It ended with Olivia bent double over the piano and Annie having to flop into a chair as they both became helpless with laughter.

When at last they sobered, Olivia rose and opened her arms. Hugging Annie made everything right in her world.

Chapter Twenty-Five

Annie

The weeks seemed to fly by. Here they were in the third week of May and living what to Annie was an ideal life.

She was loving her studies and had taken her school certificate in record time. Now she waited anxiously for the results. But it was learning to type that she'd loved the most.

Olivia's father had given her an old machine out of his office, and she'd practised and practised, even sent typed letters home! Till now she could do thirty words a minute without looking at the keyboard, and Olivia's father had arranged for her to take a typing exam too.

It seemed that life was falling into place and it was for her a wonderful holiday as the sun always seemed to shine, getting unseasonally hot enough in the afternoons to allow them to sit outside and rest, as they completed any work they had to do in the cooler mornings.

Olivia had several clients now, old and young, teaching them all music and piano or helping them to learn their own instrument. They were all at various levels and getting them through exams seemed to help her to cope with her longing to be with Hendrick.

Hendrick hadn't made it home on leave yet but at last had permission to come the moment the baby was born. Something Annie knew was encouraging Olivia on as she had flagged a lot lately.

Looking up from Ricky's letter, Annie's stomach muscles clenched with excitement, and yet worry too, that she might be too late to go after her dream.

Ricky had said that there was to be a recruitment drive for women officers and that if she was serious about joining, then she should come home and apply. As far as he knew it was scheduled to take place at the beginning of July.

Sighing, Annie looked over at Olivia sitting next to her on a deckchair in the garden. *How will she take the news that I want to go home?*

She was determined that she wouldn't even think of it if the baby wasn't born, which she felt sure wouldn't be long now. Due in June, with an estimate of the first week given by the doctor, Olivia was always tired, and the heat got her down.

But it wasn't just the birth. Olivia would need her after, too, to help care for her child.

Sighing even more heavily, Annie stood. 'I'll go and get you some of that lemonade I made, luv. You look hot and thirsty . . . and, well, I need to talk to you.'

'Oh, that sounds ominous, Annie.'

'It is a bit. As it could mean that changes are afoot.'

Olivia sat up. She went to say something, but then seemed to change her mind. Annie hurried away. She needed to prepare for what she knew would devastate Olivia but was pulling at her so strongly that she didn't think she would resist going.

When Annie came back, Olivia sat staring out to sea, her

expression creased with worry. 'I've put the drinks in the shade as I think we should move as the sun is right above us now. Give me your hand, luv, and I'll pull you up.'

This caused them to giggle over the next few minutes as they tried to get Olivia's bulk upright. They managed it eventually by gently rolling her over till she was on all fours and then Annie could help her to stand.

They were both panting with the exertion.

'Right, these chairs are going in the shed, mate, and ain't coming out again till your baby's born. We'll sit on the basket ones. That near killed me pulling you up, you lump!'

Again, they were laughing as Olivia exaggerated her waddle to get to the table and four chairs that stood under the tree.

After a couple of sips of the lemonade, Olivia asked, 'So, what's happening, Annie, love? Is it to do with Ricky's letter?'

'It is. The police force is recruiting women.'

Olivia sat up straight. 'Oh, Annie, you're going home!'

Annie could only nod.

They fell silent.

Olivia broke it. 'Annie, there's no question that you must go, love. You're ready. I just know you'll have passed your typing certificate, so that won't be a problem.'

Annie knew that saying this had cost Olivia dearly.

'But what about you? You will need help with the baby.'

Olivia's reply both shocked her and pleased her. 'I'll come too. We'll live in the apartment together. Cissy will help me while you're out at work . . . But no, of course she can't, she'll be helping Janey!'

'I know. I thought of that, and it helped me as I have been torn lately by wanting to be home for Janey's baby's birth, but as you say, she does have Cissy, so I won't go unless you have your child.'

'Well, if I come too, we'll all manage. I can keep house and look after my baby, and you can go out to work. I'll have a nice hot dinner ready for you when you come home.'

Annie burst out laughing. 'You make it sound like we'd be an old married couple. But it will work, I'm sure. It's what mums have to do, and I have faith that you can do it too, luv.'

'That's settled then, and if I'm not able to go at the same time as you, I will follow when I can.'

Annie felt a weight lift off her shoulders and could see that Olivia was happy.

'It all fits in with my plans anyway, Annie, as I have told my clients that the lessons will cease when my baby is born and probably won't start again until it's one year old. They were disappointed but most have a good grounding now. Some were already quite advanced when they came to me, but others will always be beginners. I've told them, too, that when we do resume, I'm going to start a band and a choir.'

'Ooh, a choir, I'd love to join one of those.'

'And you should. You have a lovely voice, love.'

'Ta very much. I've only ever sung music hall songs but would love to try my hand at ballads. Some of those we listen to are lovely. My favourite is "Too Marvellous For Words". I love Bing Crosby.'

On saying this, Annie burst into song:

'You're just too marvellous
Too marvellous for words
Like glorious, glamorous
And that old standby amorous!'

They burst out laughing once more.

'Amorous . . . ha-ha, neither of us are that at the moment, Annie! But, oh, I wish.'

Annie felt herself blush. She sometimes had the same thought even though she'd never experienced it like Olivia had. More and more she wanted to and had often explored down below, wanting to feel what it was like. Always she was thinking of Ricky when she did. Now she might see him soon and this made her heart flutter.

As if this had been said out loud, Annie looked away. 'Oh, look at that seagull! Noisy beggar, but I ain't seen one that big before.'

'Annie, you're changing the subject. Look, it's right that you go home. And when you do, marry your Ricky, eh?'

It was sometimes as if Olivia was under her skin and knew her most intimate thoughts. If only she could just do that, go home, tell Ricky she loved him and had missed him so much, marry him and feel the completion of herself, but something compelled her to keep focused on her ambition or she might regret it for ever. At last she had a chance to do something for herself and not others.

'I can't, Olivia. Married women can't become policewomen and I just want to achieve that one thing!'

'Well, jump into bed with him then!'

'Olivia!'

'Sorry, I didn't mean to embarrass you, love, but well, you're missing out and you shouldn't be. I am, I know, but I couldn't anyway now, and at least I know what it is I can look forward to.'

Olivia gave a heavy sigh and patted her bump. 'Come on, little one, come early for Mummy, eh? Then when daddy comes home . . .'

'It will be just too marvellous
Too marvellous for words
Like glorious, glamorous
And that old standby amorous!'

This did it. They'd never spoken in this manner before and it hadn't been comfortable for Annie, but Olivia had turned it into being hilarious, and this made them helpless with laughter. When they calmed, Annie felt exhausted so couldn't imagine what Olivia felt like. Suddenly she knew.

'Oooh, Annie! Annie, I'm all wet! My waters have broken!'

Shock took away Annie's laughter. She stood and stared at the puddle between Olivia's legs.

'Oh, Annie, help me! My baby's coming!'

It seemed that something took over Annie as she suddenly felt in command. 'Sit still a moment, luv, we have time. Don't be afraid. I'll go and ring the doctor to get him on the way, and then I'll help you upstairs to your bed. We have everything ready; it only needs laying out . . . Ooh, Olivia, you'll be a mum by tonight, me darlin'.'

For an answer, Olivia screamed and clutched her stomach.

Annie ran inside. Her mum once told her that there were those who brought the house down when giving birth and those that did it all in silence. She'd said that she was a screamer herself. Well, if that's what Olivia wanted to do, that was all right by her!

Hours later Olivia was still screaming. And not only that but cursing too. What she was going to do to Hendrick didn't bear thinking about; the latest was to cut off his balls and hang them on the line to shrivel in the sun!

Annie was past being shocked at what Olivia came out with,

294

and was no longer embarrassed by it, but just worked tirelessly, bathing Olivia down with sponges dipped in cold water, giving her drinks, massaging her back and anything else that Olivia wanted or the nurse, who the doctor had sent over, asked her to do.

At last, the nurse said that Olivia could push.

It was then that she gained control and put all her effort into giving birth. Within an hour, the room was filled with the wonderful sound of a newborn's cry and the nurse saying, 'You have a lovely little boy, Olivia. And he's got a good pair of lungs on him!'

Olivia burst out crying, then laughed, then cried again. Annie joined her in each emotion, then couldn't believe her eyes as she looked down on mother and son – never had she seen a more beautiful sight.

'So, what are you going to call him?' the nurse asked.

'Karl Hendrick.'

'Oh, German names. Well, I suppose his dad is one of them.'

Annie felt incensed. She wanted to scream out that yes, Hendrick was a German, but he wasn't 'one of them', which implied he was to be hated and mistrusted. But Olivia's look told her not to react.

After taking the baby, bathing him and then swaddling him and putting him to Olivia's breast, the nurse said, 'Well, Miss Olivia, you have Annie with you, so I'll get off.' To Annie she said, 'Just get Olivia a nice cup of tea and a bite to eat, Annie. And call me if you have any concerns. I'll call in every day to check you and baby over, Olivia, but all should be fine now. And congratulations.'

'Thank you, Nurse. My father will settle your bill. You've

been a big help and made me feel I was in safe hands . . . I'm sorry about my swearing and carrying on.'

'Don't even think about it, dear. You should hear some, they could teach you a thing or two about what to do with hubby's parts, but they all go back for more.' The nurse laughed as she left.

'Oh, Annie, I can't believe I said those things. I don't know where they came from.'

'Ha, it was funny. Like listening to the near-the-mark comedians at the music hall! Mind, me mum would have washed me mouth out with soapy water if I'd have said them!'

'Well, make sure she's not with you when you give birth then.'

This made them laugh.

But the mood changed as Olivia spoke to little Karl who was hungrily sucking away at her breast.

'Well, Karl, welcome to the world, my darling. I love you so much and Daddy will too.'

Olivia burst into tears. 'I want Hendrick. Oh, Annie, I want him here with me.'

Annie was at a loss as to what to say. Nothing could be the right thing. So, she just climbed onto the bed, knelt behind Olivia and held her. Her own tears stung her eyes. Suddenly they seemed like two lonely women with no man to support them and the responsibility of a baby to care for.

But then she thought, is this how a policewoman should react? And with the thought her strength came back into her.

'I think a cup of tea is in order, luv. You put Karl to your other breast now, while I go and get us both one. The little chap needs a variety, you know, and your left one might give him a different flavour!'

They were giggling again and the morose feelings that had taken them lifted.

While Olivia drank her tea, saying it was the best one she'd had in her life, Annie held Karl. His little fingers curled around hers. His eyes were closed, and he looked so beautiful that her love flowed for him. She ran her hand over his mop of black hair. *I'll always be here for you, little man. I'm your Aunty Annie!* The thought made her think of Janey and wonder how she was faring. In her letter she sounded so happy, and always said she was well and loved being pregnant. That Jimmy was the kindest man and always attentive to her. This had all settled her mind, and yet now, she felt a twinge of guilt at being here for Olivia but not for her own little sister.

The pain she'd suffered through Janey's and Jimmy's love seemed like a distant memory she couldn't recall now, and she was glad it had happened. If it hadn't, she would never have met her Ricky. And yet it had been the very thing that had sent her running away from him. Now, she wished with all her heart she hadn't reacted like that. Who knew, she might have been looking forward to the birth of her own child!

This thought stopped her in her tracks. These feelings she had were sending her off the track that she was determined to travel. But why she needed to prove to herself that she could achieve something in life, she just didn't know. She only knew it was a burning ambition that took precedence over all else. Marriage and baby thoughts had to wait.

Three weeks later, the second week of June, Hendrick arrived, and both were to see Annie onto the boat within a few days. She had her precious certificates and had applied for the position of trainee policewoman, giving the apartment in

London as her address. Cissy had picked up a letter for her and telephoned her telling her that an application form that was pages long had arrived and was to be lodged by the last day of July.

Before she left, Karl's christening was to take place, and as the day approached, she and Olivia were arranging for a luncheon to be served in the garden afterwards.

They bought a ham and cooked it to serve it cold with salad and crusty bread, which they were busy baking. Annie had tried her hand at making a fruit cake and was pleased with the result as they both set about decorating it, giggling as the icing ran off it at first because it was too thin, but then pleased with how it looked when finished.

Hendrick had been very quiet and seemed like a different man. It was as if he had lost all that confidence that made him debonair, and become almost wooden, waiting to be told what to do and obeying every command.

In a moment on their own Olivia expressed her concern over this. She wiped a tear from her eye as she said, 'It's as if they've drained all he was from him and replaced it with a compliant being. He's just not my Hendrick.'

Annie put her arms around her. 'Give him time, luv. We don't know what he's experienced. When the christening is done and I'm gone, you will be together on your own, then he may talk to you, and you can help him.'

'But I won't have long, not the six weeks we thought we would have.'

'Oh no, why?'

'It's to do with Czechoslovakia. Hitler wants it to be part of the Reich as it was part of the Sudetenland, which all belonged to Germany at one time. We were reading about it, remember? Well, Hitler has talked of attacking Czechoslovakia, but they are putting troops on their borders. Hendrick will be needed as part of the negotiation team as talks are expected to go on between many countries . . . It's just awful, I hate Hitler. Hendrick doesn't think it will stop there even if he is successful. He sees Hitler as a man who wants power over the whole world!'

'Oh, Olivia, it's all scary. But I'm so sorry how it's affecting you, luv. Have you never considered going to live in Germany with Hendrick?'

'I have but Hendrick won't hear of it now. If we don't see each other for years, he would rather that than me go and live there and to be part of it all . . . And, Annie, well, Hendrick isn't keen on me coming to the mainland to be with you.'

'Why?'

'He feels that it wouldn't look good. For all Chamberlain's appeasement, Hitler doesn't look on Britain as being a friend. Hendrick thinks that once the regime knows I am in England, they may try to use me to their own ends.'

'Spy for them, you mean? But how would you do that?'

'Father has a lot of connections. I never got involved with them – they are all monied and powerful, they have dealings with Father's bank. In the financial world he is a very import-ant figure. He could get me into circles where I would be party to gossip that was truth – if that makes sense. Father says he learns such a lot when on the mainland and associ-ating with them all.'

'Oh, Olivia, it's like we ain't in the know of what's really going on. We read the paper and listen to the wireless, but it seems now that they are only telling us a small part of it.'

'They are. Hendrick is very worried. He feels that if anything happens, I will be safer here. I won't be expected to know anything useful and the island is well protected. He wants me to stay.'

'And are those he works for happy with that?'

'They seem to be . . . . Oh, I could murder my so-called father-in-law. He's never bothered to visit. He doesn't even write to me. I've heard nothing from him since Karl was born. I mean, his first and only grandson! He took little interest in Hendrick when he was growing up, and yet Hendrick adores him and has put his life, and ours, in danger to save the bloody coward's skin!'

Apart from during labour, Annie had never heard Olivia swear, but now she didn't blame her. She felt like swearing herself.

'I feel helpless, mate. I ain't that knowledgeable about everything as you are, but what I do know frightens me. I've only recently found out there was a country called Czechoslovakia. Do the folk that live there want to be given to Hitler?'

'A lot do as they are German-speaking and consider themselves German, but then again, a lot don't, poor things.'

'Well, I feel sorry for them who don't want to be part of the Nazi regime. Mind, I hope that Hitler fellow never sets his sights on Britain, as he'll have a fight on his hands. Even the women would be out bashing him with their saucepans.'

The laughter that followed this lightened the moment and Annie was glad. Her heart thudded with fear for what the future held when all she wanted was the happiness of those she loved, her own fulfilment of her ambitions and then to be Ricky's wife and mother to his kids.

This thought shocked her as she realized how important the last bit was. It set up a longing in her heart for the days to pass and for her to be in Ricky's arms. So strong was the feeling that she almost gave up the idea of being a police-woman and wanted to begin life with Ricky instead. And with this came a true understanding of how being separated from Hendrick felt for Olivia.

'I need to hug you, Olivia.'

'Oh, where did that come from? . . . Oh, Annie, I've upset you. I'm sorry. It's hard facing everything, and for me to think of doing that without Hendrick was made easier by having you. It breaks my heart that that won't be so now . . . But that's of no matter. You must go, love, you must.'

They hugged as if this was the last time they would do so. Both cried on each other's shoulders. For a moment, Annie wanted to say she would stay. But suddenly, it seemed to her that there was an urgency to everything. As if time was running out.

She mentally shook herself. Of course it wasn't, she was only twenty-three! She had her whole life to live. She just wouldn't give thought to all that scared her about what Olivia told her but look forward to a future where she was a respected member of society.

That's what she wanted. She wanted to be the one that people looked up to, not the maid, not ever again the maid.

Olivia had given her this freedom of thought, treated her as an equal. Well, now she wanted to be treated like that by all. Being a policewoman would do that for her, besides fulfilling her need to help the young kids just like the policeman that Ricky told her about, and he was doing himself.

The day before she left, as if being given a gift to go home to, Annie had a phone call to say that Janey had given birth to a little girl!

To Annie, this soothed her sadness at leaving Olivia, which had hung like a cloud over them both.

'It's wonderful news, Annie, I'm so glad it's over for Janey. Soon it will be a memory, and she'll be as happy as I am with my Karl and have lots of cuddles – well, that's when Hendrick doesn't get to him first!'

'Well, poor Hendrick only has a little time with him and it's good that they are forming this bond.'

'It is, and lovely to see . . . Oh, Annie, when will I see you again?'

'I'll come back for a holiday, I promise. Ricky told me that after the few months of training are complete – if I get the job, that is – then I will be given leave. I'll bring him with me if he can get the time off.'

'In that case, make it your honeymoon, love.'

'Oh, Olivia, you're obsessed with me marrying! But not this time, luv, maybe next as all me leaves will be spent over here with you.'

Then a cheeky thought came to her. 'I might just take your other advice, though!'

Olivia looked bemused.

'You know, when you said what I should do if I didn't marry when I got home.'

As the penny dropped, Olivia burst out laughing. 'You do that, love, but make sure Ricky is careful or you'll be a shotgun bride!'

Olivia had become her confidante. She understood and dispelled the myths. She was free-thinking and easy to talk to on any subject. There were no longer any mysteries or scary bits about making love – like how painful she'd heard it was the first time as Olivia had told her the reality of some women experiencing discomfort, but for most there was no pain, just a soreness for a few seconds, and had gone on to explain what physical change happened to a woman's body to mean she was no longer a virgin and how she'd read about it all in books bought by her father for her.

'He'd been so embarrassed as he thought if I'd had a mother, she would have helped me with it all. But he obviously hadn't read it! It was meant to help me understand my periods when they started, but most of it read like a horror story to an eleven-year-old!'

'I don't think I could've taken it all in then. Me mum just said, "Well, you're a woman now, you just have to get on with it," and then ripped up some rags for me to use! After that, I heard tales from other girls and picked up what I could.'

The liberation they both felt from speaking openly on these subjects, and even a little crudely about them at times, led them to say that if ever they had daughters, they would tell them everything, not leave them to wonder and become afraid by the untrue tales.

For Annie, it was as if suddenly, everything in her life seemed to be a wonderful adventure to look forward to, not to fear, and not even Hitler could spoil that for her!

Chapter Twenty-Six

Annie

As soon as Annie stepped off the boat she was in Ricky's arms and being kissed by him and was kissing him back.

When he looked down at her, still holding her, he had tears in his eyes.

'Annie? Oh, Annie!'

'I love you, Ricky. I love you with all my heart. I've longed for this moment.'

His tears spilled over and matched her own. He seemed unable to speak, just repeat her name.

She clung to him. 'I've missed you, luv. We need to talk, but I want to see Mum and Janey and meet me little niece, and see Cissy too.'

'I'll take you to them, they are all waiting, and I have a surprise for you as well. I've bought a car!'

'That's wonderful.'

'Yes. Jimmy saw it for sale. He knew I was looking out for one, so bought it and then sold it to me . . . Ha, he said it was for the same price he got it, but I ain't sure of that – him being an East End trader, he's a proper wide boy.'

Annie found that the mention of Jimmy didn't affect her

in any way. She just giggled with Ricky. 'As long as you're happy with it and what you paid for it that's all that matters, luv.'

'I am, it's a nineteen thirty-two Austin Seven. That's it over there, the cream and black one. So, madam, your carriage awaits you!'

Ricky seemed like a big kid to her at that moment, full of joy and excitement. She wasn't sure if it was her arrival that had done that or his new car, but it was lovely to see.

On the journey he held her hand whenever he could safely let go of the steering wheel. After a while he asked, 'So, can we have that talk you spoke of? Now seems a good time.'

'Yes, luv, it'd be good to get it off me mind as it's partly about me fears for the future. Hendrick has told us such a lot of what is going on – a sort of background to what we read in the papers or hear on the wireless set. And he seems afraid. He says he has nothing specific to tell us yet, but when he does . . . Well, we might be involved.'

'How? I ain't following you, Annie.'

'It's something we would never think would be asked of us, but Hendrick is so serious about it all . . . He wants to pass on information to Olivia and for her to give it to us – you and me. But no one is to know of it except . . . well . . . he wants me to go along to the Defence Ministry and ask to speak to someone about how he wants to help by passing on secrets. He says that they will know how to proceed.'

'What? My God, Annie, I never dreamed you would say anything like that! Hendrick wants to make us into spies?'

'Yes. It's for our country, Ricky. He thinks you are ideal as being a police officer you will already have sworn your allegiance, and I would be the perfect vehicle, as he called me, for Olivia to pass things on to. She will speak in code . . . I've been trying to learn it. I have the principles of it written down, though, so can keep trying. Olivia will start giving me pretend messages from now so we can both practise.'

'I can't take this in, luv. And yet, a part of me is excited by it. I think I need to discuss it with my senior first and see what he says. If he thinks it's something I should pursue, then I'll do it, one hundred per cent, and I can see you've made your mind up to do it.'

'I have, but I'm scared for Hendrick. He'll be shot if he's found out . . . It's one of the reasons he wouldn't let Olivia come over with me. And anyway, he thinks too that if war did break out, Guernsey would be the safest place for her and Karl.'

'He thinks it might then?'

'Yes, he does. He is making so many preparations. He just doesn't seem to be the same man. It's as if trying to save us all is his mission, and yet he's not able to . . . Look, I know I ain't making sense, mate, but it's scary being around him. Poor Olivia is hoping that being on their own for a couple of weeks she can help to put his mind at rest. But I don't think she will be able to.'

'It sounds like he knows more than he is telling, though it can't be specific or he would pass it on. I feel sorry for the bloke. It's like he's being torn in two. Well, if them in authority over me allow it, I'll help all I can.'

'Ta, Ricky. I know it ain't easy for you to take this in. I found it hard to at first, but being with Hendrick it becomes real somehow.'

'I can see that but must admit this was the last thing I thought we'd be talking about.' He squeezed her hand. 'I imagined – hoped, by the tone of your letters – that things had changed for you where we were concerned, and that would be what we would talk about . . . your plans and our plans for a future together. But are you still going ahead with your application, luv?'

'I am, Ricky. If I don't, I know I will regret it for ever. Are you all right with that, mate?'

'Well, yes, but not the bit about not being able to marry. Oh, luv, I hoped . . . I dreamed, but it doesn't matter. At least you will be with me, not across the sea. I'll be patient, luv.'

'Ta, Ricky.' She wanted to say that he needn't be that patient, but she couldn't, it would make her sound like a loose woman. But she would show him. She wouldn't be able to stop herself.

As soon as they pulled up outside the flats, Cissy came running out. 'Annie! Annie, lass. Eeh, me little love, am I pleased to see you!'

When Cissy hugged her, it truly made her know she was home, as she smelled of baking and freshly laundered clothes, as she always did.

Jimmy came out next. Without any embarrassment, he came over to her and hugged her too. 'Good to see you, mate.' His face beamed.

Annie couldn't believe how it just felt normal, like greeting a member of the family. 'So, you and Janey have given me a little niece? Ta, Jimmy. I can't wait to meet her.'

As she turned back to the car to get her handbag, Annie caught Ricky watching her. She smiled at him. He visually relaxed and smiled back.

They went into Mum's flat first.

Annie's tears spilled over to see her lovely mum looking so well and smiling a smile that wasn't marred by pain. Rosie was with her. She didn't rush forward but allowed Annie to get to her mum. When she did, they cuddled, they cried, they laughed at themselves, told how they had missed each other, and then shared the happiness of Annie not going away again and the new little girl in their lives.

Rosie gave her a lovely hug after that. 'It's good to have you back, girl. And I'm glad you're staying this time.'

'Ta, Rosie. Well, I need to get upstairs to see me sis and me new niece. I'll be down shortly, Mum.'

'I'm coming too, luv. You don't think I have a hulk of a son-in-law for nothing, do you, luv?'

Mum was laughing as she continued. 'I was at the birth, Annie! I can't believe it. Janey wanted me so Jimmy did no more than carry me up there, then fetched me wheelchair up and that's continued whenever I want, or Janey wants. And I looked after her through it all. She were a screamer like me and what she weren't going to do to Jimmy, well, it would turn your hair grey!'

'Ha, you should have heard Olivia. I was shocked. I didn't know she knew such crude words. It would make your hair curl before it turned grey!'

They all laughed.

'I'd better watch out then if we have kids in the future, Annie.'

The room went quiet. Ricky looked as if he could have bitten his tongue off, but to Annie, it was a lovely thing to say.

'You better had! As by then, with me training, I'll have learned some tricks on how to give you a pasting.'

When they stopped laughing from this Mum said, 'Oh, Annie, Annie, luv. That's the best news I've ever heard.'

'Eeh, I'd better get stitching then. Them wedding gowns take some making, thou knaws!'

Again, they laughed at this from Cissy.

'Don't worry, Cissy, you've a few years yet. I'm still set on joining the police first, but me and Ricky will get wed. Mind, I think so; he ain't actually asked me yet. But a girl can dream, eh?'

'I can propose right here and now, Annie, luv.'

Mum put in, 'Do it upstairs, Ricky, when we're all together as I know that nothing will lift Janey more than witnessing that.'

This worried Annie.

'Is Janey all right, Mum?'

It was Jimmy that answered. 'She's seemed a bit low in spirit since the birth, Annie. I'm worried about her.'

Mum tried to reassure him. 'I keep telling you, its natural, Jimmy. It happens to most women. Anyway, let's get upstairs to her. She'll have heard that you're here, Annie, luv.'

Annie could tell that her mum didn't really think that Janey would be all right. Her stomach muscles tightened. *Please don't let the self-harm happen again!*

Thinking she needed to talk to Annie without them all, she said, 'We'll see you all up there in a minute, eh? Come on, Ricky, let's go up, shall we?'

Annie was glad when Ricky followed her. She was afraid of what she'd find and wanted his support.

As soon as she opened the door to Janey and Jimmy's flat, Janey called out, 'Annie, oh, Annie is that you?'

Rushing across the kitchen and through the lounge, Annie found Janey sat up in bed. Her face looked red, her eyes puffy with crying. 'Oh, Annie.'

Annie went into her open arms, noting that Janey's tears weren't tears of joy but those that spoke of despair.

'Me darlin'! What is it, Janey?'

309

'I don't know . . . I just feel . . . I should be happy, shouldn't I? I was. I was happy and looking forward to having me baby, but now it don't feel like I thought it would . . . I – I don't love her, Annie.'

Shocked, Annie held Janey to her.

'It hurt, Annie. It hurt so much that I hated me baby before she came out. I wanted to rip her out of me. I couldn't stand it, Annie . . . And . . . and when she were born, I wanted to get rid of her!'

Annie couldn't speak. And yet she instinctively knew that when she did, she mustn't tell Janey off. But how could she handle this?

Ricky came to the rescue.

'Janey, luv, most women feel like you do. I've delivered a couple of babies and both of the women didn't want the baby near to them, and I've heard tales of many women taking a few days to bond with their kids, so stop worrying about it, eh?'

'Ta, luv, you've made me feel better. Everyone seems cross with me, or impatient.'

'Right, I'll stop the others coming up and you and Annie have a chat, eh?'

Annie could have hugged Ricky. He was the most thoughtful and caring man she'd ever met.

When he'd gone, Janey asked, 'Was Olivia like this with her baby, Annie?'

'No, luv, but that's nothing to go by. Have you fed baby, yet?'

'No, and I don't want to. That hurts too. Me nipples are sore.'

'What is she having to eat then?'

'Jimmy bought a bottle and some powdered milk.'

Thinking this wasn't right and how Olivia bonded with her baby when feeding him, Annie asked, 'Can I look at your nipples, luv? Only Olivia suffered this, and we rubbed Vaseline into them. After a few days, they were fine. The nurse told her to persevere as breast milk protects your baby.'

Janey's nipples didn't look at all sore, nothing like Olivia's had.

The baby began to cry at that moment.

'Is she hungry now? Only milk is dripping from you, luv.'

'She's always hungry.'

'Let's just try, eh? I'll help you, luv.'

Janey began to cry.

Ignoring this and going to the baby, Annie felt love surge through her as she looked at the much tinier baby than Karl had been.

'Has she a name, luv?'

'No, I can't decide, Annie.'

Annie picked the baby up and held her to her. As Karl had done, her little hand stretched out. Annie took it and held it in hers. 'Oh, Janey, she's beautiful. She looks like you – her mum . . . She looks like her very own mum.'

Talking to the baby, Annie told her, 'Your mum will be like ours was, me little darlin'. She'll love you and protect you, play with you, and smack your bum when you're naughty so that you learn right from wrong – but it'll only be a tap, like your granny gave us. And she'll go to the ends of the earth for you, just like Granny did. You're so lucky to have me Janey for your mum, little one. And I'm your Aunty Annie, and I love you.'

The baby gurgled.

'You can bring her here if you like, Annie.'

'There you go. Now don't worry if she cries. That's the

only way that babies have of telling you they need something or are in pain.'

'How will I know which is which?'

'You don't, luv, it's trial and error.'

Janey went quiet. She looked down at her contented child. Annie saw love in her face and relaxed.

'Shall I help you to try to feed her, luv?'

Janey nodded.

Gently, Annie put the child to Janey's breast.

'There. How's that?'

'Not so bad.'

Janey didn't take her eyes off her baby.

'She does look like me, Annie.'

'Well, you're her mum.'

'I think I'll call her Elizabeth – Beth for short. I liked that name in that book Mum used to read to us, *Little Women*.'

'It's a lovely name, me darlin'.'

'It isn't hurting now, Annie. It feels strange as I can feel the milk running through me. It sort of tingles. And feels nice too. Look at Beth, she likes it. She's like a man with a pint of beer!'

They both laughed.

Annie sat on the bed holding Janey's hand. 'Oh, Janey, I feel all maternal and wish I could have a baby too.'

'You will, luv. And it could be sooner if you'd give this idea up of having a career.'

'I can't do that. I have to achieve something first.'

'Will it be Ricky you'll marry?'

'You'll see.'

'Oh, Annie, it should be, he loves you . . . Annie, I want Jimmy to be here to see Beth feeding and tell him her name.'

'I'll go and get him, me darlin', then we'll all come up when you've finished.'

When Annie got to the door, Janey called, 'Annie, I love you so much. Never go away again, will you?'

'I won't, and I love you, and me little Beth, so much too, me darlin'.'

The chatter amongst them all while they waited to go upstairs was of Janey. Mum cried as she told how difficult the last couple of days had been and how afraid she'd been for Janey. 'It sounds like you've sorted it, Annie, luv.'

'She did it herself, really. I didn't put any pressure on her. I spoke to her through the baby – she has a name now, but Janey will tell you.'

'Well, luv, you did a good job.'

'It wasn't all me.' Annie told them Ricky's part in it all. She'd only just finished when Jimmy came down and told them to go up. Then as if she was a feather, he picked Mum up and carried her up after them. To Annie, it was as if at last Mum didn't have to miss out on anything. She could, and had, forgiven Jimmy anything after that.

Once upstairs they were all introduced to Beth, now she had a name, and were treated to a glowing Janey who didn't seem to want to put her baby down.

It was then that Ricky stole the show. 'Well, Janey, I've been given a task to celebrate you and Beth.' He took Annie's hand and went down on one knee.

'Annie, I fell in love with you at the canal side and that love has deepened over time till I want to be with you my every waking hour. Will you marry me, Annie?'

Annie looked down at what she now thought of as his beautiful face. Its flaws, to her, made it so. 'I will, Ricky, ta for asking me, luv.'

Everyone cheering made little Beth jump. She let out a squeal.

Janey held her close and then made them all laugh. 'She's objecting. She says, she's only bloomin' just met her Aunty Annie, and you've pinched her from her, Ricky!'

When the laughter died down, Ricky took Annie in his arms. 'Ta, Annie, you've made me day – me life, me darlin'.'

To Annie, it seemed this was the beginning for her. Life had changed so much for herself and for all those she loved. For the most part they were good changes. She wished it was so for Olivia, though was glad she had Karl to cushion her pain and loneliness.

What the future held, she was yet to experience, but for herself it would surely only hold happiness and fulfilment, wouldn't it?

Chapter Twenty-Seven

Olivia

From the nursery window, Olivia, cradling Karl, watched Hendrick standing at the edge of the garden, staring out at the design of their future home.

Always he looked troubled, and his nights were peppered with dreams that had him waking up in a sweat and then shivering as if very afraid.

Up early every morning, he didn't seem to feel the chill of the dawn, but often, as now, went outside in his shirtsleeves.

She'd tried to comfort him, but though he hadn't rejected her, he hadn't once relaxed in her arms.

Seeing him now wipe his hands over his face, realization came to her that he was crying.

Her heart seemed to crack. Her anguish was such that she wanted to jump out of the window and go to him.

Looking down at the sleeping Karl and then back to Hendrick, it was as if she had to make a choice. She chose Hendrick. Karl was sleeping, he didn't need her, Hendrick did.

Tucking Karl into his cot, she hurried as much as her aching leg would let her and went downstairs. Not stopping to get a coat, she went into the garden.

The chill didn't matter to her as she ran in her wobbly fashion towards her beloved. He turned as she called his name.

'Darling, what are you doing out here this early?'

'Oh, Hendrick, I cannot watch you suffering. Please, please, talk to me.'

For a moment he stood and stared at her, then moved towards her and took her into his arms. His words, 'Help me. My darling, help me,' filled Olivia's heart with despair.

'Let's go inside. Karl is asleep. He won't wake for an hour or so.'

Once inside and having climbed the stairs to the flat, the chilled air, mixed with her fear, set her shivering. Hendrick steered her towards the sofa next to the roaring fire and covered her with the rug she'd always kept thrown over the arm.

For a long moment, he held her close.

'Talk to me, darling.'

'I'm sorry, Olivia, I haven't been fair. Coming home has been more difficult than staying away . . . I mean, the wrench on my heart at knowing it is for such a short time and meeting our darling son; knowing too that I may not see him grow up.'

Olivia pulled away from him. 'What? Of course you will. You work for Hitler himself so nothing will happen to you, darling. It can't!'

'My father can make it all go bad for me. Oh, Olivia, he is holding secret meetings with like-minded people and that scares me, and yet I am so proud of him and them. They are trying to find ways of helping the Jews, gypsies and homosexuals. It is admirable, but so dangerous for them, and it puts me in grave danger too. If they are caught and I am known to associate with them, then I

will be classed as one of them – which I am really . . .
It's just that my intention is to make the best of my time
over there to help other countries, which will ultimately
help all people. And yet I want to help them now, as my
father is doing.'

'Oh, Hendrick! I don't know what to say. We need your
father so that you can ring me safely from his friend's house,
and yet you need to sever relationships with him.'

'That will hurt me so much as he needs protecting, not
alienating.'

'But why can't he think – yes, these poor people need
help, but so does his own son! Where does he carry out this
work? Is it from his own house?'

'At the moment, though he has made a contact – a remote
farmer with the same ideas – and it is their intention to hold
meetings there and to do any rescue work from there too as
it is near to the border of Belgium. They also have several
clergymen involved and their churches are to be refuges too.'

Olivia felt torn. She wanted so much to praise Hendrick's
father. He was a hero to her now, but she couldn't forgive
him for putting Hendrick in so much danger.

'Why don't we run away together, Hendrick? Just go? We
could go to the mainland and then get a ship to America
and stay there till the day comes that Hitler is overthrown?'

'That will mean certain death for my father. How could
I have that on my conscience? And how can I abandon my
plan knowing that I have access to so much that would help
when war comes?'

'You said "when" . . .'

'It will happen, I am certain of it. Hitler is ruthless. He
wants to make Germany a superior nation, a superpower in
the world. To do that, he must conquer others and rule over

them. That is his aim. He has done it in Germany and Austria, and now we are on the brink of him regaining Czechoslovakia. Their protection of their borders is futile as he will find a way. Already, in Germany and Austria, the Nazis control the army, schools, everything! And I see so often in transcripts that are shared with his allies how he promises to take them along with him in Germany's superpower status – Japan, Italy, and to a lesser degree Spain.'

The shivers that had calmed now shook Olivia's body once more. She was at a loss.

'What can we do?'

'I think we carry on with our plan. I am in a unique position to help the countries he covets, and mark my words, they do include France and Britain – he wants the whole of Europe to be under Nazi rule.'

Though she didn't want to, Olivia agreed. It broke her heart to do so.

She could feel Hendrick's fear, almost touch it. Turning to him, she took his face in her hands. 'I will play my part, darling.'

'I know you will, my love . . . Oh, Olivia, I want you so badly. I want to hold you, to kiss you and to make love to you as if it is our last time.'

Not liking the last bit, but thrilling at his words, she looked into his eyes. 'Let us go back to bed.'

'Is it all right? I mean, after Karl's birth . . . can we?'

'Yes, my darling. I have so wanted to. I am ready, but I knew you weren't, not properly. You have so many troubles on your mind.'

'Help me to forget them, my darling, just for a little while. Release my mind from the fear and the anxiety.'

They stood, held hands, and Olivia guided him through

to their bedroom. There, they made love over and over till they lay exhausted in each other's arms and cried tears of joy mingled with tears of heartbreak and fear.

After a moment, Hendrick suggested they go to see her father and tell him everything. 'He has a brilliant mind and can make suggestions that we may not have thought of, darling.'

Olivia agreed. 'But then, after that, let us forget it all and just enjoy being a family together.' Her voice caught on a sob. 'We may never get another chance.'

Once more they held each other and didn't speak. Until Olivia thought she had to do something to bring a little light-heartedness into their lives.

'Come on, let's bath while Karl is still sleeping.'

They giggled, they splashed each other, they touched, but could go no further as both were spent. It was just lovely to enjoy each other, and Olivia did manage to put it all out of her mind. She hoped that Hendrick did too, as he looked relaxed and didn't mention anything about his concerns until they arrived at Father's house.

They found him at home. He hugged them both.

Olivia playfully patted his stomach. 'Daddy, you are getting a belly on you and your moustache is overly long. I'm going to trim it for you. I'll get the scissors.'

'Uh-uh, I'm guessing you two have something to tell me. You always fuss over me if you know you might have to upset me, Olivia. My belly and my moustache are the same as always, now give my grandson to me and sit down, my dear.'

When they were seated, Father rang the bell next to his armchair. 'Now, we'll order tea and then we will talk.'

Until the tea arrived, they cooed over Karl.

'He's always asleep! Hey, sleepyhead, your granddad wants to talk to you!'

But Karl snoozed on.

'Well, he's a contented baby, just like you were, Olivia. That's what helped me to cope when I lost your mother – my love for you. My wanting to protect you from the pain I was in, and this little one will help you in the same way.'

'That must have been a terrible time.'

'It was, Hendrick.'

Daddy's eyes went to the photo of Olivia's mother that stood on the top of his bureau – one of several all over the house.

A knock on the door brought his attention back and restored normality to the room.

Daphne, a young girl who lived in St Peter Port and worked for her father, came in with the tea trolley. Her eyes settled on Karl.

'Ooh, your baby! I haven't seen him; may I have a peep?'

Olivia smiled at her. 'You can take him to meet the rest of the staff if you like. That's if they aren't busy.'

'No. We had just sat down for our tea.'

Father spoke up. 'Well, as the boss, I am allowing you an extra half an hour to coo over my grandchild, but no longer. He must be back here then with no sign that he's been disturbed by meeting you all!'

Daphne giggled. 'Yes, sir!'

Olivia smiled as she handed over Karl. She'd always loved the family atmosphere her father created with his staff. It was never an 'us and them' situation.

As Daphne took Karl, she exclaimed, 'He's beautiful, like a china doll, and I will treat him as such. Ooh, the girls are going to love him!'

Olivia didn't say that most had met him on his christening day as they'd helped out, or been at the church, but was just glad Karl was in safe hands while they talked to her father.

Once they had related everything to him, he sat in silence at first. Then leaned forward. 'So, you definitely think there will be a full-scale war, Hendrick?'

'I do, William. I don't know when and, well, I must admit that Chamberlain's appeasement programme is working for now, though I think Hitler will play him for the fool he thinks he is.'

'He's a bloody idiot. He should be doing more along the aggressive line, to show we aren't to be messed with! But that said, he is investing in the RAF and I have heard it said that any new conflict will probably be fought in the air as much as anywhere.'

They were quiet for a moment. Olivia could tell her father was thinking deeply about it all as he had a habit of tugging his moustache at such moments.

'So, this plan of yours to pass information is bloody dangerous to my mind, and yet I see no alternative. I'm thinking that if it does happen, it might be better if Olivia worked in the bank and then you can ring her there. There are so many phone calls, and telegraphs from all over the world, that yours will just slot into them. Also, Olivia, now you are going to be on your own, maybe you should consider living back here? We can engage a nanny for Karl and refurbish your old nursery for him. How does that sound?'

'For my part, having Olivia here and being able to ring the bank sounds very good. But when I ring you on a personal level, darling, I would prefer to ring you wherever you are living, though I won't try to influence you one way or the other as to where that should be.'

'To be truthful, I'm trying to think of an objection to it all as I'm not sure that I am bank-staff material, and as much as I love living in our farmhouse, I know I will be lonely out there. But if I move here, I will miss having the classroom for my music lessons when I restart as I have changed my mind on waiting a whole year before I do. I thought being a new mum was going to be more difficult than it is.'

'Good, you need plenty to occupy you, my dear. And as for the lessons, you could conduct them here, or in the church hall.'

'The church hall sounds best . . . And thinking about it, I will always know when you have a message for me, darling, as you will ring the bank if you have . . . Yes, it all sounds good. Though moving back here would be simple, when it comes to working in the bank, I just don't know if you will ever teach me financial matters, Daddy.'

'Of course we will. I'll have you in charge of the smaller investors in no time. Besides, you should know how the bank works from the counter upwards as one day it will be yours.'

'Oh, I don't want to talk about that day.'

The truth was, she didn't want to talk about any of it, Olivia thought, but she was glad they had as Hendrick looked reassured.

'So, about your father. I know, Hendrick, that it is putting you in danger, but I very much admire him and am thinking how it is that I can help to fund him without it being found out?'

'Thank you. I, too, admire him, but am worried how much of a risk he is taking.'

'A huge one, I would say. But if he is willing to take it, then, well, it does sound like these people need someone to help them.'

'They do. I cannot tell you how awful it all is. And Father does need funding. He is talking of selling his house on the pretence of moving out of Munich and living in the country now that he is retired. He would get away with that, and I think it a good idea, but it would mean that I don't have access to a private telephone. My quarters are very public.'

'Mmm, I see . . . What about this farmer? Is there anything at all that points to him engaging in activities that he shouldn't?'

'No. There aren't any flags on him as far as I know.'

'Well, get bank details from him then and I will send a donation to his bank. We need your father in situ, or your plan, if ever it is needed, will fail at the first hurdle!'

'Thank you so much, William. I really appreciate your help.'

'I am proud of you and your father, though, like Olivia, I was angry at your father in the first place as I knew that I would have let them execute me rather than put my child in danger, but he has redeemed himself and obviously was spared for a purpose . . . Well, my dears, I do have an appointment that I must get ready for – a round of golf with Frederick and a couple of drinks in the bar afterwards.'

Olivia giggled; she'd never known anything take precedence over her father's golf. But then, he worked hard and deserved the relaxation it gave him.

'We'll go to my sitting room for a while, Daddy. We'll see you tomorrow as you invited us to lunch, remember?'

'Yes, I do. And I'm looking forward to it . . . Now, both of you, try not to worry. I know you have a lot to face just with your separation, but adding this on top, well, it's too much, especially as we have no guarantee that anything will happen that needs you to take up clandestine ways.'

Not worrying was easier said than done, Olivia thought. Hendrick's glance told her he'd had the same thought too.

Seeing Hendrick off when the time came was heartbreaking – more so than it had been the first time as it seemed to Olivia that she might never see him again.

For her, too, life was to change completely.

Not just the move back into her father's house, but it had been felt that she was better to begin working in the bank as soon as possible, so that it would be a natural part of life and not something that had suddenly happened.

'My darling, keep safe.'

'I will – well, as long as I toe the party line, I will.' He smiled as if this was a joke, but it sent shudders through Olivia that there were many pitfalls for him with all she'd learned about his father's activities.

They clung together until they had to part.

Olivia waved until the ship taking him to mainland France was just a speck on the horizon, then turned to go back to her father's house.

As she pushed the pram, folk stopped to see how Karl was progressing. Some commiserated with her, others didn't mention Hendrick.

In Olivia's mind, they were all so lucky. None of them knew what she did, but even if it happened and war did break out, she didn't see any of them being affected by it. War wouldn't come to this small island.

* * *

When she arrived at what was now her home once more, she had a sudden craving for a bath as that always helped her to relax and gave her the solitude she sought.

On her way to her room, she didn't pass anyone and knew that her father would be at the bank.

Gently laying Karl in the cot that was to be in her room until the nursery could be set up, she went into the adjoining bathroom and ran the hot water, leaving the door open so she could hear Karl if he should wake.

With the tub filled almost to the top, Olivia lowered herself carefully into the very hot water.

Relaxing back, she let the water cover her to her neck. It was then that she felt as if everything left her. All her composure, the courage she'd mustered, and her determination to do her best.

It started with tears rolling down her face, but soon it was as if her whole body was weeping – her heart, her breasts, her fingers, her toes. Every bit of her released its tension and sorrow in a torrent of uncontrollable sobs.

Life as she knew it would never be the same again.

PART FOUR

A Changing World

Chapter Twenty-Eight

Annie

3 September 1939

The usual tapping of the keys of typewriters had stopped as the tension in the police station office mounted.

The time had come for Chamberlain's broadcast to the nation.

The admin room was crowded with the station staff who were on office or desk duty. Despite it being a Sunday, there was a full complement as there was every day of the week – criminals didn't take a day off, so the station never closed.

Annie knew what their prime minister was going to say. Hendrick had prepared Olivia and so her too. Hitler's plans hadn't changed, only grown. They knew he was never going to be appeased. Knew he would not withdraw from Poland. All they waited for was to see if Chamberlain would take up the bait, but then, they knew too that he had no choice. He couldn't abandon Poland.

Betty Randal leaned forward and turned the wireless knob. A voice echoed around the office. 'This is London. You will now hear a statement by the Prime Minister.'

There was an audible intake of breath. Annie shuddered as if someone had run a feather down her spine.

The prime minister's voice filled the room. 'I am speaking to you from the cabinet room of ten Downing Street.'

After the words 'This country is at war with Germany' had been said, it was several seconds before the oppressive silence around her was broken by the sound of a sob.

Betty Randal had bent her head over her typewriter. Her wedding day was this coming Saturday. All the talk had been around if there would be a war and how the women would cope without their men and the men cope with leaving their families, jobs and having to be what they weren't – soldiers.

Most of the girls had said they would marry quickly, before their men left. Most had waited, like herself, to fulfil their ambitions of having a career in the police, which they loved and felt proud of, before taking this step.

Annie hadn't known what she would do if the announcement was of war, but suddenly she did. And she asked herself: *Why did I think that a job in the police force was more important than my love for Ricky?*

Not thinking, she stood up, sought Ricky's eyes, knew they would be on her.

'Ricky, will you marry me soon?'

Ricky found his way to her side through the now stunned silence and took her in his arms. 'I'll post the banns the moment I'm off duty, me darlin'.' Then he punched the air . . . 'Thank you, Hitler!'

The loudest cheer went up as they clung to one another and kissed – a kiss Annie would never forget.

Even the sergeant was cheering.

Once it died down, one after the other of the girls said, 'I'm going to marry my Bill, Fred, Johnny, Alfred . . .' till the sergeant shouted, 'Hey, stop! With a lot of the lads most probably going, who will I have to police the area with?'

Annie chirped up, 'Well, they'll just have to change the rules and allow married women to serve as police officers, Sarge. They should have done it long ago; we'd all have been married by now if they had.'

Betty put in, 'And would have done just as good a job as we do now!'

'A woman's job is in the home, luv.'

Annie mocked him. 'Ha, well, Sarge, I think Hitler might just change that tune!'

The sarge put his hands up. 'All right, girls, we shall see. I won't complain if you all stay on after you're married, but if you want to, and the government do change the rules, then you'll have to be careful about having babies, as they might be forced to bend the rules where married women are concerned, but I doubt they will for mothers!'

Annie felt incensed by the unfairness of this. A man has a baby, just as much as a woman does, only without the carrying and screaming bit. So why was it always down to the women to stay at home and take care of them?

But she didn't voice this as half the women in the room would be on the men's side. *Will things ever change?*

It had been almost a year now since Annie had become a policewoman. She'd found the exam easy and had passed with flying colours and loved her job.

There was nothing she didn't like but most of all she loved her work with the women and children. Understanding how they came to do what they did. The stealing and, for the women, prostituting themselves.

As she wasn't from a lower-middle class family as most

other officers were, but had sailed in the same boat they had – the poverty vessel – she knew what desperation was, and they felt this.

And, once she had qualified, for her to have landed a job in the same police station where Ricky worked had thrilled and amazed her.

Her life had changed in so many ways and achieving her ambition was just part of it as she and Ricky had become a couple without the gold band and without living together.

Their love was the most wonderful thing in her life, though it always hurt when they had to part.

And though she still lived in Olivia's father's apartment, they hadn't ever made love there as both thought it wouldn't be right to do so – like taking advantage. And in any case, they might be found out by Cissy, who still came to clean and sometimes stayed over – times that Annie loved.

There was no need for Cissy to do what she did – change the beds, laundry, and generally clean – as Annie could have managed it all but she wouldn't put Cissy out of her job, knowing she needed the money.

Mainly, she and Ricky had made love in the car, driving out into the country where they found a lane to park in, but sometimes they had made love at Ricky's home, when his mum, Lilly, who Annie loved, had gone to bed.

Those times were the best for Annie, especially in the winter on the rug in front of the fire. Always, Ricky was careful and wore a sheath, which he hated, but he knew it was the only sure way to protect Annie from pregnancy.

He was a kind and considerate lover, but passionate too, taking her to exquisite feelings that splintered her before making her whole again.

She loved him with all that she was.

To Annie, her life was almost complete – marrying Ricky would make it so. Though there would still be one hole in her life which he couldn't fill: her yearning to have Olivia by her side, and yet she'd never made it back to Guernsey.

Having to quickly apply for a job at the station where Ricky worked had meant there had been no time after she'd passed her exams to take leave. Both she and Ricky were owed a lot of time off as they found it difficult to slot leave in: Ricky because the married men with kids took precedence, and herself because there just weren't enough policewomen – they only had five stationed here.

Thinking of Olivia, Annie had a deep desire to see her before things began to happen that she hardly dared think about.

Looking up at Ricky, she asked if she could see him in private for a mo.

Others heard, so amidst catcalls and laughter saying that Annie couldn't wait, they went into the staff canteen together.

'What is it, luv?'

'Oh, Ricky, I want to see Olivia . . . I know, it's the last thing you'd expect me to say, but I do so want to see her.'

'Me darlin', you can't. It may compromise what is set up for the messages. You must keep a low profile where Olivia is concerned. I know that's not what you wanted me to say, but think about it, luv. At the moment, you're her ex-maid-companion who is allowed to stay in her apartment – but that's got to end. You know that, don't you?'

Annie felt distraught. She hadn't thought of it all like this. She'd had some fanciful idea that she could arrange a ferry, go over for their honeymoon, and have a wonderful week with Olivia and Karl.

'The War Office would never allow it, luv. And they do

have a say in your movements. You're already an important link and will become even more so. I expect you will hear that when you meet Lucy later.'

Lucy was her contact at the War Office, though she was an undercover worker, so for all intents and purposes she worked as a secretary in a journalist's office.

In the beginning they had been instructed to meet often so that they appeared to be like any other two young women, shopping together, going to the cinema and having drinks after, but that had become much more and now Lucy was very important to her and they had formed a deep friendship.

'And, luv, we have to think carefully about our future with us being at war . . .'

A sudden thought came to Annie. 'You won't have to go, will you, Ricky? Only Sarge said, "some of the men".'

'I will, luv. I'm a reservist. A lot of the coppers are. Most came from the army to be police in civvy street . . . And, Annie, luv, Jimmy will have to go too. He'll have no say as he's not in a career that's likely to be exempt.'

Jimmy and Ricky were best mates now, and with her and Janey, the four of them often went out together for pie and mash and a pint. Jimmy and Ricky loved to play darts, and that gave her and Janey plenty of time to chat. During these times, Annie had become concerned for Janey once more as she'd begun to worry about the war and if Jimmy had to go – worry of any kind wasn't good for Janey's mental health.

'Oh, God, Ricky. I can't bear it.'

'You can, luv, and you will. You will for Janey and your mum, Lilly, Cissy and Rosie. They will all need you to be strong. Not to mention your work at the War Office. That must carry on, luv. It could be the difference between us winning this war and losing it.'

Annie had never thought of her taking messages as important, but now it dawned on her just what position she was in.

'Remember, me darlin', you're a serving officer of His Majesty's Police Force, and you will do your duty. The people will need you, and not just the women and children.'

'But I will have to leave. I want to marry you, luv. I want to marry you before you go.'

Ricky looked down at the floor. When he looked up, he had tears in his eyes. 'I know and it is what I want most in the world, me darlin'. But maybe it would be better to do that when it's all over.'

At her gasp of disbelief, Ricky took her in his arms.

'It is important that you stay as a police officer. They may employ you back anyway, we don't know. We just don't know what their plans are. They could make policemen exempt even, but as I see it, and the papers are always speculating, women will be called upon to do men's jobs. If you ain't in a job, you could be sent anywhere – a factory, farming, anywhere! For your sake and that of the extra job you do as a go-between for Olivia and Lucy, and will be called on to do a lot more of, you must remain here, luv.'

Annie was astonished by all of this. 'How long have you thought this, Ricky? When you said you would marry me just now, did you know then that you would put all this to me?'

'I did, luv. But it was such a wonderful moment and in front of everyone, I thought to wait until we were on our own.'

'How will I tell them all?'

'We'll come up with something. Say you changed your mind as you put your job first, something like that. The other girls will understand that, and I'll take the ragging off the men.'

'Oh, Ricky, our lives are going to be so different, mate.'

'They are, me darlin'. I wanted nothing more in the world than to make you me wife.'

He held her closer and lay his head on hers. She clung to him as if this was the last time that she would hold him. Her thoughts went to lovely Olivia and how life must be for her. Hendrick had only made it home twice since that first time and then only for a week at a time.

That would happen for herself now.

This became a truth later that day when it was announced that a law had been passed that all men of eighteen to forty-one were subject to compulsory conscription. Exemptions were given to certain essential occupations – policemen were not amongst them.

They had gone outside together after the announcement; Ricky had said he had something to tell her.

'Annie, I should have said before when we spoke of this, but I couldn't bring myself to. But, as I said, I am a reservist, and I – well . . .'

Annie watched as Ricky took a crumpled envelope from his pocket. 'I've already been called up.'

At these words, Annie could feel her heart breaking.

When he unfolded the letter, he told her he was to report to Colchester in ten days' time.

Anger at what seemed like a deception to her seared through her, but then, looking at Ricky's expression, she knew it had cost him dearly to admit what was now the inevitable. An acceptance came over her.

'Annie, luv, shall we have a few days off together, eh?'

Releasing a deep sigh, Annie nodded.

No one catcalled or made jokes when they went back into the office this time, and Annie was grateful.

They went together to the sergeant's office and asked him to give them leave.

'Well, this isn't going to be easy, I'm afraid, every young officer is going to ask the same thing. But as you're the first, and in recognition of your sacrifice in not marrying so that you can continue to serve, Annie, I'm going to grant you both a week's leave. Let's say from Tuesday evening, eh, Ricky? Well, you no longer work here but for His Majesty's Armed Forces, young man. Make us proud, son.'

With Ricky having to report to the town hall and Annie having to meet Lucy for tea, they had to part shortly, but for a moment, outside behind the station, in the small garden that Annie and the other WPCs had planted with flowers and where the men had cobbled together a bench, they sat holding hands. Ricky looked deep into her eyes. 'I love you, Annie.'

'Oh, Ricky, ta for loving me. And I love you, me darlin'. Me heart's breaking at you having to go away.'

His voice shook. 'I know, mine is too. I cannot imagine going from seeing you every day, and in the evenings too, to not seeing you for months, or how I'm to bear it.'

'I feel the same. I know that we've done it before, but this is different. Now we are so bound together, it will sever me in two to wave goodbye to you.'

They clung to one another.

'While we're off, will you come away with me, Annie, luv? I want to know what it would be like to sleep with you and to wake up with you beside me.'

'Oh, Ricky, yes . . . Yes!'

As they came out of the hug, Ricky said, 'I thought perhaps Southend, then if we get the chance we can have a look at Colchester where I'm to be stationed for six weeks and you'll be able to picture me there.'

'That would be perfect.'

After work, Annie made her way to rendezvous with Lucy as they always did on a Sunday. Nothing was ever thought suspicious on the holy day.

Lucy, as usual, was sitting in the cafe on the side of the canal near to the Old Ford Road where Janey and Mum lived.

This was always ideal for short meetings as it meant that Annie could visit her family afterwards to make sure Janey was coping.

With her mousy hair, hazel eyes and freckles by the million covering her face, Lucy was the sort of girl that didn't attract a second look. Which suited her role – to be believable as a nondescript secretary, when she was one of the most important go-betweens the War Office had.

To save time and not have to go home first, Annie had taken her shirt, tie and jacket off and hung them in the police station cloakroom, changing into a cream twinset, which turned her formal slim-fitting black skirt, black stockings and sensible shoes into an attractive outfit that didn't mark her as anyone of authority.

Lucy stood when she entered. They hugged.

'Good to see you, Annie, I've a lot to tell you. I've ordered us both tea and one of Gill's fairy cakes. She was glad to see me as she says the place has been deserted all day, but that suits us and is why I sat in this furthermost corner so that Gill won't be able to hear. I just hope she doesn't bother us too much.'

'We could go for a walk if you like, luv. It's lovely along the towpath.'

'That's a good idea. We will after our tea.'

They chatted on about the awful announcement – just general talk as any friends would who met up for afternoon tea.

They shared their anguish over impending war with Gill, who expressed her worry over her son of sixteen.

'I hope it all ends before he has to go. I'd go out of me mind.'

'A lot will be doing that today, Gill, as their sons have orders to go now. They will need you and your cheery cups of tea, luv. I know I do. It's like I come back to me roots when I chat with you.'

'Your Janey'll feel it, Annie, luv . . . Well, you will too. I mean, Ricky will go, won't he?'

Lucy answered. 'That's why Annie just told me she'll be moving back in with Janey. You can support each other that way, can't you, Annie?'

Used to surprises dropped on her by Lucy but having been prewarned that this might happen by Ricky earlier, Annie agreed.

'I can't wait. I ain't liked it up west, but there ain't been room for me with Mum.'

'I don't know, Annie, who'd have thought – you making fancy friends that let you live in a posh apartment, eh?'

Annie thought quickly. 'They ain't me friends – I mean, they've always been nice to me, but I was a maid and companion and a sort of watchman of the apartment as Cissy couldn't get there so often. But they're closing it down now as they won't be able to come over. It was the first phone call I got as soon as the announcement was made this morning.'

'Uh, that's the toffs to a tee! You're not useful, so get out! Well, good riddance to them, I say.'

Annie stopped herself from defending Olivia. She felt Lucy willing her not to.

As they walked the towpath and chatted, Lucy suddenly stood still and made a pretence of pointing towards a few ducks making their way along the water.

'Right, there's no one around . . . Annie, you probably guessed, we want you away from anything that connects you to Olivia. Going to live with your mum and sister would be ideal and a natural thing to do.'

'But the islanders know we are the best of friends!'

'That won't matter, they have no reason to suspect anything. You haven't been over for a long time. If there comes a time that the islanders knowing you is a problem, we will have to sort it out, but I doubt it will happen.'

'But what about Cissy?'

'She isn't to go to the apartment either. You must contact Olivia with these instructions.'

'But Cissy relies on her wage. She will be devastated by thinking that Olivia's father just sacked her. How will I tell her?'

'We thought about this. We think the best thing to tell her is that the government want the apartment and have requisitioned it from the family as they don't live there. If she wonders how the government knew, just remind her that Olivia's father has many circles that he moves in, and it is known in high places that he has property here. This particular one is thought to be very useful, but neither you nor the family know why or what it will be used for. To make this more real, you and she will clear it out of all personal belongings of the family and yourself – the family ones will go into storage.'

Annie relaxed as the thought occurred to her that this was really to keep Olivia and herself safe from suspicion. Olivia's father was bound to pay Cissy a retainer and wouldn't see her suffering from lack of money. When she voiced this, Lucy agreed.

'Yes, and it would be a natural thing for him to do, thinking he would get his apartment back when the war is ended, and he will need her again. No one could suspect such a transaction – that's if they ever found out. Good thinking. Now, we must talk about how everything is to happen. Olivia's to ring the police station . . . I take it you haven't done anything silly like arranging to marry?'

'No. I wanted to, but Ricky wanted to be sure I had my job at the station and wasn't sent off here, there and everywhere to do war work.'

'Good. Janey will need you too. I hope she copes, love.'

'Me too . . . So, how will it all be arranged? I mean, private calls aren't accepted at the station.'

'No one will know. Instructions will be issued that you are to do more duties on the switchboard. You'll be responsible for manning it at a certain time every day, which you will have to tell Olivia of. This won't be noticeable at the station as the order of duties for every one of the policewomen will change under the guise of needing to cover male officers going to war. Three are going from your station as they are the only ones who are reservists. Some stations are losing most of their male officers and the women are rushing to marry, so something will have to be done. However, that's not our concern. We had to make these changes for you as Olivia's calls will be international, and therefore, if handled by other girls, they'll be classed as personal and not taken or not passed through to you. But you will need a way of none of Olivia's calls seeming to need action. Is that possible?'

'Oh yes, no problem, we get bogus calls by the dozen. I just don't know why people do that but it could be a useful ploy now.'

'Good, it sounds as though Olivia's calls will be easy to handle. We want you to ring her tonight and talk it through so you both know what you're doing. Your duty times on the switchboard will be the last two hours of the day as our time is one hour behind Germany's. This will give Hendrick time to give any information he has to Olivia as he will know that she will leave the bank at the same time you leave the station.'

'I wish none of it were happening. I wish there wasn't ever a man called Hitler. His bloody Christian name "Adolf" sounds like a reindeer, but he'd never be chosen by Santa! The pig!'

Lucy burst out laughing. 'Oh, Annie, I'll forever think of him with horns and a red nose now!'

This made Annie laugh as she conjured the picture in her mind too.

As their laughter died, Lucy said, 'Well, love, it has happened, and we'll all do what we can to beat it. Oh, I nearly forgot, your code name is to be "the Guernsey Girls". Tell Olivia that if ever she must ring you at home with a message – and she must only do so under extreme circumstances – she's to start the conversation by saying, "It's the other half of the Guernsey Girls, here, love." That way, you will know to take down what she says and decipher it after the call. Remember to always be aware that the operator may listen in. And that goes for when she phones the station too.'

Annie felt her world closing in on her. And with this last truly realized the danger Olivia and she could put Hendrick in if they weren't very careful.

'The only other thing to tell Olivia is that if she can avoid it, she isn't to ring you for at least an hour after Hendrick has rung and to ring you a lot of times when he hasn't. We don't want to raise anyone's suspicions. It may seem unlikely, but there are a lot of callous folk around who don't care a jot for their fellow countrymen, only what they can get out of a situation for themselves. If one of the operators at the telephone exchange does get suspicious, and decides to cash in, they could find a way – very unlikely it will happen, but be aware of every pitfall attached to the work you are doing.'

'You're scaring me more than I was already, Luce.'

'Well, that will put you in the mode of always being alert. What Hendrick is doing is so valuable to us and the fight against the Germans but puts him in grave danger. Anyway, on that sombre note, I'd better go and catch my Tube and you need to get to your mum, Janey and Cissy.'

'It's not just them either, Luce. Being a Sunday, and with the announcement, I'm sure Ricky's mum, Lilly, and Jimmy's mum, Rosie, will be there too. It's going to be all girls together!'

'For all over Britain, too . . . I've never said, but there is someone I'm sweet on. His name's Dan. He's a journalist. He doesn't know how I feel, and anyway, wouldn't look twice at me. He's always bringing me his work, though, and having a chat and a joke, but oh, Annie, I want so much more.'

Annie put her arm around Lucy. 'You're beautiful, luv. Never forget that.'

Lucy's head came onto Annie's shoulder and Annie knew they'd now left the realms of spies for their country and were back to being just friends.

They didn't speak any more, but stopped and stared out at the water, and watched the antics of the ducks who, thinking they might get a titbit, had swum along with them.

To Annie, even though she was with Lucy, it was a moment of feeling deep loneliness. As if the world they knew had changed, and they were different people.

It was a feeling she knew she had to face in the future when the time came for her to say her goodbyes to her Ricky – for how long, she didn't know, but just the thought of it brought tears to her eyes.

Chapter Twenty-Nine

Olivia

'Annie! Oh, Annie, it's lovely to hear your voice. I know we only spoke last week, but so much has happened! Our worst fears have been realized.'

'Yes, and I have so much to tell you, but first, how's my little Karl?'

'Ha, not so little! For a sixteen-month-old, he looks almost two! He's not just walking but running and on the go from morning till night. He drives Nanny nuts as she's adamant that he should have an afternoon nap, but oh no, not my little chap. I think he's going to be an Olympic runner! How's Beth doing?'

'She's into everything, and spoiled by all the womenfolk, including me, but even more so by her dad and Ricky. Jimmy's besotted and you'd think that no man had ever had a daughter but him!'

'Ha, that's lovely. Hendrick's the same, even though he is a long-distance father. The first thing he asks is how's Karl, when he phones, and it can be a few minutes before he remembers to ask how I am!'

'Ah, it must be so hard for you both. I ain't looking forward to me and Ricky parting.'

'Ricky has to go? Oh no, Annie! I didn't think . . .'

As Annie went on to explain about his previous service, she then said, 'I have a lot to tell you, Olivia, so I'd better carry on in case the line goes dead, like it often does.'

Olivia realized the line going dead was an intro to a code coming and got ready to write everything down. But as she did, she wondered at how Annie had worked out such an intricate one to give her such a lot of information.

Yes, they had prepared – Hendrick had seen to that. They'd played games learning codes, testing each other, and they'd exchanged a couple or so real messages and found that they had coped. But the reality wasn't a game; it was a frightening prospect and one that could lead to dire consequences for her beloved Hendrick!

And it brought it home to her then, too, that there truly was a war! They could all be killed! Why she thought this, she didn't know. She and her father and her child and all the islanders were safe. No one thought that the island would see any of the war, only feel its effects as some of their men prepared to serve. It was well protected by mainland forces and wasn't of any value to Hitler. But this last thought didn't relax her as she listened to Annie, knowing she was speaking in code.

'I wanted to tell you that I am to be given a new job in the evenings. I will be on the switchboard. No cut-offs of service there, worst luck.' Annie laughed.

Olivia began frantically deciphering what she could. 'Oh dear, that'll be boring for you.'

'Yes, but I'm glad to be taking care of Janey when at home. So my job of looking after the apartment is over too, as it is for Cissy. It's all change according to orders. Oh, everything's awful, but at least I have memories of when I worked over there with you. Do you remember we once called ourselves the Guernsey Girls? It was when we had some fun that afternoon. Well, I love those words and thought them good for our game.'

Olivia got the gist of most of it without having to study it all – it seemed she was to ring the police station from now on and that their friendship must be low key.

As Annie continued to give her information using their code, Olivia wrote all she was saying down to decipher later. But one thing did stick out from it all as it wasn't very well disguised – Annie and Cissy must leave the apartment and the story was to be that the government had requisitioned it. This she half knew as her father had been contacted and having this knowledge had given her an opportunity she never dreamed would come her way.

'Yes, I am sorry about the changes, but war brings many challenges. It has brought me one. Father has charged me to do the clearing of the apartment.'

She heard the sharp intake of breath and knew that Annie wanted to jump for joy.

'Daddy has made all the arrangements. Top brass will be informed.' Top brass was their code for Lucy.

'I will need you and Cissy to help me. And I am to pay a retainer to Cissy as we will need her after all this is over and we get our apartment back.'

Annie was very quiet as Olivia explained more. 'I will arrive early Thursday morning. Could you arrange to meet me? I will pay all of your expenses, of course.'

'Yes, it will be me pleasure to do that. Me and Ricky will meet you. We have some time off.'

Keeping in a business mode, Olivia continued, 'I will have slept on the boat, so will be fresh for the onward journey, will that fit in?'

'It will, perfectly! We'll be there to collect you.'

For all this bravado, Olivia knew that deep down Annie was scared, as she was herself. 'Well, love, we have something to look forward to now. But I must go.'

After only saying half of a goodbye, the phone cut off. This was usual and it had surprised Olivia that she'd had a line to Annie for so long.

When she'd deciphered all of Annie's news the reality of it shocked her. Yes, it made sense, but that Lucy had instructed that such precautions were deemed necessary had really made Olivia face up to just how serious their role was being taken. She liked the idea of the Guernsey Girls, though, as it somehow reinforced that they were in this together.

Her thoughts went to Cissy and how she could help her through the transition of not being able to follow her daily routine. She knew that moving into the flat that Jimmy rented to her had been a huge step for her and must have cost her a fortune, as though she said she went to second-hand shops to get all her furniture, it still must have taken any savings she'd had to set up from scratch!

She loved the idea of a retainer being paid and it would be a natural thing to do and something she was proud of her father for.

Feeling better – and that was helped, too, by Annie being upbeat about it all and already making moves to live with her mum and Janey – Olivia sat watching Karl as he tried to build up the wooden bricks that he loved to play with, often achieving three balancing in a higgledy-piggledy way, but then the fourth one sending them all tumbling, making him giggle. He was so like Hendrick, in looks but in his ways too – kind and thoughtful. Often he would bring her one of his toys if he sensed she was feeling down or offer his arms to be picked up and then he would cuddle her head and his little hand would stroke her hair, just as Hendrick had done. And now, as he concentrated, he had his tongue out to the side of his mouth – another mannerism of Hendrick's . . . *Oh, how I miss you, Hendrick, my darling.*

To stop the emotions of this encasing her, Olivia stood. 'Come on, Karl. Mummy needs to bath you now, and then it's time for bed, darling.'

Karl didn't react. Again, just like his father. If Hendrick was doing something, he hated to leave it until it was completed.

Olivia didn't pester him but waited. Willing that fourth one to sit just for a second. But no. Number three toppled before Karl could get it there.

Nanny came in as they were both laughing.

'I have come to take the little one for his bath, Miss Olivia.'

'I'll do it, Loes. You knock off for an hour.'

'Knock off? What is this?'

'Ha, sorry, dear. I meant, you can stop working for an hour and then take over again after Karl is bathed as I have some music students meeting in the church hall tonight.'

'Oh? My English doesn't always give me the sayings you have. I thought you wanted me to knock something off the shelf.'

They both laughed. They'd become friends. Loes had been found through a magazine that advertised nannies wanting to work in Britain, but she was just as thrilled to come to Guernsey, knowing it, too, was British.

A pretty girl with the expected blonde hair that she wore long and in the traditional way for a Dutch girl – two plaits fastened on the top of her head – and large brown eyes, though only nineteen, she was a very competent and loving nanny. Karl adored her. He already had his arms out to her. She didn't ignore him but went to pick him up and made him giggle by tickling his tummy.

Feeling relaxed after her lovely hour with Karl, and them making a watery mess in the bathroom as they'd played splashing and boats, Olivia arrived at the church hall a few minutes late, and was surprised to find there was no one around.

This was strange as, always eager, her students were usually all in the hall by now. She tried the door and it opened, but inside was in darkness.

Ten minutes later, Mrs Green, a woman who had put her name down to join the choir, turned up.

'Hello, it's lovely to see you, though you're the only one so far out of the twelve who had shown interest.'

Mrs Green, a portly, formidable woman, coughed, then folded her arms under her ample bosom. 'Well, with the news and your husband being one of them, I'm not surprised.'

Olivia sighed, remembering when she'd heard this before. But now, she understood.

'Oh? Well, I can't change things now, Mrs Green. Hendrick had no choice. I have none either. I have to carry on the best I can without my husband by my side, but I didn't expect to have to do that without my fellow countrymen by my side too.'

'Well, if you put it like that, I'll talk to them and see what I can do . . . You know we all think a lot of you, Miss Olivia, we have watched you grow up . . . And, well, Hendrick too. But things have changed.'

'They needn't. If we fall out amongst ourselves, what chance do we have against the Germans?'

'You're right. Though I must say, I thought twice and I'm glad I did. You don't deserve the attitude some are taking. Leave it with me. I'll see they're all here next week, I promise.'

'Thanks, Mrs Green.'

'Well, now I am here, can I show you what I can do?'

'Of course. I was going to get everyone singing "My Bonnie Lies Over the Ocean". I have the music for it here. I'm sure you will know the words as they are mostly repetitive. I'll play the first line then you come in. But firstly, as I am setting up the piano, do a few warming up exercises like this.' Olivia held her hands on her diaphragm. 'Make sure it comes from here.'

Once they began the song, Olivia was thrilled to hear that Mrs Green had a beautiful soprano voice that soared around the hall. When it came to an end, Olivia applauded her.

'Oh, I hope the others come next week, Mrs Green. We could have a beautiful choir and put on concerts, sing in the church at special festivities, and generally have a good time together.'

'Well, for me, it will be a godsend and help me get through if me Albert goes to war. He's only sixteen, so it might be over by the time he reaches call-up, but I need something to look forward to as I dread the news now.'

Olivia wanted to hug her as she could feel her anguish but wasn't sure it was the right thing to do with this strong woman.

'I hope so too. It isn't nice being separated from loved ones.'

'And that's what I'll tell them as I think they shouldn't stay away now. Hendrick was a nice little boy and a kind and thoughtful young man. Your wedding was beautiful, and everyone was happy then. I'm sorry I spoke how I did.

No young men, English or German, will be given a choice, and I can see now that Hendrick wasn't either and will make sure that folk know that.'

'Thank you. That would mean a lot.' Olivia wanted to say that many a young man would have to go to war who didn't agree with the principles of it, but she didn't want to hint that Hendrick disagreed with Hitler and hated what he was doing. How things were, anything could happen, and she would never want him compromised just to appease anyone who was bigoted.

As she walked home, she pondered on how in such a short space of time everything had changed. From feeling safe and secure and blissfully happy, she'd gone to being lonely and afraid. From being thought of as a nice boy and a kind young man, Hendrick had gone to being someone to hate and mistrust. And from having an open and beautiful friendship between herself and Annie, they'd gone to being embroiled in a clandestine association.

Would life ever be the same again?

The thought came to her that the hate she had for Hitler, and had had from the moment she'd heard he existed, had intensified as it was entwined with fear. For hers and Hendrick's future and that of the whole world.

Chapter Thirty

Annie

When Annie called in to see her mum and Janey the next afternoon, Beth toddled unsteadily towards her with her little chubby arms held up to her. Annie scooped her up and hugged her close. She smelled of Johnson's Baby Powder and gave a hug of love mixed with giggles.

As Janey joined the hug, she looked lovingly at Beth and tweaked her nose. 'She's been a madam today, Aunty Annie. I ain't been able to do anything. I wouldn't manage but for the nurses from the convent who come in to see to Mum.'

'They're a godsend. They help us too, as they're always ready with a cup of tea for any copper patrolling their street. They truly are angels.'

'So, Ricky called in earlier and told us that you and he are off tomorrow . . . Southend! Lucky you.'

'Yes, and doubly so with Olivia coming.'

'That was a shock hearing the government had taken over the apartment. It all beggars belief and makes you wonder what else will happen. Mind, they wouldn't have any use for a place in Bethnal Green, so we're safe.'

'How's Cissy? Is she still all right with it all?'

'She is. And a bit relieved if anything as even going there to see you and to help out was getting a bind for her. And she's looking forward to seeing Olivia.'

Changing the subject, Annie asked if Jimmy had heard anything about his training yet.

'Oh, Annie, he has to go to the same place as Ricky, but a few days after.'

'We'll get through it, luv. We'll always be there for one another.'

'We will, but why you and Ricky don't marry before he goes, I don't know. Ain't you ready to give up your career and be Ricky's wife, Annie, luv?'

'Oh, I am, Janey, but . . . well . . .'

Janey sighed. 'I can't understand why being a police officer is so important to you.'

And I can't tell you, Annie thought, at least not the real reason. But an idea occurred to her to quieten the constant chatter around the subject.

'To be truthful, I want to with all me heart, Janey, luv, but you've heard all the talk of women having to do the men's jobs. Well, what if we don't have a choice and are sent somewhere? Those of us who aren't mothers, of course. I don't want to have to leave you, mum and Beth, or Lilly, Cissy and Rosie. If I'm in a career, that won't happen. If I marry, then me career will go. It's a sacrifice me and Ricky have decided to make. We'll marry when it's all over.'

'Well, I never thought of that. Ta, luv, I'd never get through it without you.'

'Are you coping now, with knowing Jimmy is going, luv?'

'I ain't. Not inside, I ain't . . . Oh, Annie, I need a hug. A proper hug.'

Annie put Beth down and took Janey into her arms. 'We'll

be all right, luv. We'll have each other. We've got our own women's army with the lot of us!'

Janey giggled and it was good to hear. For now, anyway, Janey was doing all right.

'And there might be another, Annie. I think I'm pregnant again.'

'Oh, Janey! Oh, luv! That's fantastic news . . . Well, you'd better have another girl, as we can't have a lad in our army!'

This had them giggling again. Beth joined in and clapped her hands together, making them laugh even more.

When they calmed, they fell silent. For Annie, it gave her a moment of reflection on how unfair it all was and how she should be having babies and her own home and how she should be caring for them and Ricky.

A voice brought her out of this as Lilly called up the stairs, 'I'm here, Annie, girl. I'm just making tea for your mum!'

Calling back that she'd be down in a moment, Annie added, 'Pour me one, Lilly, luv. I don't know what you have to do to get a cuppa in this flat up here!'

Janey hit out at her in a playful way and Annie thought how much she was looking forward to being with her – it was as if she was finding her sister once more and she had a lovely feeling of being needed by her family.

As she got to the bottom of the stairs, Annie knocked on Cissy's door and opened it. 'Tea's up in Mum's, Cissy, luv.'

'I heard, Annie, lass. I were just finding me slippers. Eeh, make sure there's a mug for me an' all, won't you?'

Having already greeted her mum and chatted before she'd gone up to Janey, Annie went straight into the kitchen. 'Lilly! Oh, it's good to see you, luv.'

Lilly, a big woman in every way, turned, put the teapot down and held her arms out to Annie. Lilly gave the best hugs, all squishy and soft. They gave comfort if you needed it, or strength if that was what was required. Today they just gave love.

'So, that son of mine is taking you away for a dirty weekend, only in the week, ain't he?'

Annie burst out laughing. 'Something like that.'

'Good luck to the pair of you. I won't ask why you ain't marrying, it's your business, but just to say, luv, I'm on your side. We'll all see each other through this, eh?'

'I know and we will, Lilly. I've just been saying to Janey that the six of us – seven with Beth – will be a women's army!'

'We will, and one that no Hitler can break.'

When they went into the front room laden with mugs of tea, everyone was there. They were just missing Rosie who would be working her stall, having had to give up her plans to marry just yet as she would need to run the business now that Jimmy was going.

Annie looked around at them and knew she wouldn't be without any of them, and that together they would weather any storm, and keep each other going while they did.

Southend had changed as if overnight. It thronged with servicemen – mostly seamen of the Merchant and Royal Navies but a lot of regular soldiers too. The sight spoke of the reality of war more than anything had but when they went to walk along the promenade and were stopped, they knew just how frightened the government were of a possible invasion.

The landlady of the small hotel they had booked into, who spoke more like a Londoner from the East End than a seasider, had told them that Southend was the headquarters of the Thames and Medway Control and that preparations were underway to thwart an invasion. 'Even our pier's been taken over by the Royal Navy and named HMS *Leigh*.'

As they stood and gazed along where they weren't allowed to go on the Wednesday morning, they saw concrete blocks being erected. Those completed were at least seven feet high and five feet wide.

Streets leading down to the beach were blocked off and the army sergeant turning them around told them that the street they had come down was the next one to be done. 'We're making sure the Germans can't get anywhere fast, even if they manage to land,' he told them.

To Annie, it was a sad sight. Worse than the hundreds of sandbags scattered around in the doorways of London.

She and Ricky had vowed not to talk of war, but now she uttered, 'They truly could invade us, Ricky.'

'Well, if this is happening along all of our seafronts, they've got a job on, luv.'

Annie looked out to sea. Her imagination gave her warships on the horizon with huge guns pointed at the houses. A shudder went through her. Ricky's arm came around her. 'Annie, I've heard some great news, I wanted to surprise you when we got back, but because of it, it's possible that Olivia could be your bridesmaid after all.'

'What? How? Why?'

'Ha! The "what" is a gold band that says you're mine, which I am going to put on your finger on Friday. The "how" is being made man and wife, in the Bethnal Green register office, and the "why" is because I love you and because notice came through to the station that they could employ married women and should contact all officers who left to get married in the last few years and offer them their jobs back!'

'Oh, Ricky! Ricky! I can't believe it. So, this truly is our honeymoon?'

'It is, luv.'

'But what about me family? I want them all there . . . How can we arrange everything?'

'It will all be done. I told Jimmy and he is telling them all right now. He said not to worry. He, his mum and Janey, not to mention Lilly and Cissy, will have a feast ready that's fit for a king and Janey and Cissy will go to the apartment to get your wedding and bridesmaid frock unpacked and hung up. Janey has herself down as bridesmaid. And after all this they will all be there at the register office for us.'

Annie couldn't speak. She had never dreamed this would happen. It had taken the wind out of her sails.

'So, luv,' Ricky was now saying, 'you will soon be Mrs Richard Stanley!'

His laugh was infectious. Annie joined in with him and then reached up and took his face in her hands. 'I like the name Richard. And I love the person called it with all my heart.'

He held her close and kissed her nose and then found her lips.

A fire burned in Annie, and she went willingly into the alley they were passing. There, in broad daylight, standing against the paint-peeling wall, they made love.

The world receded as they clung together, and she cried out at every thrust of Ricky's body into hers. Their kisses were hungry gasps and delicious dances of their tongues . . . Then it happened.

Annie bit her bottom lip in an effort to stop herself hollering with the joy of the feelings that always splintered her into fragments of sheer pleasure.

They clung together afterwards. Giggled at their daring. Looked this way and that, but found to their relief they had got away with it.

Ricky gave a half-smile. 'I can see the headlines. Two police officers arrested for lewd behaviour in broad daylight! But, Annie, if that had happened, I would have no regrets. That was the best ever.'

Annie couldn't help giggling. Ricky always said that afterwards. But then, each time was always going to feel like the best ever. It did for her too.

The next morning, after the landlady had allowed them to have a bath if they used the same water, and Ricky had taken her literally and hopped into the bath with her, they sat in the front room. Annie was on tenterhooks.

Her eyes were constantly moving from the window to the door, thinking that she would catch sight of a car if it pulled up, or if she missed it, see the door open and Olivia would be here!

It was the noise of a car pulling up that caused Annie to shoot off the armchair. In no time they were in each other's arms, crying, laughing and both talking at once.

'Olivia! Oh, Olivia.'

'Come on, girls, let's get back into the lounge and then we can all say a proper hello.'

They did as Ricky bid. But then Olivia had to go to use the washroom.

'Oh, Ricky, she looks and feels so thin!'

'I expect she's pining, luv. Poor girl.'

Suddenly the excitement was overshadowed by the reality as Annie knew that she, too, would pine when Ricky had left.

But she had to accept that they both had their roles

to fill and even meeting up was something that shouldn't happen, but they had been given a concession to do so as the reason was a viable one and made their action a natural one.

The next few hours were taken up with the drive home and listening to each other's news. The best and what topped them all was Annie's and Ricky's wedding plans.

'Oh, Annie, I'm so thrilled that I will be there. Will you wear my wedding gown?'

'I will, luv. Ricky arranged everything, so that your gown, and my bridesmaid dress that Janey will wear, will be all ready for me . . . Oh, Olivia, I so want you as a bridesmaid too.'

'Oh, I would love that. I can wear that rose-coloured taffeta frock I have. It will look lovely and is hanging in the wardrobe in my bedroom in the apartment. It will go so well with the blue of the one Janey will wear.'

They fell silent, an excited silence that gave Annie time to dream.

She was getting married! How she wished that she and Ricky could go back with Olivia and spend their honeymoon in Guernsey, where everyone knew each other and took time to stand idle and gossip. And where, every way you looked, you were stunned by beautiful views, leafy lanes, little shops – not a Harrods-type store in sight – and all the people depended on the sea. It gave them food, brought goods to them, and provided an endless, changing backdrop to their everyday life, besides being their means of travel off the island. To Annie, it was idyllic. And yet, she would never permanently swap it for her beloved East End.

* * *

That evening, Olivia took them out to a beautiful restaurant.

'This is to celebrate your wedding.'

The food – mainly seafood for her and Olivia and a juicy steak for Ricky – was delicious.

At the end, Olivia stood.

'I'm going to propose a toast. "To Annie and Ricky, our bride and bridegroom."'

Everyone cheered. Ricky did the traditional thing and kissed Annie. A sweet kiss that sealed for her that they truly were going to be man and wife.

The champagne tasted like nothing Annie had ever tasted before, and she loved it.

Outside she felt wobbly on her legs and couldn't seem to stop giggling. Olivia was the same and poor Ricky had one of them on each arm.

Suddenly, Olivia started to sing: 'Show me the way to go home.' Annie joined in and they belted it out between giggles, rivalling anything that Ricky had done in the street when he'd taken her to the pictures.

It was when Olivia belted out, 'Any Ole Iron', that windows opened. But instead of folk shouting at them to shut up, they joined in.

Annie couldn't believe it – she had never dreamed West End folk were even human, let alone capable of doing such a thing.

Some even came out of their doors and before long the street was in uproar as men twirled women around and danced in an exaggerated skip, singing for all they were worth.

At last, with everyone out of breath, they stopped, leaned against walls, giggled, shook hands, and hugged complete strangers.

One man said, 'Well, girls, for one moment there I forgot what was happening. Thank you.'

A voice bellowed, 'Get them doors closed and pull down your blackout blinds. What the hell do you think you're doing? Have you all gone mad!'

A police officer, looking twice as big as Ricky, stood at the end of the street, his hands on his waist, his elbows stuck out.

All scampered back inside, leaving Annie, Olivia and Ricky to face the music.

'Now then, you three, I've a good mind to arrest you for disturbing the peace.' He sniffed. 'And being drunk and disorderly.'

As he reached for his notebook, Ricky stepped forward and offered his hand. 'PC Stanley, Officer, and this is Policewoman Freeman. We apologize. We didn't plan for that to happen. We are celebrating our wedding tomorrow before I go off to war.'

'Police officers! Well, you should know better. And I expect you do. But I can see this was a spur-of-the-moment thing. But even so, them lights could have—'

'Yes. I'm so sorry. It is one of my nightly duties to check no lights are showing over London and now I am part of the cause of them doing so on your patch.'

'Well, no harm seems to have been done and from what I witnessed you gave folk a bit of light relief, so go on your way . . . And, PC Stanley, I wish you good luck. I wish that I could go, but I'm too old. Due to retire in six months, which I'm dreading. But mind, the war may be a blessing in that. They may need me to stay on. Goodnight to you all.'

With this he turned and walked away.

From darkened houses came a cheer resounding louder than any Annie had ever heard.

The three of them were soon giggling and waving to shadowy figures and hearing people say, 'Thanks,' as they turned the corner into St James's Street.

Annie walked into the register office the next day feeling the happiest she'd ever felt, despite a telegram having arrived for Ricky telling him he must report earlier than expected. No war was going to put a blight on this day – the very best of her life.

It had all been a hectic rush, but they'd managed everything in time, and now as Ricky looked into her eyes and told her she was beautiful, she said, 'And you are too. The most handsome and beautiful man I have ever met.'

It wasn't that she didn't see his scar or his broken nose – both he'd since told her were sustained by a prisoner in the cells who had grabbed him, taken his truncheon and attacked him with it. To her, they'd always been a part of his beauty.

Then, when he repeated the vows and once more looked deeply into her eyes, it was to Annie as if no one else was in the room. A moment she would cherish.

When they walked outside, Janey and Olivia threw petals over them, which Annie guessed would have come from the rose bush Janey had grown in her back garden.

They ended in a hug, and then waved to folk who called out good wishes or honked their car horns.

Back at Janey's flat, where what looked like a huge buffet was laid out, they, along with Olivia, Lilly, now her mum-in-law, Janey, Jimmy, Mum, Rosie and Cissy, had a wonderful afternoon. Jimmy and Ricky had even carried Mum's piano up. They sang, they danced and they laughed, till it was time for Annie and Ricky to go to the hotel that Ricky had booked for the night.

Through it all, Annie let herself forget that Olivia was to leave the next day and Ricky the day after. He was to be in the first contingent going to France.

As Annie lay in bed and looked at the ceiling the next morning, love, happiness and sadness attacked her in a barrage of emotions. She let the love and happiness win. How, she didn't know, as her heart was heavy.

The night having been like no other helped. Yes, she'd experienced sleeping with Ricky, but never as his wife!

She sat up and looked over at him, still snuggled under the covers. He stirred and opened an eye. His sleepy, 'Morning, Mrs Stanley,' made her giggle.

His arm came around her and he gently pulled her back down to lie beside him. His lips came on hers. His hands explored her. His words were of love and wonderment at her beauty.

Slowly, he rolled and cradled her underneath him.

When he entered her, her worlds, of which she felt she had many, collided and exploded in a crescendo of feeling that had her crying out and then sobbing in his arms as he reached his own climax.

They'd never made love in such a short time before, and to Annie, it felt as though, as her husband, Ricky had gained powers over her that she never knew were there for him to take. But she wanted him to have them for ever.

They made their way to the apartment later that morning to find Olivia rushing around giving Cissy last-minute instructions of what was to go where – or so they thought.

'Oh, Annie, I can't go home today. There's been a delay; the ferry isn't leaving until tomorrow evening. But I thought

I would get this done . . . Cissy, will you be all right for a moment? I just want to chat to Annie and Ricky.'

They went into Olivia's father's study.

Olivia opened her arms to them. 'I'm so happy for you, and yet sad you have to part.'

'I know, but me and Annie have decided to treat it that I'm only going away for a few weeks and take it in slices like that. Now, what's troubling you, luv?'

'It's all this! Oh, Ricky, it all seems so unnecessary! Nothing is really happening to the apartment.'

Annie squeezed her shoulders. 'Well, knowing that, just make a quick pretence to satisfy Cissy, and not have her ask too many questions. Let her pack some things, and tell her they are all going to be picked up in a couple of days' time. We're here with you now. I know what you would move out if you were really made to, so I'll mark some of it – ha, stickers we'll be taking off again when all this is over.'

'Thanks, love. Oh, Annie, are we really going to get through it all?'

'We are. We're strong. Look, mate, you're missing Karl now, on top of missing Hendrick, and not being able to go home is a huge disappointment to you, luv. Tomorrow will come – too soon for me, but not soon enough for you.'

They hugged again, each with their own thoughts and each knowing they could do nothing to stop the inevitable.

At the station Olivia said her goodbyes to Ricky and then left them to themselves while she went to sit in the waiting room. Her train went a little while after Ricky's.

Annie and Ricky clung together, as did many couples around them, all of whom, Annie knew, didn't want to be in this moment.

Many sobbed out loud. But she and Ricky had done that after they had made love. And both had said they would wave to each other with a smile on their faces.

When the train came in, Annie's heart stopped. A shrill whistle sounded, even before the smoke that swirled around them, puffed from the funnel on the train's engine, had time to clear. A shout of, 'All board the train! And in an orderly fashion! You have your carriage number on your rail pass!' saw men marching towards their carriages.

As Annie watched Ricky disappear into his and a few seconds later reappear with his head out of the window, she smiled at him.

He smiled back.

He waved as the train pulled away, and until he was just a spec seeming to be miles in the distance.

Annie turned and hurried to Olivia.

They had so little time, so sat on the platform holding hands. Both let their tears flow.

'Oh, Annie, this is it. I feel as though it is truly beginning. And I know how you are feeling, like screaming and crying, but knowing that you can't – that you mustn't.'

'Yes, that's exactly it, Olivia . . . Hug me, before I do break, mate.'

No sooner had they gone into the hug than a strange, disorientated voice announced Olivia's train.

Olivia pulled away from her. 'Don't forget, love, we are the Guernsey Girls.'

'We are. And they couldn't have picked a better name for us as every time I hear it or say it, it conjures up our lovely time together living in your farmhouse.'

As she waved goodbye to Olivia, Annie took no heed of the tears tumbling down her face but lifted her head and let the strong young woman she'd become take over. And as if she was just another policewoman in her smart uniform, she marched towards the exit.

There was a war to be won. Ricky and Jimmy would play their part. But so would all of them.

She looked heavenward. *Just you try to beat us, Adolf Blooming Hitler, and see what you come up against, mate! We may be women, but we're women of the East End, and that's a different kettle of fish!*

And we have an ally in Guernsey! Olivia, who'll undermine you every step of the bleeding way!

With this Annie felt as if she had grown six feet tall. But then, yet another siren took all the space around and for one split second she crumbled inside.

A voice pulled her up. 'Officer, help me. I've me little one in me pram and me lad's only two. I'll never manage the stairs down to the Underground.'

Something happened to Annie. Her brave thoughts became actions, and she took charge. Yes, it was more than likely a practice run, but you never could be sure.

Calmly herding people into the Underground, acting as if this one was for real though all the previous ones hadn't been, Annie found that she coped. That people looked to her to guide them and to save them from harm. She would do that to the best of her ability and she and Olivia – the Guernsey Girls – would carry out their special duty. Yes, between them they had Hitler licked already!

Acknowledgements

Thank you to the team at Pan Macmillan for all the attention they give to my books: my commissioning editor, Wayne Brookes, who oversees the umpteen processes that my book goes through, for his cheerful encouragement and optimism – a joy to work with. My desk-editorial team headed by Laura Carr, whose work brings out the very best of my story to make it shine. And Victoria Hughes-Williams, who is responsible for the structural edit and makes sure the story flows. My publicist, Chloe Davies, and her team, who seek out many opportunities for me to showcase my work. My cover designer, James, who has done an amazing job – I love this cover. And to the sales team, my heartfelt thanks goes to you all.

A big thank-you also to my son, James Wood, who reads so many versions of my work to help and advise me, and works alongside me on the edits that come in. I love you so very much.

And to my readers, who encourage me as they await another book, supporting me every step of the way, and who warm my heart with praise in their reviews.

I'd also like to thank Paul Falla, the Guernsey taxi driver who helped me so much with my research when I visited the island. Thank you, you made my day perfect.

But no one person stands alone. My family are amazing. They give me an abundance of love and support, and when one of them says they are proud of me, then my world is complete. My special thanks to all. You are all my rock and help me to climb my mountain. I love you with all my heart.

Letter to Readers

Dear reader,

Hi. Thank you from the bottom of my heart for choosing my work to curl up with and I hope you enjoyed reading *The Guernsey Girls* – the first in a brand-new trilogy.

I would so appreciate it if you would kindly leave me a review on Amazon, Goodreads or any online bookstore or book group. Reviews are like being hugged by the reader and they help to encourage me to write the next book – they further my career as they advise other readers about the book, and hopefully whet their appetite to also buy the book.

Coming next, in 2024, is the second in the trilogy – *The Guernsey Girls Go to War*. Olivia has arrived in London to be with Annie when she receives a call that her father has been taken ill. Not wanting to put her son through the journey once more, she leaves him and his nanny and sails home to Guernsey, saying she should only be away for two weeks. But while there, Guernsey is invaded by the Germans, and she cannot return to be with her son or Annie.

This is a moving story of how the people of London

survived the Blitz and the people of Guernsey survived being under the Nazi regime. Annie and Olivia stay in contact and, with the help of Hendrick who remains in Germany, pass vital information to help the war effort, but the consequences of doing so are devastating.

I researched this series by visiting Guernsey as part of a cruise around the British Isles. We only had one day in St Peter's Port, Guernsey, and so I booked a private taxi online before we left home. This was so that I could be taken to the places I needed to see instead of joining the conventional tour. My guide was taxi driver Paul Falla of Guernsey Taxis, who greatly enhanced my knowledge and took me to un-touristy places I may never have seen or learnt about.

I found the perfect house for Olivia and Hendrick and took photos. I was taken to what was the Gestapo HQ, and to a museum run by a gentleman in an extension to his home. Over the last forty years he has collected war memorabilia and has thousands of items. It was amazing and I learnt so much to add authenticity to my work. I fell in love with Guernsey.

If there is anything you would like to ask me, or just want to say hello, or maybe book me for a talk to a group you belong to, I love to interact with readers and would welcome your comments, emails and messages through:

My Facebook page: www.facebook.com/MaryWoodAuthor
My Twitter: www.twitter.com/Authormary
My website: www.authormarywood.com

I will always reply. And if you subscribe to my newsletter on my website, you will be entered into a draw to win my latest book personally signed to you and will receive a three-monthly newsletter giving all the updates on my books and author life, and many chances of winning lovely prizes.

Love to hear from you, take care of yourself and others.

Much love,

Mary xxx

If you enjoyed

The Guernsey Girls

then you'll love

The Jam Factory Girls

**Whatever life throws at them,
they will face it together**

Life for Elsie is difficult as she struggles to cope with her alcoholic mother. Caring for her siblings and working long hours at Swift's Jam Factory in London's Bermondsey is exhausting. Thankfully her lifelong friendship with Dot helps to smooth over life's rough edges.

When Elsie and Dot meet Millie Hawkesfield, the boss's daughter, they are nervous to be in her presence. Over time, they are surprised to feel so drawn to her, but should two cockney girls be socializing in such circles?

When disaster strikes, it binds the women in ways they could never have imagined. And long-held secrets are revealed that will change all their lives . . .

The Jam Factory Girls series continues with *Secrets of the Jam Factory Girls* and *The Jam Factory Girls Fight Back*, all available to read now.

The Forgotten Daughter

Book one in
The Girls Who Went to War series

From a tender age, Flora felt unloved and unwanted by her parents, but she finds safety in the arms of caring Nanny Pru. But when Pru is cast out of the family home, under a shadow of secrets and with a baby boy of her own on the way, it shatters little Flora.

Over the years, however, Flora and Pru meet in secret – unbeknown to Flora's parents. Pru becomes the mother she never had, and Flora grows into a fine young woman. When she signs up as a volunteer with St John Ambulance, she begins to shape her life. But the drum of war beats loudly and her world is turned upside down when she receives a letter asking her to join the Red Cross in Belgium.

With the fate of the country in the balance, it is a time for bravery. Flora's determined to be the strong woman she was destined to be. But with horror, loss and heartache on her horizon, there's a lot for young Flora to learn . . .

The Girls Who Went to War series continues with
The Abandoned Daughter, *The Wronged Daughter* and
The Brave Daughters, all available to read now.

The Orphanage Girls

Children deserve a family to call their own.

Ruth dares to dream of another life – far away from the horrors within the walls of Bethnal Green's infamous orphanage. Luckily she has her friends, Amy and Ellen, but she can't keep them safe, and the suffering is only getting worse. Surely there must be a way out?

But when Ruth breaks free from the shackles of confinement and sets out into East London, hoping to make a new life for herself, she finds that, for a girl with nowhere to turn, life can be just as tough on the outside.

Bett keeps order in this unruly part of the East End and she takes Ruth under her wing alongside fellow orphanage escapee Robbie. But it is Rebekah, a kindly woman, who offers Ruth and Robbie a home – something neither has ever known. Yet even these two stalwart women cannot protect them when the police learn of an orphan on the run. It is then that Ruth must do everything in her power to hide. Her life – and those of the friends she left behind at the orphanage – depend on it.

The Orphanage Girls series continues with *The Orphanage Girls Reunited* and *The Orphanage Girls Come Home*, all available to read now.